THE BORROWED AND BLUE MURDERS

OTHER ZOE HAYES MYSTERIES

The Nanny Murders

The River Killings

The Deadly Neighbors

THE BORROWED
AND BLUE
MURDERS

MERRY JONES

THOMAS DUNNE BOOKS

ST. MARTIN'S MINOTAUR

NEW YORK

This is a work of fiction. All of the characters, organizations, and events portrayed in this novel are either products of the author's imagination or are used fictitiously.

THOMAS DUNNE BOOKS.
An imprint of St. Martin's Press.

THE BORROWED AND BLUE MURDERS. Copyright © 2008 by Merry Jones. All rights reserved. Printed in the United States of America. For information, address St. Martin's Press, 175 Fifth Avenue, New York, N.Y. 10010.

www.thomasdunnebooks.com
www.minotaurbooks.com

Library of Congress Cataloging-in-Publication Data

Jones, Merry Bloch.
    The borrowed and blue murders / Merry Jones.—1st St. Martin's Minotaur ed.
        p.   cm.
    ISBN-13: 978-0-312-35623-1
    ISBN-10: 0-312-35623-4
    1. Hayes, Zoe (Fictitious character)—Fiction.   2. Private investigators—Pennsylvania—Philadelphia—Fiction.   3. Women runners—Crimes against—Fiction.   4. Weddings—Planning—Fiction.   5. Philadelphia (Pa.)—Fiction.   I. Title.
PS3610.O6273B67   2008
813'.6—dc22

                                                              2008020340

First Edition: September 2008

10 9 8 7 6 5 4 3 2 1

In memory of my mom,
E. Judith Bloch

ACKNOWLEDGMENTS

In writing this book, I've received mega doses of encouragement and support from lots of people. Heartfelt thanks go out to the following:

Thomas Dunne, Marcia Markland and Diana Szu at St. Martin's Press.

My agent, Liza Dawson.

Janet Martin, Nancy Delman, Jane Braun and the rest of my close-knit, loving, extensive extended family.

Dear friends, including Lanie Zera, Sue Francke, Sue Solovy Mulder, Ruth Waldfogel, Michael and Jan Molinaro, Leslie Mogul and Steve Zindell, and the late Susan Stone.

The many generous readers who've written to me via my Web site.

Our corgi, Jack.

My precious daughters, Baille and Neely.

My precious husband, Robin.

My late father, mother and brother, Herman S., E. Judith and Aaron N. Bloch, each so sorely missed.

THE BORROWED
AND BLUE
MURDERS

ONE

PERCHED LIKE A FLAMINGO ON ONE LEG, I TRIED TO BALANCE the groceries on my thigh without disturbing baby Luke, who was sound asleep in his sling. Somehow, I managed to unlock the front door and juggle my way inside without dropping the lemon meringue pie that was teetering perilously on top of the pretzel packages, and I made it into the kitchen without waking Luke or losing hold of either bag.

The house still reeked of last night's beer. Judging by the empties lined up on the kitchen counter, Nick and his brothers had gone through several six-packs. Not that I blamed them, really. It was a family reunion. If not for the baby, I'd undoubtedly have joined in, drinking my share for no reason other than to avoid being what I had been lately: the only sober adult in the house. Instead of beer, I'd sipped decaffeinated mint tea, listening to them recount childhood memories, hoot over private jokes, tease each other without mercy and gradually descend into song, performing off-key renditions of their favorite oldies. It had been a long few nights. Actually, a long three nights. Ever since Tuesday, when Tony and Sam had arrived, our house had been home to a nonstop party.

Even so, the demands of daily life continued. Food needed to be bought, meals to be cooked. Shoving the empties aside with my elbow to make room for the grocery bags, I noticed a puddle on the floor next to the refrigerator. Damn. Somebody had let the puppy out of his crate again. And, as if on cue, he raced over, jumping and yipping, nipping at my ankles with joy at our return.

"Oliver, no, no." I knelt, cradling the baby's sling with one hand, shaking a finger at him with the other. "No. Do not piddle in the house."

Oliver, our almost-five-month-old Pembroke Welsh corgi puppy, still wasn't housebroken. His training kept getting interrupted; things like my giving birth and Nick having his relatives visit tended to interfere. The result was that Oliver left surprises for us all over the house. If he wasn't leaving deposits, he was chewing on chair legs or shoes, anything he could wrap his mouth around.

When I released his nose, Oliver stared at me with shiny, eager eyes, oblivious to the scolding. In fact, he was smiling, tongue dangling, panting with eagerness and delight, waiting attentively for who knew what. I had to admit he was cute. How was I supposed to stay angry with a little guy who grinned at me with such complete adoration? Sighing, I tightened the wrap that secured Luke to my body and gave Oliver an affectionate scratch before attending to his puddle.

As I looked for the paper towels, though, it occurred to me that, oops, I shouldn't have petted him. The teacher at puppy school had warned about reinforcing bad behavior. What if Oliver connected the puddle with the scratch and thought I was actually pleased with him for peeing in the kitchen? Damn. I might be counter-training him. But it was too late to take the scratch back. I'd have to be more careful from now on or we'd have an incorrigible corgi, a sociopath, completely indifferent to the concepts of bad and good. Meantime, I had to clean up his puddle.

Where were the paper towels? I hunted, scanning the sink full of breakfast dishes, the still half-full coffeepot, the stack of miscellaneous coupons and carryout menus, eventually spotting the towels behind the knife rack near the phone, which was blinking, the red light flashing, indicating that we had messages. So, grabbing a wad of crumpled paper towels, I multitasked, putting the phone on speaker, dialing our voice mail number and listening as I squatted to attend to the mess, still trying not to awaken Luke.

But I was too late; Luke's eyes were already open and alert. Any moment, he'd realize he was hungry; I had to hurry. Quickly, supporting Luke's head with my free hand, I soaked up the puddle, still hoping to get the groceries put away before I had to feed him.

"You have five messages." The computerized voice sounded impressed. "First message."

"Zoe, I'll be back Monday." It was Ivy, our babysitter, whose car had been stolen earlier in the week while parked right in front of our house. Normally, Ivy walked to work; she lived only about a mile away. But the one time she'd driven, her car had vanished in broad daylight. Ivy's voice now reported that she had spent the entire day doing the paperwork for her car insurance and she was ready to come back to work. From her tone, I could tell that she still blamed me for the theft. Somehow, she'd figured that since her car had been parked on my street, it was my fault that it was stolen. I'd been unable to convince her otherwise. Ivy took no responsibility for the loss, even though she knew the neighborhood as well as I did. The crime rate was high in Philadelphia, and it seemed to be higher than average in our neighborhood, Queen Village. The area was in transition, but it was a long way from gentrified. Robberies, muggings, even drive-by shootings were not unheard of. Addicts and drunks frequented the nighttime sidewalks that by day sported upscale perambulators. The street wasn't a place you'd let children play unsupervised. And it wasn't a place where you'd leave your parked car unlocked. But according to Ivy, the person who couldn't remember locking her car, the theft of the vehicle, like her presence on the street, was because of me. Ivy was neither logical nor easy to get along with, but Molly liked her and, despite Ivy's attitudes,

I was desperate. I needed her help. It was already Friday, and there were just eight days until the wedding— Wait. Stop. I had to repeat that fact.

There were just eight days.

Until.

The wedding.

Breathe, I told myself. Just stop and breathe. I closed my eyes and let air rush into my lungs, holding it there for a moment, letting it enter my blood. Then I exhaled slowly. I was on overload, and I had to stop spinning, get organized. But every time I even thought about the *w* word, my heart did a dizzying break dance and I stopped breathing. Excitement, nerves, joy, panic—I didn't know what. It didn't matter, either, because time was passing and there was so much left to do that I had no time for stuff like naming emotions. And, meantime, the lady in the telephone was impatiently repeating that I needed to push 1 to repeat, 2 to save, 3 to delete Ivy's message.

I stood, pushed 3 and tossed the soggy paper towels into the trash, held a soapy rag under hot water and squatted again, simultaneously telling Oliver to stop jumping on me and cooing to soothe Luke, who'd begun to whimper, awake enough to realize that it was way past time for his every-four-hour meal. I sang him the song about the Puffer Bellies, hoping to distract him for a couple of minutes, long enough for me to at least finish cleaning up the floor. So I washed the tiles, singing, while the puppy chased the soapy rag, chomping and pouncing, trying to grab it, having a wonderful time, and the phone mail voice announced, "Second message."

This one was from Anna, the special event planner from hell. No, that wasn't fair. Anna was efficient and detail oriented, persistent and organized; she was everything I needed her to be. It wasn't her fault that her voice was nasal and sharply birdlike, or that the shape of her glasses reminded me of outstretched wings. And I'd just left her half an hour ago; what could she possibly need to say that she hadn't already said? It didn't matter. Anna didn't need a reason. She called about a dozen times a day, always had one more item to discuss. I stopped singing long enough to listen to her say that she wanted to remind me, even though she'd just reminded me in person, that she needed a final count for the reception dinner. The chef at the Four Seasons required a week's notice. And Anna needed a decision about whether to go with Amaretto or hazelnut for the cake. I mentally recited the list along with her; she'd repeated it so many times, I had it memorized.

I stood, pushed number 3 to delete, rinsed out the rag, stooped again and, singing, "See the engine driver pull the little handles," rushed to wipe up the soap bubbles before the puppy could lick them up. "Puff, puff, toot, toot, off we go!" Lulled by either my singing or my repeated standing and stooping, Luke quieted down, burbling softly.

"Third message," the voice declared, and instantly a frantic soprano voice blurted that she was calling for Zoe Hayes with a message from Haverford Place about Walter Hayes. Oh dear. Walter Hayes was my eighty-three-year-old father. And Haverford Place was the retirement village where he lived. I froze, rag in hand, staring at the phone, dreading the message, praying he was all right. The soprano insisted that she didn't want to alarm anyone, but she was wondering if, possibly, Ms. Hayes had any idea where her father might be. Because, she didn't mean to worry his family, but no one had seen Mr. Hayes in a while. Actually, since yesterday. In fact, Walter Hayes appeared to be missing.

Missing? I released a breath, relieved; at least he was alive. As far as we knew, no harm had come to him. All we needed to do was find out where he'd gone. This was not the first time Dad had taken off on his own. He was stubbornly independent, unwilling to account to others for his whereabouts, oblivious to the turmoil he caused when he neglected to sign the ledger book before he went out. Probably he'd gone back to his old neighborhood, stopping by his old house, pulling the "For Sale" sign out of the grass one more time. Or maybe he'd hopped a bus to Atlantic City for some black-jack. Or gone to Delaware Park to play the horses. He was fine. Probably.

But then again, he hadn't been seen since yesterday. That was a long time, even for my father. I deleted the message and tossed the rag into a bucket under the sink, ready to call Haverford Place. But before I could, the fourth message began, sounding much like the third but less frantic. The soprano, cheerful now, asked Ms. Hayes to disregard her previous call. The search was off; my father had reappeared in prime condition, no need for concern. She didn't elaborate, offered no details. But that was fine; Dad was safe and accounted for, and that was all I really needed to know. There was no need to hunt for him.

Luke began wriggling, his little mouth rooting around for a nipple. "Fifth message." It was the last one. I whispered to Luke, asking him to wait while we heard this last message, wincing as soon as I recognized the caller's voice. Bryce Edmond was the ad-ministrator of the Psychiatric Institute where I worked, and he'd been calling all week. In truth, I'd been avoiding him.

"Zoe." Bryce sounded peeved. "I've sent you two dozen e-mails and called you eleven times." Bryce was nothing if not exact. And while he didn't want to disturb me during my maternity leave, he needed to speak with me at my earliest convenience.

Damn. Why couldn't he leave me alone? Obviously, Bryce wanted to talk about work. And I didn't. Whatever he had to say wasn't going to be good. The Psychiatric Institute was having fi-nancial difficulties; that was old news. My program in art therapy was considered by the administration to be "unessentiall"; it had already been cut in half. In addition, my three months of mater-nity leave were just about, if not already, up. So, either Bryce was calling to say that it was time to come back to my job, which I wasn't ready to do, or he was calling to say that there was no job for me to come back to, which I wasn't ready to hear. Either way, I figured that if he couldn't reach me, he couldn't deliver his news. So, as I had every time he'd called, I pushed number 3, and Bryce was deleted. I told myself not to feel bad about ignoring him. After all, it was just a week until my wedding—oops, there was the *w* word again—and there went my heart, taking off in its frenzied, dizzying spin, bouncing off my ribs. So Bryce would have to wait. He would have to understand. It wasn't just the wed—the upcoming event. I also had to care for a new baby, an energetic six-year-old daughter, Molly, an unhousebroken puppy and a houseful of my soon-to-be-in-laws. I simply couldn't be expected to deal with anything else—certainly not my job. Whatever was on Bryce's mind would have to wait until after the *w*—ceremony.

I turned off the phone, abandoning the unpacked groceries, assuring Luke that he was finally going to eat. His whimpers had escalated, turned into complaints. Poor baby had been patient all morning, riding around snuggled against my belly, tied to me by a long hand-woven shawl-like sling my friend Karen had given me as a shower gift. He'd kept me company on this weirdly warm, foggy April day while I'd shopped and picked up the cleaning. He'd nuzzled me peacefully while I'd met with Anna to taste pastries and appetizers for the reception. But now, he was finished being Mr. Nice Guy. Suddenly, he let out a howl, bellowing as fiercely as his eleven-week-old lungs would allow. And, on command, automatically, my body responded. Milk welled up and spilled from the swollen spigots that were my breasts.

"Okay," I pleaded. "Lunchtime, Luke. Just a second." Normally, I changed his diaper before feeding him, but he was wailing. The diaper, like the groceries, could wait. I hurried down the hall to the living room, Oliver snapping and nipping at my heels with all of his purebred herding dog instincts. I cooed to Luke, but he was inconsolable. He'd smelled lunch and, red-faced, tight-fisted, he let his fury rip.

Pulling up my sweater, I plopped down onto my purple velvet sofa and popped right up again, tossing an iPod onto the coffee table. Tony, one of Nick's brothers, had been camping on my sofa. Living on it, actually. Making a tiny home there. I shoved aside an afghan, removed a library book and a crumb-covered plate and, as Luke let loose with a shrill, spine-piercing shriek, sat back down and opened the cup of my nursing bra. Luke lunged, sucking ferociously, and distracted by I didn't care what, the puppy finally released the hem of my jeans.

I leaned back, settling in, closing my eyes. Peace at last. I sank against the cushions, felt the soreness in my breasts ease as Luke drank. Breast-feeding was intoxicating. It made me sleepy, maudlin and sappy; it made thinking about anything but the baby impossible. The world around us dissolved away. All that existed was Luke's downy head, sweet skin and soft smell, his purring as he nuzzled possessively against me, his sweaty, passionate breathing as he suckled. As always when I nursed him, I floated, lost in hormonal bliss. I felt cozy and brainless, fulfilled, as if my entire reason for being was to provide nourishment for this precious tiny creature. Usually, a full stomach made Luke drowsy. After I fed him, both of us tended to doze.

But peace that Friday was brief. No sooner did I drift off than Oliver began yelping. I cracked an eyelid, saw him digging on the mat by the sliding door to our tiny backyard. Maybe he was asking to go out? Picking this particular moment to get housebroken? Amazing. Oh well. He'd have to wait. I couldn't let him out while Luke was nursing. "Easy, Oliver," I pleaded. "Hold on for a little bit."

I shut my eyes again, determined to reclaim my bliss, hoping Oliver would not leave yet another puddle to mop up. But Oliver kept yipping, scratching at the glass of the sliding door. Maybe there was a squirrel out there. Or a cat. Or a UFO. I didn't care; I just wanted it to leave so Oliver would quiet down. But he didn't.

His high-pitched barks persisted. Finally, I'd had it. Unable to stand the yipping anymore, I opened my eyes and shouted, "Oliver, no!"

He stopped barking and looked at me, head tilted, baffled, clearly wondering what was wrong with me. How could I just sit there? Then he turned back to the door and barked. I followed his gaze, saw no movement. No rodent. No feline. Nothing. And still, he barked.

"Oliver," I commanded, "enough. Shut up."

Deliberately, I leaned back and shut my eyes. If I ignored him, he'd eventually quiet down. But my mind must have unconsciously registered some abnormal detail, because without knowing why, I sat up and took another, more careful look at the sliding door. And there, on the concrete, on the right side of the glass, I saw something that made no sense. Something that simply couldn't be there. Something that looked like five plump, pink toes.

TWO

LUKE DIDN'T MISS A GULP. HE STAYED FIRMLY ATTACHED TO MY breast, sucking, as I rose and approached the door for a closer look. I moved slowly, not believing what I was seeing. Toes? Yes, toes. And a foot. Attached to a leg, which led to a thigh with some pants pulled down around it. And above the thigh, where a pelvis and belly should have been, a jumble of torn, lumpy tissue and co-agulating blood, pooling around what must not long ago have been a woman. I gawked, frozen, taking in details. She'd been sliced open, her insides emptied out of her body, onto the deck.

For an immeasurable dizzying moment, I clung to Luke and blinked. What I was seeing could not be real. It was unimaginable. First of all, nobody came into our backyard patio. It wasn't locked, but there was a gate. It was a private, family space where Molly played with the puppy, where Nick grilled burgers. But no matter how I tried to deny it, the gory intruder remained, insisting that she was, in fact, still there. Still filleted, still gutted like a tuna.

A vision flashed to mind, another woman I knew. A patient at the Institute—a psychotic. Bonnie Something-or-other. She'd cut pregnant women open—four or five of them—to steal their un-born babies. But she was irrelevant—she'd been in the Institute for decades. This body had nothing to do with her. The slicing, the gaping abdomen, might resemble her work, but Bonnie hadn't done it. Someone else had.

Oddly, it didn't occur to me to run. I stood aghast, mesmerized by the bloody display on my back patio. A blue, blood-drenched sweatshirt draped the woman's neck, covering one nipple. There was a diamond stud in her nostril. She wore too much blue eye shadow. And her platinum hair had been pulled into a loose pony-tail. Who was she? What had happened here? Suddenly, I felt em-barrassed for her, awkwardly aware that I shouldn't be seeing these intimate, internal parts of her body. Nobody should. But her or-gans lay out in the open air, like exposed secrets. Oh God. A wave of nausea rose through me, and I turned away. Breathe, I reminded myself. I inhaled and smelled Luke's diaper, absurdly remember-ing that I still had to change it. Somehow, that realization snapped me back to reality. Finally, my survival instincts kicked in.

Stumbling over Oliver, I held on to Luke, who was still at lunch, and letting my sweater flop onto his face, I flew.

THREE

MY MEMORY OF THE NEXT FEW HOURS IS SPOTTY. I RECALL ISO-
lated moments. Like sitting on the front stoop, waiting for the police, feeling the fog creep under my clothing and cling to my skin.
The fog had held on, refusing to burn off even as the sun rose
high and noon arrived; it lingered, a clammy blanket of gray that
clouded my thoughts and blurred the row houses across the street.
I remember noticing how still and heavy Luke was in my arms.
Sated, indifferent to the world around him, he slept soundly in his
sodden diaper. Oliver lay beside us, leashed and finally quiet. I sat,
waiting for the police, listening for sirens, thinking that the air was
too moist, too warm, for early April, almost sixty degrees. I thought
about global warming, wondered if we'd ever have winter again. If
Luke would ever see snow. I thought about the blood pooling on
my deck, and the dead woman's nose piercing, how conventional
piercing had become.

I don't know how long I sat there, my mind bouncing from
thought to disconnected thought. Probably, it was just a few minutes, but time had clogged like the wet air, become sluggish and
stuck. It seemed that the police would never arrive. I remember
how grateful I was that Molly wasn't home, how worried I was
about what to say to her. In her six years of life, she had already
encountered far too much crime. When Luke was born, I'd promised her that our lives would be more peaceful. But now, just
eleven weeks later, a dead woman lay in our backyard. How was I

supposed to explain yet another murder to my child when I couldn't explain it even to myself?

And then I wondered why such grotesque events kept popping into our lives. I wasn't in the crime business, not a mobster or drug pusher. I was a forty-one-year-old mom, an art therapist. I was about to remarry. Corpses and criminals had no business in my life, yet they kept appearing. Why? Was I doing something wrong? Somehow attracting violence? Was I some kind of murder magnet?

The thought was bizarre, but it shook me nevertheless. I needed to connect with someone familiar who would reassure me. I made frantic phone calls, reaching nobody, leaving messages. I called Nick several times; apparently, he'd turned his phone off. I called all my friends, including the ones I knew weren't around: Susan, even though she was in the middle of a murder trial. Karen, even though she was at a Pilates class. Davinder, Liz. Nobody answered. And nothing moved on the street. No cars, no pedestrians, passed. I peered through tendrils of mist, searching for another human being, watching for a stranger lurking with a scalpel or maybe a long, sharp hunting knife. But I saw no one. Even the killer had vanished. Absurdly, it occurred to me that everyone—the entire rest of the world—had disappeared into the fog. The police would never arrive; there were no police. There was nothing and no one. I was alone, forever trapped in gray haze with baby Luke and Oliver the puppy. Oh, and the dead woman on the patio.

At some point, though, my cell phone rang, shattering the silence. I pounced on it as if for a life raft, hoping it was Nick. But the caller ID screen said: "Bryce Edmond." Damn. Bryce? Now? I stared at the phone, debating whether or not to answer. Bryce was at least alive and real, a voice that could link me to the world beyond the fog. Maybe I should take the call and talk to him. But then, maybe I shouldn't. After all, what could Bryce do about the corpse on my patio? The phone rang three times, four, and then, just as I decided to answer, I thought I heard wailing in the distance. I put down the phone and listened for sirens, watched for headlights emerging from the mist.

And suddenly, with great commotion, help arrived. Four police cars and an ambulance double-parked in front of the house, blocking the street, their lights flashing red and blue haloes into the haze. Officers ran around, in and out the door, talking on radios, asking repeatedly what had happened and whether Luke and I were okay, ushering in detectives who asked the same questions. The press had gathered beyond a barricade up the street, clamoring for details. I could barely see them, but I knew they were there, saw the glow of their lights, heard an officer complain about them.

I have no idea how long I remained on the stoop or how many times I replied, "Fine. I'm fine." Or, "I don't know. When we got home, she was just lying outside." I stayed there, watching the police and holding on to Luke and Oliver, until, finally, a man emerged from the fog, running, shouting my name.

"Nick—" I called to him.

"Zoe? Zoe, what the hell's going on? Are you okay?"

Oh wait. It wasn't Nick.

"Tony?"

Tony was Nick's youngest brother. His body, bursting out of the fog, moved like Nick's. His face, frowning with concern, looked like Nick's. And his voice, asking what had happened, why the police were here, sounded like Nick's. He raced up the steps, lifted me to my feet and wrapped Luke and me up in strong arms that felt safe and warm. Almost like Nick's.

FOUR

TONY DIDN'T ONLY HUG LIKE NICK. TONY COULD HAVE BEEN Nick's clone, only younger. In fact, all the brothers—Sam, Tony and Nick—had basically the same features, except that Nick's face had been scarred and partly paralyzed by a bullet wound. Standing together, the three looked like different versions of the same man at various ages and weights. Their eyes were all the same disarming shade of ice blue, their jaws cut at the same square angles. Their cheekbones jutted ruggedly; their hair was the color of desert sand, their legs strong, shoulders broad, grins wide and contagious. One by one, they were disarming. Three of them together were overwhelming.

There was a fourth brother, Eli. But he hadn't shown up. Sam and Nick had e-mailed him about the reunion, but they hadn't heard back, didn't know if he'd show. Eli, apparently, was elusive, a freelance photographer, always on the move. Sam had shown me an old photo of the four of them about nine years ago, the last time they'd all been together. Eli seemed to be yet another variation of the others, more muscular than Tony, taller and leaner than Sam. But it wasn't Eli who'd captured my attention in the picture. I'd been captivated by Nick, by how he'd looked before he'd been shot. His face had been unmarred, confident. Strong. I'd realized then how drastically the shooting had changed Nick's appearance and wondered how much he felt the loss. I'd studied not the brothers so much as the photo of the man I loved, of a face I'd never see. Eli remained an unknown to me, a name. And while it would be lovely to meet him, having two of Nick's brothers visiting was enough for now.

Even without Eli, it had been a happy reunion for Nick. With both his parents dead—his mother from stepping on a poisonous sea urchin and his father from a heart attack—Nick's brothers were his only family. Sam, an investment banker living in Connecticut, newly divorced from his second wife, was three years younger and looked like Nick two inches shorter and sixty pounds beefier. Sam smoked cigars, growled when he spoke, wheezed when he laughed, flashed wads of cash around, told stupid jokes and wore a mammoth diamond pinkie ring. Always on his cell phone or his laptop, finalizing some deal or softening some potential client, he seemed to assess everyone he met according to how much they had to spend, what he might sell them. Except women—he judged us by other standards. When I met Sam, he stood at my front door, visually measuring my body parts, blatantly checking out my legs and postpartum belly and bust. He all but examined my teeth before he reached out, grinning, and pulled me in for a bearlike embrace.

Tony, the baby, was twenty-nine. A perpetual student, he did postgraduate work in computer science at Berkeley. When I asked him what he did, he blanched and answered in terms I only vaguely understood. Gradually, I gathered that he was working on software designs for security systems, but Sam later explained that nobody but Tony really understood what Tony did. Tony, according to his brothers, was a genius. Whether he actually was or not, he definitely looked like one. His features were more delicate, his body more slender, than Nick's. A track star in high school, Tony moved with a weightless, unself-conscious grace, as if floating above the physical world, his mind preoccupied with abstractions. He couldn't be bothered with the material, leaving laundry wherever it fell and dishes wherever he'd eaten, oblivious to the

clutter. And he moved silently, startling me more than once by appearing behind me without making a sound.

Despite Sam's stinking cigars and Tony's tendency to float, I was
enjoying their visit more than I'd expected. I'd been raised as an
only child and was intrigued at having brothers, even if they were
only in-laws. Beyond that, through Nick's siblings I was meeting a
new part of him, the big brother part. It was fascinating how he
slipped into his old role, how easily he ordered the younger ones
around, how mercilessly he razzed them. In fact, Nick glowed in
his brothers' company. And Nick was not alone; Molly worshipped
both her uncles, climbing onto one lap or another with neither
shyness nor hesitation, as if either were her domain.

But now, our celebration had been disrupted. I stood locked in
Tony's arms, absorbing their affection. When he released me, I began to explain what had happened. But as he stared at me in dis-
belief, Sam came red faced, huffing, out of the fog, and I had to
begin the horrific story all over again.

FIVE

DETECTIVE DONALLY LET ME GO UPSTAIRS TO CHANGE LUKE'S DI-
aper. The baby stirred and yawned, but having a full tummy, he
didn't completely wake up. I tucked him into his crib, covering him
with his dinosaur comforter, my arms suddenly cold and empty
without his warmth. I stood by the crib, watching him, stalling,
avoiding going back downstairs. But voices rose. Men, agitated.

"Oh yeah? Well, I guess you're going to have to shoot me. Cuz
I'm going in."

"Step back, sir."

"Move aside, Detective. I have a right to know what's—"

"I warned you."

"—out there."

"Stop right there, sir!"

There was a scuffle. Footsteps pounded. Furniture scraped the
hardwood floors. Something slammed to the floor. Sam yelled,
"Tony?" And Tony called, "Sam!"

I ran down the stairs and, following the commotion, found
everyone in my living room, suddenly silent and motionless.
Donally and another detective stood beside my overturned wingback, hands at their hips, ready to draw their guns. Two uni-
formed officers stood near the fireplace, weapons already drawn.
And Sam and Tony, like bug-eyed twins, stood side by side, oblivious to the police, staring out the patio door.

"Okay? Happy now? You two seen what you wanted?"

On the patio, forensic workers froze, gaping at the scene in my living room.

"Oh, this is bad." Sam's growl was lower than usual. "Zoe said there was a body, but this—I didn't expect this; did you?" He waited for a response, but Tony didn't say anything. Tony didn't move, didn't blink.

"This is bad." Sam rubbed his face. "This is— This is bad."

"Okay? Now, if you will, gentlemen, back away from the door." Detective Donally stepped forward, arms out, apparently protecting his crime scene.

Ignoring him, I stepped over my wingback and joined the brothers.

"Ma'am." Donally glowered my way. "That includes you. Step back. Unless you want me to arrest the whole lot of you for interfering with a homicide investigation."

But we didn't step back. Sam reached for my hand, shaking his head. "This is bad." It seemed to be all he could say.

Tony remained dazed, his eyes riveted on the body, his skin the color of a kosher dill. The detectives watched us warily, the officers' guns still aimed at us as if they thought we might storm the patio.

Gently, I touched Tony's arm. "Tony?"

Tony blinked, as if suddenly awakened. Without a word, he pivoted and ran from the room. Nobody stopped him as he dashed past police with drawn weapons, heading for the powder room. Slowly, Sam and I moved away from the sliding door and slumped onto my sofa. When the guns were holstered, I made proper introductions and, then, the questioning resumed.

SIX

I TOLD DETECTIVE DONALLY WHAT I KNEW AND WHAT I'D SEEN, which didn't amount to much. No, I did not know the woman. I'd never seen her before. I'd heard nothing unusual. I had no idea why she'd come onto our patio. I'd been out all morning with the baby. I hadn't touched anything.

Sometime during my statement, Nick appeared. At first glance, I thought it was Tony. But then, I saw the scar etched into Nick's face. Thank God. Nick was here. We would all be all right. I thought he'd embrace me as Tony had, but he didn't. He turned to Sam, furious.

"Sam, what the hell went down here?" As if Sam, the next eldest, should have taken charge, should have somehow prevented the murder.

Sam hunched slightly, as if dodging blame. "Tony and I came in and this is what we found. We tried to call you."

"Yo—Stiles?" Detective Donally seemed surprised to see Nick. In the confusion, no one had thought to mention that Nick, a senior homicide detective, lived in the house. "What brings you here?"

"Do I need your permission to be here, Detective?" From Nick's tone, I guessed he wasn't a fan of Donally.

Donally eyed Nick. "I took the call, so I repeat my question: What brings—"

"Don't repeat. I live here."

"What?" Donally was stunned. "No shit."

Nick scanned the room, then the patio, coldly, quickly, taking in details.

"We got to talk, Stiles."

Nick raised a hand, making Donally wait as, finally, he stooped and took my hands, his blue eyes searching me. "Are you all right?"

I nodded. I was, now that he was home. "But I have no idea what happened."

He touched my face. "Where's Luke?"

I pointed at the ceiling. "Sleeping."

Nick looked from me, to Sam, to the body beyond the sliding door. Then he stood. "Okay, then. Jim, Al? A word?" Nick put his arm on Detective Donally's shoulder and guided him to the far corner of the room where they and the other detective conferred in hushed tones, heads together.

Beside me on the sofa, Sam kept sighing, rubbing his chin. "Never saw a thing like that in my whole life. How can that son of a gun do it?" I thought he meant the killer, but he was watching Nick. "What kind of a frickin' job is that? Tell me. Isn't there a better way to make a living? Why does he do it? Dealing with crap like this? Seeing stuff like this? It's no kind of life. If he'd go into business with me like I tell him, he'd make ten times as much, believe me." He sighed again. "But that's Nick. Him and frickin' Eli. Always was drawn to the dark side. Don't ask me why."

We sat silently, watching Nick gather information, working with the small army that had set up in our home. Sam's cell phone rang repeatedly; repeatedly, he told callers he'd get back to them, a family situation had come up—the darnedest thing—and he'd tell them all about it later. Nick and the other detectives were outside on the patio when Tony finally emerged from the powder room, still pale, and delicately lowered himself onto the sofa between Sam and me.

"You okay?" I knew it was a stupid question even as I asked it; his face looked grayer than the dead woman's.

He nodded. The three of us sat unmoving as if joined at the hips, waiting.

After a while, Tony cleared his throat. "That woman?" His voice was scratchy. "I've seen her before."

I looked from Tony to Sam, who was looking at me. "Wait. What?"

"You know her?"

Sam and I spoke together.

Tony hunkered down, watching the sliding door. "This morning. I went out to get the newspaper." His voice sounded raw. "I bent down to pick it up, and she ran right into me. I mean, smack into me. Full force. Bam. I nearly went down."

"You're sure it was her?"

"Positive."

"But why—I mean, how come she'd run into you? Didn't she see you?"

Tony shrugged. "I don't know. Maybe she wasn't looking."

I didn't know what to say, and I had no idea what the significance of the collision might be.

"Are you sure it's the same broad?" Sam used words like *broad*.

"Christ, Sam—yes, I'm sure. She just about fell on top of me."

"But how can you be? That chick out there—she's all messed up."

"Sam. It's her. Her face isn't messed up. And I recognize her sweat suit—it's University of Michigan. Her ponytail. Her eye shadow. How many women joggers were dressed like that this morning on this street? It's her. I'm absolutely positive."

Sam seemed unconvinced.

"She slammed into me, Sam. She grabbed on to me to steady herself. We both almost hit the ground. We were like holding on to each other, face-to-face, and—I don't know. We had a moment."

"You had a moment?" Sam blinked. "You? With a dame?"

Tony shrugged. "Not everything is about sex, Sam."

What? Wait, what were they saying? Was Tony gay?

"Says you."

"I'm telling you, we had a moment. A purely nonsexual one, a human-to-human moment. It was intense. Like her eyes bored a hole into my head."

Sam paused, as if absorbing the information. "This is unbeliev-able. You're telling us that this morning, that dead dame came on to you."

"She didn't come on to me—"

"But it's the same broad. You're positive?"

"How many times do I have to say so? Yes. I'm positive."

"Son of a gun." Sam shook his head, baffled. "The kid doesn't even like women, but he goes out for the paper and some hot blonde jumps him."

"She didn't jump me. She collided with me."

"Whatever. A few hours later, she ends up gutted like a deer. In the back of the place where you're staying."

Again, for a moment, the three of us sat silent. I wondered why Nick hadn't mentioned that Tony was gay. Not that it mattered, but still. And I didn't know what it meant that Tony had seen the victim before. In fact, I wasn't sure it meant anything at all. But, clearly, the police had to be told. I stood to go get Nick and almost tripped over Oliver, who'd been watching us beside the wingback. Damn, I'd forgotten about Oliver—it had been hours. He must need to go out. But I couldn't let him out back; it was a crime scene with a body on the ground. I'd have to take him out front. I knocked on the window, motioning Nick to come inside.

Oliver gave out an accusatory bark. Then, watching me, slowly and deliberately, he lifted a leg and piddled on my hardwood floor.

SEVEN

By three o'clock, the fog had mostly burned off, and Sam and I waited at the corner for Molly's school bus. Sam tried to divert my attention from the crime by talking about various time-share properties he was selling, pushing me to think about investing in the Bahamas or Playa del Something-or-other, just outside of Cancún. After all, with two kids, Nick and I would want a place for family vacations. I tuned Sam out, watching for the bus, wondering how I would explain to Molly why police cars were blocking the street, double-parked in front of our house where the bus normally dropped her off. At least there were no sirens or flashing lights.

Finally, the bus pulled up to the corner, and Molly burst out the door and bounced down the steps, yellow curls flying as she looked up the street. "Mom, what happened?"

Not "hello." Not a kiss or hug. Molly greeted us with a wide, suspicious gaze and a direct question.

"How was your day, Molls?" I dodged. Actually, her question hadn't entirely startled me. Molly had an unflinching way of confronting trouble. But so soon? Even before hello? My explanation wasn't ready. I glanced at Sam, who glanced at me.

"Here's my girl." He reached for her, scooped her off the ground. "Give your uncle a hug."

But Molly wouldn't be distracted, even as she perched in Sam's hefty arms. "Why are you guys here? You never wait for my bus."

Ouch. She was right. I hadn't greeted her bus in months, not since Luke was born. Did she feel neglected? Guilty, I fumbled for an answer. I never lied to Molly, but I hadn't fully figured out what I was going to say. The day had passed in a blur, and suddenly it had been time for her bus to pull up. How could I explain the confusion going on inside her house? The place was still crawling with police and forensic people. The body had been removed, but blood stained the back deck and yellow tape surrounded the yard. Molly watched me, waiting. From Sam's arms, her eyes were level with mine.

I took a breath, deciding to be blunt. "Well, actually—"

"It's so warm out, we figured it was a good day for you to take me to the zoo."

The zoo?

"The zoo?" Molly frowned, peering into Sam's face, perplexed. "But it's a school day." To her, the idea of going to the zoo on a school day was clearly preposterous.

She turned to me. I closed my mouth, trying not to look surprised at Sam's invitation.

"It was a school day," Sam acknowledged. "But it's Friday. No school tomorrow. And it's not a normal Friday, either. First of all, it's finally nice outside. And, second, your uncle's visiting and needs a young lady to escort him around town."

Molly looked from him to me, from me to him. My daughter was no fool, and she wanted to know what was up. I made myself smile. "Molls, it's okay. You can go if you want."

"Something happened, didn't it? On our street."

"Everybody's okay, Molls. We'll tell you all about it later."

"What happened?" She wouldn't be put off. "Where's Luke?"

"Luke's fine. He's home with Nick."

"And Uncle Tony?"

"Tony's fine, too. We're all okay, but—" Oh dear. How to say it? "But somebody got hurt. A woman—"

"The police are taking care of it," Sam interrupted. "But while we're standing here yakking, time's wasting. What do you say, Molly? Let's go. We've only got a couple hours till they close."

"You mean you want to go right now? This minute?"

"Yes, ma'am. This very one." Sam set her down and helped her remove the book bag from her shoulders.

"But, Mom, I have a project. It's due on Monday."

"No problem. You have all weekend. I'll help you."

"Mom?" Molly was still suspicious. "Luke's really okay?"

"Yes. I told you. He's with Nick and Tony."

"Wait—Nick? Why's Nick home so early? Because of the woman? So she's dead? Why didn't you tell me she was dead? Who was she?" Molly's mind worked quickly, putting facts together. Too comfortable with murder, too familiar with Nick's work.

"Molly." I knelt to look her in the eye. "Nick came home early because Tony and Sam are visiting, not because of the woman." I omitted the part about her being dead. It wasn't a lie.

And, apparently, my answer satisfied Molly. "So it's okay if I take Uncle Sam to the zoo?"

"It's absolutely okay. Have fun."

"And you'll help me with my project?"

"I will."

Nodding, she gave me a quick kiss and took Sam's hand. "Do they have elephants at this zoo, Molly? Because I know lots of elephant jokes."

"Elephant jokes?" Molly glanced at me. "What's that?"

"Here's one. What weighs five thousand pounds and wears slippers?"

"I don't know."

"Cinderelephant." Sam laughed out loud, wheezing, winking at me as they started across the street. "Get it?"

"Yeah, I guess." Molly was unimpressed, but I was certain she'd hear a hundred more before they got home, maybe even before they got to the zoo.

They walked off toward his Lexus, and I stood alone at the curb, holding a loaded book bag.

EIGHT

By THE TIME I GOT TO TALK TO SUSAN, IT WAS ALMOST TEN. By then, everyone in Philadelphia had heard about the murder. It had been a feature on the six o'clock news. People had been calling ever since, but we hadn't answered, letting the voice mails pile up. Molly, wearing a zoo T-shirt and holding a new stuffed elephant, had finally gone to bed. I'd fed Luke, so he was set and happy for another four hours, and the brothers had stopped hovering over me long enough to eat. Dinner was pizza in the living room with a couple of cold six-packs. Grabbing a slice of mushroom, I'd retreated to the bedroom with a glass of seltzer and my cell phone.

Susan Cummings was my best friend. A prominent criminal defense attorney, she was also the very married mother of three girls, an incredible homemaker and cook, an avid volunteer for a dozen charitable organizations and president of the Home and School Association. For Susan, life was a matter of juggling projects. Her projects ranged from dieting to decorating, fund-raising to child rearing, attending *Carmen* to arguing in court. Susan attacked every project with passion—baking, shopping, defending clients, being married to Tim. But for all the commotion in her life, Susan was a constant friend; normally, she steadied me. Her home, her presence, even her voice grounded me. Whenever I faced trouble, I sought her out.

"Finally," she scolded me. Her voice was angry and very ungrounding. "Why didn't you answer my calls? I tried the house.

I tried your cell. I was about to come over there and break the door down."

"I couldn't call you or anybody. The cops were here until just now."

"Well?"

Well. What should I say?

"Zoe. Are you all right?"

"I'm fine. We're all fine."

"Of course you are. And the pope's a Hindu."

She was right. I wasn't fine. I was numb, way too calm. Probably in some kind of shock. "I mean, under the circumstances. We're fine under the circumstances."

"Okay. So, spill."

I spilled, recounting events as if telling her would somehow make them less unfathomable, as if words might diminish the grisliness of the woman's death. They didn't, but as I finished, I felt somehow validated by Susan's reactions, her occasional "damn" or "no way."

"So. Do they know anything yet? I mean do they have any leads? What does Nick say?"

I gave her the latest update. "They don't know who she is, but they think the murder was about drugs."

"Well, duh. That's obvious."

It was? "How is it obvious?"

"Get real, Zoe. Why else would they cut her open?"

"So, you knew about that?" I hadn't. I hadn't any idea that people swallowed bags of drugs and transported them across borders in their stomachs, primarily to get the drugs past Customs.

"Of course I did. You mean you didn't?" She paused, and I didn't answer. "Of course you didn't. You're Zoe."

"Don't start." Save me, she was going to start her "you live in a bubble" routine again, depicting me as a completely naïve and idealistic airhead.

"But it's true. Zoe, you live in a bubble, ignoring unpleasant-
ness, shutting out whatever you don't want to know. You simply
refuse to accept the ugly parts of life."

"That's not true."

"It is true."

I wanted to say, "It isn't," but she'd just say, "It is," and we'd go
back and forth, arguing like a couple of six-year-olds. Still, I'd
seen my share of ugliness, and I was irritated at the way she repeatedly claimed to be worldlier, more knowledgeable, than I. "So
what are you saying, Susan? That people commonly jog around
the neighborhood with bellies full of heroin?"

"Maybe not. Could be full of cocaine."

I leaned back against my pillows. Damn. Was she right? Was it
really common, mainstream knowledge that people swallowed
bags of drugs to transport them inside their bellies? Couldn't be.

"Susan, the only way you know this stuff is because you work
with criminals. You defend drug dealers on a daily basis. The un-
derbelly of society is your bread and butter, so your viewpoint is
skewed. The average person has no idea—"

"The average person is a moron—forget about him. Tell me
more about what Nick said."

"He just said what I told you. That the cops think it was drugs.
One theory is that one of the bags burst in her belly and killed
her, so they had to cut out the other bags. Another is that maybe
she was holding out on the dealers, making off with a bag or two.
Whatever the reason, they think she got cut open to retrieve drugs
she was carrying. But all they really know so far is that she was already dead when she was cut open."

"Well, that's a blessing."

A blessing? "I guess." I pictured the blood and body parts,
couldn't see their owner as blessed.

For a moment, Susan didn't say anything. I stared at my pizza
slice. The cheese had cooled and hardened; grease had congealed.

The tomato sauce had darkened into clots. I picked a mushroom slice off the top, put it in on my tongue. Chewed.

"Okay. So that explains why they cut her open. But it doesn't explain a more important question."

I swallowed. What question?

"Why was she on your patio?"

Oh. Right. That question.

"I mean, out of all the gates in the alley, why would she pick yours?"

And that one, too.

Staring at my sorry pizza slice, I drifted, letting Susan go on as I considered possible answers, so that, when her voice stopped, I had no idea why.

"But please don't pick the hazelnut. And God, not the Amaretto—nobody likes that. Go with chocolate mousse? Please?"

Oh, she was talking about the cake. How could she think about the cake now, when a woman was dead? But she went on.

"Anyhow, the jury should be in, the latest by Tuesday, so how about a girls' day out? I can show you my dress—Zoe, I swear, I look twenty pounds lighter in it. If I don't watch out, I might out-shine the bride. But we'll go out for lunch. A leisurely, expensive lunch. And then, we'll have a massage and a pedicure. Yes, that's what we need: a spa day. How's Thursday?"

Susan went on, her voice lilting and chirpy, as if she were having a normal conversation with a normal bride-to-be on a normal night. What was with her? How could she be so blasé about the murder? Were sliced bodies and drugs really not big deals anymore? Was the world just, ho-hum, another bloody mess in the backyard, let's go get a facial? I didn't know, but I couldn't listen anymore.

Abruptly, I interrupted with a lie. "Susan—uh-oh, Luke's crying. Got to go." And I hung up suddenly, drained, not certain that I even said good-bye.

NINE

I LAY THERE FOR A FEW MINUTES, STARING AT NOTHING. I WAS
irritated with Susan but knew it would pass. Susan was blunt,
honest and painfully practical. She didn't dwell on subtleties; she
said what she thought and moved on. Sometimes, that was what I
loved about her. At that moment, though, it wasn't. I wanted to be
comforted, or at least reassured. But Susan, for all her fine quali-
ties, wasn't in a comforting or reassuring mood. She was in the
mood to think about chocolate mousse cake and matron-of-honor
fashions. Since Nick was occupied, I was on my own, would have
to comfort and reassure myself.

Maybe some television would help. I could watch a sitcom and
vegetate, lull myself with canned laughter. I reached for the remote, but it wasn't on the nightstand. I leaned on an elbow and
looked across the comforter, to Nick's nightstand. No remote.
Where was it? Maybe on the floor or under the bed? Okay. If I
wanted to watch television, I'd have to get up, either to search or
to turn the thing on the old-fashioned way. No sitcom was worth
that amount of effort. I lay there feeling lonely and neglected,
fully aware that I could go downstairs and join the brothers, par-
take in some actual human companionship.

But I didn't. If I went downstairs, I was sure that Sam and Tony
would fuss over me and hover as they had all afternoon and into
the evening.

"Zoe shouldn't be alone," Tony had told Nick earlier. He'd said it right in front of me as if I weren't there. "She's vulnerable. A woman with small children in a high-crime area. She should have somebody with her."

Nick hadn't argued. He'd pulled on his beer and watched me.

"I'm fine on my own," I began. "I've lived here for ten years, and I have a babysitter part-time. The neighborhood's actually safer than it used to be."

"But you've got kids now," Tony persisted. "And somebody got murdered on your back porch. You need to be more—"

"Nothing's going to happen to me or the kids." I looked to Nick for support.

Nick returned my look but didn't say a word, and I couldn't read his expression.

"Seriously, Zoe," Sam chimed in, selling real estate. "You guys should take the kids and move somewhere safer—I can get you guys a deal, believe me. What do you want? A condo? A nice house in the burbs?"

"This is our home. We like it here." I made my voice flat, trying to sound final.

Sam scowled. "Look, I'll gather up some information on properties. No pressure. When you're ready, you and Nick can look it over—"

"But for now, you've got bodyguards," Tony had volunteered. "As long as Sam and I are here, you don't need to worry. You won't be alone."

And, for the rest of the day, while Nick worked with the detectives, his brothers had followed me, a tag team, wherever I'd gone. They'd taken turns. For a while, Sam had disappeared into my office to talk on his cell or work on his laptop, but Tony had stayed glued to me. If I turned around too fast, I bumped into him. Tony had stayed with me while I bathed Luke; he'd watched as I measured the kibble to feed Oliver. Then, when Sam had finally emerged from my office, they'd switched places. It was Tony's turn to disappear and Sam's to be my shadow. I'd had to insist that he wait downstairs when I went up to the bathroom. One or the other had been with me every second, watching but not necessarily helping as I cleaned up the kitchen, tossing out empty beer bottles and finally putting away the wilted lettuce and other groceries I'd bought that morning. Sam or Tony, together or apart, had shadowed me as I'd ordered pizza, as Molly and I had made salad, as I had emptied and refilled the dishwasher. They'd backed off a little when Nick came in, gathering around him to hear the latest from the police. Finally, when the pizza had arrived and they'd been distracted by food, I'd escaped, tucked Molly into bed and taken refuge in my bedroom, where I'd called Susan. I didn't want to stay in my room all night, but if I went downstairs, I risked reactivating my security detail.

Wait a minute, I told myself. This is your home, not theirs. It's not even Nick's yet. They are all merely guests here. And they have no right to crowd you or make you a prisoner in your own home. Go on downstairs and, if they bug you, tell them to back off. Since when have you been shy?

On the other hand, since when had I had family? Never. As an only child, I had no idea how to coexist with siblings. What were the rules? These men were Nick's brothers, and I wanted to become close to them. I wanted them to accept me, even love me, so I hadn't complained once since they'd arrived. Not made one peep. Not about the way they were taking up every spare minute of Nick's time. Not about how both Sam and Tony kept using my private home office repeatedly for hours at a time without even asking. Not about Tony spilling coffee on my purple velvet sofa, not about them repeatedly letting Oliver out of his crate so he kept peeing on the floor, not about the clutter Tony left in the living room or the raised toilet seats or the shaved-off whiskers lining the bathroom sinks—

Wait, whoa, I told myself. Stop. Do not go down the list-ofresentments path. I reminded myself that Sam and Tony were family, that they would be there only for another week and that no mess, no inconvenience, no invasion of privacy could compare to the joy their presence brought to Nick. Besides, Molly was getting to know and adore her uncles. I needed to stop being a sulky spoiled brat and go join them.

And so, smoothing my hair, taking a deep breath and putting on what I thought might pass for a sisterly smile, I got out of bed and winced as my bare foot land on something hard and rectangular. The remote control—good. I'd found it.

I knelt to pick it up, but it fell apart in my hands. The plastic was demolished, the case all mangled and rough-edged. Damn it. Oliver. He'd struck again, had chewed the thing to smithereens. Shoes, chair and table legs, books, wallets, wires, purses, underwear, socks, key chains, pillows and now a remote control. It was no big deal, I reminded myself. It was just another casualty of the puppy.

Even so, tears flooded my eyes. I bit my lip, scolding myself. Stop it. You can get another remote. They're cheap. They are only pieces of plastic, nothing worth crying about. Still, the tears welled up. What was wrong with me? I hadn't cried at the sight of a carved-up woman, but I was bawling about a broken TV remote?

From downstairs, the brothers' voices rose, overlapping, interrupting each other in heated, animated conversation. I listened, suddenly jealous. I needed Nick. I wanted to be with him, and I didn't want to share him with Tony and Sam. I wanted Nick's undivided attention.

I was being childish, and I knew it. Nick loves you, I reminded myself. He's going to marry you; his brothers are no threat to you. You don't have to isolate yourself. Nick wants you there with him; so do Tony and Sam. Join them. You're not alone. You belong to a family now. Go be part of it.

And so, drying my eyes, I stood up and marched down the

steps. I continued along the hall to the living room, and without hesitation, I walked in to join the group.

And as I did, Tony nudged Nick; Sam shifted his eyes and cleared his throat. Nick stopped talking mid-sentence. The conversation abruptly stopped; the faces became blank with feigned innocence, as if I'd caught them stealing cookies. All three turned my way, fumbling a welcome, smiling awkwardly, probably wondering how much I'd heard.

"Zoe." Nick finally greeted me. "Finally. Come join us." He patted an empty spot on the sofa beside him.

Obviously, they were excluding me. But, because I ached for Nick's company, I did join them.

TEN

Later, in bed, I asked Nick what the three of them had been talking about.

"When?"

"When I came into the living room. You all stopped talking. It was like you didn't want me to hear."

He half-smiled and kissed my forehead. "Don't be so sensitive. Probably, they were just telling me how hot you are."

I wasn't amused. "I'm serious, Nick. What was going on?"

He sighed. "Nothing. You surprised us; that's all. Nobody heard you coming and, suddenly, you were just standing there."

I wasn't going to let him off that easily. I'd seen the alarm on their faces. "Why won't you tell me?"

He released a long, tired sigh. "What's this about? Do you think I'm lying to you? There's nothing to tell." He looked at me, all innocent and offended. His eyes were so blue and steady, so impossible to read. He rolled over and held me. "Look, Sam and Tony think you're way too good for me. Maybe that's what they were saying when you walked in."

I didn't believe him. But why would he hide the truth?

"Anyhow, it's been a hell of a day. I'm wiped—you must be, too. You had a hell of a time. How about it, Zoe? Hang on to me and let's go to sleep."

His breath smelled of beer and toothpaste, and his voice was fading. Nick was already half-gone. I lay in his arms as he fell asleep, and I stayed there until the baby monitor broadcast Luke stirring. He was almost an hour early but probably hungry again. Gently, I lifted Nick's arm, rolled away from him and went to feed the baby. When I came back to the bedroom, Nick was sound asleep. I climbed in beside him, tucking myself under his arm. Finally, even though he was unconscious and rattling the room with his snores, it was just the two of us, snuggled up together, peaceful. And, best of all, alone.

ELEVEN

SATURDAY MORNING WAS STILL UNNATURALLY WARM, STILL GRAY. I woke up sluggish and aching and, seeing that Molly was already up, plodded through the process of getting Luke fed and dressed, letting other people answer the endlessly ringing phone. When I came downstairs, Nick was pouring milk into Molly's cereal, ending a call. "Yes, I'll tell her. . . . No, no. . . . Thanks."

Sam's face was buried in the newspaper even as he was talking on his cell phone, assuring somebody that everything would be fine; things didn't always go as planned, they'd work out; he'd take care of it himself.

Tony was pacing, complaining. "I just don't see how they can do that without a person's permission."

"You were there. It's news. That's how." Nick sounded tired. His phone rang; he reached for it.

"But what about my privacy? I'm a private citizen, not a celebrity. They have no right to plaster my face all over the papers—" He saw me in the doorway and stopped mid-sentence. "Zoe, you won't believe this. Look—"

He grabbed the newspaper from Sam, who interrupted his conversation to slap at Tony's hand. "Hey, I'm reading that—"

"Guess what, Mom?" Molly jumped out of her chair, arms out to embrace Luke. "You're famous!"

"I am?" I looked at Nick, who, ending his phone call, glared at Tony.

"I'll call you as soon as it's done. I promise." Sam ended his call and went after Tony. "Give that back; I was in the middle of a story."

"Chill, Sam." Tony shuffled the pages, searching for something.

Molly, meantime, began kissing Luke, tickling him and cooing. "Hello, Little Lukie; good morning, sweetie pie." She was all over him, but he didn't seem to mind.

"Sit down, Molls. Finish your breakfast."

"Give it back," Sam growled. "I'm serious, punk."

But Tony paid Sam no mind, too busy reassembling the paper.

"Can I hold him, Mom?" Molly reached out for Luke.

"Your mom said to finish your breakfast." Nick motioned for Molly to sit down.

"So then, when I'm finished, then I can hold him." Molly wasn't giving up.

"We'll see." It was an absentminded answer; my mind was on the newspaper. The house phone rang again. Looking haggard, Nick picked it up, covering his ear so he could hear the caller. Sam stared, fuming, as Tony rustled the pages apart.

"You mean I can't? Why can't I?" Molly sat, but she was digging in. She wasn't going to drop the subject until she got her way. "Emily holds her baby cousin all the time."

"Emily has nothing to do with it."

"Please, Mom. Pleeeeeze."

"Maybe. After you eat."

Suddenly, moving faster than I'd have imagined a man of his bulk could, Sam stood and darted behind Tony. In a single swipe, Sam grabbed the newspaper—or most of it—out of Tony's hands.

Instinctively, Tony whirled around and took a fighting stance. "What the hell, Sam." The two faced each other, nostrils flaring like angry bulls. I glanced at Nick, but hanging up the phone, he seemed distracted, as if his thoughts were elsewhere. Molly and I, though, watched the brothers, amazed. Silent and stunned, we waited for one of them to charge.

Thankfully, neither did. After a couple of seconds, Sam snorted and turned away, arms filled with rumpled pages.

"What the hell's your problem?" Tony taunted him, trying to save face. "I was going to give you the whole thing back in a second." Muttering obscenities, Tony plopped the remainder of Section A onto the counter and smoothed out the front page.

"Take a look at this, Zoe."

Nick finally joined us. "Sit down, Zoe. Let me take Luke—" He reached for the baby.

I sat and looked at the paper. The headline screamed: "Ripper Slaying in Queen Village," and beneath it, taking up the right central portion of the front page, sat a photo of my house. A police officer, Tony, Sam, Luke and I clustered on the front steps.

"See, Mom?" Molly hopped out of her seat again, pointing to my picture. "There you are. And Luke and Uncle Tony and Uncle Sam. I told you."

I nodded, felt the blood drain from my head. "You're right. Eat your cereal, Molls."

Nick patted Luke's back, scowling at Tony. "I said this should wait till after breakfast."

"Well, I thought she should see it."

I sat back in my seat, staring at the story. Behind me, Tony was complaining about our pictures being out there, in the public eye where anyone could see our faces, and Sam told him to stop being so damned vain.

"Trust me on this, little brother. Nobody, not one fricking soul, cares about seeing your pretty face in the damned paper." He turned to me. "Can you believe this guy? He's been going on about his photograph all morning."

"Actually, I think you look pretty good, Tony." He did. He looked like Nick. "You're very photogenic."

"Are you kidding? Look at his nose. It looks huge."

"Huge? Like an elephant's?" Molly giggled and squinted, studying Tony's nose.

"Oh, by the way, Sam." Tony pursed his lips. "The airline called. They want to bill you for both the seats your fat butt occupied during your flight."

Ouch. Sam was sensitive about his size. Tension soared as we waited for his reaction. I held my breath. "You're an asshole, Tony," Sam growled. "Point is, you don't hear me crying about my fat picture being in the paper. Because it doesn't matter. Nobody cares. By tomorrow, nobody's even gonna remember you or your ugly mug. They're gonna run another picture, another headline, and you and your freakin' nose will be forgotten fish wrap. Now can you quit your whining?"

Tony faced Sam and leaned over, chin-to-chin. "My ugly face is not the point, Sam. Neither is your fat butt. The point is privacy. I don't like having my picture taken, let alone having it published in a newspaper, let alone published without my permission."

Slowly, without breaking eye contact, Sam began to stand. Tony didn't budge. Eyeball-to-eyeball, they stared at each other, breathing heavily. Sam's hands tightened into fists. No question, this time, he was about to take a swing. Tony wouldn't back away. Oh God.

"Settle down, children." Nick didn't raise his voice. He sat on a stool, holding Luke, calmly playing with his toes. "Or I'll kick both your asses."

Nick was the oldest. He took his authority for granted, and so, apparently, did the others. Without another word, Sam warily sat and Tony backed off, slunk across the kitchen and out of the room. I resumed breathing but couldn't get enough air.

I began to read the article, but suddenly Molly shrieked.

"Wait—" She dropped her spoon onto the table. "Uncle Sam—I have one! An elephant joke."

"Shoot."

"I made it up myself. Listen; here it is. Why does an elephant have a trunk?"

"I have no idea. Why?"

Molly started giggling before she gave her answer. "To hold everything it nose. Get it? Everything it knows?"

"You made that up? By yourself?" Nick was half-grinning.

"Yup."

"It's good." Sam winked at her. "Here's another one. What's the difference between eating peanut butter and eating an elephant?"

"Ewww. That's silly. Who would eat an elephant?"

"You give up?" Sam looked at Nick and me, waited for guesses, got none. "The difference is: An elephant doesn't stick to the roof of your mouth." Sam wheezed with laughter, tickled with himself.

"Good one, Uncle Sam." Molly smiled, held up an empty cereal bowl. "I'm finished. Can I hold Luke now?"

Nick took her to the living room where she could sit in the wingback to hold Luke, and I skimmed the article about the killing, about the victim's still-unknown identity, the police suspicion that drugs might be the motive. And then, while Sam slurped his coffee and commented about stocks, I studied the photograph, confused and oddly light-headed. How had a photographer gotten those shots? And when? Had a photographer gotten past the police barricade? I had no idea. And something else concerned me. Despite Sam's vow that, tomorrow, nobody would remember us, I agreed with Tony. I wasn't at all comfortable being seen by thousands, my home and my face spread across the front page.

TWELVE

IT WAS SATURDAY AFTERNOON, AND SUSAN SAT BESIDE ME OUT-
side the dressing rooms at the bridal shop, where we were waiting
for Molly to emerge after the final fitting of her flower girl dress.
Molly, Susan's daughter Emily and Anna, our wedding planner,
had been back there for over twenty minutes, long enough for me
to tell Susan that I'd been over the top with anxiety and considering asking the doctor for medication. But the medication would
show up in my breast milk, so taking it meant weaning Luke. And
Susan was adamant that I needed to nurse Luke for a year, at least.
And while I hadn't planned to do it for that long, I agreed that ten
weeks was probably not enough.

"Look. In a week," Susan went on, "your life will be sane again.
No more triplets. No more prewedding jitters. Even the murder will
be a fading—granted a nasty one but a fading—memory. But the
point is: Luke. Luke will still need you. It's a known fact that babies
who are breast-fed do better all through their childhood. They're
healthier, more resistant to sickness. There's no substitute for
mother's milk. How could you think of weaning him so young?"

How? Because I was a wreck, that was how. Susan made it sound
so clear-cut, I felt like a criminal for even considering weaning
Luke. I cleared my throat, kept my voice low. "But maybe I have
postpartum depression."

"What? You? No way. This is not postpartum. You're always
this way."

I was? Did I always feel like I was about to have a heart attack?

Susan twisted to examine my face, then sat back again. Did she think depression showed like a pimple? "Okay. If I were you, here's what I'd do. I'd wait a week before seeing the doctor, and I'd see how I felt after all the commotion dies down. I mean, what's the harm in that? What could happen in a week?"

Was she joking? I considered how much could happen. One week ago, I had my life in order. I hadn't met Sam or Tony. My babysitter hadn't lost her car and taken off in a fit. I hadn't found a woman with entrails strung across my patio, and Bryce Edmond hadn't—

"Mom? Are you ready?" A voice from the fitting room. Molly was about to make an entrance.

"Ready." I tried to refocus, to think about clothes, not comas.

Anna came out first, dressed as usual in three-inch heels and a too-tight iridescent aqua suit that contrasted too sharply with her red hair. Her hands clasped in front of her, bracelets jangling, she stood in front of the curtain like the glitzy emcee of a beauty pageant and gestured widely with one arm. "Drumroll, please." She paused, laughing way too hard. "Sorry, our drummer must be out to lunch."

Susan rolled her eyes. "Good God. Where did you find her?"

"Shh." I couldn't afford to offend the event organizer a week before the ceremony. Besides, Susan knew very well where I'd found Anna. Anna had done a wedding for Tim's niece; Susan's own husband had recommended her.

"Zoe Hayes, bride-to-be, it is my sincere pleasure to present: Your flower girl, Ms. Molly Hayes." Susan's elbow jabbed my ribs. I didn't look at her, knew she was making gag-me faces. I didn't blame her. In Anna's hands, the planning process had somehow escaped me, gone out of control. Over her shoulder, Anna whispered, "Molly, you may come out now."

For a moment, nothing happened. We sat, eyes riveted to the

dressing room curtain, waiting, wondering what little tomboy Molly would look like in an ankle-length dress of ashes of roses silk and antique lace. Molly, who refused to wear skirts or dresses to school, who insisted on sweatpants or jeans so she wouldn't look like a "girlie girl," was as rough and tough as any of the boys her age, excelling in kick-boxing, gymnastics, swimming, soccer, football—any sport she'd tried. I hoped she wouldn't complain too much about having to wear such a frilly dress. No matter. She'd have to put up with it, just for a day. I'd promise she'd never have to wear it again. I'd bribe her, if necessary. And no matter how awkward or uncomfortable she looked, I was going to rave about her grace and beauty.

In the seconds before she emerged, I rehearsed. "Molly, you look magical, like a fairy princess." No, not convincing enough. And Molly would hate looking like a fairy princess. "Molly. Oh my God. You look like a supermodel." Better.

Emily peeked out the side, between the curtain and the wall. Then, slowly, the curtains parted, and out stepped not Molly but a dream. A delicate vision in lace and silk. A porcelain doll with flowing golden hair, moving as gracefully as if she were real and alive. A small, radiant angel, glowing, with questions in her eyes.

"Mom?" the angel asked. "How do I look?"

I tried to answer, but my throat was choked. All I could do was dab my eyes.

The angel blinked, confused.

"Gorgeous!" Susan exclaimed. "Molly, you're gorgeous. Like a princess. Better than a princess. Just beautiful. Your mother can't even talk, she's so overcome. Tell her, Emily. Doesn't she look gorgeous?"

From the edge of the curtain, Emily glowered.

"Come out and take a look, Em."

"I already saw."

"Turn around, Molly. Show them the back." Anna fussed. Susan oohed and aahed.

"Isn't she just perfect?" Anna bragged.

"Nobody's perfect." Emily stomped off, disappearing behind the curtain.

"Okay. She's jealous." Susan got up and went after Emily.

"Emily's jealous? Of what? My dress?" Molly clearly didn't understand. Her eyebrows rose. "Does that mean we can't have a sleepover?"

Finally, I found my voice. "She'll be all right. She just wants to be beautiful like you, Molls."

"But she is. Emily's more beautifuller than me."

She was not.

"Okay, ladies. Let's get the dress off and hung before it gets damaged." Anna ushered Molly away.

From inside the fitting rooms, Susan's voice rose, scolding Emily. My cell phone rang. Damn. Bryce Edmond's name showed up on the screen. Again. What the hell? Why was he calling me every day? I was on leave. Didn't he understand the words *maternity leave*? I turned the ringer to silent, letting it go.

Susan emerged, fuming. "I don't know what to do. She won't come out. She's just standing there, pouting. What a prima donna."

I kept my mouth shut, unable to pretend that I disagreed. Anna rushed around with a hanger, bagging the dress, and Susan and I sat silently waiting for Molly, wondering how long it would take for Emily to thaw out. After a few minutes, from behind the fitting room curtain we heard Molly's hushed voice. "Emily, I have to tell you. Out of all the girls I know, you're my most prettiest friend."

And so there was a sleepover, after all.

THIRTEEN

MOLLY WENT HOME WITH SUSAN AND EMILY, AND I CAME HOME alone in plenty of time to feed Luke. As I came in, I heard the brothers' animated conversation coming from the family room.

". . . clothes pulled off . . . but no evidence of rape . . ." Whose voice was that? Nick's? Those guys all sounded alike.

I crept down the hall, trying to hear what they were saying.

". . . inferred that she was carrying drugs . . . but other than the condition of the body . . . no actual evidence . . ." That was definitely Nick.

I stopped near the doorway where I could hear them. I could see Tony gliding around the living room, apparently looking. He picked up cushions, peered under the sofa, while Nick talked.

"But it's got to be drugs. Why else would they slice her? Wait—are you saying somebody got his kicks out of that? Like the paper suggested—you know, Jack the Ripper?" Sam's voice was husky, strained.

"No. I'm not suggesting anything yet—"

I hadn't made a noise. At least, I hadn't been aware of making a noise. But suddenly, in unison, three heads twisted to face me.

"Zoe?" Nick bounded to his feet to greet me. "I didn't hear you come in. How long have you been standing there?"

Why would he ask that? Obviously, he wanted to know how much I'd heard. Sam rubbed his chin nervously. Tony stood up too quickly, as if afraid I'd caught him looking under the sofa.

"Where's Molly?" Nick looked around, kept asking questions.

"At Susan's. Sleepover." I came into the living room and sat on my sofa, beside the spot Tony had occupied. "Where's Luke?"

"Still napping."

"Well, I'd better get back to work." Clearing his throat, Tony grabbed his laptop and fled to my office.

"Tony," I stopped him. "Were you looking for something?"

"Oh." His eyes traveled back to the sofa. "Just—I lost some change. I had a bunch of quarters, but they must have fallen out of my pocket. No big deal." He hurried past me down the hall.

Sam pulled himself to his feet, checking his watch. "Well, look at that. It's almost five. Happy hour. Anybody for a brew? Nick?"

Nick shook his head. "Not yet, thanks."

As soon as I'd come in, the conversation had abruptly ended, and Nick's brothers had practically run out of the room. For the second time in two days, they'd avoided including me.

"What was that about?"

"What was what about?"

"Why did you guys stop talking when I came in?"

"What?" Nick fumbled. "We didn't—"

"Oh, please, Nick. I heard you talking about the murder. What are you trying to hide?"

He walked over and put an arm around me, half his face attempting a casual smile. "Zoe, don't be so sensitive. Nobody's hiding anything."

"No?"

"No. Sam and Tony are just not used to you yet. They're not really secretive. They're just shy."

Shy? Was he kidding? The word didn't fit either of them. Sam was pushy, Tony flamboyant. "Right. They're shy. Like Donald Trump—"

"I mean with you. They're shy with you."

"Uh-huh. And yet, they use my office. Sam has a room at the

Four Seasons, but he sleeps here, half the time on my carpet. Tony's made a nest out of my sofa. They help themselves to whatever's in my refrigerator—"

"They bother you." Nick tried to change the subject, to put me on the defensive. "I'll tell them not to use your office or eat anything without your permission—"

"Stop it, Nick."

"You said they bother you—"

"What bothers me isn't the point. The point is that every time I come into the room, you guys stop talking or change the subject or run out of the room. Do not try to deny it."

Nick sighed and pulled me to him, hugging me. "Sorry, Zoe. I didn't realize it. Your feelings are hurt. We're just worried about you. You seem—I don't know. Fragile."

Fragile? Me? Hardly. I stiffened, backing out of his hug. "Don't patronize me, Nick. This is not about me or my state of mind." Why was he dodging my questions? What was going on? And then, suddenly, I knew. "You think they're involved." Of course, that had to be it. "You think one of them might have something to do with it."

"With what? One of whom?" Nick pretended not to know what I meant. He backed away, but I kept after him, asking questions. Did he think Tony or Sam was involved in the murder? After all, it happened during their visit, two days after their arrival. And Nick hadn't seen them in years, couldn't really know what they were up to, and, face it, they were both kind of shady. Sam claimed to be involved in big international business deals. Maybe those deals were illegal—like maybe drug smuggling? And Tony. He said he'd seen the victim the morning she was killed. But how did we know that had been the first time he'd seen her? How did we know he hadn't been the one she'd been looking for?

"Enough." It was the same flat tone Nick had used when he'd chastised his brothers. "Stop."

I stopped.

Nick's face was stony, and when he spoke again, so was his voice. "Let's make sure I understand you, Zoe. You're saying that you suspect Sam or Tony or both of them of being criminals. Even murderers. Is that right?"

Warily, I met his eyes. "Is it wrong?"

"Are you serious? Of course it is. Completely and positively wrong." His face softened a little. "Look, Zoe. I know this is a stressful time, what with the wedding coming up. And this murder has pushed all of us—especially you—over the top. But sweetheart, please try to relax."

Sweetheart? What? Nick never called me names like that. He took my hand again.

"Look, my brothers are good-hearted. Probably, they don't talk about the murder in front of you because they want to protect you from it."

"Protect me?" I wasn't buying it. "Nick. I found the damned body. It's too late to protect me. Besides which, it's not their job to—"

"I said they're good-hearted, Zoe. I didn't say they're geniuses." Half his mouth smirked and he shook his head. "Fact is, from your point of view, I can see how they look suspicious. But when you get to know them, you'll see they're decent people. They're all bluster. Of the four of us, Eli's the only tough one. Sam and Tony are like me. Pussycats."

Wait. Nick was calling himself a pussycat? I winced. Then again, panthers were pussycats.

"In time, I hope you'll like them. But even if you don't, take my word for it. They may not be angels, but my brothers aren't killers."

He wasn't looking at me. He was looking at our hands, so I couldn't read his expression. I wondered if I could believe him. After all, Sam and Tony were Nick's blood. If Nick knew that one of them was involved in a murder, would he tell anyone, even me? I had no idea.

But, for now anyway, the discussion of homicide was over. Sam came back to the living room with a couple of beers and a bag of tortilla chips. He handed a beer to Nick, deciding for him that it was time to have one, as Tony, finished for now on his computer, emerged from my office and joined us, looking jittery. I excused myself to go feed Luke but lingered at the bottom of the steps, listening, wondering what they'd talk about after I left the room. But though I waited for an uncomfortably long time, all I heard was Sam's hoarse rendition of his profitable investment in some time-shares.

FOURTEEN

SUNDAY MORNING, WHATEVER I DID, WHEREVER I TURNED, ONE
or more of the brothers were there. Sam and Tony, apparently
committed to protecting me, stayed within a five-foot perimeter at
all times. Finally, desperate to breathe, I bundled Luke into his
puffy down snowsuit, put on my jacket and, fending off questions
about where we were going, adamantly refusing three offers to
keep us company, escaped my bodyguards and fled into the cool,
damp air. Luke and I were going for a walk, by ourselves.

Being outside felt glorious. Invigorating. Pushing the carriage, I
almost bounced with freedom as we walked two blocks along
Fourth Street, taking a smelling tour of the city. The garlic of
corned beef haloed Famous Deli. The sweet and buttery scent of
fresh scones hung outside the Pink Rose Cafe. Then, suddenly, the
stench of rotting trash and stale urine assaulted us at the alley,
and, a few steps later, the roasting of burgers already grilling at
Copabanana. An overwhelming assault of frying onions in front
of Jim's, the cheesesteak place. Every three steps, the air changed,
stunning the senses.

We turned onto South Street, where a lone shopkeeper hosed
down the sidewalk, washing away remnants of last night's partying
South Street, with its restaurants, bars and funky shops, attracted a
crowd each night, especially Saturdays. But before noon, especially
on Sundays, South Street was deathly quiet, as if the street itself was
hungover, sleeping it off. The emptiness felt disturbing, the gray

sidewalks matched the sky, and trash lining the curb lay dirty with soot. No cars passed; nobody else walked by. And even though we were outside in the open air, I began to feel the presence of another person, close by.

Stop it, I told myself. You're just tired of being surrounded by Nick's brothers. You're jangled by the murder and suffering a tad of postpartum blues. But the feeling that someone was watching, closing in on us, wouldn't go away. As we passed Eye's Gallery, I paused and looked into the glass, pretending to window-shop while checking our reflection, almost certain that I'd see someone following us. But no one was there.

I kept walking. Kept telling myself to relax. Yet my thoughts and my pulse sped along. The street was too quiet. Crime was increasing in the area. Ivy's car had been stolen in daylight right outside my house. A woman had been murdered on my patio. Every window I passed was covered with bars; every door was gated. Somewhere, not far away, a car alarm blared. Was another car thief striking in the middle of the morning? On Sunday? And then, from nowhere, police sirens wailed. Flashing lights came our way, racing along the empty street, screaming so loudly I stopped to cover Luke's ears until they faded away. Luke watched me placidly, lulled by motion and the out-of-doors, unconcerned that the city was festering with killers, car thieves, burglars and drug dealers. I lifted him, squeezing his tiny bulk, inhaling his sweet scent to mask the harsh urban reek engulfing us. His velvet face brushed mine, and he rooted around, began to suck my cheek. Lord, I loved this boy. Without hesitation, I would give my life, throw myself in front of a train, for him. The sirens faded away and, not for the first time, it occurred to me that this neighborhood might not be the best place to raise children. But then, I rationalized, this planet might not be, either. If I really wanted to keep my children safe, I'd need to take them away from Earth. No living creature was truly safe here—in fact, life itself was fraught with danger. The only absolute guarantee of peace was death.

Wait, whoa—what was I thinking? I stopped walking, scared of myself. These thoughts—where had they come from? They didn't seem like my own. I thought of what I knew about postpartum depression. That had to be it. It was my hormonal imbalance, a temporary phase that made the world seem bleaker than it really was. As Susan said, I could tough it out. Life wasn't as bad as it looked right now. It was precious. And, in a matter of weeks, summer would arrive. With daylight savings time, days would be longer. The gray skies would clear. Luke would sleep all the way through the night, so I could, too, and maybe Oliver would be housebroken. Meantime, pushing the empty carriage, I held Luke close, comforted by the warmth of his small body and the casual ease with which he observed the passing scene.

FIFTEEN

At the corner of Fifth Street, I stopped and turned around, almost positive that someone was following us. Seeing no one, I put Luke back into his carriage and, even though no cars were coming, waited for the light to change before crossing the street.

"Zoe—Zoe, wait."

I looked around, certain that I heard someone calling my name.

"Zoe Hayes! Wait!"

Yes, definitely. Someone was calling. The voice came from across the street; my gaze followed the sound, spotted its source. Oh damn. I squinted, not believing what I saw. Bryce Edmond? Here? Why? Well, whatever the reason, it was too late to escape. The man had definitely seen me. He kept calling my name, repeating it as he ran toward us down Fifth Street. But his presence here made no sense. Bryce Edmond lived out in the suburbs somewhere. Haverford? Havertown? Haver-something. And then it occurred to me—had Bryce Edmond been following me? Maybe that was why I'd felt someone watching me all morning—because someone had been.

"Zoe—" He raced past Johnny Rockets, approaching the intersection, waving both arms, breathless, shouting. "Zoe—I've been trying to reach you. Didn't you get my messages? We have to talk—"

I stood still, holding on to the carriage, wishing I could disappear, contemplating how awkward it would be to make a run for it, envisioning a woman with a baby buggy barreling through parked cars, the bespectacled, hollering Bryce at our heels. The fact was, I was in no mood, no frame of mind, to discuss work or the policies of the Institute. What was wrong with the man? Why couldn't he wait at least until after the wedding? But my thoughts were useless; there was no escape. Bryce had already started across the street. I was trapped.

"It's important—" Bryce kept yelling.

Behind him, on Fifth Street, a car suddenly screeched, accelerating, engine racing, drowning out his voice. And without warning, it veered, swerving sharply, turning to cross South Street right behind Bryce.

I tried to call out to him but couldn't make words. In a heartbeat, I saw Bryce coming up onto the curb, the car careening behind him, lurching forward, closing in. Tons of steel charged right at us, and though I wanted to, I simply couldn't move.

SIXTEEN

Bryce could, though. He leapt, actually flying off the ground. Arms extended, he hit me full force, knocking me sideways through the air. My body smacked the carriage, shoving it away, and I landed hard on cement where, banging my hip and hitting my head, I lay flat, breathless, unable to move, watching Luke's buggy roll away. For an immeasurable moment, my body seemed disconnected; messages would not travel from my brain to my limbs, even to my voice. I heard a heavy thud, an unbearable grunt. A series of harsh scrapes and bangs, and then the frantic revving of an engine, a painful grinding of metal and the roaring of an engine speeding away.

How long did I lie there, not moving, unable to make a sound? I remember straining to turn my head, blinking at the carriage a few yards away where it had rolled to a stop against a storefront window. And wailing with a stab of fear—Luke. Oh God. Was he all right? I struggled to my knees, crawled over to the carriage, desperate, afraid to look inside. But Luke was intact. He glanced my way, gurgling, completely unfazed. A miracle. I cupped his cheeks, clutched his little hands, making sure he was really all right. But touching him, I noticed that my hands were covered with grime. I shouldn't touch the baby with such dirty hands. I released him, began searching for baby wipes to clean my fingers. Where were they? The back of my head pulsed with pain, and I reached back to it, felt a tender bump, but no blood. I opened the diaper bag, rifled through diapers and teething toys, finally found the wipes, began rubbing my hands with one, realizing only then that someone was talking to me. A woman with spiked dark hair, a tattoo on her neck. A stranger, asking questions. She put her hand on my arm. ". . . all right? How about the baby?"

A young guy with a shaved head and a dozen metal face piercings ran over to her, exhaling clouds of gray. He interrupted her, asking about her dishes. "Hey—did you get the plates?"

No, she shook her head. She hadn't. She hoped he had. But he hadn't, either. Damn. Nobody had the plates. Then they discussed color. Of what—the plates? Blue? White? I had no idea what they were talking about; it didn't matter. I wanted to sit down. No, to lie down. When my hands were smudge free, I picked Luke up and held on to him, buried my face in his jacket.

"I think it was a Bronco." The woman couldn't stand still, seemed to hop from foot to foot.

The kid frowned, not sure he agreed. "Looked like an Explorer to me." He had no coat on, just a T-shirt and jeans with studs in them.

I watched them, my brain functioning in slo-mo. Bronco. Explorer. Oh—cars? Of course. They were talking about the car. The license plates. The make and model. I saw it again, coming out of nowhere, accelerating, speeding right toward us as Bryce pushed us—wait. Bryce? Where was Bryce? I turned, searching the sidewalk.

"Bryce?" My throat felt like sandpaper. "Bryce?" I spun around too fast, suddenly felt dizzy, nauseated. I held on to Luke and closed my eyes to steady myself, and remembered.

SEVENTEEN

BRYCE HAD BEEN HIT. THE IMPACT CATAPULTED HIM A GOOD twenty yards, and he'd landed in the vestibule outside Baby Gap. He lay there, his skull beside a cornerstone, caved in on one side. His forehead was wet and purple, his blood still pouring onto the sidewalk. His face seemed unbalanced, his features distorted, and his hair was slick, matting with crimson clumps.

"Bryce—" I put Luke into the carriage and knelt beside Bryce, saying his name, but he didn't respond. I took his hand, but it was limp, indifferent to my touch. Oh God. The woman and the pierced guy were pacing around, talking on their cell phones, and other people had begun to gather, gawking at us, murmuring.

I touched Bryce's face to comfort him, stroked his cheek. "It's okay, Bryce," I assured him. "You'll be fine." I held on to his hand, feeling useless, unable to recall my first-aid training: What were you supposed to do for head injuries? Should I cover him? Yes, of course. Probably. Keep him warm. I took my jacket off, laid it over him, held his hand again, not releasing it until the deafening sirens had quieted and the paramedics made me move away.

Dazed, I tried to answer a police officer's questions. No, I wasn't Bryce's wife. He was a colleague from work. I recounted the way the car had come up onto the curb, right at us, how Bryce had pushed me and Luke away, had been hit himself. He'd been a hero.

The questions wouldn't stop. I kept answering. No, I didn't

need to go to the hospital. I was fine. So was the baby. No, we didn't need to be checked out.

The paramedic didn't know, of course, about the lump growing on the back of my head. Or how his face shimmied when he moved, doing a blurry dance. There was no reason to tell him; I'd had concussions before; I knew the drill. I just needed to rest and it would get better. Bryce was the one to worry about. He'd saved us from being hurt. If he hadn't come running, pushing us away, who knew what might have happened?

The witnesses stepped up, telling the police what they'd seen. The woman who thought the car was a Bronco said that she'd seen the whole thing; the driver had aimed right at the three of us. She thought the driver was a woman. No, she didn't know how old. Hadn't noticed her race or hair color. She'd just glimpsed her briefly, had seen the outline of wavy, shoulder-length hair. But there was no question that the driver charged up the sidewalk on purpose.

The pierced kid hadn't seen the actual impact; he'd heard it and come running out of his shop in time to see a dark red Explorer disappearing down South Street.

"No, it wasn't red." The woman crossed her arms. "It was dark green, or maybe blue."

"Sorry." The kid was emphatic. "Red."

The officer turned to me. "Do you remember the color of the car?"

I tried to. I closed my eyes, replaying the scene. Bryce running, shouting. The sound of screeching tires. Bryce taking off, flying off the ground, shoving me aside—and then, a terrible thunk and a flash of light. Maybe silver? Or no, white?

"Sorry." I simply had no idea. What was wrong with me? Why couldn't I remember the car? If not the make, at least the color. Why hadn't I looked at the driver? Oh God. A paramedic handed me my jacket, warning me to keep warm, telling me about shock. I put it on, ignoring the wide scarlet stains, watching them lift Bryce's gurney into the ambulance. He showed no sign of life.

EIGHTEEN

By the time the ambulance pulled away, the police had finished taking my information, and the crowd had begun to disperse. Assuring the police that we didn't need any help, I continued our walk. Without thinking about it, I headed three blocks west and a couple of blocks north, straight to the hospital. I rolled the carriage through the emergency entrance and up to the registration desk, where I identified myself as Bryce's cousin. The woman behind the desk had a slightly out-of-focus face like the paramedics and the police, and her frown slithered snakelike above her chin as she told me that Bryce had already been taken upstairs for surgery. She had his wallet and was filling out his insurance information, wondered if I had the phone numbers of his wife or other next of kin.

I stammered, embarrassed, that no, I didn't. Not on me. I apologized, complicating my lie, explaining that I had all the family numbers at home. But it worried me that she'd asked. Did she need to contact them because Bryce was dying? Oh God. I saw him again, lying on the concrete in puddles of blood. Damn. Why hadn't I just turned around and met him on the other side of the street? If I hadn't made him chase us, we'd all have been unharmed. The car would have smashed a trash can and hit a brick wall. Nobody, except maybe the driver, would have been hurt. But what about what the witness had said, that the driver had deliberately targeted us? That made no sense; why would someone try to run us over? She had to be mistaken. The fact was that if I hadn't been avoiding Bryce, we wouldn't have been in the way of the car and he'd be completely fine. It was my fault he might die. I paced the waiting room floor, guilt ridden and worried, until Luke began to fidget hungrily. I pushed the carriage into a corner, collapsed onto a chair and, covering myself with my bloody jacket, let him nurse.

As always, as I fed Luke, the world around us seemed to fade. Luke's hunger, his fervent sucking, his needs, overtook all else. Holding him, I felt the turmoil of the last half hour settle down and my brain stop sizzling. I rested, leaned my sore head back, closed my eyes, felt my breathing begin to slow. When I opened my eyes again, for the first time I noticed other people waiting with us. A dark-skinned woman clutched her right side, moaning softly as an older woman, probably her mother, touched her back, cursing the doctors for making them wait. A man in a wheelchair sat pale and expressionless, as if waiting were his permanent condition. A miniskirted blonde in leopard-patterned high heels strutted back and forth near the doorway, talking into her cell phone.

I held on to Luke, suddenly disoriented. What were we doing here? We'd been out for a walk, and then—poof. We'd been plucked from our lives, transported to the hospital emergency room, plopped among strangers. In fact, Bryce Edmond was basically a stranger, someone I barely knew with whom I'd never even shaken hands. And now, unpredictably, that casual acquaintance had become my responsibility. But what was I supposed to do? How could I help him?

Maybe I should call the office and tell them what happened. But it was Sunday. The administrative staff wouldn't be there; their office was closed Sundays due to budget cuts. Okay, then I should call his family. But I didn't know his family. And surely the hospital would notify his wife. If he had a wife. Did he? I didn't know. In fact, I didn't know anything about Bryce Edmond except that he worked at the Institute. I certainly didn't know what he'd been doing on South Street. Or why he had been chasing us. Or what he'd so desperately wanted to tell me.

Again I pictured him, running, waving, calling my name. And again I realized what would have happened if he hadn't been there to push us out of the way. There was no doubt; by whatever circumstances, by chance or coincidence, Bryce Edmond had saved our lives. And for that reason alone, he was now my responsibility. I wasn't sure what that meant. But at the very least, it meant I would stay there, keeping a vigil for him.

Luke's tummy got full, and he fell asleep. I tucked him into his carriage, dug around in the diaper bag for my cell phone and called Nick to tell him where I was and why. Alarmed, he came right over, insisting on taking us home. But I refused to budge. So while Luke napped, Nick and I both took seats opposite the man in the wheelchair, and after I explained to Nick what had happened, we stayed there, cell phones turned off, staring at the wall or the television hanging from the ceiling or the sleeping baby or our joined hands.

A few hours later when Bryce Edmond's brother and sister-in-law arrived, we were still sitting in the waiting room, waiting for news.

NINETEEN

Bryce finally came out of surgery, but he was still unconscious, and his condition was critical. Gavin and Petra Edmond thanked us and promised to call as soon as there was any news. And just six hours after I'd begun my walk, Nick, Luke and I headed home. The lump on my head thumped a dull, persistent throb, and my vision was still not right. All I wanted was to disappear upstairs in a steamy scented bath. But as Nick pulled into a parking spot across the street from the house, I realized that the bath would have to wait. Anna, the wedding planner, was standing on the front porch in her high heels and Capri stretch pants, waiting. Even before we got out of the car, she started squawking.

"Where have you been, Zoe? You were supposed to meet me here forty-five minutes ago!"

I looked to Nick for support, but he darted out of the car and hid behind the open trunk, getting the carriage out of the Volvo. So I waved at Anna and, pulling myself out the passenger side and Luke out of his baby seat, crossed the street to face her.

"Have you forgotten that your wedding is just six days away?" Anna met us at the curb, holding up six fingers, to demonstrate the number. "Six days. That's all. We have deadlines to meet. Weddings don't just happen by themselves. They take work. The chef needs final numbers. The florist needs a final decision. The cake—my God—you still haven't chosen the cake. I picked your dress up, but you should try it on again so they can make adjustments if they have to. . . ."

She ranted on, and I watched her pink lips moving, emitting a jumble of noise. Somehow, I'd become completely detached from the wedding, didn't even mind saying the word anymore. The wedding was a detail; it wasn't important. Not when cars could come flying off the curb in an eyeblink, not when strangers got filleted in your backyard. But Anna kept on ranting.

". . . unacceptable, Zoe—I've never had a bride as uncooperative as you are. If not for your houseguests, I'd have left half an hour ago. I simply can't work like this. Without your full cooperation, I—"

"How are you, Anna?" Nick interrupted. Finally, he'd rolled the empty carriage across the street. Eyes on Anna, he took Luke from my arms.

Anna had stopped her harangue mid-sentence, mouth open. Taken aback by Nick's good cheer, she tried to curl her bright red snarl into a smile.

"Fine, just fine, Nick. Except that—"

"Well, that's good, Anna. Because, as it happens, Zoe's not very well. Zoe's had a rough couple of days, and she can use your support."

Anna's mouth opened as if she were about to speak, but she didn't.

Nick lowered his voice and leaned toward her, speaking confidentially. "We're just coming from the hospital," I heard him say. And I heard the phrase "hit-and-run."

Anna shook her head. "Oh my. How horrible." She covered her mouth with her French manicured fingers, looking from Nick to me, and back to Nick.

But Nick wasn't finished. He told her about the murder, too. "You probably heard about it on the news. The body was on our patio. Zoe found her."

"Wait—no. That—that happened here?" Anna actually gasped. "You mean the jogger? The one that was cut open?" She stared, unable to process the information. "Oh my God. I've been so busy, I didn't pay attention—"

Nick explained that given the circumstances, I hadn't been as prompt as I should have been regarding the floral arrangements.

But Anna wasn't focused on the wedding anymore. "I saw it in the paper. That poor woman's been all over the news. But good Lord. I never put it together. Wait—there was a picture. Of your house—I should have recognized it. And weren't you in it? Of course you were. And it was on television, too. But I wasn't paying attention—but, Zoe, poor dear, let's get you inside." Even in three-inch heels, Anna was significantly shorter than I was, and the arm she put around me circled my hips instead of my waist, but I let her guide me up the front stairs and into the house while Nick followed with Luke and the carriage.

"Don't you worry about a thing, Zoe. I'm here now, so you'll be able to get some rest and collect yourself. All these shocks—you must be in a state. Oh dear. And you only have a few days to recover."

Sam was in the kitchen among small mountains of empty bottles and unwashed dishes, making himself a sandwich of bananas and mayonnaise. Oliver yipped at Sam's feet, nuzzling his ankles, hoping for a handout. They both looked up as we came in.

"You," Anna called to him. "Nick's brother. What's your name?"

"I am Sam, ma'am. And you are?" He took a leisurely bite, smiling.

"I'm the one who's going to get your motor moving, Sam. Make Zoe a cup of hot tea and some toast with jam. Blackberry, if you have it. Or some orange marmalade."

Sam chewed, blinking with confused amusement at the short, officious stranger while enjoying the ample curves contained in her spandex pants.

"We've only got grape and strawberry." I wasn't sure about the grape.

"Well, that'll have to do then. Strawberry. Bring it all upstairs on a tray—along with a glass of brandy. When you're done with that, I'll show you where the vacuum is. You can start to tidy up."

Sam took another bite. Oliver whimpered.

"What's wrong with you—didn't you hear me? Get moving."

Sam put a hand up. "Okay, don't get your panties in a knot." He reached for the kettle.

As Nick came in behind us, Anna called to him, "You're in charge of the baby for now. Where's little Molly?"

"At a sleepover. She'll be home soon—"

"Good. You're in charge of her, too. We don't want any interruptions for at least two hours. Not one. I mean it."

As Anna led me down the hall, Oliver, apparently giving up on a bite of banana, barreled at Nick, yapping his greeting.

"Oliver." Anna didn't stop walking or turn to look at him. "Be quiet and sit."

Immediately, the yipping stopped. I looked back; unbelievably, Oliver was sitting, wearing a broad, eager smile. Beside him, Nick stood next to the carriage, holding Luke, watching us, looking confused and abandoned.

Tony was in the living room on his hands and knees, probably looking for his quarters again, this time under the recliner. When he saw us, he scrambled to his feet, grinning and sheepish.

"Tony, if you need change, I have a dish of it upstairs. Help yourself."

"No, it's no big deal. I just wonder what happened—you don't think Oliver would swallow quarters, do you?"

"Well, if he did," Anna barked, "it'll come out the other end. Eventually."

"Tony, this is Anna. Anna, Tony, another brother." I realized they hadn't met.

"How do you do, Tony?" Anna gave him a charming, toothy grin and led me to the stairs. "Oh, and Tony? When I come back down, I expect that you and your brothers will have cleaned the mess in here and in the kitchen, and that you will have begun preparing dinner."

Before Tony could respond, Anna pushed up the steps.

I didn't argue, didn't resist. I surrendered completely, letting Anna guide me, obeying her orders to undress as she lit scented candles and ran my bath. At her command, I sunk into hot water, letting myself float, listening to silence and the soft popping of bubbles. Finally, unbelievably, I was alone, beginning to relax. But not quite. There was a knock at the door, and Anna stepped in.

"Don't get too comfy yet, dear. Not till I get your wine order and the final decision on the tablecloths. I'd go with the Zinfandel for dinner, the port with dessert. And I'm nixing the baby's breath with roses. They're a cliché—"

"Anna." I finally found my voice. "Do whatever you think best."

She seemed confused. Her perfectly penciled eyebrows rose, disappointed. "Really? But—"

"I value your advice. You've got experience. I'm sure your choices will be excellent."

"But about the table settings—"

"Your choice."

She hesitated. "The stemware—"

"Anna." I tried to sound firm. "You decide."

"All of it?"

"All of it."

Shaking her head, she finally backed out of the room. I sunk into the water, stayed under the bubbles, soaking, until I needed to come up for air. I heard only a few sounds during the next hour. Molly coming home, with a tumult of Oliver barking and the front door slamming and loud shouting for "Mom." Nick stopping her from coming to look for me, explaining that her mom was resting. The vacuum cleaner's high-pitched whirring.

And Nick on the phone in the bedroom, escaping Anna's supervision long enough to leave a hurried voice mail for our babysitter, Ivy, confirming—no, begging her to come back to work on Monday.

TWENTY

ANNA REFUSED TO JOIN US FOR DINNER; SHE STAYED IN THE kitchen making lists and phone calls while we ate. Our meal began quietly. The brothers were subdued, on their best behavior. They used utensils properly, placed their napkins neatly on their laps. No elbows rested on the table; no one belched out loud. At first, conversation was careful, as if everyone feared that Anna might be monitoring us.

"Feeling better, Zoe?"

"Get a nap?"

And then, gradually, inevitably, attention turned to Bryce. Sam and Tony wanted to hear what happened.

"Mom?" Molly was confused. "Was somebody in an accident?"

I didn't want to upset her, so I avoided her questions. "A friend. But it's no big deal, Molls. Want another drumstick?"

Sam asked her what to send an elephant when he gets sick. "A get wellephant card."

While he was still laughing, I asked how her sleepover was and her face brightened. "Oh, Mom, I almost forgot." She beamed. "Guess what we did today?"

"What?"

Luke, lying on a comforter beside us, had been fussing, but suddenly he began to howl. I got up and brought him to the table, where Molly was in the middle of her answer.

". . . that pottery place—you know, where you can make ceramics?" Molly went on. "Susan took me and Emily."

I positioned Luke on my shoulder, patting his back, trying to help him get rid of a bubble in his tummy. His cries drowned out Molly's voice; I had to strain to hear her.

". . . a kitten, but I made a dog . . . looks like Oliver."

"Cool," I managed over Luke's wails.

". . . plus I made something else."

Sitting at the table wasn't working. The baby was squirming and complaining. He was too loud, bothering everyone, and I couldn't eat with him on my lap, anyhow. I stood to walk him up and down the hall.

". . . surprise for Luke."

I didn't realize Molly had finished what she was saying, and she watched me, waiting for my response. As I left the table, Luke's howls rattling my ears, I tried to figure out what to say. "Super, Molls!" I shouted so she could hear me, and I hoped that made sense.

"That's great," Nick offered. He was obviously trying to cover for me. "Are you going to tell us what it is?"

Her eyes remained on me, a fixed stare. "No. I'm not."

Luke wailed.

"Sorry, Molly," I apologized. "Can you tell me about it later?"

"Let me take him." Nick started to stand.

"Zoe, sit down and eat. Have Anna hold him." Sam stuffed a forkful of potatoes into his mouth.

"It's okay." I was already at the door. Seconds later, Luke burped and settled down. I came back and put him back onto the comforter, sitting with him for a moment to make sure he was calm. Finally, I sat at the table and finished dinner. The brothers had become more conversational, talking about car accidents they'd had, apparently competing for the Worst Judgment/Riskiest Behavior While Driving award. So far, Nick seemed to be winning, having, at age seventeen, spun his '65 Chevy Nova on the ice into a telephone pole, from which it ricocheted and slid into a ditch, and then, as he tried to back it up the steep incline onto the pavement, the ice gave way under it and it flipped completely over.

The men guffawed at their youthful luck and stupidity. They were so boisterous that it took a while to notice how quiet Molly was. In fact, for most of the meal, she hadn't said a word. But just as Sam was starting a story involving his Mustang and an eighteen-wheeler, Anna appeared, cutting him off with her arms crossed and her eyes glaring.

Anna spouted orders, and the brothers jumped to action. She wouldn't leave until the last dinner dishes had been loaded into the dishwasher and the last leftover stored in the refrigerator. And, before going, she handed a to-do list to each adult member of the household. Standing at the door, she reminded us again that we had only a very few days remaining until the most important event in Nick's and my life and, despite dramatic intrusions of the outside world, we had better get ourselves on board with her plans or she would not be responsible for the outcome.

As she bullied, Nick and his brothers lowered their heads slightly, avoiding eye contact, and I wondered if Anna reminded them of their mother. Despite their muscular frames and macho demeanors, the three were easily cowed into submission by a woman who was barely five feet tall. Not one of them argued or answered back. They seemed well practiced in humble obedience to a diminutive female taskmaster, a fact I filed away for future reference.

At the door, Anna gave a final warning. "I'll be back tomorrow. I expect that the items on your lists will have been attended to by then."

The door closed. No one spoke for a minute. Then Sam started, mimicking Anna, barking orders, criticizing the quality of his work: "What's this on the counter? Water stains? You left water stains on the counter?" He sounded surprisingly like her. He even stood like she did, gestured the same way.

"Water stains? What the hell's wrong with you? Slob. Moron. Incompetent screwup." Tony's falsetto sounded more like Anna than Anna did.

The two of them kept it up. "You—Nick's brother. What's your name? If you want to be in this wedding, you'll need a haircut—"

"—An eyebrow wax—"

"—A chest wax."

"—Botox. You can't be in a wedding with that face. It doesn't go with the centerpiece."

Nick didn't join in. He got up, stretched and walked over behind me, rubbing my shoulders. "You all right, Zoe?"

Before I could answer, he'd absently planted a kiss on my cheek and moved on to get a beer, and his brothers trailed him, leaving Molly and me alone with Luke, who was gumming a fold of blanket. Molly remained oddly quiet as she plopped onto the blanket beside him, lay down and covered him with her arm.

"Lukie, Lukie." Her affection was strained. "Sweet Little Lukie." She rolled him onto his back, tickling his tummy a little too energetically.

"Molly. Be gentle."

She continued to tickle him, her voice a little louder, sharper.

"Stop tickling, Molly. Just cuddle him." Not that he seemed bothered. Luke stared at his big sister with delighted, adoring eyes. But something about Molly wasn't right. Her smile was off-balance, distorted. "Molly? What's going on?"

She didn't answer. She revved it up a notch. "Tickle tickle, Lukie. Tickle tickle."

"Molls?"

"Tickle tickle tickle." Her eyes gleamed, and her tickles became jabs.

"Molly, stop."

But Molly didn't stop. She escalated. "Tickle tickle tickle tickle." The pitch of her voice rose, became cloying, and her hands formed little claws, fingers stiff and wriggling.

"I said stop." I grabbed her arm, but she pulled it away and went after Luke again

"Lukie, Lukie—" Defying me, she pawed at his belly. Luke looked confused and, predictably, dissolved into tears.

"Molly. Cut it out." In a one movement, I swooped at her, yanking her by the arm away from Luke and up into the air. She screamed, a window-rattling, nerve-piercing sound. I caught her, tried to hold on to her, but she squirmed away and bolted out of the room, cradling her arm, wailing, and Nick came running in, leading the herd of Stiles brothers, asking, "What happened? What the hell's going on?"

By then, Luke was howling. Upstairs, Molly slammed her bedroom door. In the dining room, Nick, Sam and Tony gaped at me, asking questions. My head throbbed. I wanted to cry or scream, to disappear altogether. Instead, I picked Luke up, cuddling him so he'd quiet down. "It's okay. It's nothing."

I couldn't tell Nick that Molly had tried to hurt our son, couldn't quite believe it myself. In all of her six years, I'd never seen Molly be mean to anyone, much less a smaller child. In fact, Molly and I had never before had a really angry, let alone a violent, moment. But, suddenly, poof. For no apparent reason, she'd snapped and attacked a baby. And I might have dislocated her shoulder.

"What's with Molly?" Nick wasn't going away. "She having a tantrum?"

I rocked Luke. "You could say so."

Nick nodded at the baby. "Because of him?"

I blinked, absorbing the question. "Why?"

"She's been too cool about having a baby brother."

She was?

"I mean you'd expect her to be a little jealous, wouldn't you?"

How would I know? I didn't know much about siblings.

"You were jealous, growing up." Sam grinned, punched Tony's ear.

"Apparently, you still are." Annoyed, Tony swatted Sam's belly.

Nick smirked. "Both of them have always been jealous of me. I was the oldest and Dad's favorite."

"You?" Sam's mouth dropped. "In your dreams."

"If anyone was jealous, Nick, it was you. Who used to whine that Mom never got mad at me?"

"Well, she never did. It was pitiful." Sam's eyes weren't laughing. He was only partly joking. " 'No matter what you did, you never got in trouble. Poor little Tony has the sniffles. 'Let me fix you a hot cocoa, Tony.' Or how about, 'Tony, let Mom buy you a new car'?"

"Oh, cut it out. You guys got cars, too."

"What? A '74 Pacer? Nick and I got a pile of rusted scrap metal on wheels. But not baby Tony. Little Tony got a brand-new Toyota—"

"I saved for that—"

"You paid, what? A hundred bucks?"

"Face it, Tony." Nick folded his arms. "Mom spoiled you rotten."

"Well, why not?" Tony shrugged, a smug grin spreading across his face. "I was the baby—"

"Actually," Nick interrupted, "you were the baby. But Eli was her favorite."

"Eli? She was always pissed at Eli. She grounded him ninety percent of his childhood—"

"Because she expected him to be perfect. She had her eye on him always. No, for sure. It was Eli. I was Dad's favorite, and Eli was Mom's."

"No way."

"You're full of crap."

Tony pouted. Sam snorted. Nick snickered.

Sibling rivalry, I guessed, was as common as siblings. I'd read about it, studied it in family psychology courses. I should have recognized it, prepared Molly better for it. But having been raised alone, I'd been insensitive to sibling issues, and now I'd let Molly down. Her world—the world she and I alone had shared—had been invaded, turned upside down by a little alien. And only six years old, she couldn't know why she felt the way she did, couldn't be expected to deal with her conflicted feelings. Molly was understandably jealous: Luke was tiny and cute and grabbing all kinds of attention that would otherwise have been hers. And I had been completely oblivious, not anticipating the feelings of my own daughter.

"Here." I handed the baby to Nick, left the brothers to their squabbling and hurried upstairs to Molly. I wasn't sure what to say. Nick and his brothers would be better qualified to explain this phenomenon than I was. But at least I could reassure her, remind her how much I loved her and how incredible a person she was. But, as it turned out, words didn't really matter.

Molly must have heard my steps in the hallway, because before I got to her door she burst out of her room and ran into my arms, clutching onto me, sobbing. "I'm sorry, Mommy. Don't be mad. I'm sorry."

TWENTY-ONE

AFTER WE FINISHED HUGGING AND DRYING TEARS, THE REST OF the night was just us girls. First, we tackled her school project, which turned out to be, aptly, to make a family tree. We got markers, old photographs and poster board and traced her ancestry as far back as we knew, which was only two generations back. We talked about family as we worked, and I asked how she felt about having a brother.

"It'll get better." She was probably assuring herself. "We'll have more fun when he can do stuff. Now he just cries and sleeps."

"And he takes a lot of my attention."

"It'll get better, Mom. He's not going to stay a baby forever." Now, she was reassuring me. She concentrated on drawing a line connecting Nick's name to Sam's.

"Molls, do you ever miss the times before he was born? You know, when it was just us?"

Molly looked up from her work. "Not really." Her eyes were solemn. "I'm bigger now. It's Luke's turn to be the baby."

Oh dear. Once again, Molly's thoughts went deeper than I'd imagined. We pasted on pictures of our family members, admiring our design.

"But how do I finish it?" Molly frowned.

I didn't know what she meant. "It isn't finished?" We didn't have photos of Nick's parents or my mother, but we'd made silhouettes for them. The thing looked done to me.

"No. What about my other family?"

Her other family? Oh God. How could I have been so insensitive and obtuse? Molly was adopted. She had a whole other biological family.

"Aren't I supposed to make them a tree, too?"

Oh dear. "I suppose, except we don't know their names."

"Right." She stared at the poster, and I thought she seemed sad. "Maybe I can do that some other day."

Molly had her bath, then, and we blew her hair dry and painted our finger- and toenails. When they were dry, we went through my jewelry box and I gave Molly a locket I'd worn as a child. We cuddled up and read books we hadn't looked at in years, her favorite picture books from her early childhood, *Where the Wild Things Are* and *Goodnight Moon*. We snuggled on her bed until she was about to fall asleep. Then I put my mouth to her ear and whispered, "I'll always love you, Molly. No matter what."

"I know."

"You were my first baby. You always will be special to me."

"Uh-huh."

"You can always talk to me if you feel unhappy. Or jealous. Or mad."

"Okay."

"There's no one else like you. You're beautiful. And smart. And funny. And kind. And cuddly and huggy. And—"

"I get it, Mom."

She did?

"I get that you love me." She yawned, repositioned her head on her pillow so she could look at my eyes. "It's just that—don't take this the wrong way, but you always pay more attention to Luke. Don't deny it. You send me off to play with Emily or to the zoo with Uncle Sam, but you take Luke for walks and you're always holding him, and when I want to tell you something you're either taking a nap or Luke's hungry or crying, so I can't even talk to you. I know he can't help it because he's just a little baby, but sometimes he makes me mad."

I kissed her forehead, smelled vanilla shampoo. I couldn't argue with her. She was being honest, and it was all true.

"Here's what I'd like to do, Molls." I took her hand. "I'd like us to make special time for just us."

"You mean like make play dates?"

"Kind of. More like ladies only dates."

She grinned. "No boys allowed dates?"

"Exactly. Mom and Molly dates. Once a week. Okay?"

"Okay." She held up a pinkie. I linked mine around hers, a pinkie swear, more binding than a signature.

I kissed her good night and started for the door.

"Mom?" Her voice was sleepy. "It's a piggy bank. I made Luke a ceramic piggy bank. For when he's bigger."

"He'll love it."

She didn't answer. I think she was already asleep.

TWENTY-TWO

Nick was waiting in the hall with Luke, who was hungry again.

"Everything okay?"

I nodded, taking the baby. "She's asleep."

Nick followed me into the bedroom, asking about Molly, waiting while I positioned myself and Luke began nursing. Nick sat beside us and I felt a wave of tenderness. The moment was precious and intimate, with just the three of us in the bedroom. No brothers. I realized that, except to sleep, I hadn't been alone with Nick since Sam or Tony had arrived. Nick and I hadn't really talked, hadn't taken time to connect with each other. Everything was for Tony or Sam, Sam or Tony. Nothing was for us.

"Tony wants to use your office to do some work. Okay?"

Naturally, the first time we were alone in days, Nick's first words would be about one of his brothers. But I was confused. Sam and Tony had both been using my office all week, and no one had asked my permission before. Why now? "I guess."

"Thanks for being so patient, Zoe."

"They're family." I wanted to feel that way, realized I was having my own brand of sibling rivalry.

"But I know it's a lot for you, all at once."

Nick sat beside me, kissed my neck. "I called the hospital." He began massaging my shoulders. "No news on Edmond."

No news. Well, at least that meant he was still alive. I closed my

eyes, letting a small moan escape as Nick worked away the tight-
ness at the base of my neck. Actually, my whole body felt sore.
The tenderness in my milk-swelled breasts melded with that in
my shoulders and back; a single ache spread over me from the
bump on my head to the bruises on my hip where I'd landed after
Bryce shoved me. Nick's touch was soothing, and I wished he'd
keep it up, move his strong fingers down my back, my calves and
ankles and feet. But he stopped at my shoulders, whispering, "I'll
be downstairs."

Slowly, I opened my eyes, saw Nick's shadow passing outside
the bedroom door. Luke purred and gurgled, happily drawing
nutrition out of my body. And I lay back on the pillows, miser-
able.

I told myself that I had good reasons to feel that way. In fact, I
listed them. I was still dealing with the double shocks of the murder and the hit-and-run, plus the minor injuries I'd sustained in
the latter, plus I had fluctuating levels of postpartum and milk-
making hormones, and probably some postpartum depression.
Not to mention nerves about getting married. As if those items
weren't enough, there was the matter of my home. My house
wasn't a private domain anymore. Anna and Ivy worked there, re-
arranging stuff, putting it where I'd never find it. And police still
appeared on the patio, and so did the press. That morning, Sam
had caught a guy peeking over the back fence, taking pictures of
the yellow tape surrounding the bloodstained deck. And speaking
of Sam, he and Tony were everywhere. I'd found Tony moving
furniture in the living room, looking in desk drawers in my office.
And even though Sam had a suite at the Four Seasons, I doubted
he'd spent ten minutes there since he'd arrived in town. One or
the other of them was always underfoot. Their toiletries and dirty
socks or shirts were everywhere. No used bath towel went un-
dropped. No whisker stubble got rinsed from the sink, no dirty

dish removed from the sink, unless, of course, the dishes in the dishwasher were clean, in which case they'd unerringly mix clean and dirty together—

Stop, I told myself. Don't start this again. Nick's brothers were here for just a week. It was a chance for us to get to know each other. They felt at home here, and I should be glad about that. I was focusing on them because they were nonthreatening and their issues weren't frightening. It wasn't my houseguests, Tony and Sam, who were upsetting me; it was my own sense of security. My home, normally a place where I felt safe, had been the scene of a hideous murder.

Admitting that to myself calmed me down. I assured myself that, after next week, the murder would be history, maybe even solved. The press would move on to another story, and the brothers would go back to their own lives. Nick and I and Molly and Luke would have a chance to attain a sense of normalcy.

I leaned back, picturing what it would be like. Normal. I saw Nick going to work in the mornings. Molly getting on the school bus, or going to tea with me at the Pink Rose Cafe. And Luke— what would normal be for Luke?

I looked down and saw him staring up at me, gazing with dreamy, loving eyes. His body was fleshy and so yummy that I had the urge to bite him. Lord, he was intoxicating. I wondered did he look like me at all? His eyes weren't brown like mine, but they were more almond shaped and a deeper blue than Nick's. Luke's hair was pale baby down, glistening, not dark like my brunette. His nose was still undefined, a rounded pinch of flesh, and his cheeks were fat and solid. I couldn't see either Nick or me when I looked at Luke. All I saw was a perfect baby boy. When he was finished eating, I lifted him to my face and slowly, gently, pressed my mouth against his cheeks, his eyes, his chin, his tummy. I smelled his sweet milky breath as he sighed, and I saw his eyes roll, overcome with sensation. I kissed him again. And again, watching him react each time with the same intensity.

Finally, I put him down beside me, his hand firmly grabbing my pinkie. I lay back on the bed, feeling depleted and stressed. But Luke was there with me, keeping me company. My troubles seemed faraway and petty; in his presence, it was difficult to wallow.

TWENTY-THREE

MONDAY MORNING, IVY CAME BACK TO WORK, ALBEIT WITH ATTI-
tude, arriving in an insurance company rental.

"Loaner's a piece of shit." She hung her coat on the rack near
the front door and poured herself a cup of coffee. "Thing smells
like cigarette smoke and air freshener."

"What'd they give you?" Sam eyed her openly, head to heels
and back again. Ivy had an ample figure, and she arched her back,
posing.

"A damned Ford Taurus. Can you believe it? A neon blue Taurus? What the hell is that?"

Sam sympathized, but I only half-listened, busy fastening Oliver's
leash onto his collar while he yipped and strained, eager to go outside for a walk even though he'd already peed in the house. Besides,
Molly was running late. Her school bus would arrive any second.

"Molly?" I heard her racing around her bedroom.

"Mom." She sounded panicked. "I can't find my book bag."

"It's down here. By the steps."

More frantic footsteps. "But where's my project?"

"In your book bag. So is your lunch." I held out her coat.
"Come on—you're late."

She thundered down the steps, Nick behind her. "Hey, Molly?
No kiss?"

She pulled her coat on, blowing him one up the stairs.

"Wait." Sam broke off his talk with Ivy. "What's that? That's not a kiss. It's a poof of air."

The bus pulled up and honked.

I opened the door to wave at the driver, and Oliver scampered outside, barking. Molly ran around the kitchen, dispersing kisses, leaving an extra one for Tony, who was busy on his laptop in my office.

"What? You haven't seen me in a week, and don't even say hello?" Ivy tugged at Molly's jacket. "I thought you were my little girl."

Clowning, basking in attention, Molly ran over and gave Ivy a hug. "Hello, Ivy."

The driver beeped again. Molly sped to the door as Ivy took Luke from his rocker, holding him as she resumed her chat with Sam.

"Ivy," I interrupted. "I'll be out for a little while. Luke's clothes are laid out on his changing table."

She didn't even look at me. The only indication that she was listening was that she stopped talking until I finished. When my voice stopped, immediately she continued where she'd left off. The woman knew how to bear a grudge. But I'd hired her, had no one to blame for her presence there but myself. In fact, I'd interviewed nine women before hiring Ivy. Ivy had seemed to care about the children more than the others, so even with her superior, often abrasive attitude toward me, I'd chosen her. Now, she acted as if she outranked me in my own home, and I'd have to deal with it. But not now.

"Zoe?" Nick stood at the door, waiting for a kiss. He'd been sleeping when I got up. "Morning." His eyes were still puffy.

I pecked at him, following Molly down the front steps. "I'll be back soon."

"But we'll be gone. We're leaving as soon as I get Tony up."

I glanced back at Nick, wondering where he was going. But Oliver was pulling me down the steps, chasing Molly, so I waved, "Call me later," and ran after them, stopping Molly on the steps of the bus, yanking her hood. "Wait. You forgot something." I leaned forward, pointing to my cheek.

"Mom." It was a gasp. Molly looked mortified. "Not here." And she ran into the bus, leaving me without a kiss, without even a poof of air.

TWENTY-FOUR

OLIVER WAS IN RARE FORM. I PRACTICED THE COMMANDS WE'D learned in puppy obedience school.

"Sit." I imitated the teacher, speaking with authority, but Oliver wasn't impressed. Remaining on all fours, he pulled at the leash until he couldn't breathe. Gasping, he pulled me down the street; I heard his rattled breathing as the collar choked him.

"Oliver." Hearing his name, he glanced at me, and I held up a Cheerio, one of his favorite treats. "Sit."

He seemed to consider sitting, because he slowed down for a few steps.

"Sit." I pulled on his leash, standing still, resisting his tugs.

He turned his head, grinning, eyeing the treat. And, incredibly, he sat.

"Good boy!" I felt like dancing. He'd obeyed. I fed him the treat and, before it was off my finger, he was racing ahead again, choking himself, oblivious to anything I had to say.

It went that way for the next half hour. If I held out a treat, Oliver would obey me long enough to get it. But no treat, no deal. The dog clearly understood what I wanted. He knew how to heel, sit, lie down, stay. But clearly, he saw no reason to respond to my commands. Mere praise would not do it; he required bribes. And I was beginning to wonder how I would convince him that of the two of us, I was the dominant one, since I wasn't quite convinced of it myself.

I couldn't keep it up for a full half hour. After maybe ten minutes, I'd had enough. The walk was over. As we rounded Third Street and turned onto Monroe, I saw Sam and Tony pile into Nick's Volvo and pull away. I'd forgotten to ask where they were going. No matter. At least the house would be quiet. Ivy would watch Luke and Oliver, and I'd be able to grab some time for myself.

As we came inside, though, the house seemed oddly quiet. Ivy wasn't in the kitchen, but her half-full coffee cup sat beside the sink, complete with lipstick stains. In fact, all the cups were there, along with an empty box from an Entemann's coffee cake. I continued into the living room; Luke was there, lying in his playpen, kicking air and pawing at a mobile, but there was no sign of Ivy.

I took off Oliver's leash, and he raced upstairs. Ivy must be up there, maybe straightening Molly's room. But that wasn't right. Ivy shouldn't have left Luke out of earshot. And she could have put her cup, if not all of them, into the dishwasher. Lately, but especially since her car had been stolen, she had been difficult. It was time to talk about it. I stood at the foot of the stairs, listening for her, hearing nothing.

"Ivy?"

No answer. I climbed the stairs and stood in the hall, heard a faint whoosh in my bedroom. Someone was in there. But if it was Ivy, why wasn't she answering? Was she all right? A pulse of fear jolted through me, along with visions of entrails.

"Ivy?" Again, that whoosh. What was it? It sounded like rustling. Like fabric? "Ivy? Is that you?" I called again as I headed to my room, throwing the door open, ready to pounce on an intruder.

"Ivy?" It was all I could think of to say.

There was no intruder, but Ivy was in there. Alone. And she looked splendid. Ravishing, even. But then, why wouldn't she? She was wearing my wedding dress.

TWENTY-FIVE

"What are you doing?" I finally managed.

Her eyes bulged and the pale white of her face and throat instantly splotched with pink. She took a step back, away from my mirror. But she didn't answer. For a long awkward moment, we stood gaping at each other.

"You said you were going out," she snapped. "What are you doing back so soon?" Apparently, from Ivy's point of view, it was my fault I'd walked in on her.

"So, while I was gone, you thought you'd try on my wedding dress?"

She shrugged, making light of it. "I wanted to see how I'd look—I might be getting married soon myself."

Was she serious? My fists tightened. I wanted to throttle her. "Take it off. Now. And hang it exactly the way you found it."

Our eyes locked. Her chin rose; a smug smile spread across her face. But she made no move to take off the dress.

"Ivy. I mean it." Okay. Now, I was mad. Furious. The woman had crossed an uncrossable line. She was fired. Not only fired. Banned from the property. For life. Still, she stared at me defiant and unapologetic, not removing my gown. Where did she get the nerve? What was wrong with her? "Now. This minute."

"Or what?" She tossed her head back, scoffing. "You'll rip it off me? You think you're better than me, don't you?"

"Excuse me?"

"You with your upscale brownstone house, your cute little kids, your big strong handsome man, your fancy education and your degrees in—whatever. You think you're better than me."

What was she talking about? "No, Ivy. I don't. But—"

"Bullshit." We talked over each other, voices rising. "Oh yes, you do. You look down on me. You look down on everybody—"

"—How I look at you isn't the issue. The issue is—"

"—like me. You know what? You're just plain spoiled. You don't even know how good you have it. You take it for granted—"

"—that you're wearing my gown—"

"—that your life is perfect. You don't even have to work. Your man takes care of you. And you have all this nice stuff—"

"—and you need to take it off." But still, she didn't take it off. She continued ranting, gesturing, twisting her body. Oh God, was she going to burst a seam? I needed to calm her down, to figure out what was going on.

"—Do you appreciate it? No, you think you have it coming. But you know what? You're nothing special. In fact, you're pitiful, trying to pretend you're not getting old, having a baby so late. When Luke's a teenager, you know what? You'll be in the Old Folks Home, drooling into a cup. You don't deserve to have him."

Ivy paused for a breath. Her face was covered with angry red blotches and she was out of breath, nostrils flaring. Good Lord, I'd known she blamed me for the theft of her car, but other than that, I'd thought we got along. I'd trusted her with Luke and Molly; I'd had no idea Ivy harbored such hateful feelings. I was flabbergasted. Her outburst reminded me of patients at the Institute, and so, automatically, I shifted into professional mode, standing my ground, repeating what I'd said before, but even more firmly. "Take the dress off, Ivy."

With a wail, she started forward, her hands tightened into fists. I braced myself, ready to fight, wondering if I could deck her without damaging the gown. I'd start with her hair—didn't want to draw blood. But she stopped short of punching me, stood facing me, nose-to-nose.

"If not for you, I'd be fine." Her voice was a hiss. "It's safe in my neighborhood. I'd still have my car. I saved three years for that car. I paid for it myself, with money I worked for. If not for you, I wouldn't have had to park it outside and it would never have been stolen. If not for you, I'd be working someplace with less crime, not in a house where somebody got murdered—"

"Fine." I was about to say she wouldn't have to worry about working there anymore, but I checked myself. I needed to remain in therapist mode, treating Ivy as a patient.

That was ridiculous, though. If Ivy had been a patient, the orderlies would have taken her away instantly. And she'd never have had access to my gown. Nonetheless, Ivy's behavior was bizarre, her thinking inconsistent and irrational. In one breath she called my house upscale; in the next, a tawdry robbery and murder scene. First my life was perfect; then it was too dangerous to be around. Ivy was in some kind of crisis state, and it would be unwise to provoke her. I needed to sound understanding, even sympathetic, but definitely in control.

"I had no idea you felt that way, Ivy. But I can see that you've been under a lot of stress." Now, would you please take off my damned dress before you stretch it out? Ivy was about twenty pounds heavier, about three bra sizes larger, than me.

"You bet I have—"

"Maybe you should take some time off."

"And how am I supposed to afford that—"

"I'll give you two weeks' pay." Severance pay, I thought. "You rest. Do what you need to. At the end of two weeks, we'll see how you feel."

She frowned, suspicious. "You think you're cool, don't you. Throwing a few weeks' pay my way like you won't even notice it."

"Ivy, think about yourself. You need the time."

"You'd pay me for time off? Why? Why would you do that?"

Because I want you to take off my dress, you maniac. "Because from what you've just said, you need a break. You've helped me. Now it's my turn to help you."

She sniffed, wiped her nose with her fingers. "For real?"

"For real." Don't touch my dress with those fingers.

She watched me a little longer; then, as if it were no big deal, she reached around to unzip the dress. "I just wanted to see how I looked—it's a little small on me."

"Here, let me get that." I rushed to her side, lowering the zipper carefully, peeling pearl-adorned, hand-embroidered layers of form-fitting lace and silk off her ample torso, lifting it over her head and laying it gently on the bed. I wasn't a fashion hound, but that dress was a one-of-a kind work of art, and I positioned it delicately on the hanger while Ivy reached for her sweater and pulled on her jeans.

"When you're dressed, Ivy, just go. Take off."

She stepped into her sneakers. "Wait; what about the check?"

Oh, right. The check. "Come on downstairs."

I made her go first, so I could be sure she was leaving. And in single file, we headed to my office, where I made out a check for two weeks' salary

Ivy snapped it up, hesitating as if about to speak. But she didn't speak. Silently, wearing a secretive grin, she sashayed out the office door. I waited in the hall as Oliver chased after her, listening for the front door to close. And suddenly, I remembered: her key. Damn. I didn't want her to keep the key.

"—Ivy?" I ran after her, hoping she hadn't gone yet. "Ivy—wait. Leave your key—"

Down the hall, the front door slammed shut. I followed her, opening it, only to see her climbing into a blue Taurus up the street. I shouted her name again, but she didn't look around. By the time I got down the stairs, she'd probably have pulled away.

And then it occurred to me: Ivy didn't realize that she'd been fired. She believed she'd be coming back, so she'd probably followed her usual routine. I went outside and looked at a cluster of decorative stones surrounding the planters on the front stoop, and sure enough, Ivy's key was where it belonged, just like always, hidden in a big fake rock.

TWENTY-SIX

"SHE WHAT?" SUSAN WAS APPALLED.

Shaken up, I'd called her after Ivy left.

"Nobody puts on someone else's wedding gown. That's just plain scary. Is she obsessed with you?"

Obsessed with me? "Well, according to Ivy, I don't appreciate my life. I take everything for granted. I'm spoiled—"

"Zoe, she's unbalanced. It's good you got rid of her. You don't want her around your kids. God only knows what she'd do—"

"Let's not talk about that."

"All I'm saying is it's a good thing you found out how messed up she is before something worse happened."

Worse? "Susan, please. She wouldn't hurt the kids."

"You don't know that." Susan sounded offended.

"Look, I can't deal with Ivy right now. Bryce is still unconscious. The police haven't found out anything else about the murder. Anna's on my case—"

"I know you're stressed, Zoe. I am, too. You're not the only one with stress. I'm talking to you while preparing my closing for a murder trial—"

"Oh, right. Sorry." Oh God. Ivy was right. I was selfish and insensitive. How could I forget about Susan's trial?

"It's okay; don't worry. Look, I'm done today or tomorrow. The jury won't take long on this one. And then, I'm at your service. I'll help you with the kids, the wedding, the triplets. Whatever you need. Okay?"

Susan needed to get back to work. I needed to let her. "Susan, do you think she's right? Am I spoiled?"

Susan exhaled, impatient to get going. I pictured her, pushing a lock of hair off her face. "Spoiled? Compared to what? Compared to most of the world, yes, of course you are. But so is everyone else in this country."

"But that's not what Ivy meant. She said I think I'm better than other people."

"Only someone who thinks you're better than she is would say that. The problem is about her, not you."

What? I couldn't untangle that thought, but I thanked Susan for it and let her get back to work.

And, alone again with Luke and Oliver, I faced the rest of the day.

TWENTY-SEVEN

THE GOOD NEWS, OBVIOUSLY, WAS THAT IVY WAS GONE. THE BAD news, though, was that Ivy was gone. Once again, I had no help. So what? I told myself. Without her there, I felt lighter. Relieved. Nick and the brothers were out; I had my house to myself. I double locked the door and, seeing that Luke was sleeping, I hurried back upstairs to examine my dress. I held it up, found no stretches or damage and carefully replaced it in the closet, humming. I was in charge—not Ivy, not Anna. I alone was deciding what had to be done. No cops were wandering through the hall to the patio. No brothers were in my office or pestering me to invest in a time-share or scattering used dishes or clothes or bottles or towels wherever they fell.

Oliver wasn't overstimulated, freaking out at newcomers and commotion. In fact, he was unusually calm, and so was Luke. The house was quiet. Peaceful. And, for a change, so was I. I picked Luke up and carried him in his sling, and together we went from room to room, as I reorganized my kitchen, rearranged pillows, folded afghans in the living room. But somewhere in the process, my lightness evaporated. The fact was that my home felt altered. Violated. The patio was no longer a crime scene, but ribbons of yellow tape and the bloodstains remained. And though the brothers weren't there, their presence, even their smells, lingered.

I tried to reclaim my private space, but it was no use. Even after I straightened up, the place seemed sullied, off-kilter, and it occurred to me that maybe it wasn't that the house had changed; maybe it was that I had. I sat on a kitchen stool, replaying Ivy's angry words, seeing her acid gaze. Where had all that bitterness come from? Despite Susan's reassurance, I wondered if there weren't a kernel of truth to Ivy's accusations. Did I take my life, my relationships, for granted? Was I insensitive and spoiled?

The answer hit me hard, right in the gut. Yes, I was. Spoiled and self-absorbed. In the last few days, a woman had been slaughtered at my door and Bryce Edmond had almost lost his life trying to save me and my child. But this morning, I'd been outraged, not because of the murder or the hit-and-run but because my babysitter had tried on my dress. Because of a stitched-up bundle of cloth. What was wrong with me? I'd lost my perspective. Who cared, really, about a dress, any dress, when life was fleeting and fragile and relationships so precious?

I had to get over myself, focus on others. With Luke draped to my body, I went to the phone, called the hospital to check on Bryce. I called the Institute and talked to his secretary about his condition. I returned phone calls to friends, even checked in with Anna to find out what she'd decided about the flowers and the wine. I focused on others, caught up on their news and lives. I'd been locked in my own cloud and needed to come back down to Earth and put my feet back on the ground. But when I did, I was too rash. Climbing off the stool, I stepped into a pile Oliver had deposited, probably while I'd been immersed in conversations on the phone.

TWENTY-EIGHT

WHEN NICK CAME HOME, HE WAS PREOCCUPIED WITH THE events of his day. While Sam had luxuriated at the Four Seasons Spa, Nick had gone to the Roundhouse, trying to find out what was going on in the murdered jogger case. Tony had insisted on going with him, and Nick worried that Tony was too invested in the case not just because of his natural sensitivities but also because of his early encounter with the victim.

When I finally got a chance to tell Nick about Ivy trying on my wedding dress, he didn't even blink. In fact, his biggest concern was what we were going to do about a sitter. "Christ, Anna's not filling in again, is she? Why don't we call your old sitter—what's her name? Angelina?"

"Angela. And she doesn't sit anymore. She has a baby of her own to take care of. But we don't need anyone," I assured him. "I'm fine; I can take care of my own kids."

Nick blinked at me. "You're not serious."

"Why? You think I can't?"

"Zoe. It's only—what—five days until the wedding? You're going to want to get your hair done and stuff, aren't you? Who's going to watch the kids?"

"I can manage." I wanted to prove that I wasn't really all that spoiled. I could do my own chores, take care of my own children.

Nick shook his head, but I was confident. That day, I'd already fed and bathed Luke, taken Oliver for his obedience practice and walk, run three loads of laundry, answered three days of phone calls, met Molly at the bus and, using a dusty old cookbook, prepared roast beef and baked potatoes for dinner. Molly and I had even baked. It was a packaged cake mix, but still, we'd baked it, just the two of us, while Luke cooed in his portable baby chair. When the brothers wandered in, I'd welcomed them with smiles and hugs.

Good work, I'd congratulated myself. All day, I had focused on others, not on myself. I was doing fine, taking care of my home and family. I put Luke to bed, took Oliver out, helped Molly with her bath, washed the dishes, read with Molly and tucked her in. And, finally, I was ready to relax with my soon-to-be-husband and brothers-in-law. I came downstairs, hearing their animated discussion in the living room.

"No, uh-uh." I thought the voice was Tony's. "It wasn't like that—"

"But then, why?" Nick's voice, pressing him "Give me another even remotely sensible explanation—"

Without interrupting, I popped my head in, and immediately the conversation stopped. It was a pattern. Whenever I walked in, the talking halted. Three almost identical faces adopted three almost innocent smiles and turned toward me, stumbling over each other to pretend they weren't suddenly changing the subject.

"Zoe." Nick half-grinned too cheerily. "So. Molly in bed?"

"Great dinner, Zoe. Where'd you learn to cook?"

"Anybody hear from Anna today?"

They sat there, smiling stupidly, as if I wouldn't know that, seconds ago, they'd been talking about something else entirely. Why? What were they hiding? Information about the murder investigation? Details of Sam's shady investment deals? Whatever it was, I was tired of being excluded, and I glared at Nick, resenting the forced levity crossing half his face, shutting me out. Without answering any of their silly questions, I turned and left the room.

"Zoe?" Nick stood as I turned.

"Uh-oh," the brothers joined in.

"She's pissed."

I didn't hear the rest. I was heading upstairs, and Oliver was barking as he chased after me.

TWENTY-NINE

Upstairs, I went into my room and closed the door. It opened almost immediately.

"What the hell, Zoe?" Nick was scowling, eyebrows furrowed. He looked different. Unfamiliar.

"You tell me." I tried to sound aloof.

"You stomped out, pouting like a petulant child."

Oh good. First I was spoiled, now petulant. "Clearly, I wasn't welcome to join your conversation."

"Of course you were."

"Really? Then why did everyone clam up when I walked in?"

"Christ, Zoe. Don't start this again."

"Christ, Nick," I mocked him. "Don't deny this again."

I sat on the bed, arms stiffly folded. He sat beside me, watching me, blue eyes digging at mine. "We aren't keeping anything from you, Zoe. We're just talking. We're brothers. We share history. We have private jokes, private issues. Tons of unresolved crap to talk about." He took my hand. "You simply can't relate, being an only child."

"So, having history with them means you have to exclude me?"

"Of course not. No one's excluding you."

"Oh please."

"Zoe. My brothers and I haven't been together for years; you know that. We have a lot to talk about. Old times. Old gripes. Eli. Trust me, it would bore you."

Trust him? I studied his eyes, trying to read them. How come I could never tell if he was telling the truth? "Shouldn't I get to decide if I'm bored? Maybe if I heard some of those private jokes, I'd get to know you better. Maybe I'd become part of the family. But that can't happen because the three of you shut me out."

Nick sighed, half-shrugged. "Sorry, Zoe. Nobody's trying to shut you out. But they're my blood."

His blood? "What?"

"Eli. Tony. Sam. They're my blood."

Oh. I got it. He meant that they were related by blood, but I wasn't. And I never would be, even after we were married. Neither would Molly. In our little family, only Luke would actually be Nick's blood. Did that mean Luke would be privy to family talks and Molly and I would be shut out? Would Nick favor Luke over Molly? I couldn't imagine that. And what about me? I lived with Nick. I was about to marry him, become "flesh of his flesh," or whatever the passage read, but even flesh wasn't blood. And it occurred to me there were whole sides to Nick that I didn't know. For example, his childhood, his youth, were blanks to me. And Nick the brother, Nick the blood relation—those guys were strangers. How many other unknown parts of Nick were there? And where did his loyalties lie? If Nick was ever put to the test, would bonds of "blood" trump those of marriage vows?

I needed to know. "So. Being 'blood' means what, exactly?"

"Oh, come on, Zoe."

"I want to know."

"You know what it means."

"Tell me."

He let go of my hand, annoyed. "It means we're connected. For life. No matter what, we take care of each other, watch out for each other."

"No matter what?"

"That's right. We're blood."

I thought of Sam and his deals. "So, if one of your brothers was doing something wrong? You'd protect him?"

"What? Why would you even ask that?"

Why did he look so blank? He had to know that Sam was probably some kind of con artist. "Just hypothetically."

"There is no hypothetical to discuss here, Zoe. Because none of my brothers is doing anything wrong."

"Really. How can you be sure?"

"How? Because I know. Because they're my brothers."

I couldn't believe that Nick, the homicide detective, could be that simpleminded. "That's it?"

His gaze was flat and absolutely final. "That's it."

For a minute, neither of us said anything. Nick had drawn a line, ordered me not to cross it.

And so, I didn't. Jealous of his loyalties to his brothers, afraid to challenge it, I didn't say another word. Nick's eyes had become steel, so I didn't tell him that I suspected Sam was a crook, a con man. I held back my suspicions, knowing that if I was going to find out what Sam was up to, I'd have to do it on my own. I couldn't rely on Nick.

After all, he wasn't my blood.

THIRTY

AT FOUR IN THE MORNING, LUKE AND I WERE THE ONLY ONES awake. Soon, I hoped, he wouldn't need a middle-of-the-night meal and I could get a complete night's sleep, something I only vaguely remembered. Eyes drooping, I rocked him, snug in the old caned rocking chair, not fully awake. Luke's night-light glowed softly, projecting silhouettes onto the wall. The slats of the crib, the head of a bear. Cloaked in gentle shadows, I focused on Luke's contented humming, trying to ignore the rhythmic thunder resonating from downstairs. Clearly, Sam had once again not made it back to his hotel room, had fallen asleep in the reclining chair. And the house trembled with his snores.

Covering Luke with kisses and his coverlet, I left him and, half-asleep, wandered back toward my bedroom, wondering how the noise of his own snoring didn't awaken Sam, let alone Tony, presumably sleeping on the sofa in the same room. How had two women married Sam? Maybe they'd had separate bedrooms? Maybe it was why the marriages had ended? I climbed back into bed, closed my eyes and tried to drift off but couldn't, so loud were the honks, snorts and howls emanating from downstairs. I tossed. I put a pillow over my head. Finally, I got up to close the door.

Standing, though, I remembered the cake Molly and I had baked. Half of it was still in the kitchen. Moist yellow cake with fudge icing, sprinkled with chopped pecans. If I had just a small slice of that with a glass of milk, I'd probably be able to sleep. So I went downstairs, not caring if I woke the brothers up, not minding if Sam stirred and stopped his trumpeting din, but no noise I made seemed significant by comparison. I turned on the lights and moved around the kitchen, cut myself a slab of buttery cake, licked the knife, poured myself a mug of fat-free. Sitting on a stool, stuffing my face, vibrating along with Sam, I glanced into the entranceway, noting the clutter. On the floor, Molly's book bag and a few pairs of shoes. On the hall table, a pile of unsorted mail. Underneath, Sam's leather briefcase.

I sucked my finger to get the last bit of icing, swallowed the last gulp of milk. Leaving the dishes for the morning, I turned out the light and started for the steps. But I didn't go upstairs. Instead, I stopped in the hall and put the light on, staring at the brothers' trail of clutter. And, as Sam continued his serenade, I began to clean. I hung jackets, picked up laptops, a half-empty bag of tortilla chips, a wad of laundry. My arms were pretty full when I grabbed Sam's briefcase, so I dropped it. And, apparently, it was unlocked, because when it hit the floor, something clattered and folders spilled everywhere.

The snores were regular and rattling, undisturbed. The noise hadn't awakened anyone. Quietly, setting the pile I'd gathered on the floor, I knelt to replace the items into the case. The files were marked with names. Costa Rica. St. Martin. St. John's. Taiwan. Albania. Albania?

Finally, I reached for the metal box, the thing that had made so much noise when it fell. What was in it, I wondered. Money? Coins? Diamonds? Maybe it would reveal what Sam really did for a living. I couldn't resist. Looking around again to make sure that no one was watching, I opened the lid. And then I stopped breathing. It wasn't money or diamonds; it was a gun.

THIRTY-ONE

A GUN. A BIG AND COLD, SHINY, SINISTER-LOOKING GUN. I SAT on the floor, staring at it. Why would Sam, a businessman, a guy who invested other people's money in stocks and vacation real estate, need a gun? It wasn't like he had to personally transport luxury condos or piles of cash. Or travel in dangerous neighborhoods at odd hours. No. Sam would have no apparent reason to carry a gun. Unless he wasn't the person he claimed to be.

My mind began racing. Maybe Sam really was a criminal. Maybe he carried a gun because he used it for work. But would a con artist need a gun? Oh God. Maybe he wasn't just a con artist. Maybe Sam was a killer. A hit man. The deals he discussed on the phone—were they covers? Were the conversations encoded to hide the identities of clients and victims?

Stop it, I told myself. It's late. Your nerves are wired. Your imagination is flying. But I couldn't stop myself. I was on to Sam, and I needed to know what he was up to. His briefcase wouldn't tell me anything else, but I knew another place I might look. Since he'd arrived, Sam had spent half his time on his computer.

I picked the thing up and took it into my office, aware that I didn't know how I was going to search. I didn't have Sam's password, wouldn't have a clue how to trace his correspondence. I tried to guess, realizing I didn't know him well enough. Didn't know his birthday or his ex-wives' names. I tried the brothers' names, though, and Molly and Luke. I tried the city Sam was born in. I tried his parents' names. And I was about to try Dixon, the name of the elementary school where the boys had gone, when warm hands landed on my shoulders. I jumped, hit the keyboard and spun around.

Tony's hands tightened, and he frowned. "What are you doing, Zoe? What's going on?"

THIRTY-TWO

"NOTHING." I TWISTED MY NECK TO LOOK AT HIM.

He didn't release me. Not his hands, not his gaze.

"I couldn't sleep. I decided to check my e-mail." Why was I explaining myself? After all, this was my office, my house.

"But this is Sam's computer." Finally, Tony let go of my shoulders.

Damn. I couldn't think of an excuse.

"What are you really doing?"

Don't tell him, I told myself. He'll get mad. Remember, Tony and Sam are blood.

"Are you trying to guess his password?"

Then again, I'd seen them almost rip each other's eyes out, arguing over the newspaper. Tony and Sam had issues, even if they were brothers.

"Um—" Brilliant answer, I congratulated myself. "I couldn't sleep." That made no sense, but I had to say something

Tony smirked. Scratched his head. "You want to read his e-mail? Why?"

"Sam has a gun." Damn. Why had I said that?

Tony looked baffled. "What?"

"Sam has a gun. In his bag."

"You looked in his bag?"

"Of course not." I didn't want to explain. "But why would he have a gun?"

"Wait. If you didn't look in it, how do you know it's there?"

"I spilled it. It fell out."

Again, he scratched, this time his armpit. "Wow. I don't know. Lots of people have guns."

Go ahead, I told myself. You might as well ask. "Tony, I know he's your brother. But how much do you know about what Sam does for a living?"

Tony folded his arms, cocked his head. "What are you getting at?"

"Those deals he's always making. The way he's always trying to get people to invest—"

"You think Sam's running scams." Tony said that too quickly. Had he been thinking it himself?

"Maybe. Or worse."

"Worse?"

"What if he's involved in something bigger than scams?"

Tony's eyebrows furrowed. "Zoe, what exactly are you saying?"

"Why would he carry a gun? Why would he bring it into my house, where there are children? He must be up to something dangerous. Maybe something with drugs. Maybe Sam was the one who was supposed to meet that woman—maybe he was her contact."

Tony's neck tilted so far that his head was almost at a right angle to his body. As if he was trying to see me sideways. "Are we talking about the same guy? Sam. My brother."

Go ahead, I urged myself. "Think about it, Tony," I began but stopped. My mouth was dry, my voice unsteady. "If he has a gun, maybe he's involved in this. Maybe Sam killed her."

"What?"

I couldn't repeat it. I waited for him to replay what I'd said in his mind.

"You think he killed her?" His voice sounded so loud. "Sam?"

I shrugged, ready to point out how Sam had been unperturbed about the dead woman, how he'd never mentioned anything about carrying a weapon, how he might be using his so-called international investment deals as a front to cause a diversion—

But I didn't say any of that. Even if I had, Tony wouldn't have heard me. My words would have been drowned out, lost in his peals of uproarious laughter.

THIRTY-THREE

"SAM?" TONY GUFFAWED. "SAM? YOU CAN'T BE SERIOUS."

My face was red-hot.

"He passes out when he gets blood drawn. He faints at the sight of a needle. Sam went fishing. Once. He threw up not because he was seasick but because there was fish blood on the deck. The man can't eat rare steak. He might look like a bully, tries to act like one. But, and you can take this to the bank, Sam Stiles is a wimp, pure and thorough."

"Really? He wasn't the one who ran to the bathroom when he saw the body on the deck."

"But, if you recall, he didn't stand up, either. He sat plastered to the upholstery. If he'd had to stand up, he'd have hit the floor. I promise you. Sam's all bluster. A marshmallow. A pussycat."

He'd seemed that way, amusing Molly with jokes, cuddling Luke. But that might be part of his cover.

"Relax, Zoe. I can't swear that he doesn't scam people. In all honesty, I've suspected that some of his business deals might be a little shaky. But a killer? No way. Besides, the jogger wasn't shot. She was cut. Sam can't even cut rare steak."

"But why the gun?"

"I don't know. Maybe for protection. He's got two pissed-off ex-wives, remember. And he's involved in megabuck deals, whether they're legit or not. Whatever his reason, though, it's not to kill anyone. Not Sam. You've got him confused with Eli."

Tony was still chuckling as he said good night and walked out of my office. I stayed, thinking about what he'd said. Maybe I was wrong. Or maybe Tony was so close to his brother that he couldn't even imagine Sam doing anything truly evil.

Either way, I wasn't going to figure out his password or find anything on his computer. I hoped Tony wouldn't say anything to Sam or Nick. Would he? I told myself he wouldn't, that Tony was honorable; our conversation would remain private.

I knew I should go up to bed and try to sleep. It was only a few hours until morning, less than that until Luke would wake up. But my pulse was still racing, alert. As long as I was in my office, I might as well read some of the e-mail that had been piling up for weeks.

I booted up my computer and typed in my password, and the electronic voice welcomed me, telling me that I had mail. In fact, I had 293 messages. Good Lord. I hadn't been online in two months, since Luke's birth, but I'd had no idea I'd missed so much e-mail. I scanned the list, most recent at the top, eliminating some of the spam as I went, noticing message after message from edmdbry. Bryce Edmond had e-mailed me over and over again, maybe twenty times. What had been so urgent? Why had he pestered me almost to the point of harassment? At random, I picked one of his early e-mails and opened it, expecting to find a request for a signature for some employee benefit program or maybe an informal notification that my position was about to be eliminated. But I was wrong.

Bryce Edmond's e-mail was a few paragraphs, followed by a list of names. I read his note. And, suddenly chilled, I knew why he'd so doggedly tried to reach me.

THIRTY-FOUR

BEFORE I'D TAKEN OFF FOR MATERNITY LEAVE, I'D KNOWN THAT the Psychiatric Institute was floundering financially. A drastic reduction in federal funding and grant money had led to the loss of several important research programs and elimination of staff positions, and "nonessential" employees like me had their hours slashed. My art therapy program had been chopped in half, affecting not only the patients but also my health insurance and retirement funds.

Bryce had written to inform me of the latest, even more dramatic changes. Recently, due to further funding cuts, a number of patients whose care had been paid for by the Commonwealth of Pennsylvania had been released. Some of these patients had been institutionalized by court order due to criminal acts, but having been treated for multiple years, they had aged and been deemed harmless or rehabilitated by Institute staff and the Commonwealth. As a courtesy, Bryce was writing to inform me of those newly released, formerly violent patients with whom I'd worked.

Slowly, cautiously, I let my eyes move down the list, recognizing the first name, Kimberly Gilbert. Kimberly? Oh my. How could they let her leave? The Institute was the only home she'd known for decades. What would happen to her? How would she survive? Kimberly was a schizophrenic who, years ago, had slaughtered her family, believing that demons had disguised

themselves as her husband and mother. Kimberly, even med-
icated, wobbled in and out of reality. I was appalled that they'd set
her out on her own.

But Kimberly wasn't the only surprise. They'd also released Troy
Dunbar. I pictured Troy, a too-handsome forty-some-year-old man,
lanky, charismatically intense, Nordic looking and bipolar. At the
age of twenty, he'd shot his grandmother to death, nearly killed his
sister and himself. I wondered if he'd try again, on his own.

I scanned the list, stunned, unable to believe that some of the
most disturbed patients I'd worked with, who had committed
the most violent crimes, had simply been released. I told myself
that most of them were no longer dangerous. Most of them had
responded well to medication and had probably mellowed over
time. But how could anyone be sure these people would take their
medication? Bonnie Osterman, for example. Her name was on the
list. Bonnie Osterman was the woman who, years ago, sliced open
the bellies of pregnant women. Now, she had been set free. She
was out in the world again on her own.

Bonnie Osterman. The very thought of her made my toes curl.
She was a solid, squat woman, probably in her mid-sixties, hospi-
talized for maybe thirty years, ever since a gas company worker had
discovered tiny human bones in Bonnie's backyard. Investigators,
as I recalled, had turned up the remains of five infants behind her
house and pieces of a sixth in her freezer. Bonnie, it turned out, had
craved the tender flesh of unborn infants, killing their mothers to
get them, pulling them from the warmth of the womb and tossing
them into the heat of a stew pot.

According to Bryce, the Commonwealth had determined that,
after decades of intense psychiatric treatment, Bonnie Osterman
had overcome her ghoulish appetite and been cured. But I
wasn't entirely convinced. Before I'd gone on leave, Bonnie had
been unusually attentive, fascinated by my expanding middle,

commenting on the chic styles of my maternity clothing, asking if I'd learned the baby's gender. Her attention had chilled me at the time, but I'd assured myself that she was harmless, safely contained within the brick and concrete walls of the Institute, guarded by security staff, nurses and orderlies.

But now, she was free. Out on the street.

And a woman's belly had been slit open on my back porch.

I stared at the computer screen, rereading the message. Unconsciously, my hands had risen, protecting my middle. Slow down, I told myself. It's just a bizarre coincidence. Bonnie Osterman could not have killed the jogger.

No? Myself answered back. Why not?

Because—I fumbled for an answer. Because she's old now. And probably passive—she's been institutionalized for thirty-some years. And authorities have determined that she's no longer criminally insane.

None of that convinced me. The jogger's gaping wounds reappeared in my mind, almost exactly duplicating those inflicted by my former patient.

But wait, I reasoned. Even if she still wanted to, Bonnie Osterman couldn't overpower a lithe young jogger. Bonnie wasn't fit or strong enough. And, most important of all, the dead jogger hadn't been pregnant—whoever killed her had opened her up, but not to get a baby. The killer had pulled out her intestines. Searching not for a baby but for drugs.

No matter what I told myself, though, I was unnerved. I worried about Kimberly, Troy, Henry, Olivia and the others—those patients, without care and supervision, were likely more dangerous to themselves than to others. But Bonnie Osterman. She was unlike any patient I'd ever worked with. No matter how I tried, I couldn't relate to her, could find no common ground, no vulnerability, no empathy for others. Her art projects included tangled, sinuous abstract distortions, detailed but minuscule, lost in emptiness of indifferent space. She seemed, even at her best most-medicated times, to be a monster. And now, she was among us.

I read the list of names again and again, thinking about Bryce. He'd been determined to tell me something, and now he was lying in a coma. Was there a connection? I replayed the hit-and-run in my mind, trying to recall the driver. Could it have been one of the patients? Kimberly? Troy? Henry? Bonnie?

Of course not. How would any of them have known that Bryce would be on the corner of Fifth and South streets at that exact time on that date? They couldn't have. None of them. Unless the driver had been following Bryce. But why would a patient—any patient—want to follow Bryce Edmond? Bryce wasn't involved with patient care. He was in administration. The patients probably didn't even know him.

But they knew me. All of them. What if the driver had been following not Bryce but me? I closed my eyes and saw it again, the car plowing over the curb, charging right at me—and Bryce pushing me away. It was possible, maybe even likely, that I had been the target. But who had been behind the wheel? I tried to remember, to picture the driver, but saw only Bryce's body flying at me followed by a great commotion of motorized steel.

Again, unbidden, Bonnie Osterman popped into my thoughts. "You're beginning to show, aren't you?" Her questions had made me queasy. "You want a boy, honey? Or a girl?" She'd eyed my belly, pursuing me even as I ignored her, guiding her attention back to her art project. But she'd persisted. "Is it moving? Can you feel it kicking?" Whenever she'd been in art therapy, I'd felt her creepy gaze following me no matter where I went, even as her fingers worked.

Oh Lord. Wasn't that the same creepy feeling I'd been having lately? Of somebody watching me? Oh my God. Could Bonnie Osterman be stalking me?

Impulsively, quickly, I closed the e-mail and pushed DELETE, erasing Bryce's message and Bonnie Osterman's name from the screen, if not from my mind. I got up, stood at the window, paced the office floor, as questions too horrible to articulate began to hammer at me. Had I been sensing Bonnie's presence? Had she been obsessed with my pregnancy? Planning to come after me to steal my baby? Had she been driving the car that hit Bryce?

Oh God. In a heartbeat, I ran from the room, sped up the stairs, found Luke safe in his crib. I didn't care if he woke up. I grabbed him and held him close. And then, watching the street outside through the window, I sat in the rocking chair, holding on to him for the rest of the night.

THIRTY-FIVE

FIRST THING TUESDAY MORNING, I CALLED THE HOSPITAL TO check again on Bryce. His condition had not changed. I told myself it wasn't my fault he'd been hit, even if the driver had been a patient. I hadn't released anyone from the Institute. I hadn't told Bryce to chase me. Still, guilt hounded me, and I spun through the morning, unable to rest.

Before the others were awake, I took Oliver out, congratulating him for performing his business in the bushes, only to realize when we came back inside that he'd gnawed the backs off yet another pair of Molly's sneakers. I searched the hall closet and finally found her old blue pair, as yet unchewed, and put them up on a dining room chair, safe from his jaws. I fixed a pot of coffee for Nick and the brothers. I fed Luke. I kept moving as if being busy would protect me from thinking, but it didn't. No matter what I did, the events of the night stayed with me. There was no escape. I needed to go someplace quiet to think, to sort things out. Of course. A shower.

Not wanting to wake up Nick, I used Molly's bathroom down the hall. Hot water cascaded over me like guilt about Bryce, suspicion about Sam. I thought about what to say to Nick. Should I tell him about Sam's gun? Would he laugh at me as Tony had, dismissing my concerns because of "blood"? Would he scold me for snooping? Defend Sam's basic right to bear arms? Probably. And what about the Institute patients? Nick would no doubt reassure me, tell me not to worry about them. But he had never met Troy

Dunbar or Kimberly Gilbert, didn't know how off-kilter they could get. He didn't know Bonnie Osterman, had never seen the mocking evil glint in her eyes. Nick would remind me that I could do nothing for patients who'd been released, and that, surrounded by three strong men, the kids and I were perfectly safe.

With steamy water pouring over my head, I could hear Nick's comments almost as if he'd actually spoken them. What was the point of talking to him, I wondered, if I already knew what he was going to say? Did I really know him so well? I soaped myself, smiling, thinking about Nick. About how, in a few days, we'd be married.

Married? I stopped washing, stood stock-still. In just four days, it would be the weekend. The weekend of our wedding—there. I'd said it: our wedding. I said it out loud, again and then again. Somehow, with all the upheaval that had been going on, the *w* word had become less threatening. Under hot water, I pictured the ceremony, candlelight and roses. My white-haired father, elegant in his tux. Molly, angelic in her flower girl dress. Susan, glamorous as matron of honor. Nick—but at the thought of Nick, something surged in my chest, and I actually felt dizzy, had to put a hand on the tiles to steady myself. Oh God. It was really going to happen. Nick Stiles was going to be my husband.

My husband. What was it about that word that made my knees buckle? What would *husband* mean with respect to Nick? Would he and I be different next week after the wedding than we were now? What would change? And I would be a wife again. Thoughts of last time, my last marriage, swirled in my head; I closed my eyes, ducked my head under the faucet, trying to rinse them away. No. Michael, my ex, was not welcome in this shower. Not today. Not ever. My new marriage would be different. This one was about respect. And love. But wait—hadn't I loved Michael, too? Stop it, I scolded myself, resoaping my body. You're older, more mature. Plus, Nick is different from Michael. You can trust—

But I stopped right there, mid-thought. Trust had been an issue between Nick and me, a big one. I'd come to terms with it, though, accepting that Nick was secretive by nature. Plus, as a cop, he kept the truth close and under his control, sharing only what he had to. Trusting Nick didn't mean thinking that he would always be open with me or even that he'd always be truthful. Trusting Nick meant having faith in his intentions, believing that he would never willingly hurt me. See that? I turned, letting hot water flow down my back. I'd learned a lot since Michael. I was more mature now, had more realistic expectations.

Besides, it wasn't just us. Nick and I had Molly and Luke. We were a family; the wedding would make it official. Nick would be my husband, I his wife—

Somebody knocked on the bathroom door.

"Yes?" I thought it was Nick. "Nick?"

No one answered. I shut off the water, squeezed my hair, stepped out of the shower, grabbed two towels, one for my body, one for my head. Wrapped in terry cloth, I opened the door, glanced up, then down the hall. Nobody was there.

I peeked in on Molly, but her alarm wouldn't go off for a few more minutes. She was still asleep. Luke gurgled in his crib. Nick snored softly, undisturbed. Obviously, Tony or Sam had come upstairs. One of them had knocked on the bathroom door.

I dried my hair and, by the time I was finished, Molly and Nick were awake. The day, our normal routine, had begun. But no matter what I did or where I went, I felt as if someone unseen was watching me. I spent the day off-balance, as if surrounded by secrets. As I made Molly's lunch or took Oliver and Luke for a walk, my thoughts ricocheted, bouncing from Sam's hidden gun, to plans for my wedding, to Bryce's condition, to the possibility that a psychotic former patient was stalking me, and as I met with Anna to finalize the musicians' contracts and selections, my emotions continually seesawed between terror and joy.

THIRTY-SIX

A LITTLE AFTER NOON, NICK SURPRISED US, COMING HOME UN-expectedly, bearing cheese steaks from Pat's. Just the way I liked them, with grilled onions and mushrooms. We ate at the dining room table, right off the white wrapping paper. No plates. A can of soda or of beer. Lots of ketchup. Neither Sam nor Tony had eaten these Philly specialties before, but they dug in with the same gusto I did. In minutes, the steaks had been inhaled in silence; no one had stopped chewing long enough to make conversation. But when we were finished, Nick straightened his back, folded his hands on the table as if calling a meeting to order.

"Turns out our jogger was penetrated." He announced it just like that. No introductory phrases to prepare us for the topic. No segue or transition from food to forensics. "Both vaginally and anally."

For a moment, nobody spoke. All eyes were on Nick.

"So she was raped." Sam picked something from his teeth.

"Well, that's still a question." Nick leaned back, crossed his legs. "There were some pretty brutal rips and bruises, but no DNA, no semen, no definite proof that the motive was sexual. The penetration could have been for the same reason as the disembowelment—"

"In other words, they were searching for something." Sam mirrored Nick's posture, executives at a conference. "Looking for drugs anywhere she could stash them."

"That's one theory."

One theory? "What do you mean, 'one theory'?" Were there more?

Nick sighed. "They've just released this. They've got an official ID on her." He stopped, building the dramatic effect.

"Really." Sam leaned forward. "Who was she?"

"Her name was Jennifer Harris." Nick paused. "She was a federal agent."

Sam and I spoke at once. "No shit," he breathed while I asked, "You mean a narc?"

"No, technically, she wasn't a narc. They're DEA. Harris was Homeland Security."

Wait. What? I tried to digest what I'd just heard. The dead woman had a name, an identity. Jennifer Harris. Jennifer Harris must have had friends, family. People who would mourn her loss. Maybe a boyfriend or a husband, maybe a child.

"Homeland Security?" Sam's eyes were popping. "So what does that mean? What was this Jennifer Harris doing on the patio— hunting terrorists?"

Oh God. Good question. Homeland Security agents tracked terrorists, didn't they? Did Jennifer's presence here mean that there was a cell in our neighborhood?

Nick took his time answering. "It's not clear what she was doing. The feds don't give out a whole lot of information. In fact, since she's one of theirs, they're trying to lift the case. But there's some talk going around. Not to be repeated, okay?"

We all nodded. Okay.

"The talk is that there might be links between drug traffickers and certain terrorist groups. There's a lot of money in drugs, and terrorists need a lot of funding. I doubt they'd be picky about where the cash is coming from."

"So if she tracked the drugs, she might find the terrorists." Sam snorted.

"If it's drugs." Tony hadn't said a word during the whole

conversation. Now, he stood, began pacing. "But they're not sure it was drugs. I mean, are they?"

"No. The feds aren't telling us what she was doing, and nobody else is sure of anything."

"What else could it be?" Sam growled. "I mean there's not much room in your average—" He stopped and glanced at me, cleaning up his language. "Um, orifice."

"Whatever is the size of a suppository or a condom would fit. Could be a weapon of some sort. Or a piece of one. Something biological, maybe." Nick spoke casually, discussing disasters.

"But drugs are still a possibility, right?" Tony sounded hopeful.

"I guess. But I think the feds would tell us if she'd been carrying drugs. Drugs are passé. They're everywhere. There would be no reason to withhold that information. In my opinion, whatever the killer was looking for, the feds probably know what it is. But they aren't telling."

Sam reached for another beer, popped it open. "Christ. What could it be?"

The brothers began to hypothesize, brainstorming about what would fit in a woman's intestines or private spaces. Vials of a virus or other biological weapon. A tiny atomic bomb or part. A toxic chemical agent. Some kind of poison gas. A secret formula for a lethal or destructive compound.

The list went on, got vaguer and raunchier, but I was considering a completely different possibility: Bonnie Osterman. I told myself that it was unlikely that she'd killed Agent Harris. It had to be just a coincidence that the agent's murder had so closely resembled those committed by my former patient. And just a coincidence that the agent had been killed so soon after Bonnie Osterman's release. Bonnie Osterman, in all likelihood, was no threat to anyone anymore, just as the Commonwealth had determined.

The brothers were still theorizing about what Jennifer Harris might have been carrying. Embryonic cloned cells. Engineered mutant cells. Robotic self-reproducing killer cells. I crumpled up the wrappings from the cheesesteaks, rolled them into a wad, went to the kitchen and tossed them into the trash.

Then, standing at the window, I scanned the street, wondering not what Jennifer Harris had been carrying but what a Homeland Security agent had been doing on our street. What had she been doing on our back patio? And if it hadn't been Bonnie Osterman, then who had killed her?

THIRTY-SEVEN

"It wasn't her." Nick stooped to catch Oliver so he could attach his leash. "Don't worry about it."

See that? I assured myself. Nick agrees; Bonnie Osterman didn't kill the agent. "How do you know? I mean she could have. And she could have rammed her car into Bryce, too—"

"Now you're getting paranoid." Just as Nick was about to grab him, Oliver darted away. "Come, Oliver. Time to go out." Oliver sat down a little more than arm's length away and grinned at Nick, panting.

"How is it paranoid?" I had to compete with the dog for Nick's attention. "You don't know this woman. You're underestimating her. Nick. She made beef stew out of infants."

"Baby goulash. Now that's ghoulish." He pounced suddenly, but the puppy darted away. But now, Oliver was convinced that they were playing a game. Again, he sat eager and panting, positioned just beyond Nick's reach.

I glared. "Dammit, Nick. That's not funny. I'm trying to talk to you, and you're trying to lasso the dog."

Breathless, sprawled on the floor, Nick seemed surprised at my tone. "He needs to go out." Nick pulled himself to his feet, brushing off his pants. "But okay. You want to talk? We'll talk."

I went into the kitchen, sat on a stool, Nick trailing me, Oliver trailing Nick. "Those babies were real, Nick. As real as Luke. It's not a joke. She killed them."

"I know." He didn't apologize. "It was gallows humor, Zoe. When you deal with homicide all the time, you see stuff you can't handle. You let out the stress. You make stupid jokes. It happens."

I didn't excuse him. "So. If Bonnie Osterman didn't kill her, why did Agent Harris just happen to be in my backyard? And why was Bryce Edmond hit when he just happened to be standing with me and my infant?"

Nick rested a hip on a kitchen stool and shrugged. "I don't know."

Great. I crossed my arms, ignoring Oliver whining at my feet.

"This is what I do know, though. I know that federal agents like Harris are highly trained and in peak physical condition. They know how to make themselves all but invisible in public. The only reason Tony remembered Harris was because she bumped into him. Otherwise, she would have blended into the sidewalk and run off unnoticed."

I wasn't convinced. Nobody was invisible. Certainly not an athletic young blond woman.

"These people operate among us but out of our reach, on their own plateau."

"So you think they're infallible?"

"No, but someone like your Bonnie Osterman wouldn't have focused on someone as strong as Harris. She wouldn't have selected Harris as a victim. Harris wasn't pregnant. And she would have made a tough opponent."

"But Harris was here. At our house. Maybe Bonnie wanted our baby and, by some twist of fate, Agent Harris was in her way—"

"Zoe—it didn't happen." Nick stopped me, put his arms around me. "Luke's fine. He's in his playpen."

I knew that. And I knew that Tony was with Luke, and that Sam was near them, in my office with a gun in his briefcase, checking stocks or making investment deals on his computer. I also knew that Bonnie Osterman was unaccounted for.

"Okay. Let's say, for argument's sake, that Bonnie Whatever-her-name-is—"

"Osterman."

"Let's say she did want to kill Agent Harris. Your patient is what—sixty-five? More? And she's been institutionalized for decades, so her muscle tone is gone and she's been eating too much starch. No way is she going to be strong or agile enough to harm Harris. Harris would deck her forty ways before your lady could lift her arm."

Of course he was right. Bonnie Osterman was stout, thick legged. She moved slowly, with effort.

"It's much more likely that Agent Harris was killed by one of the people she was tracking, like a drug dealer or narcoterrorist who cut her open looking for drugs he thought she was carrying."

Much more likely, yes.

"Besides, your Bonnie wasn't released onto the street all on her own. She must have been sent to live under some supervision somewhere—a halfway house or something, right?"

I didn't know. There wasn't much money for halfway houses; the ones I knew of rarely had space. But I nodded anyway, seeing no point anymore in speaking. Nothing I said seemed to make an impression. I'd told Nick about Bonnie's murders, the babies, the small legs and thighs found in her freezer. I'd described their mothers' violated, gutted bodies. But he'd seemed unfazed. To Nick, the curiosity Bonnie had shown about my pregnancy, the threat she might pose to our baby, the coincidence of a gutted woman on our porch, the hit-and-run attack on the man who'd warned me that Bonnie was loose—none of that seemed to merit concern. Nick humored me by letting me talk, but his muscles never tensed.

So, I gave up and stopped talking, partly to see if he would notice.

After a few too many silent seconds, Nick reached out, touched my cheek. "Zoe. Hey. Look at me."

I looked at him but found it hard to breathe.

"So. All this is really upsetting you."

Bingo. The man was amazing. A genius. I blinked and looked away.

"What, now you're not talking to me?"

Wow, he was right twice in a row. Nick's accuracy was mind-boggling.

"You really think this Bonnie woman's a threat?"

Still silent, I shrugged. She might, might not be a threat.

He sighed. "Okay. It's not worth having you this upset. How's this? I'll have her checked out. We'll find out where she is."

I waited, said nothing. My silence was clearly having more effect than my voice.

"All right. If I find out she's anywhere in the area, I'll have her picked up for questioning. I'll talk to her myself and see what she's been up to. There. Does that make you feel better?"

I nodded. "Yes." It did, and, relaxing, I smiled.

"Good." Nick half-grinned. "Anything to get you to stop pouting." He leaned over, brushed his lips against mine.

I grabbed his shirt and stood, pulled him closer, planting a big one on his mouth. One arm, then another slid around my back. My hands reached up behind his neck. We stayed that way for a while, bodies pressed together and mouths locked, Oliver yapping at our ankles until we had to break for breath.

And then Nick took him by surprise, dropping down and attaching the leash quickly, before Oliver could run off and piddle on the floor.

THIRTY-EIGHT

THE BROTHERS WERE OUT FOR A NIGHTCAP, THE KIDS IN BED, THE puppy asleep at my feet. I sat in bed, staring mindlessly at reruns of *Law & Order: Special Victims Unit,* a half-emptied cup of tea and half-eaten box of Mallomars on my nightstand. And leaning back, too drowsy to move, I heard someone in the house, creeping around, searching for drugs—or no, not drugs. A bomb. And it wasn't just one guy. There were a bunch of them, all over the place. Dangerous, dressed in long dark coats and hats, they were tearing open the velvet cushions of my purple sofa, upending tables, tossing collectibles off the shelves, shooting flashes of light up the chimney, rolling up the rugs. But why were they looking under the rugs? You couldn't hide a bomb there—it would make a lump. But then I realized that they weren't looking under the rug for the actual bomb. They were looking for a trapdoor, a place to hide the bomb. As I watched, the intruders tore apart my kitchen, the hall closet, the hutch in the dining room, the file cabinets in my office. I could see them scurrying about, watch them in every room at once like an infestation of insects, invading each crevice and corner. Suddenly, I'd had enough. I was outraged. This was my home, and I wasn't going to allow them to destroy it. I grabbed Nick's spare gun from his nightstand and rushed down the hall, shouting. "Get out," I screamed. "Get out of my house or I'll shoot." Their hat brims hid their faces as they came at me from all sides, so I couldn't see who they were. I just shot. They rushed me, shouting at me to stop, but I fired again and again, trying to fend them off, still recoiling from the blasts, when suddenly they dropped to the floor and disappeared in a flash of white. The room glowed, the house melted away, and there was nothing but the blinding heat of their bomb, exploding.

I opened my eyes in a jolt, found myself face-to-face with Oliver's snout. He must have moved to Nick's pillow while I'd been dozing, and now Oliver slept peacefully, undisturbed. No bomb had gone off. No spies in dark coats had invaded the house. It had just been a dream. Still, seeking comfort, I put my hand on Oliver's soft head. His eyes half-opened, registered me and closed again. Nothing, according to Oliver, was wrong. Still, I was shaken, and I lay still, recovering, listening to the televised dialog of the cops interviewing a perp. The rhythm of their voices was soothing, normal. As always, Detectives Stabler and Benson would catch the bad guys. I boosted myself up against the pillows, turning to the screen, only vaguely noticing the creak in the floor.

But then there was another one. The house is getting old, I told myself. Old wood makes noises. And at night, houses settle; floors creak. Nothing's wrong. I tried to focus on the interrogation. Elliot lost it, as usual, pushing some suspect up against the wall, pushing his nose into the guy's terrified face. This time, there were two creaks, one right after the other. Like footsteps. I sat up straight, alert, waiting.

Beside me, Oliver snored. Wait a second, I thought. Dogs are supposed to have better hearing than people. If someone was creeping around the house, Oliver would bark, wouldn't he? He'd smell a stranger. He'd warn me. But the puppy was content and calm. I was still on edge because of the dream; that was all. I reached around to the nightstand and got a Mallomar, popped the whole cookie into my mouth, stuffing my cheeks with chocolate and marshmallow, and chewing, basking in sugar, I heard a definite, unmistakable, unsettling set of creaks.

Okay. There was no mistaking it. I sat, frozen, listening. I muted the television, waiting. And again, after a long silence, I heard a creak. The floorboards were groaning under somebody's feet. Someone was in the house. Sneaking.

The dream was still fresh in my mind. Probably I was still in its clutches, imagining things. But then, I heard the muted pad of footsteps outside my bedroom door. Nick's gun—I remembered it from the dream. I rolled over, slid the nightstand drawer open and pulled the gun out, felt its cold, reassuring weight. Now what? Molly and Luke were down the hall, defenseless, and someone was out in the hall, creeping around. Oh God. Was it Bonnie Osterman? Was she here to take Luke? Well, if so, she was going to have to get past me. Oliver lifted his head, watching me as I got out of bed, holding the gun in both hands, arms outstretched like the cops on the television, and stepped slowly toward the door.

THIRTY-NINE

THE HALLWAY WAS EMPTY, THE FEEBLE GLOW OF DINOSAUR AND puppy night-lights spilling from the children's rooms. I looked both ways, measuring the stillness, then stepped out, the gun still raised. On tiptoe, I moved to Molly's room first, found her soundly sleeping. Her mouth hung open; her golden curls haloed her face. With the gun, I nudged her closet door open but found no one hiding there. I drew a deep, relieved breath. But I didn't let it out; behind me, I heard a soft rustle. And then, behind me, just outside my peripheral vision, something moved. I spun around, knees bent, arms extended, ready to fire. And saw Oliver smiling up at me. Damn. What was wrong with me? I'd almost shot the puppy.

Finally, I released the breath, but I was shivering and unsteady. Settle down, I told myself. Relax your shoulders. Breathe deep. But I couldn't. Someone—maybe a drug dealer or a narcoterrorist or maybe Bonnie Osterman—was in the house. I had to check on Luke. With my back to the wall and gun still raised, I edged out of Molly's room and headed to Luke's. Shifting my weight slowly from foot to foot so the floor wouldn't creak, I stepped through the darkness, body taut, arms out, Nick's weapon leading my way. Oliver scampered, circling me, nipping at my ankles, and I was afraid that he'd bark, warning the intruder. But then, even if Oliver didn't, the roaring thumps of my heart might. The hallway between Molly's door and Luke's was less than ten feet long, but somehow that night it extended, and with each step I took, the distance seemed to grow. As I neared the baby's room, I realized that too much light was spilling out, more than just the bulb of the night-light. Luke's lamp was on. Could I have left it on? Could Nick? My heart stopped its pounding, plummeted into my stomach.

I hadn't left the light on. Neither had Nick. Someone else had. Oh God. Was Bonnie Osterman in there? God help her if she was. And, if she had harmed Luke—

With my blood curdling, my finger tightening on the cold metal trigger, I stood outside my baby's bedroom, tightened my finger on the trigger and charged.

FORTY

AND STOPPED SHORT, GAPING INTO THE DIM LIGHT, GUN STILL drawn.

The person in Luke's room wasn't Bonnie Osterman or any of my former patients. It was Tony, and he was standing beside the crib with Luke in his arms.

"Tony?" What was he doing there? I hadn't heard him come in. Why wasn't he with Nick and Sam? And why was he decked out, neck to toe, in tight black cat burglar clothes?

He turned his head as if surprised to see me. "Oh crap—don't shoot." The voice wasn't Tony's. It was smoother. It glided, made "Oh crap" sound like butter. I squinted, trying to see his face more clearly. No, he wasn't Tony after all. He was more angular. More glamorous. The man smiled, white teeth glistening. He eyed the gun.

"Put my baby in his crib. Now." I was trembling with sheer maternal instinct, still ready to kill.

"Okay. No problem." Gently, he laid Luke down and covered him with his dinosaur comforter.

"Put your hands in the air." I'd watched *Law & Order*, knew how to mimic a cop.

He obeyed, carefully. Oliver ran to him, jumping and sniffing. "Hey, little guy. What's his name?" The man's eyes were twinkling; his voice sounded relaxed, even friendly.

Why wasn't he scared? I had a gun aimed at his chest, but this intruder, this possible kidnapper, was asking my dog's name.

"Who are you?" I already knew but felt compelled to ask.

No answer. Just a broad, engaging smile with dazzling teeth.

"You're Eli."

"Guilty as charged."

Of course he was. He looked just like Nick and the others. But I'd been warned, knew that Eli lived on the edge, might be dangerous, so I kept the gun on him.

"And you're Zoe. Soon to be my sister." His eyes smiled, and he moved his arms apart as if inviting a hug. His shoulders were huge.

I kept the gun on him. "So, Eli. What are you doing here?"

"What do you think? My brother invited me." He smirked. I knew that smirk, or half of it—it was Nick's. "Can I put my hands down?"

"No, you may not. Why are you sneaking around my son's room in the middle of the night?"

Eli didn't answer; he merely tilted his head toward the dresser. Cautiously, I followed his gaze. An open camera case was lying beside Luke's freshly folded laundry.

"Wait." I tried to make sense of it. "You're saying that you're here to take pictures?"

He shrugged. "I'm a photographer."

I'd been warned about Eli, that he was slippery. "You broke into my house to take pictures?"

"Hold on now. I didn't break in—"

"No? Then how did you get in?"

"The key." He said it as if it were obvious.

"What key?"

"The spare. Nick left it outside."

Nick left it? No, I didn't think so. Nick wouldn't leave a key outside. Nick was a detective, didn't believe in leaving keys around. He'd have been furious if he'd known where I left Ivy's key.

Eli's arms sagged, hung out to the sides instead of over his shoulders. "Look. He left it where we always kept our spare growing up."

"Where exactly?"

"In a fake rock. On the porch."

In the rock? Damn. Nick hadn't left it there; Eli had found Ivy's key.

"Nick must have left it for me in case I showed up when nobody was home. So I used it. I didn't break in, Zoe."

"You didn't exactly ring the bell."

"I didn't want to wake anyone up. I don't have much time, and I wanted to see my nephew. He's the first of the next generation of Stiles boys."

Eli's arms drooped in the air.

"I swear. I'm not here to hurt anybody. I just want to take some pictures. He's beautiful, Zoe."

So was Eli, his eyes playful and teasing, almost asking mine to dance.

"Beautiful like his mother." Eli smiled, blatantly flattering me. I felt my face heat up. "Thank God he doesn't look like his dad."

I watched Eli, assessing the confidence of his jaw, the fiery eyes that seemed to savor some secret joke even as a loaded gun was pointed at his heart. So this was Eli, the fourth brother. The one the others were somehow in awe of. Dashing, mysterious, elusive and talented. Probably, I decided, I wasn't going to shoot him.

"Okay then, Eli." I lowered the gun. "I guess you can lower your arms."

His smile widened, revealing perfect teeth. But, instead of lowering his arms, he extended them, offering a brotherly embrace. "It's nice to meet you, Zoe. Welcome to our dysfunctional, messed-up family."

I stepped toward him tentatively, self-consciously, suddenly aware that my hair was a mess and that I had on neither a bra nor makeup, trying to be casual about tucking the gun into the waist-band of my pajamas, concerned I might accidentally shoot my butt off, awkwardly realizing just in time that if I put the heavy gun there, its weight would pull my pants down. So, fumbling first to place, then to remove the gun, I finally left it dangling in my right hand and placed my left on Eli's shoulder. Instantly, he swooped, arms encircling me, squeezing the air from my lungs, lifting my feet off the floor as he planted a kiss firmly on the side of my head.

When he set me down again, he was beaming, and I was breath-less and aware of a sore spot near my hip. I backed away, glancing at his waist to see what might have jabbed me. And, buckled se-curely into his belt, I saw the sleek, dangerous-looking hilt of a large folding knife.

FORTY-ONE

I STIFFENED AND STEPPED BETWEEN ELI AND THE CRIB.

Eli, still beaming, looked puzzled. "What's wrong?"

I remembered the brothers' stories. Eli was elusive about his work, but they joked that he might be a government agent, working undercover, or he might be a hit man for the Mafia. Either way, I decided to postpone discussing the knife.

Just then, Luke gurgled a complaint. We were disturbing him. Wordlessly, I took Eli's arm and led him into the hall, Oliver trailing along with us. Eli was taller than Nick, who was over six feet tall. I had to strain my neck to look up at Eli, and when I did, I blinked and looked away. His gaze was too intense. His eyes, focused on my face, actually radiated heat. They seemed to beam through my skin, melting my thoughts, and, as my face sizzled, it occurred to me that these eyes were the opposite of Nick's. Nick's were cool icy blue. I felt Eli studying me, and even in the dim light, I grew painfully aware of every unplucked eyebrow hair, age line, blemish and clogged pore on my face. I wanted to excuse myself, at least long enough to slather on some mascara. But I was being ridiculous. This man was not here to flirt with me; he was Nick's errant rascal, possible criminal kid brother. And he had a lot to explain.

So, bracing myself for the steamy impact of eye contact, I craned my neck, riveted my stare and let my mouth rip in a hoarse whisper. "Okay, Eli. Now that we've gone through the 'beautiful baby' crap, why don't you tell me the truth? Like why you're wearing a weapon in my house."

Again, his eyes laughed. "Weapon?" All innocence. "Oh. This?" His hand went to his belt. "I always wear it."

"Bullshit, Eli. You're dressed like a damned cat burglar. You sneak into my house in the middle of the night—"

"Zoe, it's not even midnight. That's hardly—"

"—And you creep around, picking up my baby—"

"—the middle of the night."

"—in secret instead of calling ahead and arranging a visit like a normal person."

"Look, I just wanted to shoot some candids."

"So tell me, if you're here to take baby pictures, why are you wearing a knife?"

"I always wear that knife. Ever since the military. I'd feel naked without it."

Uninvited, thoughts of him knifeless and naked flashed in my mind, and I blinked, forcing them away. More than Tony or Sam, the man was a clone of Nick, a newer and improved, scar-free version. Eli carried himself like Nick, only younger and saucier, and approached me knowingly, as if he could see into my head. Like Nick did.

Eli sighed, moved closer and placed his hands solidly on my shoulders just as Nick did when he wanted me to calm down. And Eli's touch, his grip, was confusing, too familiar. Too much like Nick's.

"Zoe. Believe me. I'm not going to hurt anybody. I didn't want the others to know I was here. I wanted to surprise them. And, since I've blown it, I might as well tell you—I've been putting something together for you and Nick. Kind of a wedding gift."

"The pictures?"

He nodded, attempted a sheepish expression that came across wolfish. "A candid photo study."

Candid? Wait. "So you've been following us? Like a stalker?" My neck was aching from looking up at him.

His eyes sparkled, but he squirmed almost imperceptibly. "No, nothing like that. Just, when I've had the chance, I've stopped by and taken—"

"You mean you've been here before? What are you saying? You've been sneaking around here, peeping on us?" I felt self-conscious, undressed. And I was furious, ready to draw the gun again. "What are you, some kind of pervert?"

"No—I mean, well, yes, I've been here before, but no, I'm not a pervert. At least I don't think I am. I mean, maybe some people might think I am, but that's because they're prudes. Look, I'm not sick or anything. I haven't been peeping—just taking pictures. For you and Nick. Come on, Zoe. Trust me."

Trust him? Was he nuts? As he said the words, his face became Nick's, and I heard Nick's voice echoing: Trust me. How often had Nick said to me those very same words, wearing that same puppy dog expression? It was uncanny how the two resembled each other. But Eli was still talking.

". . . Only a few times. I swear . . ."

But I didn't pay attention. I was wondering if Eli's presence had been what I'd sensed lately when I was alone. Maybe it hadn't been my imagination, hadn't been Bonnie Osterman or any of the other former patients. Maybe it had been Eli who'd been tailing me, waiting for the perfect shot.

". . . I wanted it to be a surprise. I guess that was stupid. I'm sorry that I scared you—"

Eli stopped mid-sentence, his eyes flaring an alert. A moment later, Oliver bolted down the stairs, yapping, and I heard the key in the lock, the front door opening, Sam's hoarse voice in the middle of some story. The brothers were home.

Eli stood still, silent.

"They'll be ecstatic that you're here." I touched his arm. "You're all they talk about. You'll have to tell me if any of their stories are true."

He still didn't move, but his eyes flickered that he'd heard me.

"Come on, Eli. Let's go see them." What was the big deal? "Forget about the surprise. You're busted anyway—I found you. Come and see your brothers."

He lowered his gaze, gave me a hesitant smile. Eli had reverted, become a picked-on younger brother. I tugged at his sleeve, but he resisted, his hand covering mine, and he leaned over, whispering.

"My whole life, Zoe, I never could be cooped up."

"Okay." What was he talking about? His hand was firm, almost urgent in its touch.

"I needed to meet Nick's son and I'd never miss the wedding. Nick's always, well—I love the guy. That's why I'm here."

"Nick loves you, too, Eli. Just wait—he'll go nuts when he sees you."

I took my hand away and ran to the top of the stairs, calling softly so I wouldn't wake up Molly.

"Nick? Hey, Nick."

Nick was in the kitchen, and Sam was still talking—something about a rabbi and a priest in a bar. I went down a couple of steps, calling again. "Nick—"

"Hi, Zoe—I'll be up in a sec."

Sam continued his story. Apparently, I'd interrupted his joke just before the punch line.

I went down a few more steps, calling again. "Nick. It's important. You guys need to see something—"

Two voices erupted in laughter—but where was Tony? He wasn't with them. Nick stuck his head out the kitchen door, half his face grinning. Before his shooting, he and Eli must have been identical.

"Come here—" I gestured. Suddenly, Nick's grin inverted, became a puzzled scowl.

"What the hell, Zoe? What's with the gun?"

The gun? Oh. I'd forgotten. I was still carrying it, still had it in my hand. Nick came toward me, reaching out for it.

"I have a surprise for you." I grinned.

Nick took the gun, a question in his eyes.

"Eli."

"Eli?" Nick's eyebrows popped up.

"He's here."

"Here? Where?"

I nodded, grinning. "Upstairs."

I was still nodding, my head bobbing up and down, yes, Eli was here, yes, upstairs, as Nick raced to the stairs, followed by his half-in-the-bag brother Sam, and the two of them collided, stampeding up the steps past me, calling Eli's name.

FORTY-TWO

ELI, OF COURSE, WAS GONE. NO REAL SURPRISE. HE'D TAKEN HIS camera, his knife, his Cheshire cat smile and glowing ember eyes and snuck out of the house, probably the very second I'd left him. Quietly, trying not to wake the kids, Nick searched every room upstairs, every closet, even under the beds and in the bathroom cabinet. But, of course, there was not a trace of Eli. I was angry, felt set up. But although they were frustrated, Sam and Nick seemed to take the disappearance in stride.

"No sign of him." Sam's belch smelled of beer. "What did you expect? They train guys like him to disappear from a lot tougher places than this."

But I couldn't accept that he was gone. "He was just here. How could he—poof—disappear?"

"This is only the second floor, Zoe. It's not the top of the Empire State Building. He went out a window."

But he couldn't have. Nick had checked the windows. "Then how come they're locked? From the inside?"

"They have devices that fasten the latches, that's how."

They? Who were "they"?

"Unless"—Nick tried to look scary—"he's still here. Invisible. You know, the government might have him working on some experimental cloaking device—"

"Hush up, Nick." Sam chewed his cigar butt. "If you're right,

Eli's here listening. And if he realizes you know his secret, he'll have to kill you."

Half of Nick's face smiled, the same smile Eli had worn. Nick put his arm around my waist, led me downstairs, asking questions.

"So, what happened, Zoe? What did he say? How was he?"

"Tell us everything. I haven't seen that kid in what—six years?"

"No, it hasn't been that long."

"Well, when was the funeral?"

Funeral? Nick's arm tensed around me; he glared at Sam over his shoulder.

"What? She knows you were married and your wife died. It's not against the law to mention it, is it?"

We'd arrived at the bottom of the steps, and Nick, his eyes spitting anger, spun around to face Sam. Before Nick could speak, I slipped between them. "Of course I know." I also knew that Nick's dead wife had shot him in the face, that he'd been suspected of killing her. I knew the whole story. So what was upsetting Nick?

"It wasn't the funeral, Sam. The last time you saw Eli. You know it wasn't the funeral."

Sam feigned innocence, tried to look baffled. "When, then?"

"Think about it."

Tensions were soaring. I tried to diffuse them. "Where's Tony?"

Nick and Sam were in a staring match. Neither looked at me. But Nick answered without moving his mouth, "Tony's looking for a parking space."

Oh. I wished he'd get here. He might have a clue about what was going on.

"Nick, you're right. I forgot all about that—"

"Just don't pretend it never happened."

"I forgot; that's all. Look, I made it up to him; he got every dime back. It was a misunderstanding."

"Did he?"

"Yes. Every last one."

They were eyeball-to-eyeball now. What the hell were they talking about? Had Sam bilked Eli out of some money?

"You know, you're probably the reason Eli took off. He probably figured he couldn't afford to see his brother Sam again."

"Oh, fuck off. Eli and I are totally cool. It was a loan."

"Not the way I heard it. A loan is made willingly; you don't just take money."

"How was I supposed to ask him if I couldn't find him? Besides, I knew he'd lend me the cash if I asked him. And I paid him back. With interest."

"Did you now. All of it?"

"Yes. I swear. This—him taking off again—had nothing to do with me. You know him. How he is. Eli never sticks around. He's probably undercover, working a case or something—"

I couldn't stand it anymore. "What's going on? What are you two arguing about?"

Two faces turned to me as if surprised that I was there. They stared mutely.

"Let's all have some coffee." I went into the kitchen, taking Nick by the hand. From the way their tempers were flaring, they'd both had enough other liquids for the night.

FORTY-THREE

COFFEE SEEMED TO BE THE CURE FOR THE FLARE-UP. EVEN AS IT brewed, Sam and Nick cooled off, laughing as they recalled Eli stories.

After being trained in Special Operations in the military, he'd floundered for a while. He'd worked briefly as a repo man, sneaking onto properties, taking cars from people whose payments had lapsed. Sam relished the tales of Eli's narrow escapes when a few men discovered him in the process. One apparently ended up in his carport impossibly tangled in the garden hose. Another owned guard dogs, which happened to fall asleep after eating Eli's special-recipe hamburgers, thus failing to protect the automobile.

The stories went on, each accompanied by gulps of coffee and bites of glazed donuts, each topping the other. Eli's elusive identity, his vague career progressing from repo man to possibly undercover cop. To maybe secret agent or even government spy. I could see how the labels could fit Eli, his easy movements and taunting eyes. But most of what Nick and Sam said was playful conjecture, affectionate lore they themselves had created. Listening to them, trying to sift facts from fantasy, I gathered that Eli had served with the Army Rangers and now professed to pursue a career in photojournalism. A freelancer, he traveled constantly, followed story to story without forming ties or planting roots. The brothers, of course, saw this job as a perfect cover for a CIA or Homeland Security or FDA or any other brand of secret agent.

With Eli's training, they also speculated that he'd make a perfect assassin.

They went on recounting anecdotes, and, chewing a donut, I thought about Eli, dangerous, dressed all in black, carrying a knife in his waistband. And I realized that, yes, Eli might actually be an undercover agent. In fact, he might be working on a case now. Here, in our area. Maybe he was working for the CIA or Homeland Security. And—oh God—maybe he'd been working with other government agents. Like Jennifer Harris from Homeland Security, who'd just coincidentally been found dead on my patio. I took a gulp, almost choked on my coffee, trying to clear my thoughts.

But it made sense, didn't it? Eli might not be here for our wedding or to meet our baby; he might be here for work. Maybe he was supposed to have been Agent Harris' contact. Or maybe—the thought made my heart stop, but there it was: the other possibility. Eli might not have been her contact; he might have been her killer.

No. Good God. I shut my eyes, had to stop this line of thinking. Eli wasn't an assassin. He was Nick's kid brother, his blood. Eli's eyes danced—would a hit man have eyes that could polka? And Eli looked like Nick; his voice sounded, his touch felt, like Nick's. A man like Nick couldn't—no, correction: He could. But he *wouldn't* be a professional killer. I told myself that Eli was a photographer, that the only thing he shot was pictures. That my suspicions were the result of the late hour and the exaggerated tales.

And the tales were still being told. Sam was recounting Eli's skill with a knife, giving details about the way he could carve up a Thanksgiving turkey, whittle a walking stick, bone a bluefish, gut a deer, amputate a wounded buddy's arm, and the list was just getting started when he was interrupted by a knock at the door.

It had to be Tony. Finally. It had taken him an awfully long time to find a parking spot. Nick started to get up, but I was closer to the door, so I was the one who opened it. And I was the one who screamed.

FORTY-FOUR

Tony could barely stand; his face was covered with blood. Blood spilled from a cut at his hairline, clumped around a nasty gash behind his ear, oozed out of split lips. His left eyebrow and his nostrils were coated with a dark red crust. I reached out to help him inside as Nick appeared, responding to my shriek. Sam stood behind Nick, his mouth hanging open, squeezing a donut.

Sam was the first to speak. "Holy shit. What the hell?"

Stumbling into the foyer, Tony tossed Sam his car keys. "What does it look like? I stopped and got a makeover." Holding his ribs, he let himself fall against Nick; together they hobbled down the hall to the easy chair in the living room. I got some ice, the first-aid kit, a few damp washcloths, and followed, began dabbing away blood, putting cool pressure on Tony's wounds. The cuts were long but not deep; he might not need stitches. I gave him an ice pack for his eyebrow. The whole time I was giving first aid, Nick kept asking questions.

"Who did this? Where did it happen?" Somehow, Nick had gotten his jacket on, was ready to gather a posse and go out and search.

"Forget it, Nick." Tony's words were distorted; his lips didn't want to move.

"Tell me what happened."

"Two guys hit me."

"What did they look like?"

"I don't know. They were young. White—"

"Tall? Short? What were they wearing?"

"Nick, it's no use. They're gone. Don't even bother—"

"Don't tell me what to do. I can get cars combing the area in two minutes—"

"Easy, Nick." Sam put a hand on Nick's arm, interrupting. "Everybody take it easy. Tony, just tell us what happened."

Tony watched Nick with his one open eye. "I don't know. I got a great spot. I parked at the corner, right on Fifth Street. I got out, locked the car, and boom."

"Boom?"

"I went about three steps and something hit me, boom, smack in the side of the head." He touched the cut near his ear and winced.

Nick frowned. "I'm going to call it in." He started for his phone, but Tony grabbed his arm.

"Forget it, Nick. It was just a mugging."

Nick frowned. "Just a mugging?"

"They happen every day around here. You know that. I don't feel like dealing with all those cops and their questions."

"Really." Nick crossed his arms. "All those cops are trying to protect people like you—"

"Hey, Nick. Don't take it personally." Tony winced as I pressed on his sore cheek. "It's just not worth it; the cops never find guys like these."

Oops, Nick would definitely take that personally. And, sure enough, Nick pulled over a wingback chair and sat facing Tony as if preparing for an interrogation. "So, you're an expert on police effectiveness?"

"Come on, Nick." Tony closed his eyes as I took away the ice pack and cleaned his eyebrow. "I'm just not up to it, okay?"

"So, tell me again. You'd just parked Sam's brand-new Lexus. You were only three steps away from it when two young white guys mugged you. But for some reason, although they must have seen you get out of a late-model, top-of-the-line car, they didn't take the car keys."

"Wait—that doesn't make sense, does it?" Sam pulled the other wingback up beside Nick's. "You'd think they'd take the car."

Tony was trembling; I got an afghan off the sofa, wrapped it around him. "Nick," I said. "He might be in shock."

"He'll be all right." Nick didn't look at me. He leaned forward, elbows on his knees, waiting.

Tony's good eye darted from Nick to Sam. "They took the keys."

Sam shook his head. "But you have them. You said—"

"They took them and one guy went into the car while the other one kept me down."

"What did he do in the car?" Nick was in his element, probing. "Could you see him?"

"He was looking for something. He went into the glove box, flashed a light under the seats. Opened the hood, the trunk."

"Oh shit." Sam was worried. "They didn't, like, plant a bomb or anything?"

We all looked at Sam. Why would he think somebody might plant a bomb in his car? Where did the idea come from?

"I didn't see anything. They seemed to be looking for something, not leaving something."

"And they didn't take the car."

"No, Sam. Your car's fine, right where I left it."

"And they just gave you the keys back? Like, 'thanks, here are the keys'?"

"They dropped them on the ground."

"So they didn't take the car," Nick pressed. "What did they take?"

Tony shrugged. "I'm not sure. They searched me. They emptied my pockets and went through my wallet. I suppose they took the usual. My cash."

Grimacing, Tony leaned forward, reached into his pant pocket and retrieved his wallet. Nick reached for it.

"You mean they gave the wallet back?" Again, Sam was confused.

Tony shivered. "Just like the keys. When they were done, they threw it on the ground. I must have picked up everything. I don't really remember."

"Your credit cards are here. And they apparently missed this."

Tony gaped at the wad of cash in Nick's hand. "Look, Nick, I don't know what you're trying to imply. I don't have any idea who those animals were and I don't have a clue what they wanted."

"Nick." I put my arm around Tony. "Tony should see a doctor—"

"Uh-uh, no, ma'am, no way." Tony shook his head. "No doctors, no police, no thank you. I'll be fine." He held the ice pack to his eyebrow. "Aren't I supposed to get a steak for this?"

"Fat chance." Sam grunted. "Any steak around here, we're not wasting it on your sorry eye."

"As usual, Sam, your heart is outweighed only by your stomach." Tony struggled, even then, to hold his own.

"Look. I always said you should learn to fight. You got to be tough, especially considering your special preferences."

"Lay off, Sam." I stood close to Tony, protecting him. "If he'd fought back, they might have killed him."

Sam winked at me, no doubt intending to remind me that, unlike Tony, he was straight and lustful, but when his eyelid flickered, it looked uncontrolled, like he might have a bug in his eye.

"Did they say anything?" Nick went on with his investigation.

"Yeah." Tony nodded. "It was weird. They asked, 'Where is it?' Told me I had no idea what I'd gotten into, that I'd better hand it over." He looked from Nick to Sam, from Sam to me, then back at Nick. "I have no idea what they were talking about."

"Repeat exactly what they said."

"I can't exactly. They were punching me and then I was on the ground, trying to get them off me."

"Okay." Nick rolled his eyes, impatient. "Just repeat what you remember."

Tony shook his head. "Like I said. They wanted to know where 'it' was. The heavier one kept telling me to give it up. I told them I had no idea what they were talking about. I asked what they wanted. They just kept repeating, 'Give it up.' And, 'Where the fuck is it?' And when they finally decided I didn't have whatever it was on me, they said they'd be back and I'd better find it because until I gave it to them, they were going to make my life hell."

For a moment, we were all quiet. Nick stood, turned toward the wall and walked away from us. At the wall, he turned back to us. We watched him, waiting for his conclusions. "Eli's in town." That was all he said.

FORTY-FIVE

TONY'S JAW DROPPED. "WHAT?" HE STARTED TO SMILE BUT stopped, put a hand to his bloody lips. "Eli? Where? Wait—how do you know? Did you see him? Was he here?"

Nick didn't answer. He looked at Sam, who met his eyes with complete comprehension. Apparently, Tony and I were missing something.

Sam nodded. "He's right, Tony. Eli and you are only a few years apart. You look alike, especially in the dark."

Tony leaned back against the headrest. "So you think they mistook me for Eli?"

"It wouldn't be the first time." Nick shrugged. "Everyone got us confused as kids, but especially you two. And, if they thought you were Eli, well, who knows who they were or what they wanted? You know Eli."

"Shit." Sam shook his head. "Nick's right. If those guys thought you were Eli, it would explain everything. Who knows what he's working on? Who knows what he might be carrying? We assume it's small, since they thought you had it on you. Could be some secret formula. A hit list. Hell, could be some new micro-biological weapon or a chemical. Who knows what Eli might have on him?"

Well, I thought, he might have a knife. At that moment, as I was taping gauze behind Tony's ear, it occurred to me that the mugging was Tony's second tussle; he'd also been accosted days before by the dead agent. A question tickled the back of my mind, some fragment of a thought, but Tony was asking me about Eli, wanting to hear all about his clandestine visit, and I had to tell the story all over again. Nick sat on the sofa, frowning in thought, and Sam poured brandy and passed us each a snifter. One snort wouldn't hurt Luke, I thought, and I took a long swallow, closed my eyes, felt the soothing heat sliding down, warming my belly. And, for a while, although I'd sensed it had been important, my question slipped from my mind.

FORTY-SIX

TONY SWALLOWED SOME TYLENOL AND FINALLY FELL ASLEEP IN the recliner around two. Sam had already dozed off, snoring on the sofa under an afghan. Soon, Luke would be up and hungry, and I didn't know if it was even worth it to go to bed. But I went upstairs with Nick and was brushing my teeth when I remembered my question.

"Maybe it was the jogger!" I blurted it out, but Nick had no idea what I'd said; my mouth was full of toothpaste. Excited, I speed-rinsed my mouth, talking the whole time. I was sure I'd figured out a key part of what had happened.

"The jogger?" Even after he understood my words, Nick had no idea what they meant. He lay back on his pillows, staring at the ceiling.

"Remember? She ran right into Tony and fell on him—remember what he said? How they held on to each other, how they shared a moment? So, I was thinking. What if she didn't really trip—what if Agent Harris deliberately bumped into him, you know, pretending to fall—"

"Why would she do that?" Nick rubbed his eyes.

"I don't know. But she was a Homeland Security agent. What if somebody was chasing her? A terrorist or something. What if she knew she was about to be caught—maybe she even knew she was going to be killed. And she's running away and she sees this guy getting his newspaper, and she thinks, hey, maybe she has a chance to protect whatever she was carrying—"

"You're saying she planted something on Tony?" Nick's voice was clipped.

"You think it's a dumb idea." Oh well.

His eyes moved across the room slowly, landing on mine. "No. In fact, I think you're a genius."

With that, he was out of bed and at the hamper, pulling on the pair of jeans he'd just taken off. "When's the last time you did the laundry?"

Was he serious? "This morning."

"Really? Our hamper's pretty full."

"I did the kids' stuff."

"So what about the rest of it?"

I was getting annoyed. "Nick, if you want the laundry done, you can run a load yourself once in a while. I have enough to do, especially without Ivy and with company staying here and our wed—"

But he was out the bedroom door, heading down the hall toward the steps. "Where are Tony's clothes?" He assumed I was behind him. "The ones he was wearing that morning?"

Oh. I began to understand. He wasn't criticizing my house-keeping; he was looking for clues. "I don't know. Probably on the floor somewhere. He leaves everything where it falls." I scurried after Nick, rounding the banister, pounding down the stairs. Finally, we came to the living room. Oliver, sleeping on the floor beside Tony's feet, opened a groggy eye, blinked at us, yawned, settled down again. Sam snored on the sofa, his brandy snifter on its side, next to him, licked clean.

FORTY-SEVEN

TONY'S CLOTHES WERE CRUMPLED IN A PILE BETWEEN THE BOOK-shelf and the sofa.

"What was he wearing that morning?" Nick asked as if I should know. As if it were my responsibility to keep track of what people wore. The worst part was that I actually knew; at least I had an idea. Tony slept in his underwear. I hadn't found that out on purpose; the man was sleeping in my living room, and Oliver tended to run in there when I wanted to take him out in the morning. Anyway, going out to get the newspaper, Tony would have put on his pants. And whenever we'd had coffee in the morning, he'd been wearing sweatpants, the same pair with the same old gray hooded sweatshirt. I was pretty sure he'd have worn that ensemble the morning he'd encountered Agent Harris.

Sam's snores shook the walls, rattled the windows, but nobody woke up as we turned on the lights and rifled through Tony's worn and soiled clothes. Tossing aside underwear and T-shirts, socks and sweats, I finally retrieved the sweats. Nick examined them carefully, turning out pockets, shaking out fabric.

"Damn." He dropped the clothes back onto the floor. "Nothing."

Sighing, I gathered up the rest of the clothes and brought them into the center of the room. Maybe whatever had been in the pockets had fallen into the pile. Or maybe I'd been wrong about what Tony had been wearing.

Together, we searched the clothing, item by item, not knowing what we were looking for. Maybe a key? A coin? I thought of Tony, searching for his lost quarters. Or maybe a stamp, like in that old movie *Charade*. Or maybe something we wouldn't even recognize. A computer chip or some new technological device.

"Look for anything, no matter how small, even the size of a pinhead."

I found some Life Savers, and Nick found a ChapStick, a comb, a condom, some breath spray and a piece of butterscotch hard candy.

"How about this?" I passed along a button that had been lurking in a shirt pocket.

Nick held it up to the light, turning it slowly. "Huh. Look's like a button. Feels like a button." He bit it. "Tastes like a button."

The clothes, now scattered across the living room floor, revealed nothing unusual, certainly nothing that might have cost a government agent her life. Nor did the items on the coffee table: Tony's watch, keys, class ring and the wallet the muggers had already searched and rejected.

Nick stared at the pile, as if expecting something to jump out.

"So, there's nothing here. Sorry, I guess I was wrong. She didn't plant anything."

"It was an excellent theory, though. It makes perfect sense. In fact, I'm annoyed that I didn't come up with it myself." He gazed at me, his eyes gleaming and proud.

Wow. Nick thought my theory was excellent. I felt myself blush.

"Well. It's so late it's early. Would you consider accompanying me to bed, Ms. Hayes?" Nick offered his hand, and I took it.

"It would be my pleasure, Detective Stiles."

As we turned out the light, Sam and Oliver snored in harmony and Tony, out cold, was beyond being disturbed. Nick and I headed up the stairs, arms around each other's waists. I thought I might have two hours before Luke woke up. I might even sleep.

But, as Nick and I headed toward our bedroom, a voice called behind us.

"Mommy?" Molly stood in her doorway, chin quivering, rubbing her eyes. "I had a bad dream, Mommy. Somebody was in my room, and they wanted to steal me."

Maybe she'd sensed Eli, I thought. Not for the first or last time, I talked to Molly about her nightmare and promised her that it was over and she was safe, but she couldn't stop trembling. Finally, I tucked her back into her bed. Minutes later, climbing under the covers, dozing off, I snuggled up, body curled against body. Blanketed with love, I felt oddly safe, protected from muggers and murderers, and even from bad dreams. And I wondered only briefly how Nick was doing, down the hall, sleeping alone.

FORTY-EIGHT

WEDNESDAY MORNING BEGAN WITH A PULSING ELECTRONIC shriek when Molly's alarm went off at seven. She had an old-fashioned, beeping alarm, not a clock radio, and at first I thought it was the phone, then maybe the doorbell. I jumped out of bed, running in bleary-eyed circles, trying to identify the sound and kill it at the source. And, gradually, as my brain came awake, it occurred to me that I was in the wrong bedroom. Molly's? And oh dear—I hadn't gotten up to feed Luke; I must have slept through his early-morning cries. In a panic, leaving Molly to deal with the maddening beeps, I flew into the hall and ran to Luke's room, found him lying in his crib, staring at his dinosaur mobile, playing absentmindedly with his feet. At first, his eyes gleamed, seemed happy to see me, but in seconds he seemed to remember that he was hungry. His calm face contorted, his mouth opened in accusatory rage, and he roared.

I picked him up, covering him with kisses. "What a big boy you are, Luke. Sleeping all the way through the night." I cooed as I changed his sodden diaper and put him to my breast. Molly joined us seconds later, wearing fresh underwear and socks, dragging a yellow hooded sweatshirt and matching pants, apparently her chosen outfit for the day.

"Mommy, you slept in my room." She pulled her leg into her pants, pleased.

"How do you feel, Molls? Better?"

"Better? From what?" She pulled the sweatshirt over her head. "Mom, did you make my lunch yet?"

She seemed to have no memory of her scary dream.

"It's in the fridge."

"Oh, shoot. Is it peanut butter again? I'm sick of peanut butter."

She was? For weeks, peanut butter was all she'd even consider taking for lunch.

"Since when?"

"Since forever. Do we have bologna?"

Bologna?

"Danielle gets bologna, and Lauren gets roast beef or sometimes turkey. I'm the only one with peanut butter."

Molly went on, elaborating on her classmates' luncheon fare, and gradually I began to understand. Apparently, her friends rarely ate the food their parents actually sent with them. They switched, and peanut butter had low trading value. Molly wanted bologna or maybe tuna, and wheat bread, not white, so that she could exchange for maybe chicken salad or pastrami. I wondered why she didn't simply ask for chicken salad or pastrami but decided not to get involved in the black market for first-grade sandwiches. It was better not to know. Molly kept on chattering while Luke nursed until, downstairs, the doorbell rang and, instantly, Oliver started yapping.

"Mom. Somebody's here—" Molly started for the door.

"Molly, stop." She knew better. We lived in the city. She wasn't allowed to open the door by herself.

"But nobody's up yet. And you can't get it."

The bell rang again, and Oliver was going nuts. Downstairs, nobody moved to answer. If Sam could sleep through his own snoring, he could certainly sleep through a doorbell. And Tony was probably in no shape to get up.

"Go wake up Nick."

Molly sped down the hall, calling Nick's name. He ought to be up by now anyway. Sure enough, he'd been in the shower. I heard Molly banging on the bathroom door, shouting, "Nick, somebody's ringing the doorbell."

He said something I couldn't hear.

"No, she's feeding Luke."

Nick said something else, possibly that whoever it was would just have to wait.

"Should I go tell them?"

I'm sure he said no, because Molly ran back into Luke's room, breathless and concerned. "Mom. He said he'll go in a minute. But the people—"

Whoever they were, the people were impatient, even rude. The bell rang a third time, followed by fists pounding the door. Oliver was barking madly; I pictured him jumping, running in circles. Who the hell was out there? What nerve, to bang on our door, especially so early in the morning.

"It might be an emergency." Molly's eyes bulged, urgent.

But Nick was out of the bathroom; I heard his steps charging down the stairs, out of sync with the banging on the door. I heard his hesitation as he peeked through the peephole, viewing the visitors. I heard the unbolting of the lock and the opening of the door, and Nick's voice. "What's going on?"

Somebody, a man, barked an answer including the words "federal agents, FBI," and "some questions."

Downstairs, people entered the house as Nick protested the early intrusion. As Nick reminded the agent that he was a homicide detective, his voice was indignant but resigned, explaining that we weren't up or dressed yet, that his wife—he used the word *wife*—was a nursing mother, and asking for a few minutes' delay while he made sure the family was awake. The FBI agent was unimpressed, advised Nick to gather everyone together and cooperate with the investigation.

The next few minutes involved waking up Sam and Tony and

grabbing some clothes. Luke finished nursing, and I managed to put him back in his crib long enough to brush my teeth and pull on some jeans. Molly clung to my side, asking questions. "Who are those people? What do they want?"

I tried to explain. The agents, I said, were there to find clues about the lady who'd been killed on the patio. Molly didn't understand, though. "I know. But why are they here, Mom? Do they think somebody in our family killed her?"

"Of course not, Molls." I tousled her hair, trying to seem unfazed at the ease with which she discussed a murder. "It's just their job to ask everybody questions."

I popped a clip into my hair and joined Molly in the search for her sneakers. While Molly grabbed her book bag, I hunted, finding one sneaker under her bed. Oliver whimpered at Molly's feet, and a sense of dread washed over me as I guessed what had most likely happened to the missing shoe. Sure enough, when we found it in the corner of Molly's room beside her bookshelf, we saw that the toe had been chewed away. Demolished.

"Oliver," I screamed. But Oliver, the perpetrator, had fled the scene.

Molly's chin wobbled. "That's the millionth pair of my shoes he's eaten. I hate him. I really really hate him."

I didn't know what to say. At the moment, I wasn't real fond of him, either. "He doesn't mean it, Molls. He's a puppy. He's teething."

"But now what am I supposed to wear? Those were my only shoes with yellow in them. I can't go to school. I'm staying home."

Wait, what? Molly had never been fashion conscious. She was only six years old and something of a tomboy. But suddenly, on that morning, she'd decided that her sneakers had to match her sweats.

I opened her closet, dug out an old pair of sneakers from the summer.

"Are you kidding?" She pouted, crossing her arms. "Those don't go."

"Of course they do, Molls. They're blue. Blue goes great with yellow."

"I hate Oliver." She sniffled but accepted the shoes.

"Zoe?" Nick called from downstairs, sounded annoyed. "Are you almost ready?"

The FBI was waiting. But that was too bad. No one invited them, and I had to help Molly put together her ensemble.

"Well, I don't really hate him. I just, you know, hate him."

"I know." I kissed her head and, hand in hand, we headed down the hall to get Luke. We were running late; the bus was due any second. Two agents stood in the hall, and Nick was in the kitchen, pacing. Without a word, I handed him the baby and pulled some bread and a package of sliced turkey out of the refrigerator. Molly stood in the doorway, staring openly at the agents.

"Molly, did you eat?" In the commotion, I'd forgotten about her breakfast.

She shook her head. "I don't have time."

"You have to eat." In a flurry, worried that the FBI would think I was a bad mother for not feeding my child, I poured a glass of milk, handed it to her, reached into the fruit basket for a banana and told Nick to grab a cereal bar for her while I was slapping turkey and mayo onto the bread, retrieving the peanut butter sandwich from her lunch bag and replacing it with the turkey.

"I got turkey?"

"Yep. Want a pickle?" I felt the agents watching, resented their impatience. This was my home, my family, and I wasn't going to skimp on Molly's lunch just to suit them. I took my time wrapping the pickle even though I knew the bus would pull up any second. In fact, it was outside now, at the curb.

"Bye, Mom." Molly had a milk mustache and a mouthful of

banana. "Bye, Nick, bye, Luke. Bye, Uncle Tony and Sam—" she yelled. Eyeing the agents, she ran out the door, and I walked after her, waving at Pete, the driver, watching her scamper down the front steps and into the reassuring normalness of the big yellow bus.

FORTY-NINE

FOR OVER AN HOUR, WE SAT SEQUESTERED IN THE DINING ROOM, sipping coffee, not saying much while the FBI agents took turns questioning us in the living room. Nick was steaming, barely controlling himself. He'd made irate phone calls, complaining about the method, the lack of courtesy, the attitude and demeanor of the agents, but neither his rank nor his contacts made any impression. The agents went methodically about their business and spent a huge amount of time with poor Tony, undoubtedly interrogating him ad nauseam about his contact with the victim. When it was my turn, I was appalled at the mess Tony and Sam had left, couldn't help apologizing as I began to straighten up.

"Nick's brothers are crashing here." I picked an afghan off the floor, folded it, noticing Oliver curled up behind the easy chair.

"Ms. Hayes." One of them wore glasses. "I'm Agent Buford, and this is Agent Morris."

I nodded.

"What can you tell us about what happened to Tony Stiles?"

To Tony? What? I thought they were here about their dead colleague. "He was mugged."

Agent Buford seemed to be in charge. He seemed to doubt my answer. "What were the circumstances? Was he robbed?"

Wait. Why were they asking these questions? "I don't know for sure. You'd have to ask Tony."

"But I asked you."

I said nothing about Tony. "I thought you were here about the dead FBI agent."

The agent frowned. "Ms. Hayes, do you know the penalties for impeding a federal investigation?"

Wait, was the man threatening me? Instantly, I was on my feet, indignant. "Agent Buffart—"

"Buford."

"—Are you implying that I'm lying? I don't take that lightly. You are in my home, sir—"

"Relax, Ms. Hayes." His tone was patronizing, amused. His partner, a lean bald guy, watched attentively from my wingback, his face bland and bored. "Sit down."

I didn't.

"Please."

I glared, but I sat.

"Let's start again. Tell us what you know about the mugging."

I shrugged. "Tony was mugged. He was the *victim* of a crime." I emphasized *victim*.

Buford's voice remained calm, his eyes steady. "Go on."

"That's all. He was parking his brother's car, alone in the middle of the night. I have no idea who did it or why."

"Have you noticed any unusual objects in your home recently?"

What? "Of course. We have two guests—"

"Other than their belongings, I mean."

So I didn't have to tell him about Sam's gun.

"No. What kind of unusual objects are you talking about?"

The agents exchanged a glance. "Possibly a small statue or vial. A cigar holder, maybe. Or a small package. Anything that could fit in, say—"

He paused and I waited to hear what word he'd use for *asshole*.

"—your fist."

Fist? No, I shook my head. I'd seen nothing like that.

"Can you tell us anything else about the mugging then? Anything?"

Again, I shook my head no. I didn't repeat the threats the muggers had made or the search they'd conducted in Sam's car. And I didn't mention Eli or his late-night ephemeral visit that same night. I wasn't at all sure why I wasn't more forthcoming. True, I resented the federal agents, their abrupt manner and bullying attitudes. But I sensed that my reticence was due to something deeper, something involving greater loyalties. Tony and Eli were Nick's brothers, Luke's uncles. Almost like blood. My instincts told me it was up to Nick and Tony to reveal what they thought best. So, for better or worse, I withheld information from federal investigators. I wasn't sure what the consequences of that might be, but I said nothing, made not a peep beyond the most basic facts.

FIFTY

WHEN THE AGENTS LEFT, IT WAS STILL EARLY, JUST AFTER NINE. I wanted to ask Nick if I should have said more, but he was remote and uncommunicative, sitting in the dining room, his dazed brothers beside him. I changed Luke, fed him, attached him to my body with the sling, and then the group of us, including the wounded and still wobbly Tony, ventured out for brunch. We sat at a large booth at PhilaDeli, and mostly didn't talk. Mostly, we chewed in silence, each nursing his or her own thoughts, emotions and omelet. At one point, Sam made an announcement.

"I'm going to stop at my car on the way back." Sam chewed. "See for myself what they did to it."

"They didn't do anything to it," Tony insisted. "They just looked."

"I had some stuff in there. I'm going to check it out. And you should get that ugly mug looked at."

More silence.

"Tony, maybe you should see a doctor today." It was just a suggestion. His hairline was purplish yellow, his nose swollen. I wanted to wince when I looked at him.

"No, uh-uh."

"But what if—"

"Zoe. Forget it. I'm fine."

Nobody picked up the cause, so I let it go.

We finished eating. Nick, brooding, hadn't said a single word.

Even when he'd offered to hold Luke, he'd done it wordlessly, with a gesture. We were all exhausted and feeling bruised, and walking home, I cradled Luke's baby sling with one hand, Nick's fingers with the other, and thought about how tired I was. I would forget Anna and her list, forget returning phone calls, forget every task on my to-do list. I would put Luke in his little portable chair and sink into a bubble bath, and then I would collapse in bed for a long, uninterrupted nap.

As we walked up the steps to the house, Tony was obviously sore. Holding his ribs, he leaned on the railing, catching his breath. Nick stopped to help him, so Luke and I went in alone.

And I was the first to see the upended furniture, emptied cabinets, hall closet contents tossed onto the floor. While we were out, somebody had come in and torn the house apart.

Without a word, I carried Luke into the living room, found his little chair, belted him in and gave him a teething ring. Behind me, Tony and Nick came in and, grasping what had happened, went ballistic. Nick rushed from room to room, cursing, occasionally calling my name. I didn't answer, though. I kept my eyes ahead, my feet moving resolutely upstairs to start my bath.

FIFTY-ONE

I HAD MY BATH, BUT SADLY, MY NAP WAS NOT TO BE. BUT I LIT candles in the bathroom and turned off the lights. I soaked for a while beside soft flickers, closing my eyes, letting steam and soapy bubbles work their magic. I emptied my brain, concentrating on heat, letting my muscles give in, relaxing them one at a time, inhaling the vanilla scent of melting wax. After a while, shards of memories came to the surface of my mind, and I didn't fight them. I allowed them to drift by like flotsam on a river. I saw Bryce Edmond's smashed skull. Agent Harris' gaping wounds. Bonnie Osterman's squat, hungry figure. Tony's battered frame, stumbling through the front door. The FBI agents intruding and probing. And Eli. Beautiful Eli. Secretive Eli, sneaking through the shadows, in and out of bedrooms. I pictured him, a stranger creeping in the lamplight, holding baby Luke.

Suddenly, my eyes popped open. With absolute clarity, I was sure I knew the truth: It was Eli. Eli was the center of it all, had to be. Eli was the reason Tony had been mugged—the muggers had mistaken them. And Eli had visited us only in the middle of the night—why? Just to see Luke and take his picture? Doubtful. Obviously, Eli had other reasons. Such as finding something that Agent Harris left here or, maybe, leaving something here for safekeeping, or—who knew? But I was certain of one thing: Eli was involved with this mess, and Nick and his brothers knew or suspected it. I was certain that, just like me, they hadn't mentioned

Eli to the FBI. He might be a spy or an assassin. But, more important, Eli was blood.

When my skin had withered like a prune, I pulled the plug and
got out of the tub, considering loyalties. What if Eli was actually
involved in the agent's murder? How far would Eli's family go to
protect him? Would Nick, a homicide detective, cover for him?
Would he conceal evidence? Risk his career, not to mention his
freedom? I wasn't positive, but I thought, yes, he probably would.
Rather than have his brother arrested for murder or worse, Nick
would probably hide evidence. Wrapped in a towel, I wondered
about my own role. Was I abetting a criminal? What was right or
wrong here? What were my responsibilities and obligations? I was
confused, uncertain about what I knew, much less sure of what I
should do.

As I stepped into some comfy sweatpants, Nick came in, bringing Luke for another meal. Telling me not to worry, Nick sat with
us as Luke nursed. Whoever had been here had been in a hurry,
had made a mess but hadn't done much damage or, apparently,
taken anything. A window in the dining room had been broken;
that was how they'd gotten in. Nick went on, reassuring me, making it sound like no big deal that yet another crime had been committed in our home.

When Nick finished his update, he stood. "Well, if you're okay,
I'll go finish straightening—"

"Wait," I interrupted. "Tell me about Eli."

Nick stiffened. His eyes shifted just a tad. "Eli?" Nick tried to
sound confused.

"Please, Nick. Don't pretend it's all coincidence."

"What are you talking about?" He sat again, blinking too fast.

"What am I talking about? Your brother Eli? Eli the former
Ranger? Eli who was trained in Special Ops? You know, Eli the
trained killer and suspected undercover agent is in town just when,
by chance, a federal agent is cut open on your back porch. Then,

the very night I find Eli skulking around in the dark, your brother Tony is mugged and threatened and searched by people who think he has something they want. The next morning the FBI shows up, and that same day the house is ransacked by people who are obviously convinced that something they want is here."

"And you think this is about Eli?"

I met his eyes, didn't say a word.

"Zoe, you're stressed out. Anyone would be."

"Do not condescend to me, Nick. You're the one who told me the stories about Eli. That he was trained to be invisible, to eliminate problems and disappear. No one really buys the idea that he's a freelance photographer—"

"Photojournalist."

I frowned at him.

"Okay. To tell the truth, Tony and I were just talking about this with Sam."

"Sam's back?"

Nick nodded. "His car is apparently undamaged."

"So?"

Nick's face was grim. "So. Tony is convinced that Eli has nothing to do with any of this. He insists that Eli has grown up and is just as he claims, traveling the world to cover interesting journalistic stories."

"And you? What do you think?"

Nick sighed. "I guess it's possible that Eli might have settled down. But I doubt it. The truth is Eli has a side to him . . . Let's just say I wouldn't be surprised if he were involved. Like you said, he's had the training. He knows how to kill. And he's capable of it. Sam thinks Eli's some kind of covert agent, but he can't begin to guess for whom."

I pictured Eli, his strong hands. Dangerous hands. Holding my baby.

That same baby had fallen asleep in my arms. I carried him to his crib and tucked him in. Nick watched, waiting for me to say something, but I didn't until we were out of the room.

"No matter what"—I met Nick's eyes—"this is our home. It's the place where our children live. If Eli has any involvement, I don't care if he's a federal agent or a spy or a photographer or your brother. I don't care who he is. He needs to stay away or, I swear, I'll turn him in myself."

Nick reached for me, held me close, kissed my forehead. "I know."

We stood in the hallway, hugging, but, even then, I wasn't sure where Nick's loyalties lay. I thought about Eli, the possibility that he was some kind of covert government agent, whatever that meant, and questions rushed through my mind. But with my head pressed against Nick's shoulder and my body enfolded in his arms, I couldn't ask them. I couldn't find the words.

FIFTY-TWO

WE JOINED TONY AND SAM IN THE LIVING ROOM. TONY SAT IN the wingback, one leg twitching, but he couldn't stay still. He popped up, moved a pillow, sat, twitched, got up again, straightened a cushion. Sam sprawled in the recliner, stroking Oliver, sucking a beer.

"We set all the furniture straight."

Obviously, Sam had finished helping. Tony paced, circling the room, eyes darting around my knickknacks, making me nervous. "Looking for something, Tony?"

"What?" He sat again. "No, nothing. Just trying to, you know, figure out what they were looking for. If anything's missing."

I went to the shelves, began replacing collectibles. The Japanese doll from Uncle Dave had toppled in its glass case, which was on its side on the floor. Great-grandma Bailey's mortar and pestle had separated and rolled behind and under the sofa. A Wedgwood vase, amazingly undamaged, sat upside down beside it. Nick helped me and, as we worked, the brothers talked.

"Zoe knows about Eli." Nick handed me a crystal candy dish. "I told her what we'd been saying."

"Wonderful." Sam grunted. "Why not call the papers? Broadcast it."

"Excuse me, Sam." My hands were on my hips and my face was hot. "You're in my house. Nick is soon to be my husband. It's time you stopped treating me like I'm some outsider—"

Nick put his hand out, trying to calm me, but I was just getting started.

"I've had it with you three whispering behind my back. I don't know or care about your family secrets. But if your brother Eli is putting my family in danger, I have a right to know about it, and if any of you is hiding that kind of information from me, I swear I'll make you regret it."

"Stop her, Nick. I'm scared." Sam feigned fright, his hand clutching the puppy.

Nick remained silent, but I wasn't finished. I demanded that they tell me what they knew. "So, what do you think? Do you think Eli was Agent Harris' contact?" I looked from Sam to Tony, back to Sam.

"Who knows?" Sam shrugged. "Knowing Eli, he might have been. And he might even have knocked her off."

"Stuff it, Sam," Tony snapped. "Eli's not an agent. And even if he were, why would he kill another agent? They're on the same side—"

"Unless she was crooked," Sam offered. "Or he was."

"I'd like to see you say that in front of Eli." Tony sat up too fast, held his ribs.

"If he'd show his face, maybe I would."

"Trust me. He's not involved."

"Okay, girls, quiet down." Nick finally spoke. He was putting my Japanese tea set back, piece by piece. "The fact is we don't have a clue what happened. Or what role, if any, Eli has in any of it."

"He was her contact, I'll bet you a hundred bucks." Sam gulped beer. "Maybe he didn't kill her, though. Maybe her cover got blown and she got killed before she could connect with him."

That was one possibility.

"Look, there's no way Eli was her contact." Tony was adamant. "He has nothing to do with any of this. Why does everyone always blame Eli?"

Nick dismissed him. "Stop defending him, Tony. You don't know any more than the rest of us. Eli might or might not have been her contact. And he might or might not have killed her, for reasons we don't know and can't begin to guess. But no matter what, we know that Eli is a problem."

"I'm telling you, Eli didn't kill her." Tony winced and held his side, gingerly repositioning himself.

"Hey—maybe Eli's cover got blown just like the dead broad's." Sam ignored him, conjecturing. "That would explain him laying low, sneaking around in the dark. And it explains why Tony got mugged. The fuckers—excuse my French, Zoe—the fuckers thought he was Eli."

"Point is"—Nick faced me—"there are a lot of possibilities, none of them good. Whatever Eli's role is, the bottom line is that this house has become a focal point for the feds and whoever mugged Tony and killed the agent. We don't know who they are. They might be spies or terrorists or drug dealers or space aliens. They have nothing to do with us, but they seem to have something to do with Eli. And since Eli is ours, his problems are ours, like always. Only this time, he's gone too far. This time he's endangered Zoe and our kids."

Our kids. Plural. I was touched; Nick referred not just to Luke but also to Molly as "our."

Tony stood up again, defending Eli. "You guys. Eli is not re-sponsible for half the stuff we blame him for—"

"And we probably don't blame him for half the stuff he's done, either," Sam growled.

"But, like I said, this isn't just about Eli," Nick continued. "I agree with Zoe. This is our home. And now our home has been put into jeopardy." He faced me, took my hand. "Zoe, you and the kids need to be safe." His eyes were misty, maybe apologetic? "I think the three of you should move to a hotel for a few days. Just until things settle down—"

"Whoa, Nick—hang on." Tony was suddenly animated. "That's simply not necessary."

Nick glared. "Says who, you? The expert on security and safety precautions? The one with the bruised ribs and smashed head?"

"No, seriously, hold on—cool it for a second." Tony raised his hands, a peacemaking gesture. "Whoever wanted to search me has searched me—if they think I'm Eli, then they think they've searched Eli. By the same token, whoever wanted to search the house has done it. If they found what they wanted, they're satisfied and won't be back. If they didn't find it, they know it's not here, so they won't be back. Either way, they won't be back. Not for Eli, and not for the house."

Nick rubbed his eyes and sank onto the sofa, deflating.

"You know? I think the kid's right, Nick." Sam stroked Oliver. "They blew their wad here. They're done."

The doorbell rang and Oliver leapt to the floor, barking, interrupting our family meeting. I started to get it, but Nick beat me to it. "You stay here."

I didn't. I followed him, asserting my own will. It was my house, after all. It had been mine for years before I'd even known Nick, and, at the moment, I didn't appreciate being told what to do in it. Even so, when I saw who was at the door, I wished I'd stayed in the living room.

"What's the matter with you people? Don't you answer your phone? I've been calling all day." Anna was carrying a dry-cleaning bag. Oh dear—I'd forgotten about my father's tuxedo. I was supposed to pick it up. In fact, I'd forgotten the entire list Anna had given me. All day, I hadn't thought once about, hadn't done anything for, the wedding. Anna would raise hell.

But Anna didn't raise hell. She stood speechless in our little foyer, gaping, appalled at the mess that surrounded her. "Good Lord. What have you done?" she accused Nick. "Look at that closet." She hung the tuxedo in it, spinning around, scolding us. "And my God—what happened to the kitchen?"

Anna shed her coat and scurried around, picking up cereal boxes and dish towels, stacking plates and pots. The doorbell rang again. This time it was Susan.

"The verdict came in." She beamed. "We won. I got him off." She danced across the threshold, but her winning glow faded as she noticed that the disarray in my home was markedly worse than usual. "Good Lord, Zoe. What happened? The place looks like it was ransacked."

Thankfully, Susan didn't wait for an answer, because she glanced into the kitchen. "Is that Anna in there?"

I nodded. "Great." Susan rushed off, joining Anna in the kitchen, introducing herself even though they'd met before. "Anyhow, you're the expert; I've got a question: What are the rules concerning borrowed and blue?"

The two worked together, discussing what Susan should lend me for the ceremony: Would a sapphire count as both borrowed and blue, or did she need to provide two separate items, and, by the way, what piece would go best with Susan's matron-of-honor gown, and where did she think the colander or the cake pans should go? Oh God. They were straightening up my kitchen. When they finished organizing it, I'd never find a thing.

While Anna and Susan tidied up, Nick and I were left alone, facing each other in the hallway. With the commotion, I could have left our conversation unfinished. But I didn't want to. I'd thought about it, and I'd made a decision. I was going to tell Nick that even though I didn't want to, if he thought it best I would honor his opinion and take the kids to a hotel. I never actually voiced that decision, though, because before I could speak, Nick put his hands on my shoulders, his grip gentle but firm.

"You're right. This is your house." His hands tightened, squeezing. "Stay home."

"Are you sure?"

He nodded at the kitchen. "There's a crowd here most of the time, so you'll be safe. And Eli's hanging around somewhere nearby; you're probably safer here than anywhere else. He wouldn't let anyone hurt you or the kids."

I thought of Eli, his knife, and I saw again the gaping slices on Agent Harris' torso. "But what if Eli's not—"

"Forget Eli. Even if he's not around, it's like Tony says: Whoever these guys are, they're done with us. They've been here and done their thing. They probably won't come back."

He kissed me, watching to make sure I was okay. Then, releasing me, Nick headed back to the living room, leaving me to deal with the kitchen, where Susan and Anna were having a heated argument about where to put my coffee mugs. Stepping into the kitchen, I slid in a puddle, realizing that, again, we'd forgotten to take Oliver out.

FIFTY-THREE

WEDNESDAY NIGHT, I LAY AWAKE, SPOONED AGAINST NICK AS HE slept. He'd been especially attentive in bed, as if apologizing with his body for the upheaval his family had brought to us that week. His touch had been soothing and slow, his kisses lingering and gentle. His fingers lifted the tension from my back and neck; our skin melted together, merging with a healing glowing warmth, synchronizing our heartbeats.

But after that, as Nick faded, I felt alert and restored. I felt him breathing, his steadiness. And I thought about the day, the conversations that had been unfinished. Nick had taken Molly, Luke and Oliver to the playground after school so that Molly wouldn't have to see the state of the house. Tony was preoccupied with e-mails and his laptop, but by the time Nick brought Molly back, the team of Sam, Susan, Anna and me had all but restored the place to its normal level of chaos.

But, as we worked, I'd become more and more uncomfortable with Sam and Tony. The only reason they'd included me in their conversation about Eli was that I'd insisted. If I hadn't, Nick and his brothers would have kept me out of the loop. In fact, secrecy seemed to run in Nick's family. Eli, they said, had an entire secret identity, but what about the others? What did I know about any of them, really? It had taken a long time to uncover the truth about Nick's past, his first marriage and dead wife who'd shot him. But what about Sam? Obviously, he was slippery, maybe devious.

Why was he so secretive about his business? And why did he carry a gun? How crooked were the deals he was always pushing? Could he be involved in not just investment scams but something bigger? Something that might involve contact with an FBI agent?

And Tony, the softer, less rugged version of Nick, was helpful, gentle with Molly. Tony had given me a back rub that had ironed out my kinks and relaxed muscles I hadn't known were tight. But he wasn't easy to know. Granted, being gay in a household of macho brothers, he may long ago have become secretive to protect himself and his privacy. But Tony had been the one person in the house to have contact with the dead agent. And he was also the person who'd been mugged by people he claimed not to know, who he'd said were looking for something he claimed not to have.

The fact was that it wasn't just Eli who might have a double life. Neither Sam nor Tony seemed to be simply who he claimed to be. Nick, Sam, Eli and Tony were all, in their own ways and for their own reasons, devious. And, lying beside Nick, I became certain that, deliberately or not, one of them had endangered us all.

I was still awake, still contemplating that conclusion, when Luke woke up with a howl. I went to him and rocked him, but though I changed his diaper and nursed him, he fidgeted and cried, didn't fall asleep until morning, so, once again, I was up all night.

FIFTY-FOUR

THURSDAY, THE MEN HAD TO PICK UP NICK'S TUXEDO AND DE-
liver my father's so he could try it on. Nick wouldn't leave me
alone, so he asked Anna to come over, even though I told him I
preferred that she didn't. All I wanted to do was sleep. But while I
was sipping coffee and reading the press' latest account of the un-
solved FBI agent's murder, Susan called.

"I'll pick you up at ten thirty for our girls' day."

I hesitated; I'd forgotten all about it.

"You forgot?"

"No, of course not—"

"How could you forget? I asked you days ago—"

"Susan, I didn't forget; I just—"

"Forgot. Well, tough. We have appointments at eleven at Top-
pers and reservations at one thirty for lunch, so I'll pick you up.
Oh, wait—you fired Ivy."

"Anna's here."

"That's great. Is she going to fill in now?"

Fill in? "Susan. She's an event planner, not a sitter."

"But at least until the wedding. Without Ivy, you're going to
need somebody. Especially this week."

Of course, Susan was right.

"Ask her. You're her current project anyhow. I bet she'll be
happy to stick around."

I was sure she would, remembering how she'd relished taking

over my household and how the men had reacted. "I don't know, Susan. She's tough to be around." I whispered it, in case Anna was listening.

"What are you going to do, hire a stranger?"

Susan was right. No strangers. Anna was pushy, but she was a known quantity.

So, as soon as I got off the phone, I decided. Anna was reliable and honest. I would ask her to help me at home, just until the wedding was over. There. At least that problem was solved. I went to the sink, put my coffee mug into the dishwasher and gazed out the window. The sun was trying to peek out of the clouds. Buds were bursting on the few spindly trees that lined the curb. Traffic was light. And Ivy was standing on the sidewalk, staring at the house. Oh Lord. What was she doing there? I went to the front door, opened it and stepped outside.

"Ivy, can I help you?"

She stepped forward, met me at the bottom of the steps. "Where's my key? It wasn't in its place."

I hesitated, confused. What would she want with the key? Was it possible she didn't grasp the fact that she'd been told not to come back? I tried to sound calm, make my voice steady. "It's not your key, Ivy. It's ours. And remember, you're not working here now."

Her eyes darted to the door and the fake rock near the planter, avoiding mine. "But I could be working—"

"We decided you should take a break."

"I want to see the kids. I take good care of them—"

"Ivy. Please. You need to go." She didn't seem to understand her situation. Maybe she was even less stable than I'd thought.

"No, see, you need to listen to me. I've been here since that baby was born. I've been taking care of him and Molly all this time, and then—you have a hissy fit and tell me to take off? How come you think you can do that?"

Oh Lord. Poor Ivy might be off-kilter, but she was clearly attached to the kids, bereft without them. I tried to be kind but firm. "Ivy. I paid you for the next two weeks, and we said we could talk again after—"

"Talk? You took those children away. Is that fair?" She was hollering now, holding her stomach with one arm, gesturing with the other. White foam coated her lips; she looked rabid, almost like she was having a seizure. "After all the care I gave them, all the meals I fixed, the walks I took them on and the sniffles I dried and the diapers I changed, after everything I did for them, you think I should just get lost? No way. I take good care of those children. They love me. Now, what did you do with my key?"

"Ivy." She was over the edge. I had to be patient and speak slowly or she'd never get it. "Okay. I've changed my mind. I don't want you to come back in two weeks, after all. Let's call this relationship over, okay? You're fired."

"Wait, I'm what? You think you can fire me? You can't—"

"Oh yes, I can. It isn't open for discussion." That's right; be firm, I urged myself. Ivy looked lost, brokenhearted, but I was a therapist, knew not to enable her behavior. I had to be consistent, clear and calm. Leave no room for distortion. "We no longer need your assistance here." I turned to go back into the house.

But before I could get inside, Ivy dashed up the steps and grabbed my arm. "They do, too, need me. The kids need me." Her eyes were desperate. I didn't understand why she was behaving so bizarrely; her job must have meant a lot more to her than I'd imagined.

Still, I was not going to be bullied into rehiring her. She was obviously unbalanced. How had I not seen that before? "Ivy, I'm sorry if you're disappointed. Good luck." I took my hand from hers and stepped back inside the house, wondering if I should recommend a therapist.

Ivy didn't move. "Okay," she called after me. "We'll do what we said. I'll call you next week. Monday morning. I can start then."

I started to say that no, she should not come back, that she'd been fired. But she whirled around and sped away, and she didn't look back.

FIFTY-FIVE

ANNA EAGERLY ACCEPTED WHEN I ASKED HER TO WATCH THE kids for the week. The more control over our lives she had, the happier she seemed. By the time Susan came by at ten thirty for our girls' day, Anna had pretty much rearranged Luke's room and started to reorganize Molly's.

"You look wired." Susan pulled away from the curb, assessing me. "What did you do, stick your finger in an electric socket?"

Susan was unfailingly honest. "I don't need sockets. I have my life. Ivy was just here—she refuses to be fired."

"Poor Ivy. She doesn't want your stinking job. She wants to be you. She wants your life."

"Right now, she can have it."

"Now, now. Don't even joke about that. You'd never give up Nick and Molly and Luke. You're just going through a rough spot. And this day is the antidote for rough spots. It's an anti-stress, celebrate-the-moment day. Let's have fun."

Fun? What an alien concept. "Sorry. I don't know how to do 'fun.' All I do is nurse and wipe up puppy piddle. And blood-stains."

"That's why you need to get spoiled for a day."

I was ready to strangle her. "Stop being so cheerful, would you?"

She stopped at a light and turned to me, sighing. "Zoe, you're not going to believe me, but listen anyhow. Luke won't be an infant much longer. In an eyeblink, he'll stop nursing, and your hormones will settle down. Your body will be yours again. Your wedding a memory. The brothers will go home and the puppy will get housebroken. The horrible murder will be history. Life will calm down and move ahead, and you will wake up one morning and wonder where the time went. You'll long for these days."

I would? What? I didn't respond, couldn't. What Susan was saying was absurd.

"So, relax. It's your first day away from Luke. Enjoy it."

Oh dear—she was right. It was my first day away from Luke. And, to emphasize that point, at the thought of him my nipples dribbled. Perfect. I'd go to the spa drenched in milk. "Damn."

"What?"

"Look at me. I even think of the baby, I even hear his name, and I gush."

Susan laughed, nodding knowingly.

"Don't laugh. It's not funny. I feel like a milk machine, constantly spouting and dripping."

"Zoe. You feel like a milk machine because you are one. But it passes. Trust me, before you know it, Luke will be done with your breasts and chugging beer."

I pictured it, little Luke, swaddled and diapered, holding a beer can.

"Today, just for a few hours, forget what Luke needs; forget what Molly needs. Forget the wedding, the murder. Forget Bryce's hit-and-run. Just think about Zoe and live the moment. Okay?"

How generous Susan was. I smiled, and our eyes met. Friends. We drove for a while in comfortable, peaceful silence. But as Susan pulled into the spa parking lot, she broke the stillness.

"Oh, Zoe, I almost forgot—I found the perfect blue lace handkerchief. If you borrow it, it can be both the borrowed thing and the blue thing. But Anna says they really should be two separate things, you know, one borrowed, one blue. So I'm thinking you should wear my sapphire earrings and the hankie. That gives you two of both—then either way you cut it, you're covered. Or, if you want to use the earrings as blue, you can borrow an ivory hankie—"

She described alternatives, including choices for a new or old silver dollar in my shoe, until we were inside the spa and changing into our terry cloth robes. And while I couldn't pay close attention to her every word, I didn't tune her out, either. The sound of Susan's voice was cheery and enthusiastic, and I heard it not as conversation but as a refreshing melody or a rhythmic spiritual. Or even a team cheer.

FIFTY-SIX

THE NEXT HOURS WERE TIME AWAY. I LAY IN SEMI-DARKNESS, eyes closed, smelling fragrant oils and incense, hearing soothing tones of sitar music as skilled hands made mush out of my tensions, pressing and kneading the pain out of places I hadn't even known were sore. The masseur rubbed spots on my feet that felt connected to my stomach or my back, and places on my head that connected to my feet. When he was finished, I lay limp, my muscles empty and somehow cleansed. And then, after a cup of healing tea and a warm shower, I met Susan in another room where our feet and fingers were soaked, rubbed and scraped, our nails buffed and painted. From there, we got our hair washed, trimmed and blown dry. And finally, it was time for our catered lunch. Still in our robes, we sat in plush cushioned chairs beside a gas lit fireplace and ordered chicken walnut salads with croissants with iced green tea.

"Well? How do you feel?" Susan was pleased; she knew the answer.

"Tingly. Glowing all over. Thank you. This day has been incredible."

"We should do this more often. Every few weeks."

Every day would be fine with me.

Susan wanted to know about my massage, the details of what felt best. I was still too relaxed to feel like talking, so Susan carried the conversation by herself. She told me how she carried stress in her lower back and was sure that the whole spa had heard her moaning as Armando worked there. She admired my haircut, suggested that I color away my strands of gray, wondered if I thought she should have hers cut shorter than chin length. By the time the chicken salad arrived, she'd discussed her kids' and husband's lack of enthusiasm for household chores, and was voicing her desire for a professional wife, someone to organize and manage her home.

"I mean Tim and I both have demanding careers. And when I get home, I have to cook and clean—the cleaning people don't do it properly. And I have to do everything a mom does, help with homework, arrange dentist appointments, drive to swim practice. I'm a cliché. I'm Supermom, and that's so nineties. I mean it. It's the twenty-first century, and I need to hire a wife."

"Why a wife, not a husband? Why do you assume it's a woman's job to do all that?"

She sipped iced tea. "Get real, Zoe. The last thing I need is another man. Look what goes on in your house with the triplets there. Men are basically useless in the home. It's always been and always will be the woman's job to run the family and the house. It's biological. We evolved that way from caveman times. Men do the hunting and gathering; women keep the hearth."

Whatever. I didn't care, didn't think it mattered. My body was still too happy, my brain too empty, for gender role discussions.

"Which brings up the subject of Ivy."

It did?

"What are you going to do to replace her?"

I had no idea. "Anna's filling in."

"But next week?"

Oh Lord. I hadn't thought that far ahead, hadn't wanted to. And Ivy had promised to show up next week. "I don't know."

"Be careful, Zoe. Ivy was way too into your business. And although I love Anna, for such a pint-sized person, she's kind of pushy."

Really? You couldn't fool Susan.

"But never mind." She stretched, catlike. "Ivy's history, and next week you'll have your house to yourself again."

I imagined the house with just Nick and the kids and me and smiled. No more living in a fraternity. No more cigar butts on my ceramic plates. No more beer bottles lining my kitchen counters. No more daily pizza deliveries or randomly dumped piles of dirty clothes or late-night barhopping.

Susan forked chicken salad into her mouth. "I bet you'll miss those guys. They're like big hunky teddy bear triplets."

Quadruplets. I thought of Eli as I chewed a walnut.

"Who knew when you met Nick that he had clones?"

"But they're not like Nick." Maybe it would help to talk to her about them. "Those guys, they're—different than he is."

Susan buttered her croissant, frowning as if I'd said something stupid. "Of course they are."

I thought about answering, telling her how Sam's business dealings seemed shady, how Tony had been behaving oddly, sneaking around the house ever since the murder. That Eli had snuck around in the dark carrying a knife, that Sam packed a gun. My suspicions lined up in single file in my head, preparing to pour out. But, somehow, all I poured was more iced tea. My mouth didn't release them, not one. In fact, it didn't open at all, except to let in more food. Talking took far too much effort for my currently limp and completely relaxed brain. Instead, I let myself appreciate the sensations in my body parts. All of them, head to toe, felt alert and alive. A ring of energy seemed to surround me, cushioning me like a corona. I was wrapped in soft terry cloth, listening to timeless music, tasting flavorful food. My best friend was beside me, and my life, my heart, were full of love and promise.

Susan eyed me, munching croissant, talking while she chewed. "What's wrong, Zoe? Stop worrying about Nick's brothers. True, Sam's kind of pushy, but hell. It's not like you're marrying him.

Although, from what Anna said, we're about the only women who haven't. How many exes does he have—four?"

I smiled at Susan, not even thinking about answering her question. I was admiring the sparkle of her eyes and healthy shine of her neatly trimmed hair. I took another sip of cool tea and savored the butter melting on my flaky croissant. For once, I realized, I was living in the moment. I really was. And for that moment, even if it wasn't going to last, I understood the word *bliss*.

FIFTY-SEVEN

BUT BLISS, LIKE EVERYTHING ELSE, PASSES. AN HOUR LATER, WE picked up Emily and Molly at school and Susan drove us home.

"Can we play, Mom?"

"Can I go to Molly's?"

Susan looked at me for approval, and I nodded. Of course they could. "We can only stay about an hour, Em. I have to get home."

So, after Susan shimmied her BMW SUV into a tiny spot between a pickup truck and a Dumpster, the four of us filed into the house, where Oliver ran in circles, yipping with joy at our arrival. I heard Luke's wails as soon as the door opened, and Anna was waiting, pacing the hall with Luke, who was inconsolable.

"He's been impatient." Anna handed him to me. "I told him his mama had other things to do today than feed him, and I'm sorry, but he doesn't approve. When you're finished, I have a list of phone messages for you. And a wine list for final approval."

I reached for him, my breasts overflowing after our longest separation of his lifetime. I sat on the easy chair while Luke nursed; the girls scampered off to Molly's room, and Anna and Susan sat on the sofa deep in muted conversation until Molly ran downstairs, red cheeked with excitement.

"Announcing, for the first time ever in Philadelphia, *The Em-Molly Show*. Come one, come all. Five minutes until showtime." And she ran back upstairs.

"The what?" Anna seemed confused.

"They do this," Susan explained. "They put on shows. You know, sing and dance."

"How very creative." Anna approved.

I agreed. "They plan them for hours. They make props and scenery; they argue about who'll do what; they rehearse."

Susan nodded. "The actual show is the smallest part of the process. After all the preparation, it lasts like—what, Zoe? Thirty seconds?"

Luke had fallen asleep, so I brought him to his portable cradle in the dining room. But I didn't put him down right away. I was still tingling from the massage, as if my nerves had been dusted and every sensation was more vivid and intense. I stood, holding Luke, watching his tiny mouth still sucking, even in sleep. His skin, his texture and smell mesmerized me, and having been away from him for six hours, I felt like a drunkard who'd waited all day for a nip and was unwilling to leave the bar. Finally, I put him down and covered him, but I lingered, staring at him, marveling at the power he had over me. What was it? I couldn't get enough of him, even when I was exhausted. When I looked at him, sometimes my teeth actually hurt, aching to chew his fleshy cheeks and bulbous thighs, nibble his belly. To eat him up. Suddenly, I thought of Bonnie Osterman.

Oh God—Bonnie Osterman. That's what she had done—eaten up babies. Literally. But there was no connection between the way I felt and what she'd done. I would never really bite Luke. I might nuzzle him and rub my face into his tummy, but I'd never actually nip him, much less chew on him. Still, I wondered. That urge— the almost primal compulsion to clamp my jaws around my infant's body—was it the same one that had compelled Bonnie Osterman? Had her impulse to devour babies merely been a perversion of a basic maternal drive? And if so, were her crimes somehow more understandable? Less grotesque?

No. I wasn't going to think about Bonnie Osterman. Nothing

about her or her crimes was understandable, and there was no connection between us. I would not remember her squat form darting after me, questioning me at the Institute, asking about my pregnancy; nor would I consider the possibility that she'd run a car into Bryce Edmond. I closed my eyes, refusing her image access to my mind, and I ran a finger along the curve of Luke's cheek, trying to absorb the peace that embraced him. But commotion interrupted. Oliver ran down the steps, barking, and footsteps pounded and furniture scraped the hardwood floors, being moved.

"Mom!"

"Coming." I pulled myself away from Luke and started down the hall.

"Mom—where are you? We're ready!"

"Coming," I repeated, but Emily spoke at the same time.

"Molly, no, we're not either ready." She sounded panicked.

"Come on, Emily. Yes, we are."

"No—if one of us says she's not ready, then the other one has to listen."

Oliver was running in circles, yapping, as I approached the living room. The girls stood in the hallway, face-to-face. They wore matching pink leotards from gymnastics class, and they'd put glitter in their hair and green shadow above their eyes. Emily wore a chiffon scarf around her neck; Molly held a baton.

"Okay, Emily. How are we not ready?" Molly put a hand on her hip.

"Because we didn't rehearse enough." Emily was adamant.

"But remember, Em? That's why we picked these routines. Because we did all of them before, so we already know them," Molly urged her. "It's just a different order."

"But wait. Your mom's not even here—"

"Yes, I am. I'm here." I hurried past them into the living room. Emily turned to me, pouting.

"Come on, Em. We're ready."

Emily sulked, not moving.

"Come and sit, Zoe. Have a snack." Susan moved over, making room for me on the couch. Apparently, while I'd been with Luke, Susan and Anna had been to the kitchen. The coffee table, moved to the side of the room to make way for the "stage," displayed bowls of store-bought salsa and artichoke dip, a basket of chips and several cans of soda.

"Emily, get it moving." Susan clapped her hands. "It's now or never. We've got to get home."

"But Mom, it's going to suck."

"Emily Cummings," Susan scolded. "Language."

Emily muttered words we couldn't hear as Molly told her, "Start the music, Em." The music was on a CD that they had accidentally miscued. So it took a while for them to find the right cut. Finally, we heard strains of "Sgt. Pepper's Lonely Hearts Club Band." As the girls began dancing, Oliver went berserk, nipping at their heels, trying to herd them. I scooped him up and held him on my lap, and while he strained to jump off and Emily whined that she'd warned us it would suck, they recued the music and started from the top, again.

They danced and Molly twirled her baton, to much applause. Emily juggled three balls, dropping one only twice, and the audience went wild. Molly and Emily did cartwheels and flips back and forth across the living room floor with much clapping and cheering all around. And then, they turned the music off. The two stood side by side, and Emily announced a duet. Each of them picked up "microphones," which looked to be jump drives from my computer. I'd have to discuss that with Molly later; she knew better than to touch anything in my office, let alone to take anything out of there. It disturbed me that she'd so blatantly break the rules. But the talk could wait until Susan and Emily left; for now, I sat with the rest of the audience, watching the show.

"Stop!" Each girl holding her microphone in one hand, they

gestured the word by holding the other out in front. "In the name of love." Their free hands each outlined half of a heart shape in the air. "Before you break"—they moved as if snapping a stick—"my heart." They folded their hands over their chests. They were singing one of my favorite oldies, and their voices were pretty much on key. Emily was a year older, a head taller and more self-conscious than Molly. But, no question, the two were crowd-pleasers. They did almost matching footwork while singing the verses into their microphones, repeating the hand movements for the choruses. At the end, they got a standing ovation.

After the girls had sodas and chips and dip, Susan took Emily home and I took Molly to my office, so we could have a talk.

"Let me see your microphones." I expected her to be embarrassed or guilty for taking what wasn't hers, maybe even to apologize. But she didn't.

"Why, Mom?" She seemed genuinely confused.

"I want to see them."

Shrugging, she went back to the living room and returned with the two jump drives. "Here."

I took them. "Where did you get these?" I was annoyed that she didn't even seem sorry.

"I found them."

"You found them." Was she going to lie to me? "Where?"

"Oliver had them."

Great. Now, instead of taking responsibility for her actions, she was blaming the dog. What was happening to Molly?

"He was chewing them."

"Do you know what these are?"

She shrugged. "I don't know. Key chain thingies."

"No, Molly. They're on chains. But these thingies hold memories for computers."

She seemed unimpressed.

"So, you're telling me that Oliver had them?"

"Uh-huh." She seemed uninterested. "Mom, what's for dinner?"

"Wait." I ignored her question. "How do you think Oliver got hold of these?"

She shrugged, as if it were no big deal.

"Do you think he went into my office and took these from my desk?"

Her eyes met mine, wounded. "How should I know?"

"Well, I thought you might want to rethink your story about how you got them."

"What? You don't believe me?" Her mouth dropped in indignation. "You think I'm lying?"

"I didn't say that. But it's difficult to believe that Oliver could have—"

"Fine." She stomped her foot. "Don't believe me. Why don't you just call me a liar?" She spun around and ran out of the room, and I heard her stomping up the steps, the door of her room slamming.

I closed my eyes, felt them burning. In all the six years since I'd adopted her, Molly and I had never had a conflict like this one. Never before had I caught her in a lie.

For a while, I sat with the jump drives in my hands, oddly paralyzed, my heart hurting. I didn't want to call Molly a liar, didn't want to believe she'd lie to me. But I held the evidence in my hands. What was I supposed to do? Molly and I had always been honest with each other, but then, Molly had changed. She was getting older, would inevitably have secrets from me. And she must have feelings about Nick joining our family, some of which she couldn't or wouldn't articulate. And Luke. She was jealous. But could she be so angry with me for having him that she was getting even by stealing my stuff? Oh Lord. It all made a sad, twisted kind of sense.

Okay. A few days ago, I'd promised to spend more time with her; now was a good time to start. I'd go to her, reassure her, remind her how important honesty was. We'd talk it out. Sighing,

I stood to go, setting the drives on my desk. Then, glancing at them, I sat back down.

The jump drives were a different brand than mine. Not only that. They were on navy blue chains; my chains were black. And, looking more closely, I could see that they were damaged, dented with what looked like tooth marks. In fact, one looked like it had been gnawed by a dog.

FIFTY-EIGHT

"I'M SORRY." I'D KNOCKED, BUT SHE HADN'T ANSWERED.

"Okay." Her voice was small.

"Can I come in?" Odd, I'd never asked permission before. But then, she'd never shut me out before.

"Okay."

Molly sat on the floor, surrounded by the outfits she and Emily had tried on for the show. "You think I lied."

"No, Molls."

"Yes, you do. You didn't believe me."

I sat beside her. She wasn't looking at me; she focused on sorting her leotards and tights. "I was wrong, Molly. I thought those things were mine. They're called jump drives, and they look just like mine, but they aren't mine. I was wrong to assume you took them."

"But why would you think that?"

"What, that you took them?"

She nodded. "Do you think I'm a stealer? A liar and a stealer, too?"

Oh God. What had I done? "No, Molls. I don't. I'm sorry."

"But if you don't think so, why did you say what you said?"

She turned to me, and I saw her chin wobbling, refusing tears. I reached over to hug her, but she stiffened, rejecting my arms. She wasn't going to forgive me easily.

"Molly, I made a mistake."

She bit her lip, not letting herself cry.

"I thought I was the only one in the house who had those drives. I thought they'd come from my office. But they didn't. Maybe they belong to one of your uncles."

"But you thought I stole them."

What was I supposed to say? "I didn't exactly think you stole them. I thought you might have borrowed them without asking, but I was wrong. I know you didn't do that. I do not think you're a liar or a stealer. I love you, and I think your show was fabulous. And I hope we can make up. Can we?"

She nodded. I tried again to hug her and she allowed it, but she didn't return my embrace with any enthusiasm. I removed my arms and put a hand under her chin. "Molly, I trust you. I do. I value your opinions. And I really am sorry I doubted what you said."

"I know. It's okay, Mom. Let's just forget it. We all make mistakes."

I was speechless, relieved. Not certain how to move on. For a while, I sat with her, silently helping her straighten her room up, replacing the glitter in her crafts box, putting unworn costumes into a drawer.

"So then, whose are they?" She finally spoke.

It took a minute to figure out what she was referring to. "I don't know. Maybe Sam's or Tony's." They left everything else lying around, why not jump drives?

"Maybe they fell out of Uncle Tony's pocket."

Why would she say that? "You think?"

She shrugged. "You know that corner where Uncle Tony dumps his clothes? Well, that's where Oliver was. He was sitting on top of Uncle Tony's gray sweatpants, chewing on them."

My heart did a double take. "When was that, Molls? Do you remember?" Was it before or after the house was ransacked? Before or after Agent Harris' death?

Molly's face was blank, fearful. Not wanting me to get angry again. "I'm not sure."

"Was it after the lady died out back?"

Molly nodded, positive. "Yes."

"And what about the time Uncle Tony got his black eye? Was it before that?"

She cocked her head, thinking. "No. I think maybe it was the next day, the day right after the lady died."

"The next day?"

She nodded slowly, unsure. "Maybe. I think."

"Try to remember, Molls. It could be important."

"It was. It was the next day." She beamed, elated. "Because I remember. I slept at Emily's because we didn't have school. Remember? Because it was Saturday."

And because our house was a crime scene. "And what happened when you got back from Emily's?"

"Uncle Tony was mad because our house was in the newspaper, remember? I can't figure out why he was so mad about that."

Neither could I. But I hadn't known that she'd been aware of that. Did anything get past Molly? "I think he didn't like his picture."

She giggled. "Why? He didn't look pretty enough?"

Wait. Pretty? Did Molly know Tony was gay? Did she even know what "gay" was?

"And then you took Emily and me to the park, and when we got back, we saw Oliver was chewing on something. Emily and me—we thought they'd be good microphones, so we took them away from him and brought them up to my room, and we kept them in my prop box for the show."

Oh. She put them in her prop box. A cardboard carton, elaborately decorated with cutouts and glitter, stuffed with a baton, a dozen hats, a witch's broom, a cane, pompoms, streamers, a juggling kit, magic tricks, masks and who knew what else. No wonder, I thought, that whoever had ransacked our house hadn't found the drives. No adult would willingly venture into the tangle of miscellany contained in that box.

"Mom? Why do you care when it was? What's the difference?"

I didn't dare lie to her, but I didn't want to tell her the truth, either. "I'm trying to figure out who they belong to, Molls."

She nodded soberly. "You think the person who lost them wants them back?"

"Probably. The information they saved on those things could be important."

In fact, very important. Important enough to kill or die for.

"Will Uncle Tony be mad?"

"No, Mollybear. Why would he?"

"Because maybe—I mean if they fell out of his pockets, they might be his. Maybe he'll think I stole them and then he'll be mad like you were."

"Don't worry" I pulled her to me and held her tight. "Uncle Tony would understand. He could never stay mad at you. And neither can I."

She nodded, agreeing with me, as if I'd just stated the obvious.

We went downstairs together to make dinner but found Anna already in the process of preparing meat loaf, asparagus, tossed salad and mashed potatoes. Molly and I got to work setting the dining room table. I folded napkins, replaying in my mind what Molly had told me, convinced that she was right: The jump drives had probably fallen out of Tony's sweatpants soon after Agent Harris' death. And so, the question was: Why had they been in Tony's sweatpants?

Maybe the answer was simple: The drives were there because they belonged to him. Maybe they contained records of his software designs and business reports. But if they were Tony's, why hadn't he noticed them missing? Why hadn't he asked us if we'd seen them and sent us all searching? I thought of how he'd searched for his lost pocket change. He'd told us about a lost handful of quarters; certainly he'd have mentioned lost computer files. No, his silence didn't make sense.

Unless they weren't his. Because if they weren't his, he might not even have known they'd been in his pocket, much less that they were missing. And that's where my thoughts turned grisly. The jump drives, after all, were small. Small enough to be inserted into a rectum or a vagina. If you had to, you might even be able to wash them down with water, hide them for a while in your intestinal tract. But if you didn't have time to stuff them into a body cavity, they were also small enough that you could drop them into a stranger's pocket during a feigned accidental collision. If you had to, you could pretend you were out jogging and that you'd tripped and, oops, fumbled against some guy out to pick up his morning paper and—oh my God. I got it. I understood exactly what had happened.

Agent Harris had hidden the jump drives in Tony's sweats. Knowing she was about to be caught, she'd grabbed onto Tony and passed them into his pocket. Her murderers had searched her body, inside and out, to no avail and they'd retraced her final steps, identified Tony and accosted him, threatened him, even searched the house where he was staying. Nobody had mistaken Tony for Eli. Nobody had mistaken Tony for anybody. Tony had been attacked for bumping into Agent Harris, for receiving the information she'd been transporting.

I had no idea what was on those drives, who was looking for them or to whom they rightfully belonged, but I was certain of one thing: As long as we had them in our possession, we were—all of us—in danger.

Molly carried the glasses to the table carefully, one at a time so she wouldn't drop them. I set out the plates, praising the way she had arranged the silverware, acting as normal as I could, given that two possibly deadly devices were sitting on my desk in the next room.

FIFTY-NINE

THE MINUTE THE BROTHERS STEPPED INSIDE THE HOUSE, I pulled Nick away, dragging him into my office, telling him about the jump drives.

"Wait; what? Slow down."

"These." I held them out. "This is what the whole thing is about."

He glanced at the jump drives, then at me.

"Agent Harris slipped them into Tony's pocket—she must have. And they must have fallen out or something, because Oliver got into them, and Molly took them from Oliver, and I took them from Molly."

Nick took one from me, held it up, examining it.

"That's what those guys beat Tony up for. They're what the FBI guys are looking for, and they're the reason the house was ransacked."

"Hmm."

Hmm?

"So that's what they're after. They called today."

"Who?"

"They told Tony they're coming back for these. They wanted to come by tomorrow, but we didn't know what the hell they wanted, so Tony stalled them off, saying the feds were all over him. So they said they're calling back tomorrow to arrange a pickup. At least now we know what they want to pick up."

Nick took the drives to my computer, sat down and booted up.

"We're going to look at them?"

He swiveled around to face me. "If they're any good. Oliver chewed them up pretty bad."

"But they might be secret. I mean should we know what's on them?"

"Zoe. Calm down. Let's just see if they're really what you think they are, okay?" He didn't believe me.

"What else could they be?"

"They could be junk Oliver picked up in the street. They could be Tony's or Sam's. And I don't want to rush them over to the FBI unless I'm sure this is really—"

"Well, if you think they're Sam's or Tony's, why don't we just ask them?"

"Ask them what?" Tony's head popped through the door.

Great. I'd wanted to keep the conversation with Nick private. Now, it would be a family affair.

"Are you missing any jump drives?"

He hesitated, focused his attention. "Any what?"

"You know, these memory things." I held up the one Nick wasn't using. "For the computer."

"No. I mean, maybe. I might be." He seemed edgy. "Why?"

"Molly had some, and we don't know who they belong to."

He stepped into the office, eyeing the drive in my hand. "Where did they come from? Where were they?"

"Oliver had them. Molly found him chewing on them."

"Oliver had them?" he repeated, his eyes glazing. "Molly found them? Where were they?"

"In the living room, on your sweat suit."

He touched his forehead. "My sweat suit?"

But he didn't finish because Nick interrupted, banging his fist on my desk. "Damn. The damned thing requires a password."

"A password?" Now I was repeating.

Nick nodded. "There's no way we'll be able to guess what it is. Let me try the other one."

I handed it to him, and he tried to place it into the computer slot.

"Dammit. This one won't even go in." He jiggled and finessed the drive, but it wouldn't fit into the designated hole. "That goddam dog really mangled this thing. I can't do it; they'll have to put some nerds on this."

Nick sighed and swiveled to face us.

"So what should we do? Take them to the FBI?" I wanted the things out of the house, away from my family.

Tony's eyes darted from Nick to the computer and back. "The FBI? So, you're seriously saying you think that agent passed those to me? Is that what you're saying? That those drives are the reason I got beat up? The reason she got killed?" He seemed to have trouble assembling the information.

"It's a good possibility, given everything that's happened." Nick stood, took the jump drives. "Wouldn't you say?" He headed for the door.

"So where are you going?"

"Got to follow proper channels. These need to go to the feds; they might be critical evidence. But I got to deliver them to the Roundhouse, to the detective in charge."

Tony was at Nick's tail. "Who is that exactly?"

"What's it to you?"

"Nothing. I mean, what do you think is on them?"

Nick shrugged. "Well, Harris was assigned to Homeland Security. Whatever it is, it's important."

Oh God. The information on those drives might be of grave importance, and my daughter and dog had been playing with them as if they were yo-yos. Dangerous people were hunting for them, and I wanted them gone. Out of the house, out of Nick's possession.

"So, you're taking them to the police?" Tony bit his lip. "Where, to homicide? Right now? Wait. I'll go with you—"

"No, Tony. You stay here. It's better to keep it official." Nick started to leave, then stopped. "Unless you have something to add to your account—"

"No, no. But I've been beat up over those things and someone was killed. And I don't think you should go alone. For security."

"Better if you stay here with Zoe. It's about time for Anna to take off."

"Sam's here. He can manage."

"Stay. I won't be long."

Tony was shaking and breaking into a sweat. "Trust me, Nick. You shouldn't go alone. If those guys catch up with you—"

"Nick, he's right. We'll be fine here. Take Tony along."

Nick sighed, resigned. "Fine. Let's go." He gave me a quick good-bye kiss, and the two of them took off.

SIXTY

SAM WAS SPREAD OUT IN THE RECLINING CHAIR, WATCHING A RE-
run of M*A*S*H, finishing off the last of the leftover dip and
chips. Molly was on his lap, Oliver whimpering at his feet, hoping
for a handout.

"What's up, Zoe?" Sam sucked on a beer. "Where'd Nick go?"

"Sam, have you lost any jump drives?" I knew his answer but
needed to ask, just to be sure. "You know, for the computer?"

"Jump drives?" His face was blank. "What, those memory things?
No, I don't think so. Why?"

"Just making sure."

"I found some," Molly explained. "Well, really, Oliver did."
Stretched out on Sam's belly, Molly reached back and casually toyed
with his ears as I explained the theory that Agent Harris had
slipped the jump drives into Tony's pocket.

"Okay." Sam smiled, reached for a cigar. "That explains it." He
pulled the plastic wrapping off. "You know what I think? I think
that poor girl mistook Tony for Eli."

So I wasn't the only one.

"Knowing Eli, he was probably involved in this. I'm thinking
he was her intended contact and she confused him with Tony."

I sat down on the sofa as, on television, Radar announced in-
coming wounded. What Sam said wasn't a new idea. But I listened closely as he elaborated.

"I mean, come on, Zoe. What do you think Eli's doing in town?

You think he's really here because of your wedding?" Sam shook his head. "Don't make me laugh. Eli couldn't give a rat's ass about his family. No offense, but he never did. He's here for his own reasons. No doubt some underground, undercover espionage thing. Trust me, Eli's involved in this. And I'm guessing the reason that poor broad just 'happened' to show up on this doorstep was that Eli gave her Nick's address as his local base of operations. Maybe even as their drop point."

Base of operations? Drop point? Sam rearranged Molly and shifted the recliner to an upright position.

"Point is"—Sam slipped the gold paper ring off his cigar—"that broad knew Eli would be coming to this address. She knew his brother lives here. And you know what else? Here's the way I see it: She thought Tony was Eli. She thought she'd completed her mission. Slipping those things to Tony, she thought she'd made the drop to Eli. That's my theory." Sam twirled the cigar, wheezing and out of breath.

What he said confirmed my own thoughts. I'd mistaken Eli for Tony myself. And Eli's connection to Nick might have brought both the agent and Eli here; his late-night visit might not, as he'd claimed, been merely to take pictures and meet Luke. Eli might have been here primarily to search for the jump drives. But the question remained: If Agent Harris thought she'd given the drives to Eli, why did she return to the house? Had she learned that she'd mistaken the brothers? Or was there some other reason, other data—or maybe a warning she needed to pass along? Or, oh God, maybe her body had been left here as a sign that the killers knew she'd been here and left the drives here—

"So? What do you think is on them?" Sam tousled Molly's hair, causing giggles. "Drug stuff? Names of cartel leaders—or maybe of infiltrators? You know, government informants? Could be dates of drug shipments or lab locations. Or wait—maybe it's not about drugs. Maybe it's about terrorists. Homeland Security, after all. Maybe it's some plot they've put together, and who all's involved, you know, the what do you call them—cell members?"

I bit my lip. The suggestions were unnerving. "We have no idea. It could be anything."

"It could be weapons, too," Sam went on. "Maybe bio-weapons, like that anthrax stuff. Or like on that TV show with what's-his-name? A mininuke? Could be about a dirty bomb—"

"Sam, please." He was scaring me. A dirty bomb? "There's no point in trying to guess—"

"Yeah—that could be it." Sam chewed his cigar. "A plot to explode a dirty bomb on U.S. soil—"

"Why would you say something like that?" He was alarming me. He had no reason to assume that the drives contained information like that. And the idea was too awful to think about.

"Stop it, Sam." I was annoyed. "For all we know, the data's completely nonviolent. It could be about crooked financial records or stealing from a pension fund. Or the vice president's secret love affairs. Not everything is about terrorists or dirty bombs."

Sam eyed me, eyes laughing. "You think? Well, you might be right." He stuffed his cigar into his mouth, chewed on it. "But my money's on terrorists. A plan to attack us, maybe a suitcase nuke."

"For God's sake, Sam."

"I'm serious." He twisted one of Molly's curls. "See, in my mind, nobody's going to off a federal agent for the sake of a sex life or a pension plan."

Oh dear. I had no rebuttal.

"Well"—he leaned back, relaxing—"for us at least, it's over. Nobody's going to bother Tony or you or the house or my car anymore; the FBI has the data."

Was he serious? The government may have the jump drives and whatever data was on them, but whoever killed the FBI agent was most likely not part of the government. And the people who hired that killer would mostly likely not know that the jump drives were in government hands; they would still be hunting for them. Tony would still be in danger.

"But what about Tony?" Apparently Sam hadn't considered that. "Those guys have been calling and threatening him."

"I'm sure Nick or the FBI will protect him."

"But for how long? A couple of days?"

Sam lifted Molly off his lap and set her on her feet. "Molly, go ask Anna when dinner's going to be ready. I'm famished."

As she scampered out of the room, he leaned forward. "This is harsh, Zoe. But in the scope of things, even though we love him, Tony's just one person. One person—no matter who—is not that important. Who knows what we're dealing with here? What if I'm right? What if these guys aren't working drugs or counterfeiting hundred-dollar bills or conducting your everyday kind of criminal activity? What if they are terrorists, working with something bad like a dirty bomb? Tell me. How important is any one of us, in the case of an atomic weapon?"

And there they were again, those words: *dirty bomb, atomic weapon.* What was with Sam? Why was he persisting, almost insisting on that particular possibility? Did he know something? Or was he simply trying to upset me?

"Sam, you keep talking about dirty bombs. Out of the entire universe of information that could be on the drives. Why not anthrax or chemical poisoning or whatever? Why dirty bombs?"

He looked at me. "I don't know. It's common knowledge that there's enriched uranium to be had out there. There's been talk of dirty bombs since 9/11. I didn't say anything for sure. I just said it could be that. But it could be something entirely—"

Molly skipped into the room, drowning out the end of his sentence. "Anna says dinner's ready and we should go sit down."

"Good. Smells terrific." Sam excused himself to wash his hands.

"Did you wash up, Molls?" I reached for her hands.

"Of course." She held them up for inspection, a question on her face. "Mom?" Her voice was somber. "What's a dirty bomb?"

SIXTY-ONE

"WHAT, YOU DON'T KNOW? A SOPHISTICATED CHICK LIKE YOU?" Sam stepped out of the powder room, rescuing me.

Molly blinked at him.

"A dirty bomb is a Broadway show that has so many bad words in it that nobody wants to see it."

"No, it's not." Molly wasn't fooled.

"It's not?" Sam chuckled, wheezing. "Then you tell me. What do you think it is?"

Molly looked up at me, wanting the truth. "Mom. Tell me."

I hesitated, squeezing her hand. "It's a—"

"It's what I said." Sam was insistent now, as if daring me to contradict him. "And it's nothing for you to worry about. It's just a term."

A term?

"Hey, Molly," Sam went on. "What do you say to a blue elephant?"

Molly ignored him and kept looking at me, waiting for me to answer her. I tried never to lie to her, but I didn't want my six-year-old daughter to have to deal with the dangers of nuclear warfare or terrorists. "A dirty bomb might be part of a case Nick's working on, Molls. Police business, nothing for us to worry about." There. Well done. That was true. Sort of.

Molly seemed satisfied. "Anna said to tell you she's ready to go home." She scampered back toward the kitchen.

I changed Luke and, while we ate, he gurgled in his portable rocker and the rest of us sat around the dining room table, going through the motions of a normal family having a normal meal. As we ate, Sam regaled us with entertaining and fascinating facts. Did Molly know, for example, that the reason Prussian soldiers had buttons on their sleeves was not for decoration or utility but to prevent them from wiping their noses there? Unfortunately, Molly's reaction of "Ewww" encouraged Sam, who proceeded to share even grosser shards of history. But I didn't complain. Sam was doing me a favor, keeping Molly occupied, allowing me to force a few bites of meat loaf down my throat. And when dinner was finished, Sam engaged Molly in clearing the table, announcing that they would do the dishes together, leaving me on my own. And, on my own, I wandered from room to room, closing blinds, lowering shades, locking windows. Whoever had mugged Tony had warned him that they'd be back, and that there would be dire consequences if he didn't hand over what they wanted. Where were Tony and Nick? What was keeping them so long? I picked up Luke, carried him with me from room to room, feeling locked inside the house, a prisoner, or maybe a guard.

The phone rang when Luke and I were circling my bedroom, and hoping it was Nick, I grabbed it.

"Zoe, I hope today was as good for you as it was for me." Susan's voice purred, relaxed, teasing.

What? It took a moment to remember what she was referring to. Oh, the spa. "Yes, it was. It was great. Thanks again." How was I supposed to discuss spa days and massages when terrorists might be coming after my family? Not to mention attacking the city?

"Oh dear. We're in that kind of mood again. Today was supposed to relax you. I guess it didn't last long."

"No. Really. It did. Today was wonderful." My voice contradicted my words.

Susan sighed. "Okay, spill. What's wrong now?"

"Nothing. I'm fine."

"You know, it's normal to have prewedding jitters. Trust me. I had them, too. You'll be fine—"

"Susan, it's not jitters." Why had I said that? Let her think it was jitters.

Susan waited a second. "Okay. Then what is it?"

And without thinking, without hesitating, I told her. I set Luke down on the bed and sat beside him, telling her what she already knew and what she didn't. About Bryce Edmond and Bonnie Osterman, about Tony's mugging, about the jump drives and the dead agent. I didn't mention the idea of a dirty bomb or the presence of Eli because, before I got to them, Susan interrupted.

"Wait; I'm confused." Susan sounded completely lost. "Who are you saying killed the agent? Your patient from the Institute who cuts women's bellies? Or terrorists who thought she swallowed the jump drives? Or somebody from Homeland Security?"

But Susan had missed the point. "It doesn't matter who did it, Susan. Whoever killed her, those muggers still want the jump drives. They told Tony they'd be back. They beat him and threatened him. But he can't give them the drives because Nick took the drives to the FBI—"

"Calm down, Zoe."

Was she kidding? "Are you kidding?"

"It won't help to get nervous." She sounded nervous. "Look, maybe you guys should get out of there. Doesn't Sam have a suite at the Four Seasons? Couldn't you stay there?"

"I guess. But we couldn't stay there forever."

"This won't last forever—you have just a couple days until the wedding. And then Tony will be leaving, so whoever is bothering him will have to let up."

"No. The wedding isn't going to change anything, not anything this big, and besides . . ." I paused, not ready to say it out loud.

"Besides what?"

"I'm thinking of postponing the wedding." There. I'd said it.

"No, you're not."

"But I am."

She exhaled, loudly. Kind of a snort.

"Say something."

"Zoe, look. I don't know what to say. That is the single most stupid, most irresponsible, most incomprehensible, most ridiculous thing I've ever heard you say—"

"No, it's not. Susan. People are getting killed here, being hit by cars, beaten up and threatened. My house is invaded and ransacked. My kids are in danger. How can I in good conscience put on a lacy gown and act like everything's just peachy—"

"Okay, I'll tell you how. You just do it. And you can because not to means to give in to them and to fear. You can because you can't let the bad guys—whoever they are—interfere with your life or your family. You can because you owe it to Nick, not to mention to his brothers, who've come here for the ceremony. And to me, who's bought a very expensive hotter-than-you-can-imagine matron-of-honor dress. And to Anna, who's poured her soul into this affair. And to Molly, who's going to be an amazing flower girl. And to all your guests and friends who are—"

"Okay, you can stop." She didn't get it. "I didn't say I'd decided anything. I just wanted to warn you. In case."

"Zoe, just remember you've already postponed this wedding because of your pregnancy."

She was right. Nick and I had waited to get married because the pregnancy had been high risk; I'd been on bed rest with Luke for four months.

"Luke deserves to have married parents."

"We're going to get married." She was trying to make me feel guilty. "It's just a matter of when."

She hesitated. I could almost hear her thinking. "What does Nick say about this?"

Well, he hadn't said anything. He had not a clue. "We still have to talk."

"Oh God, Zoe. Don't even mention it to Nick. Don't do it. He'll be hurt. It's bad karma, plain and simple. I get it. You're overwhelmed with what's going on, but don't postpone your wedding. Just don't."

She was still talking when I heard Nick and Tony come in. I could hear Nick, asking Molly where her mom was, heard her tell him I was upstairs with Luke.

"Susan, I've got to go. Call you later."

I hung up and lay on my bed beside Luke, stroking his cheek, listening to him coo, hearing Nick's footsteps coming up the steps, waiting for him to join us.

SIXTY-TWO

"WE STUCK AROUND TO MAKE SURE THEY WERE GOING TO THE right guys. I gave it to Schultz myself."

Schultz? Was I supposed to know who that was?

"He's attached to Homeland Security, a computer genius for the FBI, works with security and encryptions." Nick took his shoes off, sat on the bed. "He came up from D.C., and he wanted to talk to Tony. It's a good thing Tony came with me. They spent quite a while together, working out a plan. That's what took so long."

"Susan thinks we should go to a hotel." I felt Luke's breath on my hand, smelled his sweetness.

Nick stretched out opposite me, our baby between us. "Okay. I give up. Why?"

Was he being deliberately obtuse? "Nick. Those guys threatened Tony's life. And they're going to be back—"

"Shhh." He reached out, put his hand on my cheek. He was trying to be soothing. "Listen, Zoe. If people like that want to find you, they'll find you in a hotel just as easily as they will at home."

Great.

"And there's safety in numbers. We've already made arrangements so that you and the kids are never alone. There are always at least three people here. And, remember, these guys have already been here. They tossed the place and didn't find what they wanted. I doubt they're coming back—they're relying on Tony to get them what they want."

"But they said they'd—"

"They wanted to scare him."

For some reason, Nick's opinion didn't comfort me. I put my arm around Luke, shielding him from something unseen. Nick covered my arm with his hand.

"Zoe. No one is going to attack our house."

Our house? He'd called it ours. I needed to go on. "Maybe not. But there's something else." I paused; he watched me, waiting. "I was thinking that, what with everything that's happened . . ." I looked at him, hoping he'd pick up my sentence and finish it for me. But he didn't. He waited. I started again.

"Maybe, with everything that's happened, we should, I don't know, postpone the wedding?"

His hand moved away from my arm. He looked away, then back to me. He propped himself up on an elbow, then sat up. "Postpone it? Why?" He looked lost.

Susan had been right. I shouldn't have suggested it. Nick was hurt. He didn't understand. "You don't want to get married?"

"Of course I do." It was true. I did. I wanted to be Mrs. Nick Stiles. "But I don't want the wedding to be blown up—"

He smiled his half smile, relieved. "Nobody's going to blow us up."

"But Tony should lie low, shouldn't he? What if—"

In a heartbeat, Nick leaned over, covering my mouth with his, stopping me mid-syllable. His lips were tender, his kiss steady and deep. It spoke for him, assuring me that we were, that we would be, all right.

With Luke between us, Nick and I lay face-to-face, and I listened to him tell me that we'd waited long enough for the wedding. The pregnancy and Luke's birth had delayed it. A hefty chunk of the Philadelphia police force had been invited, so we would be safe. And besides, all the plans had been made, nonrefundable deposits paid. Besides all of that, he was half-Jewish.

He said that he was half-Jewish as if it held the final word about our wedding. "What does being Jewish have to do with it?" We weren't having a religious ceremony. A friend of Nick's, a judge, was going to marry us.

"In Jewish tradition, life take precedence over death."

Wait. Life over death? What? Again, he seemed to think he'd made sense. "Okay." I had no idea what he meant.

He propped himself on an elbow. "It's like this. Celebrations of life don't get shoved aside or postponed or canceled because of events of death. Or even threats of death. A wedding is a life celebration. It's not to be delayed. Even if one of our immediate family were to die, the wedding would proceed. Life takes precedence over death."

Oh. I gazed at Nick, marveling. I'd lived with this man for over a year. I'd had his child. And, until this moment, I hadn't had the slightest idea that his religious heritage had meant a thing to him. Even now, I had no idea if he held any religious beliefs or what they might be. It was startling, alarming. Shouldn't we know that about each other? What else didn't I know about him, or he about me? In so many ways, we were still strangers. Were we really ready to get married?

Luke squealed happily, holding his feet in the air, grabbling them with pudgy hands. And I looked from the baby to the father, his familiar scar, his asymmetrical smile, his cool and knowing blue eyes. It was a face etched into my being. I had come to rely on it, had tethered my heart to its expressions. If Nick wanted the wedding, we would have it as planned. After all, he and Susan both thought the wedding should proceed, and he and Susan couldn't both be wrong. They wouldn't want us to go ahead unless they were sure it was safe.

SIXTY-THREE

I TOSSED ALL NIGHT, DIDN'T FALL ASLEEP UNTIL ALMOST DAWN. And as soon as I did, Luke blared like a trusty alarm clock, waking up, wanting breakfast. By the time he'd been fed and changed, Molly was up and my opportunity for rest had disappeared. Fortunately, I was too tired to think. I wandered through the morning on autopilot, putting on the coffeemaker, getting the newspaper and taking Oliver out, giving him his kibble and Molly a bowl of cereal and some juice, letting her watch television as she ate as long as it didn't wake up her uncles. It wasn't until the doorbell rang and Anna arrived, spinning a whirlwind of frenetic energy, that I woke up enough to realize what day it was. It was Friday. The day before the wedding. Oh God. I sat on a kitchen stool, my heart pounding in my throat.

This was it. I was getting married, committing myself to Nick for life. Memories swirled in my mind of my other wedding, the first time I'd committed myself to a man for life. That was different, I told myself. That was a mistake. But, at the time, I hadn't thought it was a mistake. I'd been sure of Michael and me, hadn't I? When I'd married Michael, I'd intended to spend my life with him, get old together, raise kids, the whole shebang. But look what had happened. Michael hadn't been who I'd thought he was, or maybe I hadn't been who he'd thought I was. Or maybe we'd both been who we'd thought, but both of us had changed. Or maybe we hadn't known each other well enough to know who either of us was. At any rate, the end had come, and it had been brutal. A disaster, really. I hadn't recovered, hadn't even dated anyone for years afterward. In fact, Nick was the first man I'd seen seriously after Michael. So, in a way, I'd met Nick on the rebound. How could I be sure this time was right? I'd known Michael for years before marrying him, and that marriage had failed. By contrast, I hardly knew Nick—we'd met not even two years before.

Okay, I told myself. Stop right now. It's too late to think about your decision. Your wedding is planned. Floral arrangements have been purchased. You love Nick, and Luke and Molly are both counting on him being their dad. And besides, this wedding is completely unrelated to your prior one. You're older now, wiser. More mature. Your choice is based on more solid factors. Now breathe deeply and get hold of yourself.

I took a few deep breaths from my belly, trying to slow my heart rate. But solid factors? What the hell were those? I didn't even know what my own words meant. Oh God. My pulse was doing double time. And Anna was jabbering, handing me something. Oh. A mug—good. Maybe it was full of Scotch. But no, it wasn't Scotch. It was steaming and smelled like decaf.

". . . but it's normal; it happens to all my brides." Anna was in the middle of a thought. I hadn't been paying attention. "You're going to think you're nervous. Even terrified. But trust me, dear, you're not nervous or terrified. Those bells in your head are not sounding the alarm; they're announcing your wedding."

Bells? What? Could she tell by looking at me? Did my edginess show? I took a sip of hot coffee. My hand was unsteady. Did she see that I was shaking? But the coffee tasted a watery kind of familiar. Grounding.

"Remember: It's just adrenaline."

Adrenaline? In the coffee?

"Humans are animals, dear. When we face the unusual or the

unknown, we secrete hormones that alert us so we can prepare ourselves."

The fight-or-flight response. It was a basic principle in which hormones prepare animals for aggression or escape. But wait, what had I missed? Why was Anna giving me a psychology lesson? I was a therapist; my event planner was lecturing me on psychology?

"Look. Athletes get rushes of adrenaline before a game, soldiers before battle, actors before a performance. Adrenaline makes you jittery. Gives you butterflies, maybe a little nausea. It feels like fear, but it's not. It's excitement. Arousal. It's the body gearing itself up. Getting itself ready, saying to itself: 'Listen up. Something big is happening.'"

Okay. I got it. Something big was happening.

"So, here's what I want you to do." Anna had a hand on my shoulder. "I've got the kids covered, and I'll handle the men. If the phone rings, I'll answer. You go upstairs and take a bath or a nap. Pamper yourself. In a while, I'll bring you some breakfast on a tray."

I had no excuses. I was tired, and although I didn't want to let my children out of my sight, I knew they were safe with everyone in the house.

Anna kept talking, her voice less cloying than usual, more rhythmic, almost soothing. "The rehearsal dinner isn't until seven. The rehearsal's at five. You have nothing to do until then. Go."

And so I thanked Anna, told Molly I was taking a nap and went upstairs, back to bed. Nick was still sleeping. Without opening his eyes, he reached out, covering me with his arm. And I lay there, feeling its strength and thinking about the word *husband* until I drifted off.

SIXTY-FOUR

"I'LL BE BACK AS SOON AS I CAN."

I opened my eyes. Nick's mouth brushed mine, saying good-bye. I blinked, trying to orient myself.

"What?"

Nick was dressed. Putting his wallet in his back pocket, going somewhere.

"Where are you going?"

He half-smiled. "You didn't hear anything I just said, did you?"

"Did you say something?"

He smiled again, sat beside me on the bed, smoothing my hair with his hand. "Schultz wants to see me. And Tony got another phone call, so I've got to go in for a bit."

We looked at each other as I woke up, becoming coherent. "But you're not working. You took time off. Today's our rehearsal—"

"I know. I'm sorry. This won't take long."

"And you said we'd all stay together—"

"I know. But I have no choice, Zoe. Besides, Sam and Tony are here. And Anna. Nobody's going to mess with you while she's around. And I'll be back in a couple of hours at the most."

A couple of hours? I had no idea when that was. "What time is it?" I lifted my head to see the clock.

"A little after noon."

What? I'd slept for almost five hours. I rubbed my eyes, sat up, felt groggy. Almost drugged.

"You okay?" Nick stood, putting on a blazer, ready to go.

I nodded, not quite sure. "Just can't wake up."

"Take your time. Rest. I'll see you later." Nick kissed me again and was out the door.

The next thing I knew, Molly was on the bed, shaking me. "Mom. Luke's crying."

My eyes refused to open.

"Mom. Wake up. He's hungry."

Luke was hungry? At the thought, my nipples began to leak. I forced my eyes open. Molly sat beside me, frantic.

"Oh, finally. I thought you'd never wake up. I've been trying to get you up for like ever."

"What?" Down the hall, I heard Luke wailing. I sat up. Oops, too fast. The walls began to sway, and I fell back onto the pillows.

"Mom? Are you sick?" Molly's eyebrows furrowed.

"I'm okay." I tried again, slower this time. And I tousled her curls and, kissing her forehead, wobbled to my feet. "Coming, Luke."

I felt off-balance, and my voice sounded like sandpaper. What was wrong with me? Was I getting sick? Great, I thought. Just in time for the wedding, I'll get some kind of flu or malaria. But Molly held my hand all the way down the hall, steadying me. At the sight of me, Luke became furious. Red-faced, angry that lunch was late, he bellowed.

"I'll get him, Mom. You sit down."

For once, I simply let Molly take care of him. My limbs felt weak, and I was afraid I might drop him if I tried to pick him up. So I obeyed, sitting in the rocking chair, watching Molly lower the side of the crib and lift her brother, holding him a little too tight, carrying him to me.

"It's okay, Lukie," she was saying. "Mommy's here." But his screaming pretty much drowned out her voice.

He pounced on my nipple, and finally the room was quiet.

"Thanks for getting me up, Molls. I can't believe I slept so long."

"You slept all day."

"Why didn't somebody wake me?"

"Anna wouldn't let us. She said you needed to rest."

Why would Anna say that? She shouldn't decide what I needed. "Where is Anna?" In fact, where was everybody? I hadn't seen or heard Tony and Sam all day. "And what time is it?"

Molly looked at the wall behind me, at a dinosaur with an analog clock in his belly. "Two . . . something. Wait. If the big hand is between the five and the six, then . . . Wait. Don't tell me—"

Good Lord. I'd slept until two thirty? I never slept all day. And I felt so odd, so fuzzy.

"—Does that mean it's two thirty?"

My genius. "Yes—very good, Molls." But how had I slept so long? Since when? About eight?

"I thought you'd sleep forever."

"You thought I was like Sleeping Beauty?"

"Well, no, because she had a poisoned apple."

I remembered Anna holding out a steaming cup. Had Anna slipped something into it? No. She wouldn't. Would she?

"And that's just a story."

But she'd been talking about her brides, about keeping them calm. Could she have given me a sleeping pill? No. How could I even think such a thing? She wouldn't. Especially since I was nursing. A sleeping pill would affect the baby.

"But even if you got poisoned, Nick could kiss you awake. He's your Prince Charming."

Speaking of Prince Charming, where was he? "Is Nick home yet?"

"Uh-uh."

No? "Has he called?"

"I don't think so."

But he'd said he'd be gone a couple of hours at the most. I wondered what had happened, what was taking so long.

"Mom, could Emily sleep over tonight?"

"What?" The question surprised me.

"Anna said she was watching me and Luke because you and Nick and everybody are going out to dinner."

"That's right."

"So could Emily stay with us?"

"Not tonight, Molls."

"Why? Pleeeeeze."

I explained about the wedding rehearsal, told her that she would have to go and practice being flower girl and that then Anna would take her and Luke home. But since Emily wasn't going to be part of the wedding, she wouldn't be at the rehearsal and wouldn't be there to take home.

"So she could come after."

"Mollybear, no. It's not convenient tonight."

"Why? Susan could bring her over."

"But Susan and Tim are going to be with us at the rehearsal and they are staying afterward for the dinner. Besides, I already said no. Another time. Tomorrow's the wedding."

Molly pouted, thinking. "So, you mean, she can sleep over after the wedding?"

"Of course."

"You mean tomorrow night?"

Was she serious?

"Can she?"

Good Lord. On my wedding night, I was going to be arranging sleepovers. But what was the harm? Nick and I would be staying at the hotel, and Anna probably wouldn't mind watching one more child. "Okay, I'll talk to Anna and Susan."

Molly clapped her hands. "Yes! Thank you, Mom. I'm going to go call her."

"Molly, wait—" But she was already gone.

Oh Lord. I closed my eyes, leaning my head back against the rocking chair. Why couldn't I seem to wake up? And what was keeping Nick so long?

SIXTY-FIVE

NICK WALKED IN AT FOUR FIFTEEN. OUR REHEARSAL WAS SCHEDuled for five. We'd have to leave by four thirty to be on time. Everyone was assembled in the living room: Anna, Luke, who was sleeping deeply, Molly, Oliver and Tony. Sam had gone ahead to change in his hotel room.

"Finally. I've been calling you." Tony was frantic. "I had to talk to you. Why didn't you pick up? I was scared to death something happened to you."

As was I, but I didn't say so. I was too annoyed. Nick always turned his phone off when he didn't want to be interrupted.

"I couldn't take any calls." Nick seemed distracted, not hurried enough. He looked from face to face. Oliver yipped at Nick's shoes; Nick stooped to pet him.

We were supposed to leave in fifteen minutes, and Nick was playing with the puppy.

"Nick. Are you aware of the time?" Anna stood, looking at her wristwatch. "You have exactly fourteen minutes to change and be out the door. We are leaving at precisely four thirty." She looked as if she was ready to change his clothes herself.

"Don't worry. I'll be showered and ready." He reached into his blazer pocket, removed something and dropped it on Tony's lap. "Here."

Molly jumped off the sofa to see what Tony had, no doubt assuming it was a present. "What is it, Tony?"

Tony picked up whatever it was and gasped. "Oh dear God. The jump drives." He dropped them onto his lap as if they seared his fingers.

"Mom, look. It's the microphones." Molly looked at me and backed away, not wanting any part of them.

"Schultz wants you to hold on to them. He said he discussed the whole plan with you yesterday."

"The man's maniacal. I'm his bait."

Bait?

Nick looked at Anna. "Anna, could you get Molly a cold drink?"

She hesitated for a moment, comprehending. "Let's go have some juice, Molly. We'll let the grown-ups talk."

"But I'm not thirsty, Anna."

"I am. Keep me company." She took Molly's hand and led her to the kitchen.

When they'd gone, Nick explained quietly, "The people who lost these do not know we've found them."

Tony sulked, his brow furrowed.

"And when they called, they said they'd be coming back for them, right?"

Tony nodded. "They called again today. Twice. I was trying to reach you. They said they're going to find me within the next twenty-four hours and I'd better be prepared."

"Well, now you are. You've got the drives. You can hand them over."

"What are those, fakes?" I didn't understand.

"No. They're the real thing. The original drives."

"So, wait." The plan still wasn't clear to me. "What's Tony supposed to do? Just hold on to the drives and wait until they mug him again and hand them over?"

"Pretty much—"

"But they might kill him—"

"Wait," Sam interrupted. "Back up. I thought you two geniuses were going to give those drives to the FBI. So why do you still have them?"

I was glad he asked. I was completely confused.

"We did give them to the FBI. They copied them and have been working on decoding the data. These are the originals. They returned them after copying them."

"But why in God's name did you bring them back here?" I didn't want the things in my house. I held on to the warm bundle that was Luke for comfort. He slept, undisturbed.

Nick spoke slowly, as if to a child. "Zoe. Whoever is looking for those drives doesn't know that the information on them has been compromised. They still want them, and they'll come looking for them. And Tony should keep them on his person until they do."

I was angry. I didn't care about pleasing the FBI; I cared about protecting my family. I didn't want whoever killed the FBI agent and mugged Tony to come back after him.

"Nick, let me ask you something." My voice was shaking. "Are you crazy? Or just phenomenally irresponsible?"

He winced. "Neither. Are there other choices?"

Tony was on his feet, wringing his hands.

"Come on, Tony. Relax." Nick put a hand on Tony's shoulder. "You won't be alone. Agents are going to be watching us from now until you're approached again."

"Really? Are they watching him now?" I had no faith in that promise, had seen one of those agents turned inside out.

"They might very well be." Nick seemed confident.

"Really?" I wanted to smack him. Why was he so smarmy and calm? "Where are they?"

"You won't know they're there unless you need them. They know how to be invisible."

"Invisible like Agent Harris?"

He didn't answer.

"And by the way, Nick." My face was hot. "What gave you the

right to endanger Molly and Luke and all of us by agreeing to this plan?"

"Zoe, I didn't endanger anybody." His eyes were steady and clear, and he emphasized the word I. He glanced over his shoulder, as if making sure that Anna and Molly wouldn't hear. "Look. These people are here, whether we like it or not. They already said they're coming back to see Tony. They'll be back whether we have the drives or not. Whether the FBI is around or not. They promised they'd kill Tony if he didn't give them what they wanted. Now, Tony can give them the drives, and maybe they won't kill him or any of us. And maybe the FBI will be watching and catch them or tail them and arrest their bosses or whatever. That's the plan. Our only chance, though, is to comply."

Our only chance? Or else what? We were dead?

Tony was ashen and shaky, but he walked over and sat beside me on the sofa. "Nick's right, Zoe. I hate to say it, but he's right. They won't harm us if I hand over what they want."

"And you believe them? You believe murdering thugs?"

Tony paused, choosing his words. He put a gentle finger on Luke's pudgy cheek. "I believe that if I don't do what they want, they won't hesitate to kill me or anyone close to me."

Great. "And if they notice the FBI skulking around? Then what?"

Nick scoffed. "That's not going to happen."

"How do you know? These people aren't stupid." I glared at him, furious. Blaming him for making decisions without consulting us. Blaming him for the whole situation. I knew I wasn't being rational or fair, but I didn't care. Blaming Nick was easier than accepting my own powerlessness.

He took in my evil eye but seemed unfazed. "Sometimes, Zoe, you've simply got to trust. Look. It won't hurt for Tony to keep those drives on his person." Nick started upstairs. "Tony, take care of my bride for a few minutes. I've got to get ready for a wedding rehearsal."

Tony and I sat silently for a moment. A wedding rehearsal? We were proceeding as if nothing was wrong, no killers, no secret codes, nothing.

"What he says makes sense." Tony seemed to be reassuring himself as much as me. "They're going to come back anyway. I might as well give them what they're looking for."

More silence.

"I mean all I have to do is carry them."

And more.

"They might not even show up. But if they do, at least I'll have what they want."

I didn't have anything to say, so I didn't say anything. I let Tony go on, rationalizing his predicament. Luke slept, didn't move or yawn. Perfectly still, he looked like porcelain, like a doll.

"Mom." Molly bounced into the room. "Anna said we can get pizza later."

Anna followed Molly, checking her watch, reminding me that we had to leave in six minutes. Pressuring me because we might be running late. What did she expect me to do? Scream at Nick? Would that help? Actually, I wanted to scream at him, but I didn't. I didn't say anything. I sat and held Luke, vaguely wondering why he was sleeping so deeply and so long.

"Mom?" Molly seemed bothered, as if waiting for something. "Can we?"

Can she what? Oh—the pizza. "Sure, Molls. Of course."

Molly hung on my arm, toying with Luke's fingers. "What's taking Nick so long? I want to go—"

"Don't pester your mom; she's already stressed out." Anna clucked, pacing nervously. "We'll go in exactly five minutes."

Apparently, with or without the groom.

Anna reached for Luke. "Let me take him, Zoe. Go freshen up so we can leave the second your man comes down."

She swept Luke up and away. His eyes opened, then rolled

closed again. And I stood obediently, not knowing exactly what I was supposed to freshen but eager to be alone for a minute. I wandered past the powder room to the kitchen and gazed out the window at passing pedestrians and cars. Were any of them FBI? A man in a suit lingered across the street. Was he an agent? A taxi pulled up, and the man got in. Clever ruse. Maybe the driver and the man were both agents. Or no, maybe the Gothic-looking woman, the one walking past the house, all in black except for the magenta streaks in her hair. I closed my eyes, breathing deeply, telling myself to stop worrying. Maybe a drink of water would help. I opened the cabinet to get a glass and knocked over a vial of pills. An open bottle of Benadryl. What? I hadn't bought any Benadryl. The label warned that it might cause sleepiness. "Avoid driving or operating heavy machinery for eight to ten hours," the directions said. Whose were these? Where had they come from?

Oh God. Suddenly, I knew. And I knew why I'd practically passed out earlier, why I'd been loopy and slow to react all day. And why Luke was still sleeping so soundly. Anna had given me one of these pills. She'd drugged me. And, in drugging me, she'd drugged my milk, which drugged Luke. I had no doubts. I knew it was true. How dare she? My hands were fists; I was ready to fight.

"Anna!" My voice was a shriek. "Anna—come here! Now." I no longer cared about the rehearsal or the wedding she'd planned. The woman had slipped a drug to me and to my baby, and she was history. Out of here. I'd have her arrested. In jail.

"Okay, let's go—" Nick rushed down the hall, holding hands with Molly. Molly was giggling, skipping to keep up with him. "Zoe? Got your coat?"

"Nick, I have to talk—"

"Talk in the car—Anna's going to thrash me if we're late." He lifted Molly and carried her out the door, Tony at his heels. Oliver tried to follow and I grabbed him, stopping him as Anna, Luke in her arms, herded the others, prodding them to keep moving. The parade filed past me, but I didn't follow.

"Anna." I stopped her, Oliver yapping at my feet. "What's this?" I held up the bottle.

"Oh." She bit her lip. "That?" She smiled sheepishly. "Well, you were exhausted."

"You mean you admit it? You admit that you drugged me?" I took Luke from her. I didn't want her near him. I wanted her gone. "Anna. I'm afraid we won't be needing—"

"But you've been so tense, dear." Her voice was soothing, maternal. "You needed the rest. It happens to a lot of my brides. Sometimes we all need a little help relaxing. The pill helped you. It gave you a day to rest before your wedding. And in your case, it was a double bonus—" She nodded at Luke. "Look at your angel, how well he's sleeping. He's not fussing or interfering, so you have time to prepare for your special day—"

"Are you serious?" I was so angry, I couldn't speak. I sputtered for a moment before making actual words. "Whatever you gave me was in my milk. You drugged my baby. Don't you realize what could—"

"Don't worry, dear. This medicine won't harm him, and it has no lasting effect. He'll be himself in no time. But meantime, you can have your rehearsal and enjoy a nice leisurely dinner out."

"Are you crazy? You had no right. I should report this to the police—I should tell Nick."

"Tut-tut, dear." She smiled. Why was she smiling? "Zoe. I promise you, when the wedding's done, you'll look back and you'll thank me. Now hurry along. We're running late."

I sputtered, too appalled to form words. The woman was unapologetic, completely oblivious to what she'd done. And before I could articulate a sentence, Anna waltzed out the door, hurrying the prospective groom, best man and flower girl to the car.

SIXTY-SIX

MOLLY WAS WITH US, SO I DIDN'T RAIL AGAINST ANNA IN THE car, and when we got to the hotel the wedding party was waiting for us. The judge wanted to get started. He had another engagement and was in a bit of a rush, so I didn't get a chance to talk to Nick before the rehearsal, either.

The judge gathered us in a corner of the small ballroom where the ceremony would be, and Nick introduced him to everyone. Sam, an usher because he'd lost the coin toss to Tony, who'd won and was therefore the best man with jump drives packed in his pocket. Susan, the matron of honor, and Tim, her husband, who had brought my father, who'd worn his tuxedo, apparently thinking we were having a dress rehearsal, and, finally, Molly, the flower girl, and Luke, the tiny ring bearer. It was a small party, intimate. Anna would walk us through the procession, playing a CD of Vivaldi's *Four Seasons* so that we could hear the rhythm and step to the music, and the judge would go over our parts and tells us a bit about the content of his talk.

Angry and distracted, I watched from the back of the room as Tony and Nick strolled down the aisle. As Sam carried the tiny ring bearer along, my focus drifted. For the time being, anyway, Anna faded from my mind, replaced by Susan's graceful form floating down the aisle, weepily dabbing her nose with a tissue. Then Molly, controlling her pace, counting out the beats as Anna had instructed, did a slow and deliberate hesitation step, pretending to sprinkle flowers along the way. Finally, Anna signaled my father.

"Ready, Walter?"

My father stood and graciously offered me his arm. "Shall we? Time to get married." Tall and white-haired, even in his eighties he was disarmingly handsome, and his eyes glistened. Was he crying? "Zoe, kitten—"

Kitten? He'd never called me that before. In fact, he'd rarely expressed affection at all.

"Your mother would be so proud."

My mother? I saw in my mind's eye the shadowy form of a woman who'd died when I was as young as Molly. "Thanks, Dad. That's nice to hear."

"Truth is, I never thought I'd live to see this night. Not after that other guy."

Why? Did Dad think no one would ever marry me after Michael? I kissed his cheek, smelled his aftershave. And, instantly, the scent triggered another childhood memory: Dad, all dressed up, looking dapper and slick. Ready to go out? Quickly, the impression was gone, and Anna was cuing us to start down the aisle.

"You're the bride. Shouldn't you have worn white?" Dad scowled at my outfit, a purple sweater, black pants.

"That's tomorrow, Dad." My father had suffered a series of small strokes, and he tended to get confused. "This is the rehearsal."

He frowned. "The wedding's not till tomorrow? Then what's the fuss?" He started to sit down again, but I grabbed his arm.

"We need to practice, Dad. This is the rehearsal."

"Then why are you giving me an argument?"

He was still frowning as, very slowly, we made our way down the aisle toward the small group assembled at a silk- and lace-covered kiosklike structure set up in the front of the room. Sam had surprised us with it; a chuppah, it was called. It symbolized a home and was an essential part of Jewish wedding ceremonies, and even though Nick and I were not having a religious ceremony, Sam had insisted that we have the chuppah, repeatedly explaining its significance to me, to the judge, to anyone who would listen, mentioning again and again that it had been his personal contribution.

Now, as the chuppah waited for us, I held my father's arm, felt how frail he was and led him along more than he led me. Molly, waiting to go for pizza, was clearly bored, shifting her weight from leg to leg, whispering to Tony, who whispered back. Sam stood at attention, watching the ceiling, inspecting the chuppah, checking out Susan, dutifully waiting for the rehearsal to end. Nick stood beside the judge, his gaze steady and grounding, watching us approach. And I walked slowly, meeting Nick's eyes, holding on to my father's arm. Thinking the whole way about firing Anna.

Anna wasn't just officious, not just pushy; she was actually dangerous. How had she given me the drugs? In my food? My coffee? And what if, not knowing about her pill, I'd taken one on my own? I'd have overdosed. We'd be having a funeral instead of a wedding.

No, the woman had to go. And she had to go tonight. Molly and Luke would have to stay with us for the rehearsal dinner. Not a big deal. But then I remembered: What about the wedding? Anna had arranged everything—the musicians, reception, dinner, menu, drinks, flowers, photographer—I had no idea what was supposed to happen or when, had relied entirely on her.

"Mother of God," my father barked, wincing. "What are you trying to do, snap it off?"

Oh dear. In my anger at Anna, I'd put a stranglehold on Dad's arm. "Sorry."

The truth was, I might have to put up with Anna for another day. Meantime, we'd reached the end of the aisle. Kissing my father, I released his arm and stepped forward to take Nick's, which was waiting. And then we stepped forward together, to practice taking our vows.

SIXTY-SEVEN

WHEN I FINALLY GOT A CHANCE TO TALK TO HIM, NICK SEEMED singularly undisturbed. "It's okay, Zoe. One more day. Anna will be done with us and she'll go on to torment some other poor bride."

We stood in the lobby of the Four Seasons; the rest of the wedding party had already been seated in the Swann Café for dinner. Molly and Anna sat on upholstered chairs, waiting to go out for pizza. But I wouldn't let go of Luke; I was unwilling to entrust the children to Anna even for a few hours. With the baby in my arms, I took Nick aside to talk about firing her. But he seemed to think it was fine that the babysitter had drugged me.

"Let's just wait it out. She'll be gone after the wedding." He was unconcerned.

"No. Not one more day. Not one more hour. Not with the kids. She's dangerous, Nick."

"No, she's not."

What?

He held a hand against his forehead, drawing a breath. "Okay."

Okay?

"Jig's up. I confess."

"You confess?"

"Look." Nick avoided my eyes. "I was worried about you. You hadn't slept all week."

Oh my God. I understood. "You did it? You drugged me?"

He put an arm around my shoulder, sighing, half-smiling,

rolling his eyes. "The doctor said Benadryl was okay, and he assured me that it wouldn't affect the baby for longer than an extra nap."

"What doctor?"

"The pediatrician—Dr. Tapper."

"Wait. You called the pediatrician about drugging me? What is this, a conspiracy?" I twisted my shoulder away from his hand.

"No, I didn't ask if I could drug you. I asked if it would hurt the baby if you took a sleeping—"

"Who else is involved? Who else is figuring ways to get Zoe to calm down?" My voice was too high, shrieky.

"Oh, cut it out, Zoe. Nobody else is involved."

"Not Susan? Not your brothers?"

"No. Of course not. But what if they had been? It would only mean they cared about you. Face it, Zoe. You've been a wreck—"

A wreck? "Thank you."

"It's not your fault. You've been under tremendous stress—"

"My stress is no one's concern but my own."

"True." He nodded, pausing. "Even so, I was trying to help you get through the week."

"Nick, we've been through this before." We had. Early in our relationship, Nick had tried too hard to protect me, overstepping boundaries, hiding facts, making decisions for me. Just as he was doing now. "You are not in charge of me."

He stuffed his hands in his pockets, studied his shoes, looking bashful and penitent. Bashful and penitent didn't work on Nick. He was too rugged, too angular. He swayed from side to side like a nervous schoolboy.

"You're right. I know. But this time, there were extenuating circumstances."

I chewed the inside of my cheek, nostrils flaring. "Listen carefully. Unless I'm in a permanent vegetative state, there are no such things as extenuating circumstances. I make my own decisions."

He nodded, eyeing the carpet, his gaze making its way to mine. Exhaling slowly, he met my glare with a soft blue apologizing gaze. "Can I say I'm sorry? Can I admit I was wrong?"

Oh God. His eyes were melting me. Thawing my freeze.

"Zoe, you have every right to be furious with me."

And I was. But how was I supposed to stay furious with him if he apologized and agreed that he was wrong?

"There's no excuse for what I did. All I can say is that I had good intentions. With the agent's killing and your friend Bryce getting run down, and you being worried about your patients being released, and then the threats to Tony and the wedding and everything, I could see effects on you. The strain. I heard you pacing all night every night. I thought some sleep would help you. That's all. I was stupid. I messed up."

He had, yes.

"But, to be fair, the fault is mine, not Anna's. All she did was agree with me that you were tense. But the idea of the sleeping pill, the phone call to the doctor, the decision to give you a pill—that was all me."

Great. Nick, not Anna, had decided to drug me. Nick, my fiancé, the father of my son, had taken it upon himself to knock me out for the day. We stood silently, awkwardly, staring at each other in the middle of the lobby. People were beginning to notice; standing stiff and statuelike, our eyes exchanging lasers, we were becoming a spectacle. In my peripheral vision, I saw Molly fidgeting, swinging her legs, impatient to go for pizza. And in my arms, Luke stirred, finally waking up. He would need a new diaper and a meal.

"Look, Nick. You do anything like this again and I mean it— we're done."

Nick looked as if I'd slapped him. But if my harshness startled him, it startled me more. Even as I said the words, I regretted them. After all, I wasn't the only one who was stressed out. Nick was pushed to his limits, too, and he hadn't meant to hurt me. But it was too late. My words were making their way through his head, and I couldn't take them back. Nor could I apologize; I hadn't done anything wrong. But if Nick was the one who'd done wrong, why did I feel so bad?

I didn't dare look at Nick. I was afraid of what I'd see in his eyes. So, before either of us could say another word or do more damage, I turned away, rushing off with Luke to the ladies' room. In my peripheral vision, I saw Molly running after me, Anna trailing behind.

SIXTY-EIGHT

THE SWANN CAFÉ WAS FIVE-STAR ELEGANT, THICKLY CARPETED, candlelit, divided into sections, each hosting only a few china- and crystal-laden tables. At dinner, I sat at Nick's unscarred side, separated from him by a wedge of hurt feelings and uncertainty. As we looked at menus, he took my hand, leaned over and whispered that he loved me. I squeezed his hand, nodding, responding that I loved him, too, but in truth, I hadn't fully recovered. I was still angry, still distrustful.

Anna had gone with Molly and Luke, assuring me that they'd be home, the kids in bed, by eight. Even so, I had uneasy feelings. What if the thugs looking for the jump drives came back to the house while they were there alone? I told myself that wouldn't happen. That we'd only be away for a few hours. That I needed to get over being angry with Nick and focus on the moment. That this was, after all, the beginning of our wedding celebration; I needed to participate.

I looked around the table, noting how candlelight softened the faces around me. Susan glowed, her eyes sparkling, her smile warm. The creases on Tim's face faded, making him look less harried, more youthful. And Tony—his chiseled cheekbones and generous eyelashes cast gentle shadows over his face, creating a living study of contrasting shapes, of darkness and light. Chatter and laughter blanketed us; as the wedding party drank and ate, it became increasingly jolly. My dad and Sam hit it off, making bets about everything. About how long it would take for the appetizers to come. About how a woman at the bar would react if my father sent her a drink. About whether or not Sam could tie a cherry stem with his tongue in under ten seconds. I tuned in and out of their playful, increasingly animated voices, listening to Tim and Nick discuss the upcoming Phillies season, Susan and Tony chatting about the history and evolution of South Street. Seated at the center of the table, occasionally holding Nick's hand, I watched them, oddly removed, the only one without a conversation partner. And, soon, the only one who was sober.

As drinks flowed and the meal progressed, the table united. Every time a wineglass got filled, another toast was given. With Tony and Nick interjecting some objections and corrections, Sam went on at length, recounting Nick's lengthy and checkered history with women, crossing lines of bad taste, congratulating him on showing some surprisingly good judgment in ending up with a classy dame like me and concluding by presenting us with shares of stock in a company he'd been backing and a week's vacation at our choice of his many time-share properties around the globe.

Susan caught my attention and rolled her eyes, letting me know what she thought of Sam. As she downed the wine in her glass, I signaled her to escape with me to the ladies' room, but before we could get up, Tony clanged his glass with a spoon and began to talk about the bonds of family, and how Nick's marriage was going to extend those bonds to a new generation. Glowing with the effects of the wine, Tony expounded upon his budding affection for me and the kids. Susan clapped her hands to that and, refilling her glass, stood to give her own sincere and somewhat slurred toast.

"Zoe. You are my best friend, the woman who knows me best, the person—aside from Tim—who I count on most in the world. You are the only one—including Tim—who I know for sure will tell me if my outfit makes me look fat and who will talk to me even in the throes of PMS. Through thick and thin—I mean our waistlines, of course—I am blessed to have you as my friend."

Everyone drank and applauded. Susan's face looked blurry; my eyes were filled. Oh Lord. I didn't want to be sappy. Susan had been drinking, so she had an excuse for being sloppy and sentimental. But I was stone sober; why was I getting maudlin and weepy? I blew her a kiss, mouthed *I love you* and blinked to clear my vision.

And then my father began, looking dapper as a game show host. "Here's to our sweethearts and wives: May they never meet." He was warming up. "Here's to love: May we kiss all the girls we please and please all the girls we kiss."

His toasts were clichéd, a trifle bawdy. Some involved bad puns. "Here's to champagne for our real friends, and real pain for our sham friends."

My father's toasts kept surfacing all during entrées of Chilean sea bass, brandied duck and rack of lamb, but I was actually grateful for the comic relief, not wanting to dive into emotional pools. But as dessert was served, Dad raised his glass and stood, tapping his glass for silence.

"As a younger man"—he held his glass high, strikingly handsome and dapper—"I thought I had it made. I was a player—Zoe can tell you. Life took its toll. For a long time, my daughter and I were on the outs. I lost what really mattered: my family. But now, miraculously, in my old age, I have my beautiful daughter back. Not only that, I've got a son and two adorable grandchildren. I don't know how long I'll be here to enjoy them, but, today, I'm the luckiest guy in the world. And when I go, I'll be leaving my family in good hands." He held the glass out toward Nick. "Thanks for taking care of my little girl. You're a good man. Here's to you, Nick." Dad and the others drained their glasses.

Touched, I stood to embrace him. As his toast had indicated, my father and I had had a long-standing estrangement and had only reunited in the last year. I stepped over to kiss him, and his spindly arms embraced me. A memory, another hug, flickered in my mind. In the kitchen, his muscled arms around me. My father had been so tall, he'd had to bend down to hug me. But before I could fully capture the image, it had gone.

When I took my seat, Susan was crying. Tim was dabbing his eyes, Sam blinking to avoid tears, Tony staring into his wineglass, Nick mistily blowing his nose. They were all a little drunk and sentimental. The maître d' approached with a package, announcing that a gentleman had delivered a gift. Nick examined it, probably to make sure it wasn't a suitcase bomb, and when he deemed it was safe, I peeled off the wrapping paper. It was a photo album. Filled with pictures of our family.

Oh God. I knew right away; it was from Eli. The photographs were recent; all of them had been taken during the last week. There were candid shots of the brothers, Molly, Luke and me. Ivy was in one, Anna, Emily and Susan in a few. Oh my. He'd been around as he'd claimed, watching us, taking pictures.

My father was confused. "You mean there's more of them?"

Tim wanted to know who Eli was; Susan wanted details. Tony, Nick and Sam were only too happy to oblige, recounting Eli stories. "He's always got to pull a prank." Sam seemed annoyed that Eli's gift might take attention from his. "Always got to upstage everybody, but he can't be bothered to be here. Eli's all about Eli."

The tales went on. Eli was inaccessible; Eli was elusive. Nobody knew what Eli really did for a living. Eli claimed to be a freelance photographer but was more likely working for the CIA or the Mossad. He worked undercover; that's why he couldn't be seen in public. He moved around working on secret, sensitive assignments. The stories were familiar; I'd heard them before.

As the others talked, I leafed through the album, saw shots of Tony out jogging, of Sam sitting out on the back patio, puffing on a cigar. There was a shot of Sam and me meeting Molly at the bus stop—that had to be the day the agent had been killed. There were a few of Oliver. Of Luke alone, of Molly alone, of Luke with Nick or Molly.

Apparently, just as he'd claimed when I'd found him in Luke's room, Eli had been watching us all week, unseen, taking our pictures.

My skin prickled. The others, involved in Eli stories, didn't seem bothered by his gift. But I was. Very bothered. Eli had been peeping. Spying on us. Invading our privacy. Who gave him that right? Who knew what else he'd seen? I felt exposed and resentful. The idea of him secretly taking pictures was creepy. But my privacy wasn't the only issue. If Eli had been around to take pictures of sweetly innocuous events, what else had he been around to see? Possibly the murder of the government agent? The hit-and-run that injured Bryce? The attack on Tony? The ransacking of our house?

If Eli had been watching us all week, it seemed unlikely that he could have missed all of that. And if I ever saw him again, I resolved to have a word with him and find out what else he'd seen. The stories of Eli's mysterious antics no longer amused me; too many disturbing questions surrounded him. I was determined to find out who Eli really was and what he was involved in. I slammed the album closed, as if shutting the blinds on prying eyes.

It was getting late and the conversation was waning. The men were getting loud, clearly ready to move on to the bachelor party, whatever that involved. I whispered to Nick, asking if he was ready to leave, but he put a hand on my arm and stood. Why? Was he going to give a speech? Of course, I thought. He needs to thank everyone for being here. Saying thank you to our wedding party was the least we could do; why hadn't I thought of it?

Nick lifted his glass to make a toast. As I was seated beside him, my head came to his elbow and I couldn't see his face. "Walter," he addressed my father. "What you said before means a lot to me. In fact, this evening, this group—everyone here—means a lot to me." He paused. Was he finished? I hoped so. I was on emotional overload, didn't want to deal with any more, especially from Nick, whose expressions of love were, thankfully, usually understated or even nonverbal. Please, I thought, don't drone. Just thank them for being here and say good night. Tell them you'll see them tomorrow. But Nick didn't say any of that.

"All night," he went on, "I've been trying to think what to say. When I'm emotionally involved, I'm not always real verbal."

"That's true." Sam chuckled. "Usually, he just grunts."

Tony added. "Or pounds his fists."

Nick ignored the heckling. "But tonight is different. I have to find the right words." He turned to me, towering over me. "Because this is my chance to tell this amazing woman what she means to me. Zoe." He paused and my face began to burn. "You've given me the highest honors I can imagine. You've allowed me to be not only your partner but also the father of your children. And so, I wish I could promise you that I'm Prince Charming, that we'll live happily ever after and that you'll never wish you'd never laid eyes on my sorry face—"

"She probably wishes that now." Sam again.

"We all do—Zoe, run while you can." Tony grinned.

"But all I can promise is that I'll do my best. As a dad and as your husband. You mean the world to me." He lifted his glass, and everyone around the table stood. "To Zoe."

"To Zoe" echoed as everyone drank and applauded. People at other tables did their best not to ogle; undoubtedly our table's rowdiness disturbed their dinners. But feeling oddly weightless, I floated to my feet and reached out for Nick, who put his glass down and wrapped his arms around me, tethering me to the ground. The wedding party was still clapping as I looked into his eyes and saw a deep sea of apology there. And as we kissed, I felt him say he was sorry with his lips.

It's okay, mine assured him. It really is. And, briefly, I wondered what he was apologizing about, if it was just the sleeping pill or something more.

But that thought was gone by the time we broke our embrace and the wedding party was dispersing, ready to leave.

SIXTY-NINE

"ARE YOU SURE?" NICK OFFERED TO HAVE HIS CAB DROP ME OFF at the house. "I don't want you to be alone."

"I'll be fine. Your cab's way too crowded."

He frowned. "Well, we won't be late." His mouth brushed mine briefly as he headed off with his brothers, my father and Tim to meet his rowing and police buddies at a destination unknown to Susan or me but which, since Sam had planned the event, undoubtedly involved bare-breasted women and poles.

Susan and I stood in the lobby, watching them pile into a taxi. The plan was that we would take the next cabs available and go home. But as the men disappeared into the city lights, I realized I wasn't ready to go home.

"How about a nightcap?" Susan asked. Apparently, she'd had the same idea. A moment later, we were perched at the brass and mahogany bar in the swank Fountain Restaurant, Susan slurping up a Black Russian, me sipping black tea.

"I think Tim's going to get a lap dance." Susan pouted.

"Tim?" The idea struck me as preposterous. Over the few years, Tim had developed a significant paunch. His belly arrived places before he did, protruding farther out even than Sam's, so that when Tim sat down, he didn't actually have much lap. I pictured a poor stripper struggling to find enough room to perform and, with no surface to support her, slipping backward onto the floor.

The image struck me as hilarious and I burst out laughing, almost choking on my tea.

"What are you laughing about? It's not funny."

I tried to stop but couldn't. "Just picturing it."

"Okay, Zoe. How about this? Let's put the shoe on the other—" She pursed her lips. "No, let's put the dancer on the other lap. How do you feel about some naked-assed bitch spreading her thighs across Nick's fly?"

Susan was right. That idea wasn't funny. But she had had a lot to drink and was slurring her words. Lisping. *Thighs* came out "thizhe," and *Nick's* became "Nickth." And she was so indignant that her eyes were popping and her spit flying. I couldn't stop giggling.

"Stop it, Zoe."

"Sorry." I tried to stop, but I couldn't. I was caught in a torrent, as if all my tensions had converted to laughter and were bursting out of me in a flood.

She watched me struggle to look serious, and as she watched, her scowl crumbled, frown inverted, and suddenly we were both howling and guffawing until our ribs ached and tears rolled down our cheeks.

"Oh, man." She was holding her sides, wiping her cheeks.

I looked at her, saw mascara streaked all over her face, and that started a new round of laughter. "Your face—" I pointed, cracking up.

"Zhoe—" Susan struggled to stop laughing but slurred my name. And that, too, seemed ridiculously comical. Or maybe I was ridiculously hysterical and Susan was ridiculously blitzed. Either way, we roared until we finally couldn't anymore, and then we settled down and sat quietly, wiping tears, catching our breath.

After a while, we were finally calm again. "Your dad seems good." Susan examined a dish of complimentary salted nuts.

"He does, doesn't he?"

She frowned, pushing the dish away. "Frankly, I'm surprised at you, Zoe. Letting them go."

Letting who go?

"They're too old for that nonsense. A bachelor party? At our age?"

Oh, she was still thinking about Tim and the stripper. "What was I supposed to do? I'm not Nick's mother. I couldn't ground them." I tried to sound independent and mature. As if I didn't really care. As if I hadn't intended to prevent this abominably sexist archaic ritual.

"Like I said. I'm surprised you let them go."

Damn. She knew me too well. I was surprised, too. "Actually, I was going to ask Nick not to let Sam plan it, but . . ."

Susan sipped Black Russian, waiting. "But?"

But the truth was, what with the agent's murder, Bryce's accident, the jump drives and thugs threatening Tony, I'd forgotten all about the bachelor party. But I didn't want to go into all that. "I got distracted, I guess."

Susan nodded. Sitting beside her in dim lights among sparkling bottles, I realized again how solid a friend she was. At the most difficult times of my life—during my divorce from Michael, the terror of a serial killer in the neighborhood, a confrontation with human traffickers on the river, my reunion with my father—Susan had been there, by my side. She was my rock. I got misty, wondering if I'd been nearly as valuable to her as she'd been to me.

Suddenly, Susan put a hand on my arm. "But you know, maybe a lap dance wouldn't be such a bad thing."

I tried to refocus, confused.

"I mean maybe it would get Tim's motor moving. You know, inspire him?"

I didn't know what to say, didn't want to think about Tim's motor.

"We've been together twenty-four years this June, married for twenty-one. After all that time, your sex life can get pretty—what can I say. Routine?"

Now, I liked Tim well enough. He was patient, pleasant, a good provider and partner for Susan. But the fact was, I didn't want to confront Tim and sex in the same sentence. So I replaced him with Nick, assuring myself that our sex life would never be dull. And that Nick, at the bachelor party, wasn't likely to participate in any unsavory sex play. He'd never be interested in something so shallow. Unlike his brother Sam, Nick didn't see women as life support for their sex organs. In fact, Nick would probably be relieved when the gathering was over and he could come home. But then, I remembered that his buddies would be there. A bunch of macho cops. And buff rowers from his boathouse. And I thought about peer pressure and how powerful it could be. And I began to worry, imagining bare-naked, big-breasted women with sequins on their skin piling on top of the groom, but Susan had stopped talking and was waiting for me to say something.

"You must be nervous. I mean, at least a little."

What? Was she reading my mind?

"It's not every day that you get married."

Oh, that. "I can't tell. I'm kind of numb."

"Numb?" She considered it. "Okay. Numb's good." She grinned. Her teeth were perfect. Absolutely flawless, bright white. I didn't remember ever noticing how straight they were. "Here's to numb."

We drank together. My tea was tepid, tasteless.

"You know." She was sloshed. "I ought to warn you. Being married to someone is no small thing. It's like two corporations merging: You don't just get the assets; you get the liabilities, too. The whole kit and kaboodle." She leaned over, whispering, "For example. You know what Tim does? It's actually kind of cute. Every single day, after the shower, in his birthday suit, he flexes. In the mirror. He poses, you know, like a bodybuilder." She imitated a stance or two. I closed my eyes, not wanting to know Tim so well, imagining his belly.

Susan went on about things Tim did, and I tried not to listen, to let her presence and the steadiness of her voice soothe me. Okay, maybe I wasn't entirely numb. I did have some jitters. But the bottles behind the bar glowed softly amber in the light, and liquid sounds of the fountain blended with the gentle strokes of the harpist in the corner. I sat with my friend and drifted, becoming mellow.

Suddenly, Susan nudged me. "Don't look behind you."

Immediately, I turned to look behind me.

"Dammit, I said *don't*."

Too late. A bald, mustached man at the end of the bar caught my eye and winked. He wore a large diamond on his pinkie, a gray silk tie.

I turned back to Susan and took a sip of cool tea, pretending not to have noticed him. "He's flirting?" He was. With us. The idea amazed me.

"Don't look so surprised. We're babes." She picked up her purse. "Think Tim would mind?"

"Too bad if he does. What's good for the goose . . ." I was joking, but Susan slipped off her stool and began to walk down the bar. I grabbed her arm. "Wait. You're not serious   "

"Going to the ladies'."

Susan teetered away, leaving me alone with our drinks, the bowl of mixed nuts, the bartender and the bald-headed winker. I avoided eye contact. I stared at the bottles against the wall, the brass apron at the bar, my hands, my teacup, but the eyes of the mustached gentlemen remained fixed on me. I felt them drilling holes into my face. Finally, I swiveled away so my back was to him and noticed Eli's photo album on the stool beside me.

"Another round?" The bartender was Polynesian, maybe Hawaiian. Or Filipino? His skin was smooth, his face round and friendly.

Yes, I nodded. Of course, another round. I was getting married in less than twenty hours, and my fiancé was off somewhere getting a lap dance. Might as well live it up, have a second cup of tea.

"It's from the gentleman at the end of the bar." The bartender tried not to smirk.

I glanced at the man. He saluted. Saluted? I nodded, smiled a hasty thank-you and looked away, not knowing what to do next. Where was Susan? What was keeping her? What was I supposed to do? I grabbed the album and opened it, hiding within its pages, trying to lose myself in photos of my children smiling and playing. Yes. And there were Tony and Sam. And Nick with Sam. And Nick with Molly. I turned the pages, thinking about how good a photographer Eli was, how he captured the essence of people. Mood, fleeting expressions.

There was a whole page of Oliver. Oliver lying on his back, paws in the air. Oliver smiling. Oliver with a ball in his mouth. Where had Eli been when he'd taken them? The next page had several shots of me. In one, I was holding hands with Nick, standing in front of the house. When had that happened? And how come we hadn't spotted Eli? And below it, there was a wide shot of me walking with Luke down South Street. The opposite page had a closer view of the same walk. As I turned the page, gooseflesh was rising on my arms before I realized why.

Go back, I thought. Look at those photos again. I hesitated, suddenly cold and no longer the least bit mellow. Slowly, deliberately, I turned the page back. There we were, Luke in the stroller and me pushing him down South Street, approaching the corner of Fifth Street. Which was where Bryce Edmond had been hit. In fact, Bryce must have been running after me at that very moment, because my head was turned toward the street; probably I'd just heard him call my name. At the moment Eli took the picture, Bryce was still conscious, still unharmed. But in seconds he was to be slammed by a car, his head smashed against concrete. I stared at the picture, wishing I could freeze time and yell to him to stop or turn back. But by the time Eli had snapped the camera, it was probably too late even to yell. Because in the corner of the shot was the dashboard of a silver SUV. And sitting in the driver's seat, small but clear as the vodka in Susan's Black Russian, was a woman who looked a whole lot like Bonnie Osterman.

SEVENTY

OH GOD, THERE WAS NO DOUBT. IT WAS. BONNIE OSTERMAN. I stared, squinting, at the photo, processing the implications. Bonnie Osterman had been driving the car that hit Bryce Edmond. Bonnie Osterman, in fact, was in the background of several photographs. She was on a bench in Three Bears Park while I watched Molly climb the jungle bars. And she'd been half out of the frame, a bit out of focus, in a shot in which Molly, seated on the front steps of the house, was holding Luke.

I couldn't move. I sat stock-still, my bones frozen. Bonnie Osterman had been following me. Bonnie Osterman, who'd cut pregnant women open to steal their infants, who'd made stews out of unborn children—Bonnie Osterman had been on my street, to my house. She'd seen my children—oh God. I saw Agent Harris lying gutted on my patio. Maybe it hadn't been a terrorist or spy or weapons dealer who'd killed her, after all. Maybe—

Someone brushed my shoulder; I jumped.

"I didn't mean to startle you." The mustached man was taking a seat on the stool next to mine. "Mind if I join you?"

I must have looked frightful, because when I faced him, he ducked ever so slightly, as if shocked. I think I asked him what time it was. Or I might have said I had to get out of there, or maybe I didn't say anything. I don't remember. But I do remember pulling out my cell phone and calling home. And I remember listening to the phone ring, unanswered, until the voice mail picked up.

The man asked something, probably if everything was okay. I looked at him, trying to figure out what he was saying, what it meant that nobody answered my phone. And then, grabbing Eli's album, I jumped off my bar stool and ran.

I was dashing out of the Fountain Restaurant as Susan was coming back in, still wobbly. She opened her mouth to say something, but I cut her off.

"I've got to get home."

She did a tipsy about-face and chased after me, asking questions. But I didn't stop.

"I'll call you later," I yelled over my shoulder as I raced through the lobby to the front door. "Cab," I told the doorman, and he waved one forward. I jumped in and gave him the address, telling him to hurry, as baffled and boozy Susan spilled out the revolving door.

"Zoe—are you okay?" she shouted. "What happened?"

There was no time, of course, to explain. So I simply waved to her through the window as the cab pulled away.

SEVENTY-ONE

I COULDN'T BREATHE. I WAS DROWNING, SWIRLING. ALL I COULD think of was Luke and Molly. And the hunched, squat figure of Bonnie Osterman. In the cab, I called Nick on his cell, but, of course, he didn't pick up. He wasn't reachable; he was busy sticking money into the thongs of stripteasers. I left a message for him to come home.

It was maybe three miles from the Four Seasons to our house on Monroe Street, but the cab seemed to crawl and to get every red light. At that hour, there was no traffic. No oncoming cars. No cops.

"I'm in a hurry." The red light lasted forever. "Can't we go through?"

"You want me to lose my license?" The very idea infuriated him. "I can't break the laws, ma'am. You want someone to break laws, you find another cabbie. Not me." He gestured as if I could get out if I had a complaint.

I tried to calm down. "Okay. It's just that my baby is sick and I have to get home." The second part wasn't a lie.

He turned, glanced at me and, looking both ways to check for cars, floored it. "Your baby? A boy or a girl?" We passed Market Street, headed toward Chestnut. Another red light.

"A little boy."

"And why did you leave your little boy alone? What are you doing out so late all by yourself?"

Why was he interrogating me? Did he know I'd lied? Was he

judging me, finding it unacceptable for a woman to be out late alone? "He's not alone. My mother's with him, and I just left my husband at a dinner party." More whoppers. Why was I lying? What did I care what the cabdriver thought? No one had answered the phone at my house, and Bonnie Osterman knew where we lived, had seen my children. My stomach and heart had exchanged places, fluttering and pounding out adrenaline-soaked panic. At the thought of Luke, milk seeped into my bra. My entire body ached to feel his soft cheeks, to touch Molly's curls. Oh God, my children.

"Okay, miss." The driver seemed, if not to approve of me, at least to accept the gravity of my plight. "Sick baby boy, here comes Mommy."

We flew through a red light at Walnut, again at Spruce. He spun onto Pine Street on what seemed to be two wheels and sped from Sixteenth all the way to Fourth Street, where he turned again. The whole ride lasted only a few minutes but seemed eternal, and when we arrived in front of my house on Monroe, I pulled a twenty out of my bag, couldn't wait for change. The driver was happy.

"Good luck with your baby boy, miss. I think he'll be fine."

But I was already hurrying up the front steps, key in hand. Holding my breath, I flung the door open and rushed inside. A lamp was on in the living room, so I headed that way, and from halfway down the hall, to my relief, I saw Anna seated in the wingback chair.

Thank God. Probably she'd been in the bathroom when I'd called. Or checking on Luke, so she couldn't get to the phone in time. Probably I'd gone crazy over nothing.

"Hi, Anna. I'm back." I tried to sound chirpy and casual. "How did your evening go? The kids okay?"

Anna said nothing as I stepped into the living room, still chattering with relief. "Did Molly like the pizza? How late did she stay up?"

But Anna still didn't answer; Anna didn't even move. And as I came closer, in the lamplight, I realized why. Anna had a purple lump the size of a baseball on the side of her head. Anna was dead.

SEVENTY-TWO

I BACKED AWAY ON WOBBLY LEGS, TRYING TO MAKE SENSE OF what I was seeing, fear pulsing, instinct overtaking reason. I didn't think, didn't hesitate.

"Molly!" The scream came from my belly, sounded deep like a roar. "Molly?"

I wheeled around, flung myself out of the room, into the hall. I raced into the dining room, my office, turning on lights, searching and finding no one. Hearing nothing but my own thundering cries. Then, somehow, I was upstairs, raging into Molly's empty room and then to Luke's and switching on the overheads to find abandoned, rumpled beds. Molly's pillows had fallen on the floor; Luke's dinosaur comforter lay alone in his crib. There was not a trace of Molly or Luke, though. They were simply, completely gone.

I couldn't stop the wailing sound, couldn't straighten up. I was bent over in physical pain, holding my belly, dropping to my knees. Bonnie Osterman had been here, had attacked Anna. The monster whose backyard had been full of tiny bones, whose freezer had been stocked with the tender limbs of infants, whose psychosis had been deemed cured by the state—Bonnie Osterman had taken my children.

I remember screaming, curled up like a fetus, rolling on the floor. Bellowing, moaning, wailing. And I remember knowing that nothing, no amount of screaming, would help. The unthinkable, unbearable, had happened, and I writhed, each breath knifelike, each body part racked with pain. I don't know how long that anguished riot continued. I knew I had to call the police about Anna, but I didn't seem able to move. I remember those moments only in flashes: lying tortured and spent on the floor of Luke's room. And then, in the stillness of his absence, I imagined I heard whimpering.

Oliver. Oliver was crying somewhere. Probably he'd gotten in the way, nipping the killer's ankles. Probably she'd shoved him into a closet. I lay, listening to him whine, and it dawned on me that I had to call the police. Get help. Maybe there was hope. Maybe the police could rescue Luke and Molly. I half-crawled, half-stumbled toward my bedroom to get the phone and call 9-1-1. But on the way, I passed the bathroom; the door was closed. Oliver was inside, scratching on the door, yipping. Without thinking, I opened the door. Oliver bolted out, jumping on me, licking my legs, but still I heard whimpering, and I looked past the door into the bathroom.

In the darkness, I saw a silhouette—Molly? She was sitting hunched on the floor beside the bathtub—thank God.

"Molly!" I flipped on the light. "Are you all right?"

Her mouth opened, but she didn't move, made no sound.

"Molly—" I rushed in and reached for her. And that was the last I remembered.

SEVENTY-THREE

SOMETHING WAS SQUEAKING AND SOMETHING WET WAS TICKLING my nose. Slowly, I realized several other things: I was cold and uncomfortable, my eyes didn't want to open, and the base of my head throbbed with pain.

The tickling continued. Okay, I told an eye. Open. It resisted, but I forced the eyelid to lift. And gazed into a dripping line of small jagged fangs. Instantly, I pushed myself up, but oops, I'd moved too fast, and I fell back down, banging onto a hard surface, slamming my head. White pain shot through my skull. But Oliver continued to slobber over me, whining and whimpering. I put a hand on his head, whispering that everything was all right. My hand was wet where I'd touched him, and I glanced at it, saw blood. Oh God. I looked at him, focusing, and gradually realized that the puppy's mouth and paws were bloody. And as I sat up, more carefully this time, I tried to remember what had happened, how I'd gotten to the bathroom floor.

A small puddle of blood pooled on the floor where my head had been. I touched the base of my skull, felt a gash. Damn. Oliver sat with his paws in the blood, panting, happy that I was on my feet. But I swayed, tottering when I tried to take a step, and my thoughts were jumbled. Then a memory bolted from my chest to my brain: the children. Molly and Luke. And I raced, bumping into the sink, then into the doorknob, moving as fast as I could to the phone. Oh God. Where were they? Had Bonnie Osterman harmed them? Was Molly frightened? Where could Bonnie have taken them? I had to hurry, had to find them before it was too late. Oliver followed me, herding me, and I tripped over him, cursing, dimly aware of a banging sound coming from downstairs. Someone was pounding on the door, ringing the bell. Maybe the police?

I half-slid, half-stumbled down the steps and made it to the door, blood dribbling down my neck. Damn. The cut was beginning to sting, and I was dizzy as I reached for the knob. But I managed to hang on to it long enough to pull it open. And to recognize the furious person standing there, demanding to come in.

SEVENTY-FOUR

"WHAT THE HELL'S GOING ON, ZOE? WHY DID YOU TAKE OFF like that?" Susan's face alternated between anger and alarm. She stepped inside and caught me just as I was fading, about to slide to the floor.

I must have passed out for a second; my next memory was of Susan saying "Good God," as she pressed a kitchen cloth against the back of my head. "I think you need stitches. What happened? Did you fall?" Under the circumstances, she seemed relatively calm. Too calm. "Where's Anna? Did she go home?"

Oh. Susan didn't know. "She's in the living room."

Susan looked confused. "Anna!" she shouted. Her voice was loud, jangling.

"No—don't shout." I began to explain. "Susan. Anna's in the wingback—"

"Why? Wait, what are you saying?" Susan cut me off. "Are you saying that Anna did this? She hit you on the head? For God sakes, why?"

I shook my head no. But the motion hurt. "Anna's dead."

Susan's mouth dropped. "What?" She got up and looked into the hall toward the living room, unable to grasp the news.

"Somebody bashed in her head. Susan—" I almost couldn't say it. "Susan." My voice became a wail. "Molly and Luke are gone."

Susan didn't move. She didn't speak. She stood frozen, her mouth a horrified oval.

"It was Bonnie Osterman. It had to be. I saw her—"

"Who?" Susan's mouth still didn't move.

"From the Institute, she's psychotic." I didn't go into detail, couldn't manage. "I saw her—"

"She's here?" Susan spun around, looking behind her.

"No, I saw her in the album. In Eli's pictures." I was gulping air, trying to express thoughts that were unthinkable. "She wanted Luke. The whole time I was pregnant, she watched me, kept asking questions about the baby. She was already planning it. Fantasizing about taking him."

"How can you be sure she—"

"Susan, there are pictures of her following us." I looked into the hallway. Where had I left the album? "Wait, I'll show you." I started to get up to find it, but Susan shoved me back onto the seat.

"Sit down. You're still bleeding. Have you called nine-one-one? We've got to get help for Anna."

"Dammit, Susan." Didn't she get it? The cut on my head—God help me, even Anna didn't matter right now. "She's going to kill my babies." My face was washed with tears.

"Oh God." Finally, Susan was grasping the situation. Her eyes darted around as if looking for answers. "Okay." She rattled off words. "Okay. First, we'll call for help. Then we'll call the Institute—they'll have records. They must know where she lives. And we have to call the police. Nick—did you call Nick?" She shoved the towel into my hand, leaving me to apply my own pressure. "Where's your phone?"

The phone? Oh, right. I'd been upstairs, about to call the police, when I'd heard Oliver whining. My cell phone was down here in my purse—but where had I put my purse? Never mind—the downstairs phone was around. Somewhere. It was portable, would be wherever the last person who'd used it had left it. Here in the kitchen. Or maybe in the living room. With Anna.

Susan was already looking in the kitchen, so holding the towel to my wound, I got to my feet, heading for the living room where Anna sat slumped in the wingback. Avoiding her, I turned into the darkness of the dining room. But before I could reach the light switch, I stumbled over something massive and fleshy. Cursing, I lost my balance and fell over it onto the floor.

Susan heard me and came running in, calling my name, turning on the lights.

At first, I was confused, not comprehending what I saw. Then, I recoiled, scuttling away from the thing I'd tripped over. It made no sense, but there beside me on the Oriental carpet, her dress stained crimson, was Bonnie Osterman, looking quite dead. Another of my kitchen knives lay bloodied beside her, and the rug was spotted with darkening red.

SEVENTY-FIVE

OLIVER JUMPED ONTO MY LEGS, WHIMPERING. I SCOOPED HIM UP and held him to my chest, more for my own comfort than his.

"It's her," I told Susan. "It's Bonnie Osterman."

Susan stared at the body, frowning. "You're sure?"

Was she serious? "Of course I'm sure." There was no question. The woman on the floor was Bonnie Osterman.

Susan helped me to my feet, into a chair. "Sit." It was a command.

I sat, realizing that Susan had indeed found the downstairs phone. She made calls, and vaguely I heard her talking, probably to the police, probably telling them where we were. But I wasn't really listening; I was talking also, out loud to myself, trying to make sense of what was happening. Because if Bonnie Osterman was here, knifed on the dining room floor, she obviously hadn't taken Molly and Luke. But if she hadn't, who had?

Obviously, I answered, it was the person who'd stabbed her. But who was that? It couldn't have been Anna; Anna was dead. But aside from Anna, who else had been here? Just my children. I tried to piece it together, to remember what I knew. I'd gone upstairs and found Oliver whimpering, and then someone had slugged me. Maybe that had been Bonnie. But then what had happened? If no one else was here but Luke and Molly, then . . . I closed my eyes, picturing the possibility. Could Molly actually have killed Bonnie? Molly was slightly built, but she was agile, quick thinking, tough. But she was only six years old. Could she actually plunge a knife into someone? I doubted it. But she'd surprised me in the past with her daring and resilience. I tried to imagine it, couldn't, told myself to stop trying. Whether Molly had stabbed Bonnie Osterman didn't matter right now. Right now, all that mattered was finding Molly and her brother. But another thought occurred to me—maybe it had been the muggers. Maybe the people looking for the jump drives had taken the children. Maybe they were going to hold the children hostage until they got what they wanted.

No. No, I told myself. That couldn't be true. They'd told Tony they were going to be back. They wouldn't kidnap children in the meantime. Would they?

Oh God. I doubled over, reeling with the pain of their absence. My fingers, my arms, my entire body physically ached for them, longed to touch their solid warmth, felt only raw, empty air. Where were they? I ought to know; I was their mother, bound to them at the heart. Maybe if I just sat still and listened, I'd feel their pulses somewhere; I could follow the beat and go to them. I sat, listening, waiting, but heard nothing, felt only the screaming panic of loss and fear.

Suddenly I couldn't stay still anymore. I was agitated, angry. I didn't think about a bleeding wound or a pounding dizziness. I got out of the chair and started pacing around Bonnie's lumpy body, thinking out loud, ranting. Where are they? I demanded to know. Maybe Molly grabbed Luke and ran off somewhere safe. But where would she take him? Where would a six-year-old go in the night, on foot, weighed down with a baby? To the park? No, it was cold out and dark, and there would be no one there to protect them. Okay, not the park. Neighbors? Our street wasn't a community; people moved in and out all the time. We didn't even know most of the people on the block. Still, she might simply have rung a bell, asking for help. But she knew better than to talk to strangers, and besides, if she had, the neighbors would have called the police, who would have been here by now; it had been a while since I'd been knocked out—long enough for cops to answer a 9-1-1 call. So no. Molly hadn't taken Luke. It had been someone else. But who?

Oh God. I was mumbling, rambling, walking in circles. I wandered into the hall and back into the dining room, where I stopped, reversed my direction and backed into the hall again. Something was different there, out of order in the hall. But what? I looked around, but it took only a second glance to figure it out: Luke's stroller was gone. Where it should have been was a bare corner beside the coatrack. Whoever had taken the baby had also taken his wheels, walked off as if going for a stroll. And then from somewhere deep in my head, I heard a voice. Who would want to take not just Molly and the baby but the stroller as well? And, in an flash, I knew. Or thought I did.

SEVENTY-SIX

I RUSHED TOWARD THE FRONT DOOR, PULLING ON MY COAT, finding my handbag underneath it.

Her jaw dropped. "Zoe, what are you doing?" She started after me.

"Wait for the police, Susan. I'll call you as soon as I know something."

She dashed between me and the door, blocking me, talking, but I only half-heard what she said. ". . . police . . . hospital . . . gash—"

Actually, it was good that she stopped me; standing there, I realized I'd better take a weapon. I opened the front closet and, standing on tiptoe, reached up to the back of the top shelf for a metal case. I unlocked it, took out one of Nick's spare guns, loaded it and stuffed it into my handbag while Susan fluttered around me in frantic protest.

"Zoe? What is that? What are you doing? You're taking a gun? What the hell's wrong with you?" She squawked, waved her arms like a ruffled hen. "Answer me, dammit. Where do you think you're going?"

"I don't have time to explain, Susan—I'll call in a few minutes. I just have to go check something out." I couldn't dawdle around explaining my theory or justifying my intentions. My gut told me to fly.

"Check out what? The police can check it—"

Susan tried to hold on to me, but I couldn't sit still and wait passively for the police. My children needed me, and even with Susan grabbing at me, even with blood trickling down the back of my neck, I managed to thrust myself out the door and down the steps.

"Zoe. Stop, damn it." She came after me, pulling my coat.

"Let go," I panted. "Susan, go back. The front door's open."

"So?"

She was right. What else could happen in there? I forced myself to stop struggling and relax. "Please, Susan. Go back and wait for the police." I met her eyes, pleading. "I'll be back in ten minutes."

"Not until you tell me where you're going."

I shook my head no; if I told her, she'd never let me go. "If I find the kids, I'll call." I tried to pull away.

She had hold of my arm and wouldn't let go. We stood at an impasse, her hands locked on me, and with each second I feared more for Molly and Luke.

"Susan." I was furious; she winced at my gaze. "They're my children. Let me go."

Shivering and frowning, she left me at the corner of Fourth Street. "Fine. Go," she scolded. "But you'd better call me in ten minutes like you said. And when you shoot your foot off, remember, I tried to stop you." And she stomped away.

SEVENTY-SEVEN

IVY'S HOUSE WAS FIVE BLOCKS SOUTH, TWO WEST. MOLLY HAD
been there dozens of times. My head hurt, but I raced ahead, al-
ternately running and jogging. Along the way, I thought about Ivy
wearing my wedding dress, raging that I didn't deserve either my
children or my fiancé, demanding that I rehire her, refusing to re-
linquish her job. She'd seemed almost delusional. As if she thought
I was out to hurt her. Or no—as if she thought I was living the life
that should have been hers.

That thought chilled me. Was Ivy really that disturbed? And
more important, had she been at the house that night? Had she,
not Bonnie, knocked me out and taken the children? Had she
killed Anna and Bonnie?

My cell phone was ringing, but I didn't stop to dig it out of my
shoulder bag. It was probably Susan, anyway, checking to see if
I'd shot anyone yet. I kept on going, one step, another, running in
slo-mo while the phone rang and my mind pounded questions.
What had Ivy done with the children? Was Molly frightened? Was
Luke hungry? Would she hurt them?

My legs weren't fast enough, and my lungs were getting raw; a
few times, I had to slow down to steady myself and catch my
breath. But I pressed on as if possessed, not stopping as I passed
Fitzwater Street. The next street, Catherine, was Ivy's. I stopped at
the corner, looking up the block, locating Ivy's door in the row of
houses. The third one on the right.

The lights were on in her living room. The blinds weren't completely shut; if I stood at the window, I could see in. Quietly, heart racing, I hurried through the shadows and stood on tiptoe, peeking through a crack in the blinds. And yes, I'd been right. Luke's stroller was folded beside the sofa. Thank God.

I let my breath out, watching the stroller as if it might dissolve into dust. But it remained there, concrete and three-dimensional, going nowhere. Suddenly, tears were gushing all over my face, and I smeared them away, realizing in the dim light that my hands were crusted with blood. Whose blood was it? Mine? Bonnie Osterman's? I didn't know. Didn't care. Luke and Molly were here, inside. I'd found them. And now I was going to get them out.

SEVENTY-EIGHT

THE PHONE WAS RINGING AGAIN; AGAIN I IGNORED IT. I NEEDED to think, plan carefully. But I lacked the patience for either. I wanted to rush up and bang on the front door, barge in and take my children, but something held me back. That voice deep in my head was whispering, warning me to be cautious; Ivy was irrational, might harm the kids if she felt threatened. So I held back and did more reconnaissance, walking back to the corner, making my way around to the back of the house.

Wrought-iron bars covered the back windows. But from the alleyway, I could easily see inside Ivy's kitchen. And there, on the other side of the bars and glass, seated at the kitchen table, was Molly. I stood for a moment, watching her, letting my heart rate slow. Feeling the tensions ease in my shoulders. Watching my Molly. Her golden curls were tangled, but she appeared unharmed. Wiping away the last of my tears, I wanted to shout her name, but I kept silent as I crept through Ivy's back gate and snuck to the window, watching my little girl stare blankly at a slab of angel food cake and cup of what was probably hot cocoa.

As I watched, Ivy walked in, holding Luke, who was crying. Actually, he was howling. Of course he was; it was past time for him to nurse. At the sight of him, my nipples predictably began to spout. I hid at the window, bodily fluids spilling from my head, eyes and breasts. Ivy danced around with Luke, talking to him, offering him a bottle. A bottle? Luke had no idea what that was, wouldn't even consider sucking on it. Molly said something, maybe that Luke would never drink from a bottle. Ivy snapped something back, a severe expression on her face. She sat at the table with Luke, trying to shove the bottle into his mouth as he pushed it away in red-faced rage. Finally, Molly scowled and jumped to her feet, hands on her hips, evidently telling Ivy what she should do with the bottle. Ivy shook her head, laughing, until Molly came over and tried to take Luke, whose face had turned purple from screaming, from Ivy's arms. Ivy stopped laughing and, in a heartbeat, stood, holding Luke with one arm, smacking Molly in the face with the other.

That was it. I yanked frantically at the bars, trying to rip them off the windows, but they didn't budge. Meantime, Ivy ranted at Molly, and I saw Molly's fists tighten. No one, to my knowledge, had ever struck my child before, and I doubted Molly would take it lightly. I half-expected her to pounce on Ivy, pounding and scratching. But she didn't. Instead, jaw clenching, eyes burning, Molly walked back to her chair and sat.

The interchange had happened fast, too fast for me to react or prevent it. But I'd had enough. I fumbled inside my purse, pushed past the gun and pulled out my cell phone. I called Susan.

"Zoe. Thank God. I've been calling you—"

"Susan, listen—"

"But it's important. You need—"

"Susan. I said listen, damn it." I told her to send the police and Nick to Ivy's house, gave her the address, and without engaging in conversation I hung up. Instantly, the phone rang: Susan, calling back. But I didn't take the call, couldn't. I was focused, preparing to move. I watched Ivy trying to settle Luke in her arms, jabbing the bottle unsuccessfully at his mouth while he roared and Molly covered her ears. And as soon as my phone stopped ringing, I made a second call.

This time, I called Ivy.

SEVENTY-NINE

I WATCHED IVY AS THE PHONE RANG. SHE GLANCED AT THE BABY, then at the door to the living room, considering whether or not to answer. Damn. She was letting it ring, not answering. I stood there, watching my infant wail and my daughter fight tears, waited a couple of never-ending minutes and called again. By now, Ivy had given up on the bottle and, when the phone rang, she seemed relieved to have a reason to get out of the room. As soon as she left, I rapped on the window to get Molly's attention.

Molly looked up, not moving, staring at the window. Then, glancing over her shoulder, she scampered over, looking elated, spilling tears.

"Hello, Ivy. It's Zoe." That's all I said when Ivy answered the phone.

There was a pause. "What do you want?"

"What do you think you're doing, Ivy?"

"Nothing. I didn't do it. It wasn't me." Luke's screams almost drowned out her voice.

"Don't lie to me, Ivy. I can hear Luke screaming. I know he's there."

Molly was making hand signals, pointing toward the door, showing me where Ivy was. Her cheek was red where she'd been hit. I gestured back to her, pointing to the back door, indicating that she should unlock it.

"No, I mean Anna. It wasn't me who killed her—it was an old

fat broad. Anna was already dead. I rescued the children. I saved them."

I thought of Bonnie Osterman and realized that, in fact, maybe Ivy had. "That's why I'm calling, Ivy. I'm coming to get the kids."

"What?"

"Luke's hungry. He needs to nurse." He was becoming hoarse from yelling. Molly was struggling with the locks.

"But I rescued them, not you. You left them there. That woman came in and she killed Anna, and if I hadn't stopped her, she'd have kidnapped them. You have no idea what went on."

"Thank you for saving them, Ivy." I tried to keep her talking, to give Molly time. "But now, Luke's hungry. So I'm going to come and get him and his sister."

"No. I can take care of them. I know what TV shows Molly likes and what to do when Luke's got a bellyache. We don't need you to come."

If she hung up, she'd find Molly at the door. "Ivy, tell me how you saved them."

It was hard to hear her through Luke's wails. "Who was she? She called them tender morsels. She said she wanted to eat them up. I thought she was joking, but when Anna tried to stop her, the old woman struck her. I grabbed them and we ran. I saved them. They need to stay with me now."

Molly was still wrestling with the bolts. I told myself not to argue, just keep Ivy talking.

"What were you doing there?"

"What are you talking about?"

"Tonight. What were you doing in my house?" I heard a loud metallic click. Yes. Molly had a bolt undone, but the door still didn't open. How many locks were there?

"You know what? That's not your business, not anymore. Bottom line: I deserve them. Besides, Molly's adopted. You're not even her real mother—"

"Yes, I am." Why was I defending myself? Ivy was a lunatic. "I'm her mother, and I'm Luke's mother, too—"

"No, you're not—"

Just then, I heard another click. Thank God—Molly had unlocked the second bolt. I tried to open the door, but it wouldn't budge, still locked. I gestured to Molly to turn the knob.

"—Not anymore, you're not. You had your chance. Back off, Zoe. Remember what happened to that fat lady. She tried to take them, too, and I stopped her. I can stop you, too. Leave us alone or you'll be sorry."

She slammed the phone down just as Molly turned the knob, and she came back into the kitchen exactly as Molly opened the door. Ivy's face contorted as she realized what was happening. With Luke dangling from her arm, she bellowed, "Nooo!" and leapt forward to slam the door. And she would have, except that I'd also leapt, and my leg was jammed in the way.

EIGHTY

LIGHTNING SHOT FROM MY SHIN TO MY BRAIN, AND I YELLED IN pain. Molly shouted, Ivy hollered and Luke raged. The chorus was deafening, but I kept pushing, leaning against the door until I wriggled my way in, watching my bag slip off my shoulder in the struggle. Damn, I thought. The gun—the gun was in there. But I couldn't stop. As soon as I made it into the house, Ivy whirled around and grabbed a cleaver off her counter. Clutching Luke in one arm, she swung at me with the other; I felt the whoosh of air passing my face and ducked almost too late. Molly, meantime, sprang to action, attacking Ivy from behind, smacking her repeatedly with a giant bottle of orange soda. Ivy spun around to shove Molly away, but Molly spun with her, staying behind her and slapping, distracting Ivy long enough for me to reach for Luke, who'd spotted me, smelling dinner. Luke practically dove for me as I grabbed him from Ivy, and I pressed him against me, but I couldn't stop to exult in his soft touch because Ivy, still holding the cleaver, had turned on Molly, had shoved her against the wall. Molly stood still, bug-eyed and cornered, as Ivy scolded her for disobeying.

The gun, I remembered. Get the gun. While Ivy chided Molly, I stepped back to the door where my bag had fallen, half in, half out of the house. I turned, stooping, holding on to Luke while I reached for the strap.

"Mom!"

Molly's cry was ear piercing and primal; I didn't turn, didn't stop to look. I simply reacted; ducking and dodging, I took a dive to the right, sheltering Luke with my body. Ivy, propelled by her own momentum, kept flying forward, hitting the door with her cleaver raised and ready to strike. Ivy crashed into the paneling, the cleaver firmly wedged in the wood of the open door. Luke clung to me, sucking his fist, and Molly ran over and threw her arms around me.

"Molls." I reached for her with my free arm and, keeping my eyes on Ivy, I leaned forward, kissing Molly's head again and again. "Are you okay?" I tried to balance well enough to stand so we could get the hell out of there.

Molly nodded yes, but her eyes looked wide and haunted. "You're all bloody."

"I'm okay." I left my bag where it was and began to usher her out of the kitchen so we could run out the front door.

"There's blood all over your back."

"I know, but I'm all right."

She wasn't listening anymore, though. She looked back at the door and her eyes widened; I turned to see Ivy righting herself, freeing the cleaver.

"Mom—let's go!" Molly grabbed my hand.

"Go? I don't think so." The cleaver in her hand again, Ivy walked toward us, swiftly, deliberately, and swiftly, awkwardly, Molly and I backed away.

"Molly, take off. Run."

She didn't move. "No, Mom—"

"Molly, go on—run for help."

But Molly stayed beside me, clinging to my hand. We backed up, rapidly, until we bumped into a counter. No, not a counter. A stove. I edged alongside it, not sure what to do. Oh God. Ivy's eyes were glowing, burning. She grinned, but her mouth formed a grimace.

"Molly and Luke belong with me. They'll be better off." She stepped forward.

"You're crazy, Ivy." Molly belted it. "You're not my mother."

Ivy was undaunted. "No? Well, neither is she."

"Yes, she is, too."

As they argued about whether or not I was the children's mother, I realized that, stupidly, I'd backed us into a corner; we couldn't move any farther away. Ivy, apparently tired of debating, had the cleaver raised and ready to swing. I turned away, shielding Molly and Luke with my body, preparing for a hacking blow. Nick's face flashed to mind; I pictured him standing not at our wedding but at my funeral, beside the coffin with the kids. And then the box I was seeing wasn't a coffin anymore; it was a carton of instant hot cocoa. And beside it was a kettle, steaming.

EIGHTY-ONE

I SHOVED LUKE INTO MOLLY'S ARMS AND YELLED, "RUN!"

She grabbed him like a wide receiver catching a pass and took off toward the living room while I grabbed the kettle and lunged in the opposite direction. The commotion confused Ivy only momentarily; her eyes darted from Luke and Molly back to me, and she lunged at me, her cleaver held high. It was impossible to say which happened next, the splash of boiling water or the crash of the metal against the stove. But when I opened my eyes again, I saw Ivy writhing, contorted with pain, steam rising from the sizzling skin of her arms, chest and neck.

Oh God. I watched her, stunned, appalled. What had I done? I'd poached her. Okay, okay, I told myself. Calm down and think. What was first aid for third-degree burns? I couldn't remember. Immersion in tepid water was for minor burns. But for major ones were you supposed to soak the wound or leave it dry? I couldn't remember. Were you supposed to wrap it? Leave it exposed? I wasn't sure; my mind wasn't working, seemed disconnected. I took in images, snippets of sound. Ivy was shrieking and Luke was crying in the next room. Why could I still hear him? Hadn't Molly taken him outside yet?

"Moll—" I stopped calling her mid-syllable, not wanting her to come back and see Ivy in agony. Molly had been traumatized enough that night. Aside from her babysitter swinging a cleaver at us, Molly might have seen Anna dead in the wingback. And a stranger, Bonnie Osterman, lying in the dining room.

"Molly." I revised my message, hoping she'd hear me over Luke's cries and Ivy's moans. "Stay in the living room. I'll be right there—"

Suddenly, Ivy's shrieks crescendoed, became a continuous wail. Like a siren. Which reminded me: Where were the other sirens? What had happened to the police? I'd given Susan the address; hadn't she told them to come? Call, I told myself. Make sure they're on the way. Tell them we need an ambulance.

"Ivy." I eyed her festering, reddening skin. "I'm calling for help. They'll take you to the hospital."

She didn't seem to hear me, didn't respond, just kept wailing, rocking from side to side.

My cell phone was in my bag near the door. I grabbed the bag and headed for the living room to gather up the children and wait for the police. Maybe I'd even manage to feed Luke in the meantime. I reached into my bag as I walked, found my cell phone and began to push the buttons, 9 first. But I missed the 1, hit the 4. My fingers were trembling; I had to start over. I was about to punch the 9 again when I got to the living room and looked up to see Molly curled onto the sofa, wide-eyed, tightly gripping Luke, who was still screaming.

Just a few arm's-lengths away, her blood-soaked bodice peeking out from her open wool coat, stood Bonnie Osterman. And she was smiling.

EIGHTY-TWO

"WHAT'S YOUR NAME, SWEETHEART?" HER VOICE WAS SOFTER, higher pitched, than I remembered.

Molly remained silent, tightening her hold on Luke, eyes afire.

"It's okay. You can talk to me. I'm not a stranger. Your mother knows me, darling. My name's Bonnie."

Apparently, they hadn't seen me; they remained focused on each other, indifferent to the wails of pain emanating from the kitchen.

"My goodness, you're very shy, aren't you?" Bonnie continued, her tone sweet, almost hypnotic, and she kept smiling, holding her hands behind her back. "Well, you're cute, and you have a cute little baby brother."

Molly tightened her grip. "My mom's right in there—" She nodded at the kitchen door. Bonnie's gaze moved from Molly to the doorway. When Bonnie saw me there, she didn't budge and her smile didn't waver. If anything, her grin widened pleasantly.

"Well, well. Here she is."

"Back away from them, Bonnie." I strode into the room, taking a stand directly beside Molly. Luke's and Ivy's wails continued. We had to shout to be heard.

"My, my, Zoe. You look dreadful. Look at you. You've got— wait, is that blood all over you?"

"What the hell, Bonnie?" I was startled to see her; I'd been sure she was dead.

"You thought I was dead, didn't you? I got hurt but not bad. Just a little scratch. I wasn't dead, though. I lay on your floor and kept very very still. I was faking." Her smile was coy, her hands behind her back as she took a step closer. "Your children are beautiful."

"Back off, Bonnie."

She ignored me, edging closer to us, both hands still hidden. What was she hiding?

"I didn't let her in, Mom." Molly was worried I'd be angry. "I was going outside with Luke like you said, but she was on the porch and she tried to grab me, so I ran back inside—"

"That was good thinking, Mollybear. You did the right thing." I kept my eyes on Bonnie, trying to keep her talking, trying to stall. Where the hell were the police? "Have a seat, Bonnie. Let's catch up."

"Thank you, but no." She still smiled. "I'm quite a mess in this dress, and I really must change my clothes. We should be going."

"But you've bled a lot; maybe you need a doctor."

"No, but thank you anyway. Most of the mess isn't from me; it actually came from that gaudy red-haired creature—"

"Anna. Her name is Anna."

"Mom? Wait—did something happen to Anna?" Apparently, Molly hadn't seen Anna's smashed head. At least she'd been spared that.

"Don't worry, Molls." I didn't take my eyes off Bonnie. "Anna's okay."

"Don't you believe it, hon. I got her good. She came at me, see. Charged me like a rabid dog. Ran right at me, her head like a slow pitch flying right into my bat. Well, it was a poker, but it could have been a bat. I could hear her skull crunch. I had no choice, really." Bonnie sucked her teeth, as if removing a piece of meat stuck in her molar.

"Mom, she killed Anna?" Molly's voice was urgent.

"Don't worry, Molls."

"Let me tell you, the momentum of her running sent her head right into my swing. She looked small, but she was solid. It was tough getting her off me. I'm not young anymore, you know. But I shoved her off me and she actually landed on a chair, comfy as pie. But see this? She bled, ruined my dress." She glanced down at the crimson stains but kept her hands concealed behind her. "I'll probably have to burn it—"

"Mom? Who is this person?" Holding on to Luke, Molly moved to the edge of the sofa, ready to bolt.

"Oh, your mom and I, we go back years." Bonnie gave Molly a grandmotherly nod. "How many, Zoe? Six? Twenty? I can't recall. They kept me there so long. Days, years. Time meant nothing." She took another tiny step forward.

"Bonnie, listen to me. Keep your distance." I was exhausted, bloody. I didn't sound scary even to myself. "Don't go one step closer to my kids."

"Why, Zoe? What are you worried about? Haven't you heard? I'm cured." She paused, her smile deflating a tad, as if her feelings were hurt. "Completely rehabilitated. They said so when they let me out."

"Out of where?" Molly wanted to know.

"The asylum, sweetheart—"

"Bonnie was a patient in the Institute."

"—I was an inmate at the zoo where your mother was one of the keepers. But you know, Zoe, it wasn't the same after you left to give birth. No more finger painting—no more playing with clay."

"How did you find us?"

"Find you?"

"Here. How did you know we were here?"

She took the tiniest of steps closer. Obviously, she had a weapon behind her back. Obviously, she intended to use it. Keep talking, I told myself. The police were on the way. They had to be.

"I followed you. Isn't that obvious?" She moved forward another inch, her sweet smile still shining.

"Bonnie, I mean it. Do not take another step."

She kept her eyes on Luke, but she didn't move. "You left to get the children, so I came with you for the same reason."

Oh God. Susan. How had Bonnie gotten past Susan? Maybe there was a reason the police hadn't arrived. "Bonnie, did you hurt my friend?"

"Who, Mom? Who did she hurt?" Molly looked terrified. In the kitchen, Ivy let out a low, whalelike moan.

But Bonnie ignored my question, intent on asking her own. "Tell me, Zoe. How was it, giving birth? Did your water break first? And the labor—was it long? How bad did it hurt? Did you need drugs or did you tough it out? I want to hear all—"

"I've called the police, Bonnie," I lied, but Susan might have, if Bonnie hadn't hurt her. "They'll be here any second."

"Oh please, Zoe dear. That's a crock—"

Inside my bag, my cell phone rang. For a moment, my eyes met Bonnie's and neither of us moved. Then, as if a starting gun had fired, I dug my hand into the bag and Bonnie swung her hand forward. As Molly screamed, I saw a metallic flicker, recognizing the elegant blade of another of my Cutco carving knives. Good God. My entire set was being put to use. My hand rooted around in my bag, searching, and my phone kept ringing.

"Drop the bag." Bonnie held the knife back, ready to plunge.

"Okay."

But I hesitated, finding what I'd been feeling for, wrapping my hand around it. As I did so, Bonnie made her move, reaching past me, grabbing Molly's shoulder. Molly kicked her and tried to squirm away without dropping her still-bellowing brother. The knife arced high, the blade reflecting a sinister glint as Bonnie's raised arm extended to its fullest reach. But before she could plunge it downward, I held up my bag and reflexively held my breath. The sound of Nick's gun was deafening, time stopping. Luke's screams, Molly's wriggling, came to a sudden halt. Bonnie's arm froze; the knife seemed to hang mid-air, and then, as blood spouted from her right eye, her arm and the rest of her body collapsed, crashing heavily to the floor.

EIGHTY-THREE

THE POLICE AND AMBULANCE ARRIVED A FEW MOMENTS LATER, Susan right behind them. By then, Luke was calmly nursing and Molly snuggling quietly against me, her head resting on my shoulder. Bonnie Osterman lay at our feet under a coat I'd pulled out of Ivy's closet. Ivy groaned quietly as the EMTs carried her off on a gurney, and medics examined the gash on the back of my skull, determining that the cut was superficial and that the bleeding had stopped. I refused to go to the hospital, wanting nothing except to go home. A detective hammered me with questions and I explained what had happened, sounding oddly defensive about burning Ivy and shooting Bonnie, and when Susan informed my interrogator that she was my attorney, she seemed to polarize the situation even more.

I lost track of time; events swirled around me. I remember that Luke finished nursing and slept and a while later, reeking of booze and cheap perfume, Nick and his brothers finally rushed in with a gaggle of Nick's cop pals. Suddenly, it was a party, a police reunion, a homicide investigation turned festive, and after I answered a few more brief questions, we went home, leaving Bonnie Osterman's body and Molly's unfinished cup of hot cocoa behind.

Nick held his questions, maybe because he was half-blitzed. But that was okay; I didn't want to discuss everything in front of Molly. I worried how the events of the night would affect her, and I watched her, noting her paleness, the dark circles beneath her sleepy eyes.

"You okay?" I whispered to her in the car.

She nodded, wordless, her head pressed against me.

When we got home, we realized that, due to the abduction of the children and the attack on Anna, our entire downstairs except the kitchen had been taped off as a crime scene. Sam wanted us all to stay at the Four Seasons; after all, the wedding was going to be there and we'd have to go there anyway. But I didn't want to rush around in frenzied packing; I wanted to keep life as normal and calm as possible for Molly's sake. She'd been through enough, and it was already after 2:00 A.M. The last thing she needed was to be kept awake longer, grabbing clothes and shipping off to a hotel. No, Tony would take his tuxedo and the jump drives and go to the Four Seasons to stay in Sam's suite, since the sofa he slept on was off-limits, but we were going to stay at home.

Susan helped, changing Luke into fresh diapers and pajamas, giving me time with Molly. I stayed with her as she brushed her teeth and washed up. I helped her into a fresh nightgown, fluffed her pillows and tucked her in, sitting beside her on the bed.

"You were very brave tonight, Molls."

She nodded, pleased, and yawned.

"And don't worry; Ivy's going to be okay." Ivy had been her sitter for half a year; I assumed Molly would be worried about her.

"No, she's not, Mom. Ivy's nuts." Molly said it simply, as if she wondered why I hadn't noticed such an obvious, uncomplicated fact.

"It's sad." I didn't know what else to say.

"So what did you do to her?"

I hesitated, remembering that Molly didn't know—she'd taken off with Luke.

"I thought she was going to hurt us." She laughed, too high, too shrill. Why was she laughing? "What did you do, throw the kettle at her?"

Oh my. Once again, Molly's thinking surprised me. But her

laughter—was it a bit hysterical? Or just a much-needed release? I leaned down, kissed her forehead. "How would you get an idea like that?"

She shrugged. "It's what I would have done."

Oh my. "You're a smart girl, Molly Hayes."

She yawned again. "Do you really know that other lady? Was she really from your job?"

I nodded, holding Molly. "She's very sick."

"No kidding."

No kidding? Sarcasm from a six-year-old? "But you're safe now. And I meant what I said. Tonight you were very brave."

She nodded, thinking. How would she process the terrible events she'd witnessed? How would they affect her long-term? In her short life, she'd seen far too much violence but had somehow managed to adjust. Now, she was up later than she'd ever been, and her eyelids were heavy, her small body demanding rest, drifting off to sleep. I'd have to wait; only time would tell how she was coping. Again, I leaned over and kissed her good night, whispering that I loved her more than I could say. Then I started for the door.

"Mom?"

"Yes?"

"What if I drop the basket?"

If she what?

"Or what if I trip?"

It took me a second to grasp what she meant. But then I got it: Molly was worrying but not about being kidnapped or attacked by a murderous lunatic—she was worried about being a flower girl. How amazingly childlike and sweet. Except, suddenly, my heart and stomach switched positions, churning and pulsing, and air got stuck, clogged my throat. Oh God. The wedding—it was the next day. Or no. By now, it was nearly three. The wedding was today.

"Or what if I do the step wrong?" She'd been listing the possible things that could go wrong. Mistakes she might make.

"You'll be fine, Molly. No matter what, you'll be the best flower girl ever." I went back and smoothed her curls, but her eyes were already closed, and she seemed to have fallen asleep. I paused, watching her even breathing before I tiptoed away.

"Mom?"

I stopped at the door, listening.

"You were brave tonight, too."

EIGHTY-FOUR

APPARENTLY, NICK HAD BEEN WAITING FOR ME IN THE BEDROOM; the lamp was on and he was sitting up, but he was sound asleep, snoring. God knew how much he'd imbibed at the bachelor party, but it must have been significant. Normally, Nick would be unable to rest until he'd found out every detail of what had happened in a killing, let alone a killing involving his family, let alone a killing committed by his future bride. I sat beside him, listening to the soft rumble of his snores, considered waking him up, decided not to. I couldn't. His face was too relaxed, the purple, jagged scar almost invisible in the shadows. Instead, I watched him, comforted by his steady, noisy breathing. In less than twenty-four hours, this man would be my husband. Husband? I repeated it to myself, trying to understand its definition. But my mind was dull, my emotions numb, my head sore, my body drained. The word seemed to be just a couple of syllables with meaning I couldn't fathom.

I showered. I stood under hot clean water, soaping myself, scrubbing away clotted crusted blood, cleaning away the recoil, the smell, the ear-shattering blast of the gun. Rinsing away the sight of an eye socket spouting red, the agonized shimmy of a woman scalded. I washed, lathered, shampooed, rinsed and repeated the cycle until the water got cold. Then, beyond exhausted, I wrapped myself in my soft terry cloth robe and returned to the bedroom.

Nick still slept. Damn it. Why was he sleeping? How could he sleep after everything that had happened? And then I realized that I didn't actually know everything that had happened. The bachelor party might have been more exhausting than I wanted to know. Naked women danced into my head, slithering over, under, around and onto Nick as Sam and a battalion of men cheered and hooted. Okay, now I was pissed. I was out rescuing our children, fighting for my life and for theirs, while Nick, homicide detective extraordinaire, fiancé and father, buried his face in bare bosoms and his thighs in, well, I didn't want to think of what. I was furious.

"Nick—wake up." I shook him.

His eyelids popped open, then dropped again.

"Nick." I shook him harder.

Again, the eyelids lifted. "What?" His eyes drifted, found me. Half his mouth lifted into a half smile, delighted to see me. "Zoe?" He reached for me, arranging himself on his pillows. "Zoe. C'mere."

He pulled me to him, but I resisted. He opened an eye, confused for a moment. "What?"

"I need to talk to you."

He nodded. "Wuzzup. M'lissnin." He closed his eyes, already snoring. I'd never seen him this way.

I shook him again. "Nick."

"Pudem enyupokit." I think that's what he said.

"Put them in my pocket?"

"Notchoo. Tony."

It was no use. Nick was unreachable. I lay down, put my head on his chest, letting my tears dribble onto his skin. "Nick, I really need to talk to you."

"Sleep." His voice was content, like a sigh. "Sokay, beyokay." He kissed my head, his words blurred; Nick was only half-awake, and that half was in the bag.

EIGHTY-FIVE

EXHAUSTED, I DOZED OFF AND ON, BUT I COULDN'T REALLY sleep, unable to recover from the aching fear I'd felt for the children. I got up to check on Molly and Luke, wandering from one room to the other, and when Eli showed up a little before five I was wide awake in the rocker in Luke's room. This time, I wasn't surprised to see Eli. I didn't think anything could surprise me anymore. Instead, when I looked up to see him standing in the doorway, I simply got up and gave him a hug.

"Coffee?"

He nodded. "That would be great."

Together, silently, we went downstairs. While the coffee brewed, I explained the yellow tape and the events of the night. I told him about the rehearsal dinner and how I'd spotted Bonnie Osterman in his photograph, how his picture had saved the children's lives.

"If I hadn't seen her face there, I wouldn't have hurried home and, instead of playing dead, she'd have gone after Ivy and taken the kids."

Eli listened without interrupting. I told him all about Anna's murder, Ivy clunking me on the head. I talked about the kidnapping, burning, knife wielding and shooting, and when I got to the part about Nick being sound asleep, Eli set his mug of coffee down and reached out, gathering me in muscled arms. He didn't say anything. He just held me. And he kept on holding me until I stopped shaking.

EIGHTY-SIX

It was awkward when he released me. I'd felt his heart beating, had learned his scent. Standing beside him, I felt chilled and bare, and I averted my eyes. He watched me, though, as if waiting for me to signal what would come next. Stop it, I told myself. This man is Nick's brother. The attraction you feel is for Nick, and Eli looks exactly like him except younger. Which means that you are, by the way, more than a decade older. Still, Eli's eyes pulled at me, and I didn't dare look at him, his square jaw, his wide—very wide—shoulders. Good Lord. What was happening to me? My wedding was today. To Eli's brother. And I'd just been through a night of hell. How could I feel steamy attraction after a night of death and fear? Especially for Nick's baby brother?

It was nothing, I told myself. I was in shock, that was all, and Eli was comforting me. And I needed to change the subject before mentally pursuing the subject of Eli's rippling shoulders or tight torso any further. He didn't speak, just watched me. Waiting.

"How come they call you a spy?" I clutched my coffee mug, wandered to the steps and sat.

He followed me, chuckling. "They still do?"

I nodded. "Or secret agent. Even an assassin. They say nobody knows what you really do."

Eli shook his head; his smile seemed forlorn. "Those guys."

I sipped coffee, watching his eyes. I couldn't read them.

"It's just a game. They know what I do. I'm a photographer."

"They say that's just your cover story—"

"Because they never could accept that I'm who I am. I'm shy. I've always been shy. They take that as secrecy; they assume I'm hiding something. But I'm just—I don't know. I'm what you see. I live on the sidelines, observing. I guess that's why I take pictures. The camera gives me an excuse to keep apart."

To keep apart? On the sidelines? I didn't buy it. The man was too compelling, too imposing. Too gorgeous. There was no way people wouldn't notice him standing on the sidelines and pull him in. "Even as a kid?"

He shrugged, twinkling. "I don't know."

"They tell stories about you. Stuff you did. You didn't sound all that shy."

He didn't answer. We sat quietly, comfortably. In a little while, the sun would be up. Luke would want to nurse. But for now, we sprawled on the steps, Eli and I, holding coffee mugs, our backs leaning against the walls, facing each other, oddly intimate, silent.

"My unit was ambushed." His voice was hushed, almost a whisper.

I waited, not sure how to respond.

"Did you know I was a Ranger? In Afghanistan?"

"Yes."

"Most of the guys were killed. Nick, Sam, Tony, our parents, everybody thought I was dead, too, because they couldn't find me. But I wasn't there. I'd been sent ahead, secretly, to do recon and take pictures. While I was away, my buddies—everyone got blown up."

I watched him. "Eli. I'm so sorry."

"Like I said, for a while everybody here thought I was dead, too. I had a girlfriend then. When I came home on leave a few months before the ambush, she got pregnant." He shook his head. "Nobody knew. She didn't even tell me for a while. But when she thought I was dead, she had an abortion." He waited for me to respond.

"I'm sorry." I didn't know what else to say.

"Imagine. A baby like Luke. And she just got rid of him like—"

"Eli. She thought you were dead. She must have been devastated. I'm sure she didn't know—"

"She killed my kid." His eyes were steely, his jaw set. A warrior. "Whatever." And, in a breath, his face relaxed again. "It's history. Thing is, she died, too."

What? "What happened?"

He shrugged. "Car crash. Not long after I got back."

Oh my God. "Eli. How awful for you."

"Whatever." Another tough-guy shrug. "What goes around comes around."

Wait. Did he mean that his girlfriend had deserved to die? I touched his arm, rejecting that idea, telling myself that he'd had nothing to do with the "accident." What was the matter with me? Not every death was a murder. "You've been through a lot. I'm sorry."

"Nick's the only one who knows about the baby. I never told anyone else. Just him and, now, you."

"I'm glad you did." I met his eyes, saw something burning there. An expectation? A threat? I looked away.

"Well, you're going to be my sister now. Family. So, we can turn to each other."

"I've never had a brother before. I was an only child."

He grinned. "Really? And suddenly you have three brothers, none of us easy."

Upstairs, Luke whimpered. Waking up, hungry again.

"You guys aren't so bad."

Eli's eyes laughed, beaming a message impossible to read. "Oh, you have no idea."

I excused myself to get Luke. A minute later, I came back with the baby, but no surprise, once again Eli had gone, faded into the early-morning light.

EIGHTY-SEVEN

WITH ANNA OUR WEDDING PLANNER LYING IN THE MORGUE, THE big day did not go as planned. Most of the house was a crime scene, I had a cut in the back of my head, Nick was hungover, Molly seemed to have developed a cold, and Susan arrived at first light, fluttering, hovering and offering endless commentary and items borrowed and blue. Susan was nervous, worrying her hands and pacing, but she poured me yet more decaf and got me moving. Without her, I'd have forgotten my hair appointment, never would have remembered about my scheduled makeup, pedicure or manicure. Like a drill sergeant, Susan led me through the day, imitating Anna in her officiousness, herding our straggling wedding party toward the evening.

In fact, by 9:00 A.M., Susan had gathered a staff of my friends to help her. She delegated the catering, flowers and hotel setup to Karen and Davinder. She assigned Tim the tasks of getting my father dressed and delivered to the ceremony. She ordered Nick, once he'd slept off the effects of his party, to focus not on the murders but on his bride and to take care of Molly and Luke because their mother wouldn't be available all day. And she hustled me into the shower, reminding me that I should bathe early because, later, I wouldn't want to ruin my hair. Wow. How could she think ahead like that? How could she focus on my hair? I obeyed. But in the shower, the water didn't drown out Ivy's agonized moans; it didn't wash away Bonnie's lethal sweet smile. The water poured over my head, but nothing could cleanse the guilt I felt about Anna. Everything we did, every preparation or errand, reminded me that she was gone and that her death was my fault. If I hadn't asked her to babysit, she'd still be alive, pestering florists and bothering chefs. I kept imagining the fatal encounter. Had Anna been afraid, anticipating the knife? Or had she been fooled, seeing Bonnie as a kind and grandmotherly soul? Again, I saw Anna seated in the wingback, her empty gaze staring at air. I closed my eyes, letting the hot water run. I could take shower after shower all day; nothing could make my trembling or my sorrow go away.

"Get a move on, Zoe," Susan called through the bathroom door. "You're going to be late. My appointments are the same times as yours, and you'll make me late, too."

There was no room in Susan's voice for debate. I had to get out of the shower. Somehow I dried off and pulled on a sweat suit. Susan stood at the bathroom door, waiting while I peeked into Molly's room; she was still asleep. Susan went with me to peek in on Luke. In his crib, he held his toes, gazing happily at his musical mobile. I started for my bedroom to find Nick; we still hadn't had a chance to talk about what had happened the night before. I wanted to connect with him. I was shaken. In fact, I was shaking.

"What are you doing?" Susan stopped me at the bedroom door.

"Why do you need to know?" She was in my way.

"Are you going to see Nick? Because you can't, not today." She blocked my way.

What? "Susan, move."

She wouldn't. "Trust me. It's your wedding day. A bride and groom cannot see each other on their wedding day."

"Who says?"

"It's common knowledge. It's a rule just like the borrowed and blue rule. Don't go in there. You can't see him."

"Susan—it's too late. We slept in the same bed."

"That doesn't count as today. That counts as yesterday."

I started for the door. "I have to talk to him."

"Whatever you have to say can wait."

"It's about last night—"

"Listen to me, Zoe." Susan's voice was firm, her hands on my arms. "I understand that you're freaked out about Anna. So am I. And I know about last night. I know you shot that patient of yours—"

"I killed her."

Susan nodded. "Fine, so you killed her. But there will be plenty of time to deal with that. Tomorrow and the next day and the day after that. But not today. Today, you are getting married. And even though it sounds superficial and selfish, today you are not going to even try to deal with anything else. This is your day and Nick's. It's going to be a day you'll remember forever. And you don't want to spoil it by breaking the rules."

Was she crazy? "Susan. I killed a woman last night. I also hurt Ivy pretty bad. I need to find out if I have to see the police today. I need to talk to Nick—"

"I'll talk to him. I'll tell you what he says. But you are not going to lay eyes on that man. Not until the wedding. It's bad luck."

"That's ridiculous. It's a superstition—"

"And you're going to risk it? The way your life's been going?"

There was no point arguing; Susan was adamant. And the truth was, she was right. The way my life had been going, I didn't want to risk a thing.

EIGHTY-EIGHT

THE PUPPY SCHOOL TRAINER CAME FOR OLIVER AT FOUR TO board him for the weekend. He went with her joyfully, as if she were his true owner. While I waited for her, I called the hospital again to check on Bryce, and I almost keeled over when he answered the phone himself. At the sound of his voice, I was instantly in tears, in danger of ruining my makeup. He couldn't talk much, but he let me know he'd awakened the day before and he had no memory of the accident. Unaware of what had happened, he still wanted to warn me about Bonnie Osterman. I explained that there was no danger, that she'd been found, but for now I spared him the details that she had been the driver who'd run him down and that I had shot her. Promising to visit him in a day or two, I got off the phone relieved; Bryce was going to recover. Maybe it was a sign that life would be normal again.

The limo came to pick up the bridal party at four thirty. It was silver and took up half the block. The driver rang the doorbell and waited in the foyer, and for some reason, I didn't want him in my house. Get over it, I told myself. He was not going to kidnap the children; he was merely there to drive us to the hotel. Still, his presence made me uneasy. Why? Maybe it was that his uniform was too big for him. Or that his hair, beneath his driver's hat, was kind of long and scruffy. But bad fashion wasn't illegal. The fact was I'd killed a former patient the night before and I hadn't stopped spinning since Agent Harris had died. The problem wasn't the driver; it was me.

Susan gathered up all the garment bags containing the dresses. And Molly skipped down the steps, her blond hair bouncing in perfectly formed ringlets. The limo driver stared into the house, as if trying to see past the yellow tape. It's normal, I told myself. He's curious, doesn't usually pick people up at crime scenes. I showed him what I needed him to help us with: my overnight bag, the bag of our shoes, the diaper bag, Molly's book bag stuffed with whatever miscellany she'd packed in it. Finally, I went to get Luke. When I came downstairs, I stopped halfway; the limo driver wasn't at the door. He had stepped farther into the house, had moved into the hall and stood at the yellow tape, trying to see what lay beyond. He turned when he felt me watching him, and I noticed, beneath his professional uniform, he was wearing blue and white sneakers. Odd, I thought. Maybe his feet hurt in other shoes. Maybe he had bunions.

He smiled, revealing shiny white teeth. "Need help, ma'am?"

I shook my head no. No, I didn't need help. I rushed down the last few steps and out of the house, leaving behind the yellow tape and the scene of two murders in one week. The limo driver helped Luke and me into the car where Molly and Susan were waiting.

"Look, Mom—there's a TV. And snacks. And a refrigerator." Molly already had helped herself to a bottle of cranberry juice and a bag of popcorn.

As Luke and I got comfortable, she fiddled with the remote, trying to pick a program.

"Ready, Zoe?" Suddenly, there was a pop; I jumped, ready to bolt before realizing that Susan had opened a bottle of champagne. Foam spilled over the top onto the leather seat as she reached for two glasses. "Oops. A little bubbly for the bride?" She poured.

I rearranged Luke on my lap. "Susan, I'm nursing." What was going on? She knew I couldn't drink alcohol.

"Right." She slurped up a glass. "But Luke deserves to celebrate, too. One glass won't hurt."

"Mom, look. Willie Wonka's on."

"Great, Molls."

Actually, I ached for a drink. For several. "I'll pass." I glanced through the partition and saw the driver's eyes reflected in his rearview mirror, watching us.

"Everything okay, ladies?" His voice came over a microphone.

"Fine. We're fine, thank you," Susan sang, and slugged her drink.

"Where is the rest of your wedding party? Are they taking a separate car?"

Now he was chatting with us.

"They're at the hotel already. We have a couple of suites."

"Got a big crowd coming?"

Again, Susan answered. They conversed, but for the rest of the ride to the hotel I didn't say a word. I merely tried to stay calm. Molly munched, raptly watching the television. Luke slept. And Susan chattered and chattered with the driver like a blissful canary, putting away almost half a bottle of champagne.

EIGHTY-NINE

TONY'S COMPLEXION WAS A PALE WAXY GREEN WHEN HE MET US at the main entrance to the Four Seasons. While the limo driver unloaded our bags, I took Tony aside.

"Well." He glanced around. "This is it."

I wasn't sure if he meant the wedding or the day the thugs were going to come for the jump drives.

"Any sign of anybody yet?"

Instinctively, he touched his pockets, feeling for the jump drives with trembling fingers. "Nothing. I've been hanging around the lobby and the bar all day. Nobody even asked me what time it was. I'm thinking they may suspect something's up. They might not come."

I looked around the lobby, scanning strangers, looking for people who might want jump drives. An elegant middle-aged couple occupied a sofa, sharing a magazine and pair of reading glasses. A man in expensive pinstripes paced, checking his watch, looking out at the carport. Nobody looked suspicious. Our limo driver had finished unloading and hung around near the door. Oh dear—was I supposed to tip him? No, of course not. He wasn't a cabdriver. He'd get paid in full for the night at the end of the evening. Lord, I missed Anna. I had no idea what arrangements had been made or which transactions were still pending.

"How long are you supposed to wait?" Tony didn't look like he could last much longer. "What's the plan exactly?"

"The plan?" he scoffed. "The plan is for me to get beaten to a pulp again, it seems to me. Anyhow, I need a break. I'll go up with you guys and hang with Nick for a while." Tony looked around the lobby. "Maybe nobody's coming."

I shifted Luke to the other shoulder; he cuddled close and began sucking my cheek. He had a passion for sucking any part of me—arm, finger, face, neck. But if I didn't stop him, at the ceremony I'd have a hickey on my face. Gently, I detached his lips and repositioned him again as we started for the elevator. Suddenly, someone put a hand on my shoulder. I spun around.

"Anything else?" I hadn't seen the limo driver approach.

"Anything else?" I didn't understand.

"Before midnight, I mean?"

Midnight? What would I need at midnight? Wait. I remembered: Anna had arranged for the limo to take my father home and to deliver Anna and the children back to our house. Except, now the kids would be staying here with us and Anna wouldn't need a ride. But the driver could still take my father back.

"Midnight's fine. Actually, a little earlier." My dad was, after all, in his eighties; I didn't know how late he'd want to party.

"Okay, then. See you at eleven thirty?" The driver tipped his cap, watching us walk toward the elevator.

Molly and Susan waited there, having explored the lobby, Susan gaily commenting on the drama of floral arrangements and fountains. The bellman was there, too, ready to guide us and our belongings to the bridal suite, which, he advised us, was conveniently located adjacent to the groom's suite. When the elevator doors opened, as if on cue, Luke opened his mouth, depositing a generous blob of curdled milk onto my sweatshirt. And, as they closed, I stared into the lobby, still searching for a suspicious face.

NINETY

THE SUITE WAS ELEGANT, LUSHLY CARPETED AND LAVISHLY UP-
holstered. Karen was already there. She'd been at the hotel all day,
filling in for Anna, doing whatever a wedding planner had to do
on the day of the ceremony. She'd opened the minibar, had an ar-
ray of bottles and snacks set up on the small dining table. I
couldn't think of swallowing. When I glanced at a wad of melting
Brie, my stomach cringed spasmodically

"Wait till you see your bouquet, Zoe," Karen greeted us,
flushed and jittery. You'd think the wedding was hers. "It's exquisite."

"What about my flowers?" Molly pulled urgently at my arm. "I
need to pull the petals off and put them in a basket—"

"It's all done." Karen chuckled, took Molly's hand. "Flower
girls don't have to pluck the petals; they have it done for them.
But your basket's beautiful, all decorated in ribbons. Come see."

Karen took Molly off to inspect her basket while Susan poured
drinks. I set Luke down in his portable rocking chair, calculating
how to time his feedings so he wouldn't interrupt the ceremony,
deciding whether to get him or Molly dressed first, wondering if
he could manage not to throw up on his too-adorable-for-words
tiny dress shirt.

"Scotch?" Susan held out a glass. "Take it, just this once. It'll
take away the jitters."

"I don't have jitters—"

"Zoe. You're shaking. Look at your hands."

I held them out. They shook. I tightened them into fists and put one behind me.

"Zoe. Believe me. One shot on one day is not going to harm your baby, but it will do you tons of good." She brought it to me, waited for me to take it, refusing to let me decline. "Take it."

I took it from her, telling myself that I could just pretend to sip it. If I held it to my mouth, Susan would leave me alone.

"Here's to my best friend." She held her glass up, chin wobbling. "Husbands can come and go, but best friends are forever." She wiped away a tear and gulped her drink down, and as I held the Scotch to my lips, it occurred to me that she and Tim might be having problems.

"What's that mean, Susan? Husbands come and go—"

"Nothing. Just, you know. First Michael. Now Nick."

What was she insinuating? That I couldn't stay married? "Nick is permanent."

"Of course he is." Susan sounded tipsy. As far as I could see, she'd been drinking steadily for two days. But I couldn't think about Susan's drinking now. I had to stay on track, think about getting ready. I set my glass down, and while Susan and Karen took Molly into the bedroom to get ready I fed Luke so I wouldn't have to worry about feeding him for a while. Then I took my dress out of the garment bag. Marveling again at its simple lines, delicate lace, shimmering silk, glowing pearls, intricate embroidery, I tried not to remember Ivy preening in it and told myself that the dress did not smell of her perfume. Still, I aired the dress out, leaving it hanging on the closet door.

"Mom, look at me!" Molly twirled out of the bedroom, dazzling and aglow. "Can I go show Nick?"

I supposed she could; there was no rule that I knew of forbidding the flower girl and groom from seeing each other on the wedding day.

"Not by yourself."

"I'll take her." Karen took Molly's hand. "Then we'll go show Davinder. She's all alone downstairs coping with the florist and the photographer and the musicians and the chef. She probably could use some company."

My friends were saints. "Karen, how can I thank you guys? You and Davinder and Susan have really rescued us—"

"Zoe, please. Your wedding planner died the day before your wedding. What kind of friends would we be if we didn't help? We all love you." Blowing a kiss, she led Molly out the door. "Back in a few."

When they left, the room was suddenly quiet. Luke slept, and I thought that I'd finally have a little time to myself.

But just then, Susan called from the bedroom, "Zoe, I have the borrowed and blue stuff. Come here and decide what you want—"

"In a minute." I dashed into the bathroom, not ready to try on a borrowed necklace or blue earrings or a borrowed blue garter or whatever blue borrowed things she'd chosen, bless her. I needed to be alone.

Breathe, I told myself. Take air in and let it out. I stood against the bathroom door, eyes closed, trying to calm down. Maybe we should have postponed the wedding. Too much, far too much, was interfering. Our babysitter was in the burn center; our wedding planner was dead; I'd just shot a former patient, and not only that. Tony might get mugged at any moment by persons unknown. The jump drives were still in his possession, and he was a mess waiting for someone to show up for them.

Visions of espionage, secret codes, death and pain were not what were supposed to fill a bride's head before the ceremony. I needed to center myself. To focus on the commitment Nick and I were about to make. To focus on Nick. But when I thought of Nick, I saw him as he'd been the night before, blitheringly drunk, unconscious and snoring. I told myself to forget that, to think of Nick the way he was when Luke was born, steady and misty-eyed beside me, coaching me through the worst of the contractions. Or to think of him the first time I saw him, to remember how I couldn't think straight once our eyes met, how his aftershave drugged me, how the texture of his jacket sleeve seduced my arm. Nick. Remembering him made my chest hurt. I missed him, needed to talk to him, needed to hear him reassure me not just about what had happened last night and last week but also about what was about to happen this night and afterward.

Stop being so wimpy, I told myself. Get a grip. Slowly, I opened my eyes, turning to the mirror. And gaped at the face that gaped back at me. I hadn't looked at myself since I'd had my makeup done in the salon. The cheeks were heavily rouged, the nose and chin caked with base so thick that it would crack if I smiled. The eyelids were painted a startling shade of kelly green that clashed with the shocking pink heavily outlining my glossed lips. Oh God. How could Susan have let me leave the salon looking like this? I'd paid a week's worth of grocery money to get my makeup done, and I looked grotesque and cartoonish. Where was a washcloth? I grabbed one and dampened it, pawed my face with it. I'd have to take it all off and start from bare skin. But where was my makeup case? My hands were trembling, and the white washcloth became mottled with stains of vermilion, forest green and burnt orange. Somehow, I gathered my own sack of makeup, reapplied a light base, a hint of natural blush, a subtle blend of violet and rose shadow, a little mascara, a deep flesh-toned lip gloss. Yes. At least I looked like myself again. And, I realized, the simple process of applying my makeup had grounded me. For the first time in days, I felt in charge. I stood at the mirror, pleased with myself, admiring the dark hair swept loosely back into a simple chignon, elegant wisps framing my face, a few strands of gray adding drama. I looked almost like a bride.

Molly was dressed, but I still needed to put myself into my

gown. And I needed to find out whether Tim had arrived yet with my father. Checking myself in the mirror one final time, I stepped out of the bathroom, swathed in the hotel's thick terry cloth robe. Little Luke still slept in his chair, just as I'd left him, but Susan was sitting stiffly on the love seat, gawking at something near the door. At what? Puzzled, I started into the room. Susan noticed me and, too late, I saw her shake her head no. Why?

Moving into the sitting room, I saw Eli.

"Eli—you're here." A stupid greeting, but I was grinning, happy to see him.

He had come to the wedding, just as he'd said he would, and standing beside the bar, dashing in a black tuxedo, Eli was so striking, so commanding, that at first I didn't notice anything else, not even the limo driver standing right behind him.

NINETY-ONE

As I approached, Eli smiled. "I told you I'd be here."

My arms opened for a hug, but Susan gasped, "Zoe, don't," and the driver stepped forward, warning, "I don't think so." His voice was hushed, his eyes menacing. "Nobody touches this guy until he gives me what I came for."

I stopped, my arms embracing empty air, and glared at the limo driver. So. I'd been right about the sneakers. There had been something wrong about him. Probably, he was the guy who was supposed to get the jump drives from Tony. Probably, like everybody else, he'd gotten the brothers confused. But now, somehow, we had to steer him to Tony.

"Where are they? Hand them over." His mouth was against Eli's ear.

"No, you've made a mistake. See, he isn't—" I'd been about to say that he wasn't Tony. To explain that Tony, not Eli, was the brother with the jump drives. Mid-sentence, though, it occurred to me that I shouldn't do that. Nobody but Tony was supposed to know about the jump drives. If I said anything about them I put us all in jeopardy and ruined the FBI's whole plan. What was I thinking?

"He isn't what?" The driver revealed the gun he'd been pointing at Eli's back. It had a long, awkward muzzle, probably a silencer. Oh dear.

"He isn't . . ." I struggled to think of an end to that sentence. ". . . very healthy. He's just getting over brain surgery." Eli looked surprised, but I kept babbling. "He wasn't even supposed to be here. He said he might not make it."

"Where are they?" The driver had stopped listening and turned his attention back to Eli. "Hand 'em over."

"Does anyone know what he's talking about?" Eli looked at me; his eyes were violet.

Of course I did. But I shrugged, shook my head. Susan watched me, confused and suspicious.

"Cut the crap, dude. You know damn well what I'm talking about."

Eli blinked at him.

"Shit, man. What the hell's wrong with you? I called you yesterday told you to bring them. What are you up to? I could kill you right now."

The driver had no idea that Eli wasn't Tony. And Eli had no clue what was going on.

"Okay, look. I won't hesitate. I'll kill them." He pointed his weapon at Susan and then at me. Eyes burning, Susan glowered on the love seat like a cornered wildcat.

"No, you won't. Because, if you even try, I'll never give you what you're looking for. And also, while you're firing the first shot, I'll break your neck."

Beads of sweat were pearling on the driver's forehead. "Just give me the damned drives, pal. Nobody gets hurt. We all go on with our day."

I stared at Eli. How could I let him know about the jump drives that Tony had, or that the FBI wanted Tony to give them to the guy?

"Come on," I tried. "Stop messing around and give them to him, will you? Where are they? In your room?" I nodded toward Nick's suite. "Did you leave them next door?"

Eli didn't even blink. He got it. "What the hell, Zoe. Way to give me up."

"Your room's next door?" The driver jabbed the gun at Eli. "Shit. Let's go have a look."

"Not so fast." Eli turned to face him. His face was composed, his voice calm. "I'll give you what you want, but if you harm anyone, the women or anyone else, I'll find you. And while you're still alive, you can watch me feed your nuts to my dog. Got it?"

The limo driver opened, then closed his mouth, attempting a sneer. The gun seemed unsteady in his hand. Obviously, he hadn't been prepared for Eli the assassin; he'd expected to deal with Tony the computer geek. "Look, man. I got a job to do. I'm supposed to collect and deliver. That's all. Let me do it and we'll all be happy."

"Fine." Eli's eyes remained on the driver's. "Let's go."

The driver looked at Susan. "Wait. I can't just leave them here." He dug in his pockets, pulled out a coil of plastic rope. "Here. Tie them up. Together—I only got the one rope."

Without hesitation, Eli took the rope and tied us back-to-back on the floor. Then, with a gun pointed at his back, he led the limo driver away, and the door closed behind them.

NINETY-TWO

"THAT WAS ELI? HE'S HOT. BUT HE COULD BE TONY'S TWIN." Susan began talking the second the door clicked shut. She tried to
move her arm, yanking the rope against my rib cage. Reflexively, I
pulled back. Susan cursed. "Dammit, Zoe. Stop moving; just hold
still and tell me what's going on. What is he here for?"

"Hang on, Susan." I tested, trying to move my arms, my hands.
To squirm or wriggle. I couldn't. Eli had tied us too tight.

"Zoe. Stop pulling on the rope. You're killing me."

It was no use. Eli had left almost no slack. Why not? Whose
side was he on? Finally, I gave up, beginning to panic. "He's here
for those jump drives. The ones I told you about."

"Did you ever find out what's on them?" She was panting. Trying to have a discussion.

"No. Not yet. The feds won't say." I was grunting. "But I knew
something was wrong with that driver."

"No, you didn't."

What? "I most certainly did—"

"Why didn't you say something—"

"Well, how was I supposed to know he had a gun?"

Her butt pressed against mine. We lay there, arguing, spine-to-
spine, cheek-to-cheek.

"If I'd have been able to talk to Nick, he'd have found the gun.
But *someone* wouldn't let me talk to Nick."

"So you're saying it's my fault that some lunatic was driving your limo? You're the one who thought he was so odd; why didn't you do something?"

Oh my God, we sounded like bickering hens. In his little chair, still sleeping, Luke let out a deep sigh.

"Susan, forget all that—they've gone to Nick's suite."

"Why? What do they have in there?"

"It's a long story. Now we need to get help."

"So, what do we do? Scream?"

"We could try."

"Okay. What should we shout? 'Help'?"

"Help's good."

"Okay." I could feel her every breath. "On three."

Together, breathing as one, we counted. And on three, we belted out *Help!* with all the power of our tightly fettered lungs. Luke slept on as we repeated it again and again, until our throats were raw. But, unfortunately, the Four Seasons' boasts of thoroughly soundproofed rooms were accurate. Nobody responded. Finally, breathless, we stopped shouting.

"Now what?" I croaked.

"It's getting late. The photographer will be looking for you. Eventually, Karen or Davinder or somebody will come get you."

Oh God. People would be arriving. Nick and I were supposed to get married in an hour, and I'd just sent a gunman to Nick's room.

"Let's try to get out of here."

"You're not serious."

"We have to try. Press your back against mine and push."

She did, and I did. "Now what?"

We were like two mummies bound together. "I don't know." I'd never had to travel without using my arms or legs, much less when tied to another person. We pushed against each other, driving our thighs down to the floor. We flopped forward and back. We twisted our torsos up to a twenty-degree angle and collapsed.

"Hold on. I have to rest." Susan panted. "I'm getting carpet burn on my face."

We lay for a moment, breathing, noticing the undersides of the dining chairs and table. When Luke started to crawl, this would be his vantage point.

"Okay. Ready." Susan had recovered. Against my back, I could feel her heart, still racing. Our bodies were damp, our breathing rapid and shallow, perfectly in sync.

"Maybe we can slither to the door."

"Slither?"

"You know, push and wiggle. Shimmy."

"Okay. To which door?"

"Nick's." The door that adjoined to Nick's suite was closer than the door to the hall. Besides, the suite was where Eli and the driver had gone.

"On three." Again, we counted together. Again, I felt her muscles work in unison with mine. Susan and I didn't exactly slither; probably we resembled an inchworm more than a snake. We pushed our backs up and thrust our torsos ahead, flailed our united legs back and forth and up and down. We rolled and tipped, groaned and grunted, and gradually, one centimeter at a time, made our way to the door.

Where we lay, huffing and puffing. "Now what?"

It was a legitimate question. We couldn't reach the doorknob. We couldn't really bang on the door with our heads or feet. And depending on what was going on in the suite, we might not want to.

We tried to listen through the double door, hearing no gunshots, making out only garbled baritone sounds. And then, when we'd run out of ideas and energy, we heard the click of the passkey in the lock. The door swung open and Molly skipped in, Karen right behind her.

NINETY-THREE

MOLLY HELD MY HAND, STROKING MY FACE, ASKING QUESTIONS. Were we hurt? Had someone robbed us? Was there still going to be a wedding? Did Nick know we were tied up? Should she go tell him?

The rope was too hard to untie, so Karen used a nail scissors. It took some time to cut the plastic; it was thick and the nail scissors had short, rather dull cutting edges. Susan was busy giving instructions to Karen, so I had plenty of time to answer Molly's questions. "No. No. Yes. No. No. Everything is going to be okay."

As soon as my hands were free, I cupped her face and kissed her, assuring her that we were fine.

"But who tied you up, Mom?"

"Uncle Eli."

"Who's Uncle Eli?" Karen was confused.

"Uncle Eli?" So was Molly. She'd never met him. "But why?"

Good Lord. I needed to explain, but I couldn't, not then. "To help Uncle Tony. It's a long story."

Susan nudged me. "Zoe. We sent them next door. Should we call security?"

"No. No security." The FBI wanted the guy to get the drives; security might interfere. Might even get hurt.

Karen watched us, her brown eyes baffled. "Zoe? What can I do?"

I nodded. "Sweetheart." I took Molly's hands. "In the bedroom, there are some boxes of jewelry and hankies and stuff. Can you and Karen go into the bedroom and pick out something borrowed and something blue for me to wear?"

I met Karen's eyes; without words, my gaze told her to keep Molly there.

"Wait. Won't they both be borrowed?" Molly was no fool.

"I guess, yes. But I need two things."

"But only one thing has to be blue?"

Goodness. Why wouldn't she just go "That's right."

"Let's go, Molly." Karen hurried her along. "Why don't we take Luke, too?" She grabbed the handle of his portable rocker and led Molly into the bedroom.

As soon as they left, Susan and I ran to the door adjoining our suite to Nick's. Susan opened it, but we faced another door, the door on Nick's side.

"Listen," Susan whispered. "Hear anything?"

I put my ear to the door, shook my head. "I'll try the knob."

"Slowly."

Slowly, silently, I turned the knob as far as it would go. Then, hoping that the door was unlocked and that the limo driver wasn't watching it, I pushed against it gently until a sliver of light shone through. Men were talking in the next room. I looked at Susan, and she shook her head. Neither of us could understand. So, slowly, gently, I opened the door another centimeter, then another.

At first, all I saw was the limo driver, his gun raised. His back was to us, so he wouldn't see us opening the door. I opened it wider, and saw men in identical tuxedoes, standing, facing the wall. Eli. Or was it Tony? About four feet away was Tony. Or Eli. Sam stood on the other side of the sofa. Where was Nick? I opened the door wider and saw him about five feet away, standing at the wall like the others, and it occurred to me that, damn, I'd seen Nick before the wedding. And that was bad luck. But worse than that, the plan to return the jump drives had gone awry. No one but

Tony was supposed to have been involved. Instead, all of us had seen the guy. All of us—Susan and I and Nick and his brothers—were witnesses who, if we survived, could identify the limo driver.

Susan put her hand on my arm, pointing to the men. "Look—they've spread out." Her breath tickled my ear. "That's good—he can't aim at all of them at once. What should we do? Storm them?" She looked at the phone. "Are you sure we shouldn't call for help?"

"No—no security." But maybe I was wrong. Maybe we needed help.

No question, she thought I was crazy.

"Why the hell not?"

Was I supposed to explain the whole FBI plan there and then? "Just don't." I was too loud, glanced at the men to see if they'd heard me; apparently, they had not.

Susan gaped at me, silent.

"Trust me." Maybe I was making a mistake. But I must have been convincing; she stayed beside me, didn't go for the phone. We crouched, trying to hear what the men were saying.

The driver was talking, aiming the gun at Tony. "Enough talking. Give me what I want or these guys are hamburger."

"Dude—you're talking to the wrong guy," Eli interrupted. "I'm the one you talked to on the phone yesterday. I'll give you what you want. Just let my brothers—"

"Bullshit," Tony argued, touching the cut near his ear. "I'm the guy you mugged last week. I'm the one who has what you want—"

"Don't even listen to him—" Eli didn't know what was going on. But that didn't stop him. "He's trying to stall—"

"Shut up, both of you." The driver was sweating. He looked from one to the other, unsure and exasperated. "I'll tell you what. I don't give a fuck which one of you has my stuff. But if I don't get the drives from one of you Bobbsey twins, these two are dead men." He waved the gun at Sam and Nick.

"But it's Nick's wedding day—," Eli protested.

"So? Convenient for the family. They'll be here for the funeral."

"Forget it," Nick interrupted. "Whatever he wants, don't give it to him. We're all dead anyhow. Why would he let us live after he gets what he wants?"

Why indeed? We'd all seen the guy's face. Which changed everything. The FBI's plan had gone haywire. Now, he'd have to shoot all of us if he wanted to get away. But to hell with the drives; I didn't care what information was on them. I wasn't going to let Nick or his brothers get hurt. I made hand signals to Susan, and she made some back to me. Then she crawled to the bar, reached up into the silver ice bowl and retrieved two hefty bottles of champagne.

"I'll tell you why." Eli smirked. "He's not going to kill anyone. He can't afford to let this get complicated. If he leaves a bunch of dead bodies around, suddenly he's got a lot of attention to deal with. What he wants is to get out of here clean and quiet—"

"I don't want to kill anyone today—but make no mistake. I will if I have to."

"Of course you will. We can identify you." Nick sounded calm.

"Trust me. You can't."

What? I looked closer. His too-straggly hair might be a wig. His nose looked too large and pale for his face, might not be real. Was he really thick at the middle? Or was he wearing padding? Who knew what the guy really looked like? Maybe he knew we couldn't identify him. Maybe he wasn't going to kill us.

"Good," Nick went on. "Lose the gun, and we'll help you find—"

A sudden pop stopped Nick mid-sentence, and a snowstorm swirled. No, a feather storm. Feathers were flying everywhere. At the pop, I'd grabbed Susan and she'd grabbed me; we'd nearly tumbled into Nick's suite before we realized that the men were all still standing and the only victim of the driver's silenced gun had been a down pillow. He'd picked it up and shot it, apparently to shock them. We steadied ourselves, each clutching our bottle, poised and ready to strike.

Tony backed away from the wall, hands in the air. "Okay. Okay. Don't shoot anything else." He was trembling.

Eli backed away from the wall, too, protecting his brother. "Don't listen to him. I'm the one who's got what you want."

The limo driver shot the wall.

"Eli, cut it out." Tony's voice trembled. "It's gone far enough."

Tony's legs wobbled; he seemed about to faint. "Here. I'll give you what you want. I have to reach into my pocket, though. Don't shoot."

"You pull anything out but my drives, I'll shoot your clone first, then you."

Shaking, Tony's hand fumbled in his jacket pocket for the jump drives, but it was shaking so badly that the drives flew out onto the carpet, along with our wedding rings. Tony stooped, retrieving the drives. "These what you're looking for? I found them in my pocket—"

The driver lunged forward and grabbed them while Tony was still picking up the rings. Eli, unaware of the FBI plan, spun around, charging the driver, trying to retrieve the drives. Oh God.

"Now!" I yelled to Susan, and together we stampeded into Nick's suite, swinging our bottles. The driver whirled around, shooting, and, above Susan's head champagne and glass exploded, raining onto Susan and the carpet. Susan yelped. Eli tackled the limo driver; Tony tackled Eli. As they struggled, I stood at the driver's head, trying to slam his head as Sam dove onto the pile, trying to separate them, and Nick darted around, trying to disarm the driver, who kept firing until, suddenly, somebody gasped in pain. Oh God. Who'd been hit?

All of us froze. Then, slowly, Sam rolled off Eli, who rolled off Tony. No wounds, no blood. The blood, it seemed, was on the driver. He'd somehow managed to shoot his own forearm.

"I should fucking kill all of you." Cursing and wincing, holding the gun with his good arm, he barked at Sam to get him a towel. Wrapping his arm with it, he had me remove the belt from my robe and tie it tightly around the terry cloth bandage. Then he backed toward the door.

"Here's the deal." His wig hung askew, and his nose was smashed. "Nobody moves for ten minutes. I got people watching. Anybody leaves here, anybody tries to call for help, you're all dead." He'd reached the door, opened it and backed into the hall.

NINETY-FOUR

"WHAT THE——" ELI BEGAN. BUT THE OTHERS HAD BURST OUT laughing, giving each other high fives.

"Can you believe the asshole shot himself?" Sam turned scarlet, wheezing as he chortled. "You guys, we should go into business together. Sell somebody the Brooklyn Bridge."

"Zoe." Susan turned to me. "What the hell was that?"

"Exactly." Eli looked from one brother to another. "Can somebody explain what just happened?"

But Tony and Sam, instead of explaining, hugged Eli, barraging him with questions about where he'd been and what he'd been up to lately. Meantime, Nick pulled a cell phone out from his shaving bag and made a call.

"It's done. The delivery was made, no real collateral damage." He described the limo driver, listened, nodded. "That's right, the guy with the towel. No, not serious."

Apparently, federal agents were already following him, tracing the jump drives to their source. I stepped to the window, trying to spot the agents. Was that one, there in the blue jeans and leather jacket? Or there, in the SUV—the guy with the baseball cap? A limo pulled out of the Four Seasons' entranceway. Was it ours? Was our limo driver making his escape in the limousine? Across the street, a black sedan pulled into traffic, following. At the corner, a blue one pulled in behind. Were they all agents? Or were the cars just normal traffic?

Nick stepped over, put an arm around me, asked if I was okay, kissed my neck. His finger gently coiled a lock of hair that had fallen loose. Hell with bad-luck superstitions, I thought. And I turned, leaned against him, let myself be wrapped in Nick's arms.

Molly barreled into us, Karen following close behind, calling her.

"Mom, I picked out these." She held out a blue garter and a pair of antique gold and pearl earrings.

"I held her back as long as I could." Karen looked frazzled. In fact, the entire wedding party, gathered together in Nick's suite, looked frazzled.

Eli and Susan insisted on explanations, and Karen joined them to listen to Sam elaborate. Nick joined them, answering questions, divulging what he could.

"What was on the drives?" Susan frowned.

"I can't tell you exactly. But the dead agent was a weapons specialist."

My stomach did a somersault. So, the data was about weapons?

"Come on, Nick. We nearly got killed."

"Out with it. We deserve to know what we're involved in."

Nick knew his brothers wouldn't relent. "Okay. The drives contain information that traces financial transfers that trace dealings in weapons and materials." He paused, cleared his throat.

"What's he saying?" Sam asked. "Does anyone understand what the hell he's talking about?"

"I'm talking about foiling terrorist activities."

"You mean an attack?"

"I mean avoiding incidents. I mean stopping potential terrorist events in their planning stages."

Oh God. But the limo driver hadn't seemed like a terrorist. He'd seemed kind of like a pickpocket. Or maybe a car thief. But he was involved in funding and smuggling weapons? I couldn't grasp what Nick was saying. I was light-headed, unable to breathe or think. Molly was asking questions. Oh God. Was I going to have to explain to her about terrorists and weapons smuggling?

"What, Molls?"

"The door. Someone's knocking. Can I get it?"

The door? No, of course you can't get it. It's terrorists and smugglers. Or it's a limo driver with a gun loaded with enriched uranium. But oh, too late—Karen had already opened the door. It wasn't a smuggler; it was Tim. With my father. My father, dashing in his tuxedo, white hair gleaming, eyes aglow and ready for the wedding.

Oh—the wedding. I still had to get into my dress, fix my makeup and my hair again. Slithering on the floor hadn't done much for my chignon. Still feeling off-kilter, I floated over to kiss my dad and greet Tim. Then I started back to my suite, realizing that Tony was behind me, tagging along.

"You're pale."

I was? Of course I was.

"Sit down. Collect yourself." The advice was odd, coming from Tony, who moments before had been trembling and quaking, fumbling with the jump drives and the wedding rings. But now he was steady and grounded, and he put an arm firmly around my waist, probably just in time. Because I felt myself swoon, a damsel in distress kind of swoon. How embarrassing. How mortifying. But Tony's arm supported me surprisingly well. He was stronger than he looked, and effortlessly he guided me into a chair. I knew the chair well; I'd seen its underside. I'd studied it from the floor.

"Talk to me, Zoe. What can I do for you?" Tony leaned close; his face—so familiar and like his brothers'—was inches from mine.

"Nothing. It's just—"

"Just?"

"Well. I hope they can track that guy. I hope they catch whoever he's working for before they do any harm—"

"Oh, no question. They've got him."

How did Tony know? "Come on, Tony. You can't be sure—"

"Oh, but I can." His hand on my shoulder was very firm. "Don't worry. I promise you. This round went to the good guys."

Tony didn't sound like Tony. He sounded too confident, like Eli the spy, the undercover agent. Tony looked unlike himself, too. And I realized why—Tony wasn't nervous. His timidity was gone, replaced by a casual cockiness. His eyes blazed and his shoulders squared, as if he had adopted a whole new persona. And, in a flash, I saw Tony encountering Agent Harris, Tony getting sick when he found out she'd been killed, Tony searching for "loose change" after Oliver had stolen the drives, Tony getting mugged and meeting privately with FBI agents. And it occurred to me that maybe it was not Eli who was an undercover agent. Maybe, just maybe, it was Tony.

NINETY-FIVE

BUT THAT THOUGHT WAS INTERRUPTED. THE DOOR TO THE SUITE flew open.

"Zoe, you're still in your robe?" Davinder burst from the hallway, hair flying, arms flailing. "What's the matter with you? People are already downstairs, seated. The musicians are playing. The photographer is ranting because you missed your preceremony sitting and he says he's not going to be responsible if you're not happy with his album—"

"Okay." I was on my feet. "It's okay. I'll just be a minute." I wanted to ask Tony some questions, but he'd already gone through the door adjoining Nick's suite.

"Look at you, Zoe. You're a mess. What the hell happened? You look like you were in a brawl. Where's everybody? You need serious attention."

As if on cue, in the bedroom Luke began to cry. I went to him, and Davinder began calling for Susan and Karen, and they came in with Molly. In seconds, Luke was at my breast, and everyone else was hovering around me.

"I'll do the hair." Davinder had her hands on my head. "Somebody find her makeup kit."

"I'll get it." That was Molly. "She put it in the bathroom."

They talked like I wasn't even there.

"Where are the earrings?" Susan stuck her hand into the pocket of my robe, retrieved them and the garter. She handed the garter to

Karen, who ordered me to pick up a leg and tugged the thing over my foot and up to my thigh while Susan jabbed an earring into one earlobe, crowding Davinder, who snapped at her to back off.

"Susan, watch it. You're going to ruin her hair—"

"Move over. This'll just take a second." She missed the hole, pushed the stud so hard that she almost made a new one.

"Ouch. Susan, let me do it—"

I reached for the earring.

"Don't move!" Davinder shrieked. "I swear, if you move, the whole thing comes loose—"

Another sudden stab, and the earring was in. Molly gave the makeup kit to Karen, who leaned over me with lip gloss and mascara, touching me up, wiping away smears. Luke finished feeding, burped up a wad of curdled milk, and then, as my friends changed his diaper and cleaned him up, I disappeared with Molly.

"Molls, are you ready?"

I looked her over. She was solemn, wide-eyed, perfect as a porcelain doll in her ashes of roses lace dress. "You need to put on your dress, Mom."

"I need your help for that." I took the gown off the hanger and, not daring to mess my hair again, stepped into it, kneeling so Molly could zip me up.

She took her time, pulling the zipper carefully, as if lives depended on her accuracy. When she was finished, I stood, grabbed my shoes from their box and stuck my feet into them.

"Zoe—your veil."

Davinder charged into the bathroom and pinned the thing in place. Susan and Karen had changed into their dresses; somebody found my bouquet and thrust it at me.

"Molly? Do you have your flower basket?"

Where was Molly? I turned, found her standing in the bathroom doorway, exactly where I'd left her.

"Molls? Are you okay?"

She nodded, chin wobbling.

I went to her.

"Come on. The men are downstairs," Davinder rushed me.

"What is it, Mollybear?"

"Nothing."

"Not nothing." I touched her cheek.

"Just." She shrugged. Everybody's all dressed up. Luke looks so cute. Everyone looks so pretty."

Molly the tomboy was upset about looking pretty? "You look beautiful, Molly."

"Zoe," Susan interrupted. "Your dad's waiting to walk you down the aisle. Come on before he wanders off somewhere."

I waved her away. "Molly, are you ready?"

She nodded. "But Mom, we've been waiting and waiting for the wedding, and now, here it is. And now, it's going to be over."

And once again, Molly showed wisdom beyond her years, bringing me back to reality. I was running and rushing, hurried and harried, not even noticing what was happening. Molly reminded me to live the moment.

"Mom, you look so beautiful. I love being the flower girl. I don't want the wedding to be over." Tears flooded her eyes.

Ignoring my lip gloss, I kissed her head. "Molly, you are the most lovely flower girl ever in history. And the smartest. And the coolest. And if I could stop time, I'd stop it tonight."

She nodded, sniffing.

"You know we can't do that. But we'll have pictures. And memories. And in our memories, we can make tonight go on forever."

"Okay. I know."

"Zoe." Susan snorted. "I swear. Women are volunteering to take your place. The wedding's going to happen without you."

"Ready, Molls?" I held my hand out.

She smiled, still teary, and took it. "Ready."

We rushed to the door; a stampede of women thundered down

the hall and herded into the elevator. And suddenly we were past the lobby, around the corner from the small ballroom in which a cello, violin and harp played Vivaldi.

"You wait here." Susan pushed me aside. "I'll let them know you're here."

The others disappeared around the corner, rushing off with Molly, who watched me over her shoulder as they pulled her away. And there I was, in my exquisite pearl and lace wedding dress and high silk heels, holding exotic long lilies, standing in the corner of a hotel corridor, alone.

NINETY-SIX

THAT MOMENT IMPRINTED IN MY MEMORY: BEING ALL ALONE BE-
fore the ceremony. It was only a moment. But in that brief stretch
of time, my life seemed to collect itself, my body to find its center.
The air around me stopped swirling, calmed by the music, and I
became aware of the tremendous step I was about to take. It was
my last moment of being single, my last instant unmarried. And
my heart seemed swollen, heavy with the gravity of what was
about to occur.

And, as if from nowhere, my father appeared. "You sure?" He
watched me, and I wondered if he'd heard my thoughts. "It's not
too late to change your mind."

"Thanks, Dad. I'm sure." Was I? Was anybody ever sure?

"Because it's quite a commitment. At this stage, I'm reluctant to
make it. You understand?"

Oh dear. My father seemed confused again. Had he forgotten
what his role was, that he was there not to get married but to give
away the bride?

"Too late," I told him. "You're committed for life. You'll always
be my dad." There. I hoped that clarified it.

"Yes, indeed." His smile seemed relieved. "I guess there's no escape." He took my arm. "Did you see that baby? Who brings a
baby to a wedding?"

"Dad, that's Luke. Your grandson. He's our little ring bearer."

"Yeah? Five dollars says he starts bawling right when they say the 'I dos.'"

"Dad—"

Karen stuck her head around the corner. "The judge and Nick are already in there. Tony's on his way with Susan. Then Sam's going to carry in Luke with the rings. Molly follows. Then you guys. So come on."

My arm tucked into his, my dad elegantly led me down the hall toward the ballroom door.

NINETY-SEVEN

WE GOT THERE JUST AS TONY STARTED DOWN THE AISLE. MOLLY waited for her cue, a doll baby with a basket of rose petals. And when Karen told Molly to begin, she hesitated, glancing at me in what might have been terror, before putting her left foot half a step forward, her lips moving, silently counting the beat.

The music was louder here, and I tried to focus. Live the moment, I reminded myself. But my mind whirled, aware of my hair—was it still mussed? And the veil—was it on securely? What if it slipped? And what about the limo driver? Were his cohorts here, watching us like he said they were? Were there still FBI agents in the room, protecting us just in case?

Karen nodded, and my father whispered, "You look beautiful, Louise," calling me by my mother's name as we started for the ballroom door. He did that often, but this time it moved me. My father, in his eighties, still strained to see my long-dead mother when he looked at me, and the sadness of that brought me to tears.

Do not cry, I told myself. You will ruin the mascara and the rest of the makeup. Focus on the moment. We stood at the doorway, ready to start down the aisle. The music stopped, and everyone stood, turning, staring at us. I leaned on my father's fragile arm, noticed, among the gawking faces, my aunt Lanie and my friends Liz and Sandie and their husbands. And across the aisle from them, an entire section of cops, rowers and their spouses—Nick's friends, the guys from the bachelor party, who were probably still hungover.

They watched me now, and I felt dozens—no, hundreds—of eyes travel my body. Go on, I told myself. Start. Follow Molly's path of rose petals. But still, the music did not play. Tim, Susan's husband, popped into view, grinning broadly, giving me a thumbs-up. And Karen's husband stood smiling beside Davinder and her husband, whose name escaped me. And—oh wow—there was old friend Juree and my college roommate, Helene, and our friends Meghan and Nate, Alex and Robyn. And Amy and Jeremy, parents from Molly's school. And, oh Lord, my coworkers from the Institute—the dance therapist, Magritte, and Bryce Edmond's assistant, Sophie. My favorite psychiatrist, Dr. Tokler, and his wife. And a couple I didn't know—were they the FBI? The woman wore a striking sky blue dress. A hundred fifty people, a motley, odd gathering with nothing in common but Nick and me. Oh, and one more thing: Every single one of them was looking at me. I hung on to my dad, wanting to run for cover, wishing the music would start already, wondering if I would faint. What were they waiting for? The moment dragged on, and in the drama I realized I was once again forgetting to breathe.

What if something went wrong? What if I stumbled or passed out? What if the guys looking for the jump drives realized there'd been a setup, or if the guy spotted his FBI tail and called his "people"? No, stop it. The jump drives were taken care of. The plot had been foiled. But what if Luke began to cry during the ceremony? I was still listing what-ifs when the bridal procession music suddenly began and my father tugged too sharply on my arm, yanking me into the ballroom.

I planted a foot forward, took a deep breath and closed my eyes, trying to center myself. My father smelled of aftershave, and his gnarled hand played with my fingers as we walked, startling me with a memory of childhood—he'd always tangled my fingers when he held my hand. I opened my eyes again, letting my dad measure our steps along Molly's floral trail. Up ahead, Nick's brothers lined up like identical Ken dolls alongside the chuppah,

Sam holding little Luke. Susan, who was sniffing away tears, stood beside Molly, who was watching me, rapt and bug-eyed. In the middle, under the silk-draped bema, stood the judge.

Look at Nick, I told myself. My heart jumped into my throat, panicked at the thought. Why? I was going to marry him. I'd had his baby. What was so frightening about just looking at him? And then I knew: I felt ridiculous, all decked out, all draped in silk and jewels as if I were a nineteen-year-old innocent bride. I was embarrassed at the pretentiousness, the anachronism of the ceremony. What would he think, seeing me like this? Would he think I was pathetic, trying to be glamorous while still nursing an infant, trying to be a bride when I was already a mother? Would he look at me and see the arguments, the stress, of the past few weeks? Would he wonder why we were doing this wedding thing? My father led me along, and I kept my eyes diverted until, finally, he stopped me and lifted my veil, winking at me with twinkling eyes as he kissed me and lowered the veil again. Nick stepped forward to receive me, part of the ritual of the bride being given away. And releasing my dad, I turned to Nick. His ice blue eyes were waiting for me, riveting into mine, steadying me, and as he took my arm, my body seemed weightless, floating forward on its own. I looked up at Nick, my eyes locked on to his, and everything else faded away.